D1106989

THE
LONG
NAKED
DESCENT
INTO
BOSTON

Also by William Eastlake

Go in Beauty
The Bronc People
Portrait of an Artist with Twenty-Six Horses
Castle Keep
The Bamboo Bed
Dancers in the Scalp House

THE
LONG
NAKED
DESCENT
INTO
BOSTON

WILLIAM
EASTLAKE

A RICHARD SEAVER BOOK

THE VIKING PRESS   NEW YORK

TERTELING LIBRARY
THE COLLEGE OF IDAHO
CALDWELL, IDAHO

PS3555
A7
L6

Copyright © William Eastlake, 1977
All rights reserved

A Richard Seaver Book/The Viking Press
First published in 1977 by The Viking Press
625 Madison Avenue, New York, N.Y. 10022
Published simultaneously in Canada by
The Macmillan Company of Canada Limited
Printed in the United States of America

LIBRARY OF CONGRESS CATALOGING IN PUBLICATION DATA
Eastlake, William.
    The long naked descent into Boston.
    "A Richard Seaver Book."
    1. Boston—History—Revolutionary period, 1775–1783—Fiction. I. Title.
PZ4.E133Lo   [PS3555.A7]   813'.5'4   76-46932
ISBN 0-670-43852-9

103880

To Ricardo, Marilyn, and Sandía

TERTELING LIBRARY
THE COLLEGE OF IDAHO
CALDWELL. IDAHO

THE
LONG
NAKED
DESCENT
INTO
BOSTON

one

"The Revolution has started and it looks like a long war, Your Worship."

"You can say that again," George Washington said.

Editor Hieronymus Poxe put aside this fake piece of dialogue his reporter Isaac Braxton had written for *The New Boston Times* and tried to concentrate on this stop-the-press—what this newcomer Young Wild Tom was saying to him now.

"Everything, Master Poxe, that is right or reasonable pleads for common sense—for America's separation from England—the blood of the slain and the weeping voice of nature cries 'tis time to part! Even the great distance which the Almighty hath placed between England and America is a strong and natural proof that the authority of one over the other was never the design of Heaven."

"Let me think about that, Young Wild Tom," Poxe said. "Meanwhile, I have a balloon problem, an employee problem, and right now I can't be bothered with your Revolution problem. Run along, Young Wild Tom, and think of some more slogans." Poxe paused. "Have a good war." Poxe stared around the *Times* empty pressroom on the eve of the Revolution. "I believe all my gang are still asleep."

As everyone knows, in 1775 the boys and girls who worked for *The New Boston Times* had to sleep five in a bed in a room above the paper—times were hard.

As almost everyone knows, the Montgolfier hot-air balloon was invented in time for the American Revolution. Seventeen seventy-five. Hieronymus Poxe, the editor, publisher, and principal owner—Benjamin Franklin had a small piece of the *Times*—used a hot-air balloon to boost circulation and make money until a war came along to save the paper. Poxe charged two shillings the balloon ascension from Boston Common—the idea was to see God. As everyone knows in America, "excepting a few crackpots," God is up there someplace. In 1775, before balloons, no one had had an opportunity to go up and have a good look for

2

THE
LONG
NAKED
DESCENT
INTO
BOSTON

Him. Hieronymus Poxe had never promised you'd see God from the balloon, but certainly the opportunity was there now from Poxe's balloon. To be honest, no one who took the balloon up had seen God yet, but to be the first would be very important—more important than going to the moon, which in 1775 had not been accomplished yet either.

Some of the balloon passengers carried signs in various languages that they held up as the balloon rose, because although everyone was certain that God was American, God might not have bothered to learn the language, He being so very busy— "He" because in '75, before liberation, God was a He.

Francine, Dilsie, and Gretchen, the *Times* reporters, our heroines, our girl heroes of the Revolution, suspected that God was a woman. Their evidence was that God was capricious and a creator of all things—as women are. God's work must mean women's work. Men do very little work, "on our particular planet anyway."

As the balloon rose and Boston disappeared below, the Colonial passengers would shout out to God in all languages— Japanese, Italian, Dutch, Spanish, Scandinavian, French, Swiss, Scotch, Outer Mongolian, Australian, German—*Sprechen Sie Deutsch, mein Gott?*—Southern—Y'all hear me, God? But no one had gotten an answer so far. But this was in '75. There may have been many proven conversations and substantiated sightings since.

"After all, God's son Jesus came down once to have a good look at us," Poxe said, "and I don't think he would mind our having a good look at Him."

"Particularly if it builds the *Times*'s circulation," Gretchen said. Poxe noted no bitterness in her remark, but he would watch her more carefully in the future.

Billy Cracker, the Colonial evangelist, approved of the balloon search for God, and was of the opinion that God spoke Southern. Anyway, he always addressed God in that language. "Y'all comin' to the King's prayer breakfast, God?" Billy himself went up twice to look—no luck yet.

But there was always hope of a God-sighting if the balloon went higher—maybe God was concealed beyond the next cloud. The hot-air balloon rose until the fuel ran out—burning damp straw gave the best heat—and then descended beautifully again into Boston with much cheering from the lower classes on the Boston Common and waving of silk handkerchiefs from Beacon Hill.

Anyway, now that there was a war the balloon could be put to better use, and Poxe made a note of that. "I wonder if God is Tories or the Patriots, or will He wait like the *Times* before choosing sides to see how the wind blows?"

"Or will *She* wait to see how the wind blows?" Gretchen, who doubled as Poxe's secretary, said.

Francine, a young white woman from New Haven, and Dilsie, a young black woman from Punkhatasset, and Isaac Braxton of Roxbury, Massachusetts, were still in bed. But they were behaving themselves. The *Times* artist, Amos Lee, was sketching them from a Franklin chair by a Franklin window in front of a Franklin stove, instead of attending to business at the paper below.

"We better get our asses down below before Poxe roots us out," Francine said.

"The Revolution can wait," Lee said. "A good watercolor is worth ten wars anyway. You know, they tell me a neighbor of mine in Mount Vernon, Virginia, has a chance of leading the Patriots."

"Who that?" Dilsie said.

"George Washington."

"Who that?"

"A planter—mostly tobacco. The British just lowered the price support on tobacco. George is mad."

"What does he know about war?"

"He can learn. Dilsie, why do you take your blunderbuss to bed with you?"

"It's just by the side of the bed," Dilsie said. "If there's a war it might come in handy."

"Well, you got your war," Lee said, holding his watercolor at arm's length to see it better. "But it may all be over in a few days if the British are coming."

"Poxe wants everybody downstairs," Young Wild Tom said from the door. "Poxe has declared the Revolution is formally opened. And that's what the next editorial will say."

3
THE
LONG
NAKED
DESCENT
INTO
BOSTON

4

THE
LONG
NAKED
DESCENT
INTO
BOSTON

First they all had a drink below at the Rose and Crown, and then went through Henry Knox's bookstore to the *Times*. Having Knox's Adult Book Shoppe in the same building as the *Times* was convenient, and going through the Rose and Crown Colonial Bar was convenient, too. As any newspaperman will tell you, it's impossible to go to work without a good book and a stiff drink.

Hieronymus Poxe was disappointed, along with Francine and every lover of poetry, that the young men on both sides had decided to go off and fight a war at Concord and Lexington rather than attend the poetry reading of Lowell Cabot Loring. Lord Percy, Commander of the British 17th Royal Lightfoot in Boston, had given his King's men the choice of attending Lowell Cabot Loring's poetry reading at Harvard College or fighting at Concord and Lexington, and all but two had opted for almost certain death "over certain boredom." At Concord and Lexington, Colonel Conant had given his Colonial Minutemen the same choice and the Americans, unlike the British (98.6% percent), were a solid 100 percent for war.

Hieronymus Poxe had received a poetry reading brochure that had been sent to *The New Boston Times,* and it sounded attractive. "The University of Harvard Department of English and Other Languages announces the reading in person by Lowell Cabot Loring of choice selections from the fourth volume in his contemporary poetry series."

"I cannot understand," Hieronymus Poxe said, "how modern youth, which we all know is going to hell, could insult Harvard College, which is trying to get back on its feet after the French and Indian Wars, to say nothing of the slap in the face to Lowell Cabot Loring. I hate to think how it will look in the history books to have the Revolutionary War start because both sides wanted to get out of going to a poetry reading. Don't you find that disgusting, Gretchen?" he said. "Besides, where are the other employees of *The New Boston Times?*"

"Still in the bed," Gretchen said, taking up her plume and notebook.

The *Times* had five employees—Braxton and Lee, who had signed up with the *Times* to beat the army draft; and Gretchen, Francine, and Dilsie, because Hieronymus Poxe had discovered women would work cheap, sometimes for as little as a nice cup of tea and a pat on the ass. Unfortunately, due to hard times at the paper and through no fault of Hieronymus Poxe's, all five employees had to sleep in the same bed in a barnlike loft above the pressroom. Although sleeping five in a bed had its drawbacks—the Boston Watch and Ward Society—its compensations were togetherness and a sense of belonging, of sharing. The males, Lee and Braxton, were not only trying to beat the draft into the British or the Continental Army— they had both gone to Harvard College, which made it nigh impossible to get a job, and both the British and the Continentals looked at them askance. Poxe had hired them because he, too, had had the bad luck to attend Harvard and knew how it felt to be alone in the world. "Alienation," Doctor Johnson called it. Then, too, Harvard men would work for bed and board. Poxe had the bed and somehow he would dig up the board. Seventeen seventy-five was a hard year, but Hieronymus Poxe, despite his Harvard background, was resolute.

Gretchen Greenwinter had drifted into Boston in '74 to seek her liberation, and had found Poxe instead. He had seemed a soft touch at the time.

"Get in on the ground floor of the newspaper game, Gretchen. The media are going places. Do you have any interest at all in hot-air balloons?"

Gretchen had abandoned a rustic in Bangor, Maine—a Mainiac—whom her mother was fond of and who was now with Ethan Allen's Green Mountain Boys, but the rustic was thinking of switching to the Minutemen for the boots and pay.

Gretchen was Poxe's amanuensis, which meant that she had to scrape by on her Christmas bonus. And last Christmas had been skipped.

Francine, who slept in the straw with Braxton and Lee, Dilsie, et al., was the daughter of Professor Willingham Wilkes, who held the chair of Professor of Creative History at Yale University. Francine had fled New Haven when Yale opened its doors to the local residents and closed down the New Haven whorehouses so the students could concentrate on the Harvard–Yale game. New Haven just wasn't any fun any more since Yale ruined it. And probably never would be forevermore. Not the New Haven that

5

THE
LONG
NAKED
DESCENT
INTO
BOSTON

6

THE
LONG
NAKED
DESCENT
INTO
BOSTON

Francine had known as a child, with wide-open gambling and whoredom. Burlesque shows were held on Elm Street before Yale expanded into the center of town and incorporated the burlesque houses into its biology class under the right of Eminent Domain. The Yale Law School pulled that shenanigan in 1770. New Haven held nothing for Francine now, and when she arrived in Boston to seek her liberation, our kindly picturesque Poxe had spotted her as a comer, as he had many a wayward angel. Francine perhaps was "overreacting against her academic background." "Academic bullshit," she called it. Francine swore like a British tar and worked at the neighborhood pub, the Rose and Crown, on her day off and sometimes on her day on. Again, an overreaction against the "Yale bullshit." Poxe dwelt on this theory, but remember, Poxe was a prejudiced Harvard man.

Amos Lee, a member of the *Times* bed, was a painter from Vernon, Virginia. The wrong side of the mountain. His parents, who raised chewing tobacco on their Virginia plantation, had managed to scrape enough pence together for Lee to realize his mother's ambition of attending that fine school up North. Lee quit Harvard when he discovered his painting teacher didn't drink or go out with girls. Actually it was because his painting teacher didn't believe in perspective or any of those "goddamn foreign ideologies" and wanted to get back to good old American primitive painting. But then these are all rationalizations on Lee's part, Poxe thought. Like any alert lad who had his head screwed on properly in these modern times of 1775, Lee wanted to get in on the ground floor of the newspaper game, to get into wood block prints—BOSTON MASSACRE EXPOSED—rather than kick around perspective. Notice how the bigger an object is, the farther it is away, or just the opposite, or all lines meet in infinity if you have the patience. Which very few students do nowadays. Seventeen seventy-five. Like Lee, many young men in the Colonies realized that the newspaper was the coming medium, but unlike Lee, they did not seize the bit by the teeth.

Isaac Braxton was unfortunately from Massachusetts, born and bred. Massachusetts was the Colony which at this time was trying to con the rest of the little Colonies into abandoning the mother country and all she stood for. It had begun with the Boston Tea Party and God only knows where it would all end.

Anyway, Massachusetts did not want to be stuck with the whole war. Being from Massachusetts was a tough row to hoe because the New England accent, and particularly the Boston accent—sometimes referred to as the Boston Massacre—was incomprehensible to anyone. Which made communication with all the other little Colonies Massachusetts was trying to suborn difficult. It might not be such a bad idea after all to select a Southern general—"Has anyone here ever heard of Virginia?" That move might bring all of the Colonial Confederacy into the bag. Being from Massachusetts, Braxton had to run a tight ship and keep his mouth shut so as to not attract attention to his New England accent and let the cat out of the bag.

"You'd think that by keeping his mouth shut, Braxton would tend to write more for the *Times,* wouldn't you, Gretchen?" Poxe said.

"I wouldn't personally, no," Gretchen said, "if that's what you're getting at. Poxey, you've simply got to learn, even at your age, to pay salaries."

"At my age it's too late to change, Gretchen."

"How is a girl going to keep up with inflation?"

"Don't try, Gretchen. After the Revolution they will pass a law against inflation and everything will be hotsy totsy. Hancock and Adams swore to me that if the paper would tilt to the Patriots, they would kill inflation as the first act of Congress. Where is Dilsie, Gretchen?"

Dilsie Firstchild was a free black young woman—Poxe had once called her a colored girl and Dilsie clobbered him—from Punkhatasset, Massachusetts, an old Indian village. Dilsie had fled Punkhatasset when the Indians tried to take it back, but returned when it proved to be a false alarm. But she fled Punkhatasset for good when she inadvertently blew off the parson's son's head with her blunderbuss. As it turned out, it hadn't been inadvertent after all. The parson's son, who looked like a Boston matinee idol and was directly descended from the first Puritans on his mother's side, had been feeling his oats and had seduced all the young girls in Punkhatasset until he got to Dilsie, who blew his brains out with her blunderbuss as he was dragging her into the barn and had inadvertently turned his back. You see, the parson's son was the inadvertent one, not Dilsie, as

7

THE
LONG
NAKED
DESCENT
INTO
BOSTON

8

THE
LONG
NAKED
DESCENT
INTO
BOSTON

the trial later proved, which sent her off scot-free. But as the judge said, "I don't think it would be wise of you, Dilsie, to hang around Punkhatasset. Have you ever thought of Boston? There's an opening for a good copy reader at *The New Boston Times,* if you can stand the heat."

"Where is our good and loyal Dilsie?" Poxe asked. "She is the only one around the paper I can get any work out of, although I wish she wouldn't keep dragging that blunderbuss around with her. Do you think she's paranoid?"

"No, for a young girl the streets of Boston aren't safe."

"After the Revolution everything in America will be hotsy totsy," Poxe said. "Hancock and Adams have promised me that, if the *Times* tilts to the Patriots." Poxe sighed and looked at the ceiling and then down at the editorial he was composing. "What do you think of that can of worms, Gretchen? Apparently, if this latest dispatch from my drunken stringer is to be believed, the young on both sides would still rather fight than listen to a reading by Lowell Cabot Loring, the Dean of New England Poets. Do you believe it?"

"It's not important," Gretchen said. "The British are marching to Lexington and Concord tomorrow morning. *That's* what will interest the readers."

"I'm trying to make the *Times* a first-class newspaper," Poxe said. "We can't afford to give a damn about the reader. As an editor I have to judge whether news is in the interest of national security or the reader. The reader hasn't won yet, Gretchen. You may have a point, though. Scoop Jackson of the *Globe* might print something about the Revolution. Find Lexington and Concord on the map, that's a good girl."

When Lee, Braxton, Gretchen, Dilsie, and Francine were all gathered in the editorial office, Poxe said, "It looks like war. If not war, then the *Times*'s, the British, and the American credibility will be zero. Does anyone around here know anything about balloons?" Poxe rushed from one non sequitur to another. "I know all of you young ladies are concerned about your liberation after the war and women's job security when the boys come home. I will tell you that there will never be any job security in this country for anyone, so you're on an equal footing with men there. I believe Hancock and Adams appreciate your needs and will see if they can work women's rights into the Declaration of Independence. If not that, then the Constitution."

Ten minutes before, upstairs on the bed for five, Amos Lee had sketched Dilsie and Francine in the buff. Lee had posed the girls every which way for Braxton's article on Revolutionary Art for the Sunday *Times*.

"Revolutionary Art may be all well and good," Poxe said, "as a follow-up to this civil war." Poxe laid down Lee's pictures. "Why don't we call this war the Revolutionary War? That name should excite people and build circulation. A civil war never sold papers. And a Revolution would help your Revolutionary Art, Lee. The job of a good newspaper," Poxe said, arranging type, "is to get a war on the road. Braxton and Lee, I want you to get to the British General Gage and find out what his plans are for the Lexington and Concord trip. Dilsie and Francine, cover the battle from the Patriots' side. Braxton and Lee, after you have covered Gage's secret briefing I want you to ride to Concord and warn the people so someone will show up for the war. The Patriots have selected Paul Revere for the messenger job, but I don't think Paul is reliable. All right," Poxe said, studying what he had composed in the type case, "get your asses moving—if we don't have a war, you don't have a job. Gretchen, you stay here with me. I want you to start a column answering letters from the lonely soldiers, called 'Dear Gretchen.' "

"*I* was supposed to do that column," Dilsie said. "You said ye were going to call it 'Dear Dilsie.' You said the *Times* had to stay ahead of the *Globe*. You said the *Globe* was going to do a 'Dear Jackson' column written by Scoop, to say nothing of Lowell Cabot Loring's column for lovers of poetry."

"All right," Poxe said, "then Gretchen will stay here to keep me company. If everyone else on the *Times* gets killed, we can still keep the Revolution going. We must be careful of the British Central Intelligence Agency, and at all costs the *Times* must scoop Scoop Jackson of the *Globe*. Forget Lowell Cabot Loring. Poetry is dead—have a good Revolution."

9
THE
LONG
NAKED
DESCENT
INTO
BOSTON

two

Francine went back to tending bar at the Rose and Crown. Braxton and Lee asked for a drink for the road.

"So Poxe wants you to handle the Revere Concord–Lexington warning thing for the *Times*—the British are coming?" Francine said.

"Yes."

"You'll both need a drink," Francine said. "I hear the British are going to get an early start."

"What do you think?" Lee said to Gretchen, who was trying to put what Poxe had said into English. "Have you ever been to Concord?"

"No, but I've been to Lexington."

"They're both one-horse towns," Francine said. "If you've seen one, you've seen 'em all. I'd keep my ass in Boston if I were you, Gretchen, until these clowns, the Patriots and the British, finish their shoot-out."

"Let Gretchen decide herself, Francine," Braxton said. "Gretchen might enjoy a quiet day in the country instead of being bored by Poxey."

"Quiet day in the country, my ass! Braxton and Lee," Francine said, leaning over the bar, "don't you realize what you're getting into? Both sides have been itching to kill each other for months and you two poor bastards will be right in the middle. That will leave Gretchen, Dilsie, and me alone. Gretchen will have to go back to Maine and that rustic, I'll have to go back to New Haven, and Dilsie will have to make out with her blunder-buss. Now why don't you two boys grow up and stop playing war. The boy heroes of the Revolution. There are only two of you men. There should be three. There are three of us. If anyone can afford to go to war it should be us women. There are always more women than men. As Young Wild Tom would say, that is a strong and natural proof that the authority of one over the other—men over women—was never the design of Heaven, and I might add, a good reason for women to start a Revolution."

"Why don't you go?" Braxton said. "You could pack a lunch and get an early start."

"Because women are not damn fools. Right, Gretchen?" Francine said.

"As I said"—Gretchen looked up from her plume quill pen—"I've been to Lexington."

Dilsie came in the Rose and Crown now through the bookstore entrance. She was splattered with printer's ink and told Braxton and Lee that Poxe wanted to see them again in his office.

Poxe did not have an office. Everything was in one small pressroom.

When Lee and Braxton passed through the bookstore, Knox asked if he could have a word.

"Yes."

"Will you ask Dilsie," Knox said, "to use the front entrance? She's absolutely ruined two of my best sellers with her ink."

"Why don't you tell her yourself?"

"Because I think she might think it an affront to her natural blackness rather than to her acquired ink."

"Explain that to her."

"You know Dilsie never waits for an explanation. She just picks up a best seller and throws it at you."

"What best seller did Dilsie throw at you?"

"The Bible."

"That's heavy."

"Yes. Speak to her," Knox said.

"Dilsie is very difficult to speak to on such matters," Lee said. "She is a very sensitive young woman."

"You're telling me," Henry Knox said.

"Will you boys please shake a leg?" Poxe said from the doorway.

"We're trying to sell Knox an ad in the paper," Lee said.

"I don't advertise in a paper that's not for the Revolution," Knox said.

"What Revolution?" Poxe said. "Has there been something going on that I haven't heard about?"

"Your next line should be, Poxe," Knox said, "I only know what I read in the paper."

"That's true," Poxe said.

11

THE
LONG
NAKED
DESCENT
INTO
BOSTON

12

THE
LONG
NAKED
DESCENT
INTO
BOSTON

"It's all over town," Knox said. "The British are going to march to Lexington and Concord in the morning."

"I know that," Poxe said.

"Then why don't you print it?"

"It never occurred to me," Poxe said. "Do you think there's a story there? This Mrs. Loring thing is going to take up most of the edition. Then there's the cricket match. Mrs. Loring is sleeping with General Gage, you know. That's an exclusive for *The New Boston Times*. We can thank Braxton for that."

"Yet, I think," Knox said, "the Revolution might be worth a few lines. Jesus!"

"I will give it my most careful consideration," Poxe said, "but it will stir things up. After all, a newspaper does have responsibilities to national security. What do you think, Lee?"

"I think we would not be entirely remiss," Lee said, "if we sneaked something in about the Revolution on the back page. Christ!"

"Will do," Poxe said. "I believe in these editorial conferences. Will do. Now everything is out in the open. Will do. Don't forget, I'm sending you and Braxton to cover the whole shebang. My thought had been we shouldn't cover anything before it happens. If nothing happens at Lexington and Concord, you'll get your expenses anyway. No bar bills. Will two pounds cover it, including the horse rentals?"

"No."

"Come into my office. I've got another trick up my sleeve," Poxe said. Poxe sat down at his roll-top desk.

"I see Dilsie has left the type scattered all over my desk. I've been afraid to mention it to her after what happened to Knox. I wish one of you people would speak to her."

"Will do," Lee said.

"Now, where were we?" Poxe said.

"The Revolution."

"Of course," Poxe said. "Now this is my idea for your trip to the Revolution that I'd like to kick around with you. It's not a stop-the-press thing, but it's an idea. General Gage has promised to let you both in on the press briefing for the British march to Concord if I kill the Mrs. Loring story. As you know, Gage is living with Mrs. Loring and is expecting his wife on the next boat."

"Things that history will miss," Lee said.

"General Gage may want you to cover the briefing blindfolded, Mrs. Loring being a proper lady. But you can hear what is said at the briefing even if you can't see."

"But then we won't be able to see the map briefing."

"I'll speak to General Gage about that," Poxe said. "Maybe he'll let you have a peek. Mrs. Loring could be asked to leave briefly without hurting her feelings. But if Gage won't make this concession, that is, if he won't let you peek at the map, you fellows know your way to Concord, don't you?"

"We did until they built the new by-pass."

"Was our paper for or against the new by-pass?" Poxe said.

"Against."

"What did they by-pass?"

"Harvard."

"We should have been all for that," Poxe said. "Now where were we? Remind me to write an editorial for the by-pass. Where were we?"

"Mrs. Loring."

"Yes, I promised Gage we'd kill the Mrs. Loring story as much out of respect for his wife and kiddies as in return for his allowing us to attend the secret briefing. I've promised to hold the march story until his general, Lord Percy, is well on his way back from Lexington and Hancock and Adams on their way to the clink. That's part of the reason for the British march. Adams and Hancock are holed up in Lexington with a Mr. Clark. It might be a good idea to take out some life insurance with Hancock while you are there. You might consider making the *Times* the beneficiary. I believe Mr. Clark's is a tavern."

"I believe it's a parsonage," Lee said.

"Check that out," Poxe said, arranging the type that Dilsie had scattered until he spelled DILSIE, YOU MADE A MESS. "The plan, as I understand it, is that you are going to anticipate Revere. If you start out ahead of Revere, that's all right with me. Revere has not placed a single ad with us for his silver pots. He gives all his advertising to the *Globe*, and this ride would be a big plus for him.

13

THE
LONG
NAKED
DESCENT
INTO
BOSTON

14

THE
LONG
NAKED
DESCENT
INTO
BOSTON

It would be the equivalent of a free ad. I like Paul, I'd like to see him get ahead, but fair is fair. Agreed?"

"I suppose so," Braxton said. "What are you spelling out in that type?"

"Now?"

"Yes."

Both Braxton and Lee walked around in back of Poxe and looked over his shoulder. The type announced: REVERE PREEMPTED IN RIDE TO LEXINGTON. PAUL MAY HAVE MISSED NEW TURN-OFF. CITIZENS CONCERNED FOR REVERE'S SAFETY. WIFE MARY CLAIMS PAUL ALWAYS HOME BY 10:00 O'CLOCK. SHE SUSPECTS FOUL PLAY. BRAXTON AND LEE OF THE NEW TIMES ALERT IRATE PEASANTS. PANDEMONIUM. MUCH SHOOTING. GENERAL GAGE CLAIMS LEXINGTON-CONCORD FORAY SUCCESSFUL DESPITE MANY BRITISH SOLDIERS DEAD. CLAIMS MOST REBELS SHOT. AMMO DESTROYED. HANCOCK AND ADAMS CAPTURED AND PLACED IN DURANCE VILE. BRAXTON AND LEE OF THE TIMES FETED BY MAYOR. KING GEORGE ANNOUNCES NO CAUSE FOR WAR—YET. BUT COULD START ANY DAY. BRITISH CREDIBILITY AT STAKE. NATIONAL SECURITY THREATENED BY AMERICAN TERRORISTS. HOPE COLONISTS WILL SOBER UP AND PAY BACK TAXES. THEN NO RECRIMINATION, KING INDICATES. FULL AMNESTY FOR ALL INCLUDING THOSE WHO FLED TO CANADA. PLEASE TURN TO PAGE 3.

"That's what I call objective reporting," Lee said. "Is the paper going to increase to three pages?"

"Four, five, who knows?" Poxe said. "If the *Times* can get a war cooking. Without a war every ten years, even the *Globe* would go broke. I hope everyone connected with the Press remembers that. A newspaper can survive anything but peace."

"Whose side are we on?"

"Let's wait and find out who's winning," Poxe said, "and find out which way the advertisers are leaning. Boston, according to the latest *Times* poll, is one-third Tory, one-third Rebel, and one-third rabble. The rabble is what we call the independent vote. Let's wait to find out which way the rabble swing before we jump. If we guess right, there's a small fortune in it for all."

"Does that mean we get a raise?" Braxton said.

"Let's not be hasty," the editor said. "I always said the paper should never rush into a situation from which it cannot withdraw. Now why don't you two pop over to the horse rental place and make reservations. You will only need one horse. You can ride double, can't you?"

"No."

"Well, we don't have a Revolution every day. Get two horses, but be sure you take them by the mileage rate rather than the day rate, and if you think you're building up too much mileage, run the horses backwards for a while. No one will see you."

"But that's illegal."

"Well, we don't have a Revolution every day. Avis Horse Rentals should make allowances. If we could hold up the Revolution for a day we could get the weekend rate. Try that new outfit on Water Street called Hurtz. I believe they call it that because it hurts so much to ride the damn things."

"Save your wit and wisdom for the paper," Braxton said. "We are off."

"Remember, speak to Dilsie about her mess, and God bless, God bless." And then Poxe settled back into his editorial mood.

When our intrepid reporters, the boy heroes of the Revolution, passed through the bookstore, Knox wanted to know if they had spoken to Dilsie yet and if they would speak to Francine about her swearing. "The doors are very thin and swearing doesn't sit well with my Tory customers. I don't want to give the image of a porno book shoppe."

"Call it an adult book shoppe," Braxton said.

"I've explained to the Tories that Francine is a professor's daughter but it doesn't help. They think this younger generation should be written off now that the country's going to hell anyway."

"Any complaints about Gretchen?"

"No. Except that she hangs out with the Liberty Boys."

"Guilt by association," Lee said, as they crashed into the bar.

Francine saw them coming and leaned over the bar and told Dilsie and Gretchen to mix with the cash customers. She would take care of the two deadbeats.

"I don't wants to mix," Dilsie said. "I wants to talk to Braxton and Lee about my next editorial. Why don't you mix your own goddamn self."

15
THE
LONG
NAKED
DESCENT
INTO
BOSTON

16

THE
LONG
NAKED
DESCENT
INTO
BOSTON

"Someone has to tend bar," Francine said. "I want you to mix because there are a lot of good-paying Tories sitting in here tonight and today was the soldiers' payday—mix. Learn something."

"Everybody knows the British is going to march tomorrow," Dilsie said. Dilsie spoke incorrect English when she felt like it. It was part of her style. Like Francine, she used words as part of her personal revolution.

Lee came up to them and wondered if one of the girls had made up their room yet.

"I ain't ye goddamn slave," Dilsie said, "but I'll buy you a drink. Poxey slipped me a pound."

"That calls for a celebration," Lee said.

"I'm thinking of doing a column on women's rights," Dilsie said. "I bets the blacks gets the vote before the women. I'm also thinking of a column on love, as Poxey suggested. Something like 'Dear Dilsie,' you know, where peoples write in and says, 'My old man ain't had an erection on him in three months. Is this the fault of the war or am I doing something wrong? Dear Dilsie, I sure would appreciate it if you would straighten this out. Signed, Lonely in Massachusetts.' What do you think?"

"Never in Boston."

"How about after the war? How about a 'Dear Dilsie' then?"

"Never after anything in Boston."

"But people could write in from Pennsylvania. 'Dear Dilsie'—"

"But they wouldn't print it in Boston," Braxton said.

"I'll study that," Dilsie said. "I hear you rented some horses. Is you going to preempt Paul?"

"We'll see," Lee said. "It's going to be a busy weekend. Maybe all the horses are rented."

"If you hang around this bar much longer," Gretchen said, "the war will be over and we'll all still be British."

"I don't know," a British soldier said, leaning on the bar. "I hear the King is going to rent Hessians to take our place. I sure hope they hurry up with this rent-a-soldier thing before we make our secret march to Lexington, before I get my ass shot off."

Lee and Braxton drank up quickly and bade everyone good-bye. They said they were going to Gage's secret briefing for the secret march to Lexington tomorrow.

Outside on Church Street, Lee told Braxton they should put off the rent-a-horse until Gage had firmed up his secret march. "Then we might ride double and charge Poxey for two. I know a girl at Hurtz who will cooperate."

They passed a small stable on the way. They made a note that it displayed used second-hand horses. The sign said, WE TRY HARDER. SPECIAL RATE TO LEXINGTON. NO CHARGE FOR DROP-OFF IN CONCORD. WE BUY THE HAY. TWO-WEEK RATE TO YORKTOWN. SMALL DROP-OFF CHARGE. YOU BUY THE HAY. Lee kicked a used horse, an all-white with a black cock, and said it hadn't been driven too hard considering the shape it was in. A used-horse salesman slouched up and said financing was available and that a little old lady doctor in Chappaquiddick had owned the horse and never rode it further than the bridge.

Lee and Braxton hurried on to Gage's requisitioned brick Colonial on Mill Street, where they were blindfolded by two American slaves Gage got with the house—Ali Pomfret and Mohammed Pomeroy. The two white-haired slaves, Pomfret and Pomeroy, seemingly out of a fake stage play, hustled the worried reporters past Mrs. Loring in the drawing room. Mrs. Loring commented that Braxton and Lee were two fine figures of men and it was a pity, pity, pity they were going to be hung.

"We're not going to hang any Rebels today, Mrs. Loring," one of the American slaves, Pomeroy, said. "We are going to the secret British war briefing."

"Then I'll join you," Mrs. Loring said, "if I may."

"You may," both the slaves said.

THE
LONG
NAKED
DESCENT
INTO
BOSTON

three

The British General Thomas Gage, the Military Governor of the Colonies, was seated in the library with his tobacco and port. General Gage appeared discombobulated at first, tapping his silver Skoal snuff box, but then remarking his own importance, he quickly became combobulated again. He had four thousand British troops under him, but only two with him in the library— Lord Percy and Colonel Coudray.

"Before we get to the matter at hand," Gage said, "I want to say that Lord Percy has come up with a fine figure of a woman. Her name? Her name? Her name?"

"Her name is a military secret. National security."

"And jolly well kept."

"Hear, hear, hear."

"It is a Madame Annette de Tocqueville."

"Pass the port."

"We are about," General Gage said with gravity, "to foray out to Concord and Lexington and pick up Hancock and Adams and divers stores the Colonials have for making war. Now that Lowell Cabot Loring's poetry reading has failed, we hope by our march to raise sufficient money for the Americans so that they can buy uniforms. We cannot fight a war with ragamuffins. If there is a decent skirmish, then the Colonials will take sufficient interest in the war to raise money for uniforms. If a war must take place, it's not going to take place without proper uniforms."

"Hear, hear."

"The Colonials don't even have a proper name. They don't want to be called Colonials or Provincials. What about Patriots? I've suggested that to them."

"*We* are the patriots," Lord Percy said.

"We are the *Government*," Gage said. "It's taken for granted we are patriots. It's only the insecure that would take a name like Patriots. The more the scoundrel, the more he insists on his patriotism and the more he impugns the patriotism of others.

Through my feminine double agent, a certain Peggy, I planted the name Patriots. I believe the Americans have taken it hook, line, and sinker."

"Peggy?" Mrs. Loring said.

"Yes. And these two gentlemen are from the *Times*. The two blacks, Pomfret and Pomeroy, I believe, are from where?"

"Newark, New Jersey."

"Anyway," Gage said, "we hope our foray to Lexington and Concord tomorrow will create enough interest in the American cause so the Boston Patriots can buy uniforms."

"Clever, clever, clever."

"How do we know," Lord Percy said, "that the Patriots will use the money thus raised by our efforts to purchase uniforms? It could be squandered on rum. And can you buy a decent uniform in Boston today?"

"Any more questions?" Gage asked.

"Before we march we might check and see if the Americans have paid their taxes yet. We may be off on a wild goose chase. We don't want to shoot people who have just paid their taxes. That wouldn't be fair."

"As far as I can gather, not a single Patriot has paid his taxes in five years."

"But hasn't this always been a problem in America? Maybe it's not the King they object to paying. Maybe Americans won't pay taxes to anyone. Is that worth a war? Let's try to be fair."

"Both sides have to have a war about something," Gage said.

"I still don't think the Colonials will spend the money on uniforms," Percy said. "I think they'll get their backs up and continue to pot us from behind trees in overalls."

"It's a chance we have to take," Gage said. "As the Commanding General, I'm here to take that chance."

"But some of our lads will be killed," Mrs. Loring said.

"As the Commanding General, I will take that chance. The King informs me he is going to rent Hessians, then it won't be our British lads killed."

"What language do Hessians speak?"

"I forgot to ask," Gage said. "I wonder if the King knows. Does anyone know?"

"I believe they speak Hessian," Braxton said.

19
THE
LONG
NAKED
DESCENT
INTO
BOSTON

20

THE
LONG
NAKED
DESCENT
INTO
BOSTON

"Good boy," Gage said. "I hope you get some of that wit into the *Times*. What does your latest poll show on the war?"

"Thirty-three percent for, thirty-three percent against, and thirty-three percent don't know."

"What does the poll show on those who will flee to Canada?"

"Thirty-three percent will flee to Canada, thirty-three percent will stay here, and thirty-three percent don't know where to go."

"Are these polls honest? That is, is it a fair sampling of Boston or just certain middle-class sections?"

"The polls," Lee said, "are assigned by our editor, a Mr. Poxe, to Dilsie Firstchild, a competent researcher."

"Yes," the taller black named Pomfret said, "Dilsie is fair. She asked me."

"And you replied?"

"I'm for Canada."

"You wouldn't opt to go back to Newark?"

"Not now," Pomfret and Pomeroy agreed.

"Well, now that everything is settled," General Gage said, "where was it we were going tomorrow? Lexington, of course. All in favor of the war say 'aye.' All opposed, 'no.' "

"No," Mrs. Loring said. "But I realize that I have no right to have an opinion. Being only a woman and it being only the latter part of the eighteenth century."

"Tut, tut," Lord Percy said.

"I only want to say," Mrs. Loring said, "that I don't want my children killed in a war."

"But you have no children that we know of."

"I don't want my children that ye know not of killed in a war either," Mrs. Loring said.

"Hear, hear," Lord Percy said.

"Whose side are you on, Lord Percy?"

"Hear her out," Lord Percy said.

"Killed in a war," Mrs. Loring said, "to raise money, uniform money, for the Boston Patriots, or because neither side wants to go to a poetry reading."

"Poetry, I am afraid, will in time make a comeback, and we have no say," General Gage said, "what the Patriots do with their money. We just hope they'll buy uniforms. It is their money, they can do what they like with it. They'll probably buy some ammunition, some cannon. If it's a serious war, contraceptives—"

"Contraceptives?"

"Yes, the lay mind," General Gage said, "and there is no pun intended here, but the lay mind cannot conceive of the complications of war, the sheer bulk of logistics that a professional soldier like myself must be concerned with. The lay person thinks we pass out guns and say, 'Lads, have a go at it.' It's not that simple at all."

"Hear, hear," Lord Percy said.

"That is why, before taking this fatal step—is fatal step a cliché?"

"Yes, I'm afraid it is," the slave Pomfret said.

"Do you spend all your time in my library?"

"Most of the time," Pomeroy said.

"Anyway," General Gage continued, "that is why, before taking this serious step of war, we British, being British, are willing to listen even to Mrs. Loring."

"You listen, pet," Mrs. Loring said, "and then you men go off and do exactly as you like. That goes for both sides. You're all determined to have your war even when you have no excuse for it except to skip a poetry reading. You'll all be out there shooting at each other tomorrow—the devil take the hindmost. You admit the Patriots don't even have proper uniforms and you say the Colonials haven't paid their taxes. You people haven't paid your taxes. I know you haven't, Tom," she said to Gage.

General Thomas Gage turned very sober and put down his maps. "I intend to pay them, Kate. There's a great deal of difference between their refusing to pay and my intending to pay at some nebulous date."

"True, true," Lord Percy said.

"I can't see it," Mrs. Loring said.

"Women become hysterical. No logic."

"True, true," Lord Percy said.

"Now if it was a war for women's rights," Mrs. Loring said.

"She is becoming hysterical," General Gage said, taking full blame for Mrs. Loring on himself. "You will observe, Kate, that regardless of who wins this war, people of my high income and position will never pay any taxes. That's why we invented the

21
THE
LONG
NAKED
DESCENT
INTO
BOSTON

22

THE
LONG
NAKED
DESCENT
INTO
BOSTON

tax-exempt bond and the middle class. Someone must pay to keep the armies of the world going. Any middle class would rather starve to death than not have an army, and an army, to justify its existence, has to have a war. Whichever side wins gets to write the propaganda and that is called history. Liberty is always a good slogan. Liberty, gentlemen, corrupts, and absolute liberty corrupts absolutely."

"Hear, hear."

"People are always willing to kill other people to establish the tyranny of the majority called mobocracy—are you taking this down, Lee, Braxton?"

"No."

"Because the reporters are justifiably miffed," Lord Percy said, "by having to wear blinders. What in God's name aren't they supposed to see?"

"Mrs. Loring."

"But they have seen Mrs. Loring," Colonel Coudray said.

"Take some snuff," General Gage said, passing the silver Skoal box. "Now, take the supposition," Gage said, that two gentlemen of the Press have seen Mrs. Loring in *deshabille* at the Gage residence the day before Mrs. Gage arrives. Take the supposition that Mrs. Gage steps off the boat and picks up a *Times* paper and reads, MRS. LORING FLEES IN THE BUFF AS ELIZABETH GAGE'S SHIP SIGHTED OFF BOSTON HARBOR. GENERAL GAGE FACES MILITARY INQUIRY INTO HANKY PANKY. 'NO ORGIES IN WIFE'S ABSENCE,' THE FOXY GENERAL ALLEGES IN WEAKENED VOICE. ELIZABETH GAGE WILL STAND BY HER HUSBAND IN 'HIS DRAINED CONDITION.' UNKNOWN RELIABLE SOURCES THAT DO NOT WISH TO BE QUOTED INDICATE GAGE STARTS WAR TO HUSH SCANDAL. BOSTON PATRIOTS DEMAND EXPOSURE. COUNTRY MUST BE RETURNED TO PURITAN ETHIC. BOOKS IN BOSTON SHOULD BE BURNED. GAGE SCANDAL POINTS UP NEED FOR WAR. PLEASE SEE FOLLOWING EDITORIAL ON WHY WE FIGHT. Is that a fair supposition, gentlemen?" Gage said to Lee and Braxton.

"I see you read the *Times*," Lee said.

"Yes."

"Well, it depends on who writes the article. The paper *never* prints what we report. If a rewrite man makes that mistake, they put him to reviewing books—they claim he has no imagination. If Poxey writes the news, it tends to be dull because he claims the paper has to find out who's going to win the war before the paper jumps. Dilsie tends to favor the Patriots because it gives the paper more zap. The section you quoted sounds like Dilsie."

"It sure enough does," Pomfret said.

"Gretchen would be more conservative and Francine more obscene," Braxton said.

"It seems to me," Lord Percy said, "that your editor, Mr. Poxe, believes in hiring women. Is that a consciousness-raising activity—will you please pass the port—or what?"

"It's more a money-raising effort. Poxey has discovered that women will work for a pat on the head or ass."

"Dilsie?"

"Poxey slipped Dilsie a pound note yesterday."

General Gage, Lord Percy, and Colonel Coudray tried to evince interest in Dilsie and her pound note by nodding their heads in wonder, but tomorrow's war kept nagging at the back of their minds.

"I suppose you two, Braxton and Lee, are going to trot off on the morrow to warn the Patriots in Lexington," Gage said. "You know Revere was supposed to do that. Paul has his signal lanterns arranged and everything. In the old North Church, I believe."

"Paul is determined to hog the whole show," Lord Percy said.

"You could tell the country people that Paul is on his way," Colonel Coudray said. "Then he wouldn't entirely be left out of it."

"I say leave Revere out of it in toto," General Gage said in a commanding voice. "Think of all the bad poetry that would save the world. 'One if by land and two if by sea, and I on the opposite shore will be.' "

"Hear, hear," Lord Percy said.

"I believe, in view of the circumstances," the taller black, Pomfret, said, "that some accommodation could be made to history."

"Whatever that means," the other slave, Pomeroy, said.

"It means the American Revolution awaits," General Gage said. "Now, let us have a look-see at the maps. Here we have

23
THE
LONG
NAKED
DESCENT
INTO
BOSTON

24

THE
LONG
NAKED
DESCENT
INTO
BOSTON

Lexington and here, up here, we have Concord. I see that this cow path is marked as an Inter-Colonial. Can we make it through? We must consider the Sunday buggy driver."

"And the rustics potting us."

"Yes. Who made this map, a hay company? I don't see Boston. Where are we?"

"We're right here," Lee said, lifting his mask. "Your British Army is here. The Colonial Army is there. This is a *New Boston Times* map. Boston is not included because everyone knows where we are."

"Sensible," Lord Percy said.

"But we must start from a given point," General Gage said in a correct tone, remembering his past wars. "Otherwise we will not arrive at a predetermined destination."

"Now we are cracking," Colonel Coudray said.

"Now," General Gage said in his command voice, "we will jump off at oh-six-hundred. Both regiments, the Lightfoot and the Seventeenth Grenadiers, on the ready, we will take to the boats and force a landing here at Phipp's Farm in the marshes. We will allow time for the men's feet to dry and then quick-march to Concord."

"Why don't you simply march across Boston Neck here," Mrs. Loring said, pointing to the map, "by way of Roxbury and keep the men's feet dry?"

"Because women know nothing of the art of war," General Gage said.

"I'm sorry, Tom," Mrs. Loring said.

"I don't want to hurt your feelings, Kate," Gage said, "but this is men's business. Why don't you retire to the drawing room and let us have a go at this."

"I suspect," Pomeroy said in a gentle voice to Mrs. Loring, "that, as my colleague Pomfret has suggested, it would be a further accommodation to history if we allow the generals to map the campaign."

"Quite," Lord Percy said.

"Fuck off," Mrs. Loring said.

"Kate, there are reporters present."

"Don't mind us," Braxton said.

"It was rude, and I apologize," Mrs. Loring said to the two slaves.

"Not rude," Pomfret said. "Simply gauche. It's the war. It's difficult on everyone. Let us move along, Mrs. Loring, and leave the brave new world in lesser hands."

"What do you suppose Pomfret meant by that?" Lord Percy said when they were gone. "Do you suppose he was suggesting that we are not clever?"

"The council of war is over," General Gage announced. "The decision is that we hope for the best. That we toodle off and play it by ear. If Colonel Coudray's regiment blunders into a trap, then we can send out Lord Percy's relief column to blunder into the same trap. I'm pulling your leg, Lord Percy." Gage filled Lord Percy's glass. "Do you suspect I might have offended Mrs. Loring?"

"Those black chaps are bucking her up," Colonel Coudray said. "I'll have one drink for the road, General. What did you think of Mrs. Loring's suggestion that we stay on the Inter-Colonial and keep the lads' feet dry?"

"If we stay on the road," Gage said, studying the map, "there's really no need for a general. Mrs. Loring might as well be running the war as myself. I find that unacceptable."

"Quite."

"She had a point," Lee said.

"Take off your masks. Mrs. Loring has fled. Now what do you know about war, Lee?"

"I know," Braxton said, moving in, "that Phipp's Marsh is the silliest place in New England to make a landing. You'll be up to your ass in water for three miles, and Old Man Phipp will turn his dogs loose on you. He has the place posted with NO TRESPASSING signs."

"Are you certain? Legally posted?"

"Yes."

"That puts another light on the matter," General Gage said.

"Perhaps Mrs. Loring's suggestion," Lord Percy said, "isn't bad by half."

"Is Peter Finch's marsh posted?" Gage asked.

"No."

25

THE
LONG
NAKED
DESCENT
INTO
BOSTON

26

THE
LONG
NAKED
DESCENT
INTO
BOSTON

"Then we will land there," Gage said.

"You'll still be in the marsh."

"But we will be the King's men," General Gage said. "And led by Lord Percy. Need we say more?"

They all very quietly and with a kind of decorous solemnity had one more drink for the road. Braxton and Lee joined in the silent toast with glasses raised to Providence for help and any and all outside aid—as Mrs. Loring exploded into the room followed by the black retainers, she demanding to know if they were going to drown the army in Phipp's Marsh.

"No, Phipp's Farm is posted," Gage said.

"But you're still going to have your silly male war. Kill people?"

The two blacks raised their hands in a gesture indicating that they had done all they could to reason with her.

"I have instructed Colonel Coudray and Lord Percy—I won't be there, Kate—I have instructed them to watch out for NO TRESPASSING signs, and above all, no unwarranted killing of civilians."

"Are you suggesting, Tom, that there is such a thing as warranted killing?"

"I'm suggesting, Kate, that if you think you can run the British Army better than I can, why don't you have a go at it?"

Mrs. Loring left the room, insouciant. Her nose in the air at men's childish and manic manners. As though the world would not survive the month, the hour, if males were not all sent to bed without supper.

General Thomas Gage straightened his uniform, poured each soldier and Lee and Braxton one more drink, then spread his blue and golden tassel and silk-accoutered arms in the air and said, "The war has begun. Gentlemen, need we say more?"

four

Braxton and Lee were standing on the corner of Main and Claremount streets in Lexington, letting their rented horses blow and get a second wind. Dilsie and Francine came up quietly on used rented horses but their steeds seemed in fine fettle.

"Your steeds seem in fine fettle," Braxton said. "Where did you rent them?"

"What I want to know," Lee said, "is who is minding the store? You know Poxey doesn't want the whole staff killed, particularly if there's no story in this Lexington–Concord thing. Have you been alerting the countrymen?"

"Yes, if there's anyone home," Francine said.

"Do you tell them the British are coming and rush on, or do you tell them Revere will fill them in on the details?"

"We tells them everything," Dilsie said. "We tells them the whole goop flat out. Then Poxey has us leave a piece of notepaper that says—here," she said, "you read it."

Braxton took the piece of paper that read, YOU LEARNED ABOUT THE START OF THE REVOLUTION FIRST FROM THE NEW BOSTON TIMES.

"Good, then we're scooping Scoop Jackson of the *Globe*."

"Yes."

"When you tell the farmers, Francine, the British are coming," Lee said, "what has been their reaction?"

"It varies," Francine said. "Some said, 'Do you realize what time it is?' Some said, 'Are you Francine Wilkes, Professor Wilkes' little daughter?' Some said, 'Up your ass, sweetie.' Some just rushed out and shot up the whole town. I would say their reaction has been individual, depending upon the person's background."

"Let's alert those people," Braxton said, pointing at a blue and white and gold house across the street. Dilsie and Francine dismounted and began to fire rocks at the windows.

28

THE
LONG
NAKED
DESCENT
INTO
BOSTON

"Don't overdo!" Braxton hollered.

Francine fired a rock right through a leaded glass window. "Wake up, you lazy sons-of-bitches. The British are coming."

Six windows were opened all at once and six girls appeared at six windows and six voices screamed, "Come on, boys. Payday!"

Now the six girls disappeared from the six windows and tumbled out the front door and tied up the four night visitors' horses and ushered *The New Boston Times* staff into the parlor of Madame Annette de Tocqueville.

"Vive le Roi!" the madam greeted them from her throne chair of blue sateen that matched her blue hair. *"Vive le Roi!* Tell me, *mon petit cher,"* she said to Braxton, who seemed to be the leader of the bunch, "have the good King's troops at last arrived?"

"They are coming up the pike, madame."

"Champagne pour tout le monde! Their American Revolution has ended before it has begun," she said through the yellow glow of candelabra. *"Vive le Roi!"*

Now Madame de Tocqueville's girls formed into patterns for the minuet. There would be a celebration for the arrival of the King's troops. Madame de Tocqueville had suffered much humiliation from the rabble for many months now. Her Palais de Joie had been closed by the Revolutionary Committee of Safety, her girls humiliated by the Revolutionary Committee of Sexual Temperance, her very house threatened by the Lexington First National Mortgage and Loan, and Madame de Tocqueville herself threatened by the mob hoping to cleanse our country of foreign corruption and divers perversions practiced on said premises by said Madame de Tocqueville, who is bisexual or French, whichever the case may be.

"And how do you plead, madame?" the rustic who headed the Revolutionary Committee for Thirteen Clean Colonies had asked.

"If the British get here in time," Madame de Tocqueville said to Braxton, "we will have a hung jury. The King's men will hang them all," she said, raising her glass to Braxton and Lee. "What right do they have to pillory me? Trial by jury—why, it's a comedy."

"If you haves any complaints," Dilsie said, "write a letter to the editor of *The New Boston Times*. Mr. Poxe is his name, circulation is the game."

"So you represent the Press," Madame de Tocqueville said, clapping her hands for the ladies to commence the minuet, "and you have come to hear my complaints?"

"We have ventured out into this benighted hinterland," Braxton said, "on a bad horse, at Poxey's wish, to cover the war in general."

"La guerre c'est moi," Madame de Tocqueville said.

"C'est vrai. A votre service," Lee said, genuflecting and kissing madame's rubied hand as the landlady of the Palais de Joie swung and swirled beneath the cut crystal sparkle of twenty chandeliers to three fifes, two violas, and one violin played by six silk-caparisoned eunuchs from Tangiers. The seventh musician played a comb through toilet paper "because the rabble had stolen his French horn to melt down into cannon for the Revolution."

"To shoot me," Madame de Tocqueville whispered to Dilsie and Francine.

"Madame, I will not hear of such talk," Braxton said, polishing off another magnum of champagne. "Here you are on the eve of being rescued from the mob by the King's men and you dwell on death—impossible, madame," and Braxton gathered madame in his arms and pressed her to his leather jerkin and twirled her in the minuet.

Now scattered shots were heard, then the *bim bam boom* of distant cannonading. The shots increased, the cannonading came closer, the music slowed, then ceased. Now bullets and shot entered the ballroom, pocking the plaster, cutting down candles, exploding the wine, cowering the musicians as a line of bullet holes was writ above their heads. A cannonball entered the ballroom unannounced through the side of the chateau. The ball, as large as a pumpkin, as black as pitch, as quick as light, smashed into the great ballroom mirror, causing myriad and strange dazzle. Then the cannonball continued on its way through the chateau, through the orangerie, the potting shed, the slave quarters, where the slaves quickly patched with quilting the hole caused by the ball entering, then covered the hole where the ball left. The cannonball went through the pear orchard, pruning the pear trees, before it died at the edge of Swan Lake, rolling slow now and entering the water calmly as though nothing had happened—

29

THE
LONG
NAKED
DESCENT
INTO
BOSTON

30

THE
LONG
NAKED
DESCENT
INTO
BOSTON

nothing for which it was to blame. Another ball entered the ballroom now, but this time the ladies had time to scream and dart about and show their mettle by pulling up their skirts as the ball, as though with a resolute mind of its own, rolled fast back and forth on the hardwood alley ballroom floor, knocking down the ladies in ninepin fashion; sometimes nine of the ladies would gather in a triangle shape and the ball would strike the leading lady, say the tenpin, and the leading lady would knock all the rest to hell for breakfast, so the cannonball by striking only one civilian could sometimes get as many as eleven, as a lady could ricochet out and knock down two musicians. Of course, cannonballs are not supposed to strike down civilians in cold blood; they are supposed to be used only against soldiers in the passion of battle, but the British under Lord Percy had been fired on by the Colonial "terrorists" on the North Bridge, so were shooting their cannon at any target of opportunity, and even sometimes of no opportunity, such as was the case now. The British were understandably determined to get to John Hancock and Samuel Adams before they accomplished more mischief, before the Revolution got off the ground. The British were also dismayed at being shot at, as any normal group of people always is. The fact that they were also British and represented the King only compounded the crime.

The great doors of the chateau opened and Lord Percy entered. The cannonball, seeming to sense something wrong, stopped. The girls ceased screaming, too, as though they abruptly felt themselves in the presence of God or Lord Percy; as though they were on the abyss of a historical happening that would be harkened from grandchild to grandchild, lost, and then recaptured in the ninth telling, but memorial to them now, history alive and ominous in a lone house between Concord and Lexington on a cold night; no stars, no angel watched.

"Lord Percy!" Then Madame de Tocqueville collapsed at his feet without being struck.

"Madame de Tocqueville," Lord Percy said, bending over her. *"Ma petite,* the Colonial barbarians are routed. Lord Percy is here."

"Have you hung the Colonial jury that indicted me?"

"Yes."

"Already?"

"Patience, Madame de Tocqueville. If Lord Percy says it is done, it is as good as done. We will hang the American jury in the morning. So you already have a hung jury, madame. Everything is going to be all right again, madame," he said, soothing her brow with his command hand, her hot brow that had been touched by the ball that ended up in Swan Lake. "Lord Percy has arrived," Lord Percy said.

The *Times* staff, led by Francine and Dilsie and followed by Braxton and Lee, fled the French Colonial chateau, piled out the cannonball hole, sped through the slave quarters, and got to their horses and away in haste to alert every Middlesex village and farm that indeed the British were coming, that in fact Lord Percy had arrived.

They clop-clopped down all sorts of narrow lanes, searching for the main Inter-Colonial road. The Patriots had removed the direction signs to confuse the British. They had turned some signs about and written over others; the TAKE THE NEXT EXIT TO CONCORD now read simply, TAKE NEXT THREE EXITS TO BROOKLYN.

Four tired horses finally pulled up in front of a green brick house and would go no further for now. The horses blew out great gusts of air and swung their hammerheads to catch a quick glimpse of the people who would not get off their backs and lead them back to Boston. The horses did not give a damn for history. The fact that they had arrived in Lexington before Revere and had been an accessory before the fact of independence made them laugh, not sing, made them querulous with much snorting and pawing of hoof. Before becoming a rent-a-horse, the blaze under Francine had belonged to a marauding one-eyed Indian who was made of sterner stuff than these Revolutionists.

The sign on the front lawn of the green brick house read, BRITISH COLONIES LUNATIC ASYLUM. A Patriot had crossed the sign out and rewritten, AMERICA—HOUSE FOR THE MENTALLY DISTURBED.

"Shall we tell these people the British are coming?" Dilsie said.

31
THE
LONG
NAKED
DESCENT
INTO
BOSTON

32

THE
LONG
NAKED
DESCENT
INTO
BOSTON

A gentleman opened the front door of the green brick house and waved a cane at them in the faint light.

"The British are coming," Francine called apologetically.

"And late again," the gentleman with the cane called back. "The damage has already been done. Have you seen what shape the country is in? It's far too late to do anything about it. But come in anyway and make yourselves at home."

"We are not the British," Braxton said.

"Come in anyway—make yourselves at home." The gentleman waved them to dismount. "The damage is done, I'm afraid. The country will never be the same again, agreed? It's Hancock and Adams that have accomplished the mischief, along with *The New Boston Times*. Agreed?"

The *Times* people made themselves cozy in the living room of the asylum and the good doctor, for that is what the kind gentleman with the cane proved himself to be, busied himself with fetching tobacco for Francine's pipe, which Dilsie shared with her in quick puffs like Indians. The boys had hot rum in a mixture the doctor called a New England Flip.

Then Braxton asked the good doctor if the *Times* had been scooped, if a reporter named Jackson from the *Globe* had arrived yet.·

"That queer man who is always running?"

"Yes."

"No."

"Good."

"And has Paul Revere arrived yet?"

"No."

"Good."

"So you're beating out Revere of the Patriots and Scoop Jackson of the *Globe*," the good doctor said, stirring the Flip, then giving Dilsie a fresh light from a long taper. "Jolly good. That's jolly good. Never did care for Jackson, who is one day for the war, next day against the war, depending on how the wind blows. Never did care for Revere either. I think Paul's a bit cuckoo, dashing about the country instead of tending his silver shoppe. What about his wife and kiddies? He has nine, you know. I delivered six of his children. I don't know how the others got here or where they came from. Oh dear, your pipe's gone out again," he said to Dilsie. He relit it and said, "You have a very good color, a healthy tan, my dear. You must get a lot of exercise."

"I tries to," Dilsie said.

"It's too bad you people did not make it a minute sooner. You just missed the King of Spain, the Prince of Denmark, the Emperor of China, and the next President of the United States—a former gentleman named Jimmy. You are looking a bit peaked," he said to Francine, setting down his Flip. "A bit pale around the gills," the doctor said.

"That's because I'm sitting next to Dilsie, who is black," Francine said. "I am naturally white. I feel fine. I never felt better in my life," she said, passing the pipe to Dilsie. "I was born this color. I was born peaked and pale and white around the gills. Smoking has nothing to do with it. I am naturally white."

"And you were born black?" the doctor said to Dilsie.

"I presumes so," Dilsie said.

"And you two gentlemen," the doctor said, turning to Braxton and Lee, "are here to see me about what? I am sorry to inform you that we are full up. Since the Revolution began, all the sane have been placed in mental institutions. The insane are in the army."

"Which army?"

"It doesn't make any difference which army," the doctor said. "It doesn't make any difference which side you are on. The important thing is that you take a stand. You are either for us or against us or cuckoo. In any war, both sides have tremendous respect for the enemy. Whom they both hate is the pacifist. The angry only feel safe when the soothsayers are in a nuthouse. And they put them in here in a trice, before you can say 'ali kazam,' certainly much before you can say 'Our liberties we prize and our rights we will maintain' or 'God save our blessed King.' Not until the others are put safely away in here, in jail, or in a newspaper office, does the warrior feel safe to go about his heroic business of saving his country from a fate worse than death. Come to think of it, Braxton and Lee," he said, pointing with his hot-rum-stirring stick, "you're out stirring up the country, trying to start a

33
THE
LONG
NAKED
DESCENT
INTO
BOSTON

34

THE
LONG
NAKED
DESCENT
INTO
BOSTON

Revolution. Well, you'll have one in a trice. Why can't you let the King's men march up the hill and march back again? That's all they want to do."

"Because they are men," Dilsie said, forgetting to pass the pipe to Francine and smoking thoughtfully. "They don't wants people marching all over them."

"In order not to cause trouble, the King's men purposely marched to Lexington and Concord," the doctor said, "before even the farmers are normally up. Why are you awakening the countryside?"

"Because they are men," Dilsie said, passing the pipe.

"Because," Lee said, taking a drink of the Flip, "because Poxey thought it a good circulation idea for *The New Boston Times*. Poxey claims all wars are started by newspapers. Poxey says if we don't start the war, Scoop Jackson's *Globe* or some other newspaper will. Certainly if we don't alert the countryside, Paul Revere will. I think I hear Paul now."

There was the noise of gravel being thrown against the window. No one rose; they all remained as quiet as mice. Now a stone shattered the window and Doctor Neat went to the window, opened it, and smiled out in time to catch a rock in the kisser.

"Oh, Paul," Doctor Neat said.

"The British are coming," Paul Revere said.

"Oh, Paul," Doctor Neat said.

"I've got to get moving," Paul Revere said.

"Stay a while."

"No, I've got to get moving," Paul Revere said.

"How are the wife and little nipper-nappers?"

"I've got to get moving," Paul Revere said.

"Paul, get hold of yourself," Doctor Neat said, holding up a candle lantern. "Let me see your tongue. Just as I thought," Doctor Neat said, leaning out the window. "We're going to have to put you to bed with Mrs. Revere or a nice hot-water bottle, no pun intended."

"I didn't get no pun," Dilsie said.

"I've got to get moving," Paul Revere said.

"I didn't get no pun," Dilsie said, tamping down the tobacco in the long clay pipe that she and Francine puffed. "And I works for a newspaper. Would you repeat that?"

"The British are coming," Paul Revere said.

"No, it was something I said," Doctor Neat said. "Come in, Paul, and make yourself at home."

But Paul Revere was gone, making incontinent sparks from steel hoofs and shouting from his nasal pharyngitis and strep throat, "The Witish are woming."

"Revere is beginning to drop his 'b's' and 'r's,' " the doctor said, "and make his 'c's' soft, and seems unable to add the diphthong."

"What is Paul saying?"

"Sounds like 'Witish are woming,' " Dilsie said. "In all my time at the newspaper I've never heard anything like that. Braxton and Lee, you know what Poxey said about drinking on the job."

"Whatever Paul is saying now," the doctor said, coming back with his lantern candle and making more Flips at the open fireplace, "whatever Paul is up to now, we will learn shortly. This house is in a new Colonial development. All the houses look alike and the road makes a complete circle, so Paul will be back here in a trice."

"And he started out on a horse," Braxton said, drinking.

"Make a note of that," Lee said. "Those are the curiosities that Poxey likes to know. He could do an editorial on it." BOSTON HAS NEW FISH TO FRY. MUCH CONSTERNATION AFTER REVERE'S RIDE. GOVERNOR INDICATES THROUGH UNDISCLOSED SOURCE THAT REVERE HAD TOO MANY FLIPS TO FLY. DOCTOR NEAT TO TESTIFY. NEVER SAW PAUL. HEARD STRANGE NOISES IN NIGHT. MYSTERY DEEPENS. MORE. PLEASE TURN TO BACK PAGE.

"Our housing development here," Doctor Neat said, " 'to change the subject,' was started by the late Lord Levitt, the well-known alcoholic who stole the land from the Indians. Can I freshen your drink? As I said, the development turns back on itself, so Paul will be back anon. Shall I hide you? I have room. My patient the King of Spain has joined the American Minutemen, and the Emperor of China and Jimmy have hopped off to Boston to hide in the peanut gallery."

"Why should *we* hide?" Braxton said.

"Paul will know we've been here anyway," Lee said, "when he smells Francine's and Dilsie's pipe smoke."

35
THE
LONG
NAKED
DESCENT
INTO
BOSTON

36

THE
LONG
NAKED
DESCENT
INTO
BOSTON

"Why should we hide at all?" Braxton said.

"Because you've preempted Revere," Doctor Neat said. "If I know Paul, he'll be mad as hell."

"We work for *The New Boston Times*."

"Not good enough," Doctor Neat said. "I'll think of something better. What about dementia praecox? I could write you out a prescription. I know you don't like to make excuses, but I think it's something Paul would understand and forgive. He might even be afraid his little nipper-nappers might get dementia praecox and pop off in a trice."

"No, we'll stick by our newspaper cover," Lee said.

"Poxey would think better of us if we stood by our guns," Braxton said. "Since we're Harvard men, he would expect it."

"I didn't know you were Harvard men."

"They don't tell everyone," Dilsie said. "I think I hear Revere now."

"No, that's the garbage man," Doctor Neat said. "He always makes that much noise."

"Poxey could use that," Lee said. MYSTERY GARBAGE MAN TESTIFIES NOISE THAT BRITISH ARE COMING COULD HAVE BEEN ME. REVOLUTION DELAYED. EXPECTATIONS UP. STOCK MARKET SINKS.

"If we are going to alert Hancock and Adams," Braxton said, "we'd best be off."

"There's no hurry," the good Doctor Neat said.

"Tide and time—"

"But war waits for everyman. Let me make you out a prescription for dementia praecox," Doctor Neat said. "It will be in Latin. No one will be the wiser unless you tell them."

"We are off," Lee said. "We have business."

"What will I tell Paul?"

"Tell him if his side wins the war, the Colonials will write the history books. They can say what they wish about Paul's ride; no one will be the wiser."

"I'm sure Revere would not allow a lie like that."

"If he doesn't, Scoop Jackson will. Onward, Christian soldiers," Lee said, and all followed and got on their steeds in time to see Paul Revere take the wrong turn at the third Colonial house on the left.

five

"No more drinking," Braxton said. "History is in enough trouble if you let it work its way normally. For the sake of our children and our children's children we should try to behave ourselves and set a good example."

"That's what Poxey always says," Dilsie said.

A dark rider rode up, dressed in black and wearing a face mask of black and riding a black horse. His horse had been abused and was foaming lather and giving great heaves.

"You have abused your horse, sir," our hero Amos Lee said, coming right to the point.

"What I do to my horse," the *Globe* reporter said, "is none of your business. At least I have the honor to work for a newspaper that owns its own steeds. A paper that is not reduced to rental horses."

"We of the *Times* may be poor," Dilsie said, "but we be honorable."

"I am not in the habit," the masked rider said, "of being addressed by slaves."

"I must demand you retract that statement, sir," our young hero Lee said, allowing his poor horse to come up to the handsome steed of the masked rider.

"You better listen to what our young hero say," Dilsie said.

Lee grabbed the silk cloak of the masked rider. "Retract! Retract, sir!"

"The *Globe* never retracts, sir."

"So," our young hero Lee said, "you are Jackson of the *Globe*."

"I be that."

"Then, sir, I must ask you to withdraw your insult to our dear poor Dilsie."

"I may be dear," Dilsie said, "but I ain't poor."

38

THE
LONG
NAKED
DESCENT
INTO
BOSTON

"Retract, retract, sir," Lee said, shaking the cloak of the ruffian.

"I am not a ruffian, I am Jackson of the *Globe*," Jackson of the *Globe* said. "You are destroying history, sir, and I am out to stop it."

"You mean preempting Revere?"

"That, and your making fools of both sides."

"They did it, I didn't do it."

"Nevertheless, most history shouldn't be revealed. It is the job of a respectable newspaper to make people happy. To present a proper history of rectitude, *sans* wit, *sans* truth, *sans* life, *sans* everything but a history that will not corrupt the young."

"Lee is a gentleman from Virginia," Dilsie said. "He ain't corrupting no young. We all works for the *Times*."

"The *Times* is a rag," Jackson sneered.

Our young Southern hero Lee, who was not quick to anger but was consumed by growing affection for Dilsie and *The New Boston Times,* struck the masked ruffian with a smart blow that tumbled him off his expensive steed.

No sooner had Jackson hit the dirt than he demonstrated that the only play he knew was foul, and drew in a trice a dirk from his cloak and advanced toward our hapless hero.

"Ye drop that dirk, Jackson of the *Globe*," Dilsie said, pointing her blunderbuss.

Jackson dropped the dirk.

Francine gave Jackson's steed a smart crack that sent it flying back to Boston.

The *Times* people turned their horses toward Lexington and Concord's North Bridge, leaving the masked rider from the *Globe* without a horse or a window to throw it out of. Jackson had to walk back to Boston to the *Globe* to write about the start of the American Revolution without even seeing the start of the American Revolution. That is why history is what it is—it happens all the time. And there doesn't seem to be a thing we can do about it.

"Now let's try to find out where Hancock and Adams are and tell them the British are after their ass," Francine said. "Where do they hang out normally?"

"At Clark's place."

"Is that a tavern?"

"No, a house."

"Then let's look for a likely house," Lee said. "Have you noticed, since Lord Levitt, all the houses look the same?"

"Clark's house, where Hancock and Adams are hiding out from the British, is white with green shutters with a cupola on the roof and on top a zinc cupid weathervane shooting an arrow in the direction of the wind or the British."

"Or up someone's ass," Francine said.

"Which reminds me, Francine, who's looking after the Rose and Crown?"

"With the British out of town, business will be slow. Nothing but Continental paper—who needs it?"

They paced their horses hither and yon, looking for Parson Clark's house. But the *Times* people could find no especial white house with green shutters and cupola with weathervane on top because all the houses were look-alikes. All had been built by Lord Levitt Enterprises in one sweep, so you could not only not tell Parson Clark's house from the others, so it would be impossible to tell a Tory's house from a Patriot's, or as some said, a Loyalist's house from a Rebel's. So that when the Loyalists hung the Rebels or the Rebels hung the Loyalists there would be wrong bodies hanging on each side's gibbets, all due to the lack of planning by Lord Levitt. It would never do to protest; orders would be writ and solemnly sealed to hang the man with the red nose in the white house with green shutters, and your house is not only white with green shutters, but you also have a red nose. As did every Patriot in New England and every Tory too—New England rum.

When the war was over, Braxton thought he would like to write his *True History of the Revolution (Being a Candid and Accurate Account of What Happened)* right here in Concord or Lexington. Lee would go back to Virginia to raise other Lees to fight other wars. Braxton could settle here with Gretchen or Francine or Dilsie or all three and live happily ever after. Lee could move in, too, if he insisted—a *ménage à cinq*, as it was now. Five in a bed. There are worse things that can happen to people. Living conditions are tight all over. Or good, depending on your attitude. If the Patriots won, five in a bed would be out. Each bed

39
THE
LONG
NAKED
DESCENT
INTO
BOSTON

40

THE
LONG
NAKED
DESCENT
INTO
BOSTON

would contain a maximum of two persons and not less than one, excepting on major holidays with visiting relatives, when the allowance would rise to three in a bed of the same sex and political persuasion. Knox's Adult Book Shoppe would be closed tighter than a drum, as well as the Rose and Crown, as would any and all divers places in Boston where people seemed to be enjoying themselves. If the British won, things would muddle along as they were. Without a thought for the morrow. With sin. With taxes that could not be collected—with all sorts of myriad and dreadful happenings that brought shame to our American hearts and a flush of red to our proud cheeks.

"If the British win, the South will rise again," Lee said.

"What if the Rebels win?"

"The South will rise again," Lee said.

"In that case, what would you call yourselves?"

"There's nothing against using the same word, Rebels, twice," Lee said.

"But it will confuse people as to which war is being discussed."

"It will work itself out," Lee said. "One war at a time."

"Men will always have one war at a time, one right after the other," Dilsie said, "until women whips men's asses once and for all and stops their fighting."

They all agreed to this, including the Virginian, Lee, and the New Englander, Braxton, but they could not agree which of the green and white Lord Levitt houses hid Hancock and Adams—a failure history will not forgive nor quickly forget, Braxton thought.

Their rented horses were giving out and sweating bubble foams of lather. A horse will foam more frequently from nerves than fatigue. A rented horse will lather willfully to embarrass the rentee. When the horses were returned to Boston they would have to be rested a few blocks from the horse rental lot and the lather wiped off so that the extra charge of two shillings and sixpence could be avoided for "straining ye horse."

"Why did you bring along your blunderbuss, Dilsie?" Braxton asked.

"Is that what that thing is?" Lee said, leaning over his bay mare to look. "Can I see it?" he said, holding out his hand.

"No," Dilsie said. "This is *my* blunderbuss."

"Then fire three quick shots in the air," Braxton said. "That should bring out Hancock and Adams."

"In fright and flight."

"Yes."

"I can't fire three quick shots," Dilsie said. "The blunderbuss takes five minutes to reload. It would sound like one shot fired at five-minute intervals."

"Try that," Lee said.

Dilsie got down from her horse, untied the blunderbuss from the saddle thong, said, "Don't rush me, I've got to study this," removed the ramrod, poured down the wide horn muzzle powder and shot and wadding, tamped this down, then leveled the gun and poured powder on the pan—carefully so she would not get a mere pan flash—then inserted a fresh flint and cocked the hammer, pointed the blunderbuss skyward, and said, "Everybody stand back."

The gun went off like a Roman candle cannon, and two houses down a window went up, a musket was leveled at them, and the voice of John Hancock said, "One move, Lord Percy, and you're dead."

"We be from *The New Boston Times*," Lee shouted.

"The what?" Some fresh faces appeared at the window.

"*The New Boston Times*. We're doing an in-depth story on the Revolution."

"On the what?"

"The Revolution."

"Has it started yet?"

"That's what we want to talk to you about. The British are coming."

"The what are coming?"

"The British."

"Why?"

"To pick you and Adams up."

"What for?"

"'Sedition. National security. The BCIA have a file on you both a mile long."

"Paul Revere was supposed to deliver the message," John Hancock said.

41

THE
LONG
NAKED
DESCENT
INTO
BOSTON

42

THE
LONG
NAKED
DESCENT
INTO
BOSTON

"There's been a mixup."

"All right, come around to the front door. I'll be down as soon as I make myself decent," Hancock said quietly and disappeared.

At the front door, Hancock, without any niceties, wanted to know what had happened to Revere.

"He's on his way."

"But I gave him a first," Hancock said. "I've been making historical notes and I've given him full credit for the ride. I'll have to change all that now."

"Let it stand," Dilsie said.

"Thank you," Hancock said. "Paul will appreciate that."

"We don't wants no credit," Dilsie said. "This ride is just a circulation builder for *The New Boston Times*. No big history deal. We just wants some feed for these rentals."

"Happily," Hancock said, relieved at not having to rewrite history for the sake of mere facts. "Happily, happily, happily." And he commanded the good Parson Clark's slave to do just that and invited them in "as you are," he said. "We can excuse your costumes in these troubled times."

John Hancock being a billionaire, Braxton and Lee knew he was not one to rough it out here in the country. Hancock was in hiding because he was in trouble with the British for strange bills of lading and keeping three sets of books. And, egged on by Adams, he'd recently taken to words like "liberty" and "freedom." Hancock had a queer handwriting of which he was "justly proud" and took three minutes to draw his signature.

"But I do quite believe in the Revolution," Hancock said, still wearing his golden nightcap. "It sounds dashed exciting and I do appreciate you ladies and chaps going out of your way to tell us of the Revolution's commencement. The others will be down anon. I suppose there should be some celebration before we blaze away at the King's men. But I'm being rude. What can I get you to drink?"

"Nothing," Lee said.

"We had drinks and smokes at Doctor Neat's," Dilsie said.

"Rum up to our ass," Francine said. "We're lucky we made it this far with the message."

"You sound like Professor Wilkes' daughter," Hancock said.

"I believe we became acquainted at the Rose and Crown, was it? How are things in New Haven?"

"The same," Francine said.

"That *is* too bad," John Hancock said, busying himself with glasses. "I'm going to insist you all have a drink and make yourselves comfy. Who's for tea?"

"If you insist, we'll have rum," Francine said.

"Then it's rum all around," John Hancock said. "What a pleasant way to start a Revolution."

43

THE
LONG
NAKED
DESCENT
INTO
BOSTON

six

Hieronymus Poxe had founded *The New Boston Times* in Boston so it would be close to an institution in Cambridge called Harvard, whose graduates could be hired for next to nothing because they knew next to nothing. They knew phrenology, Sanskrit, hieroglyphics, the girls in Charlestown, Professor Rollbach's dog, a long-forgotten Japanese language, and a certain Miss Mary Tyler Lessing.

Boston was loaded with young men with doctorates who were unemployed and unemployable. They formed themselves into gangs they called fraternities and roamed the streets shouting Greek slogans, writing Sanskrit on the walls, and cursing the Queen—they had not yet learned that King George had ascended the throne. Since talk of Revolution, the gangs from Yale had arrived in Boston loaded down with master's degrees—they had not yet learned what a doctorate was. They soon found out when they met the Harvard boys. They thrashed each other on Water Street, on Milk Street, and the Common. They gouged each other's eyes out in what was called in Boston the Harvard–Yale game; chased each other bleeding and naked through the streets with the girls in between until they all ended up in the army or jail where they were taught a thing or two about discipline, self-respect, obeisance to authority, regard for others' rights, attention to the Sabbath, the Boston Blue Laws, the price of ham on the hoof, Mrs. Loring, how to spell, read, count to ten, pray properly for what ye got as well as what ye had not got—in general, how to be proper Bostonians. Which Harvard thought it had taught, but in the excitement of Sanskrit had not taught; and neither had Yale.

"Witness modern youth today," Poxe said. "Here it is already

Seventeen seventy-five and all youth can think of is their own goddamn selves, not any thought for love of country, their parents, the value of money, the difficulties of the publishing business, which is going to hell in a wheelbarrow. Only of themselves do the young men think. And that," Poxe said, fuming and picking up a cheap paperback reprint of *Pilgrim's Progress* his firm was pirating, "is why I have taken to hiring women."

"When you hire someone it is an old custom to pay them, isn't it?" Gretchen said, putting down her dictation notebook.

"We don't go by custom here," Poxe said. "At *The New Boston Times* we try to innovate. Our job is to get out a modern newspaper and we expect cooperation all around. I don't draw a salary either. Where was I?"

"Not paying women."

"Before that."

"Youth have no respect for the elderly."

"Before that."

"The country's going to hell."

"Before that."

"The Benjamin Franklin saying for today."

"Small strokes fell great oaks."

"We have used that, Master Poxe."

"Use it again. I think it's a winner," Poxe said. "What happened to Braxton and Lee?"

"You sent them to cover the Concord–Lexington thing."

"Are you happy here, Gretchen? If we are not a team, we are nothing. I thought when I got out of Harvard I could conquer the world. Now I have learned I need a woman to help me over the bumps."

"What about Mrs. Poxe?"

"Don't change the subject," Poxe said. "I'm a lonely man, Gretchen. I seem to have all of the good things of this world," he said, looking around his newspaper dump. "Riches, fame, people willing to work for nothing. But there is something missing, Gretchen."

"A dog?"

"A female."

"A female dog?"

45
THE
LONG
NAKED
DESCENT
INTO
BOSTON

46

THE
LONG
NAKED
DESCENT
INTO
BOSTON

"No, goddamn it, Gretchen, it's you."

"The week before it was Dilsie, the week before that it was Francine. Next week it will be Braxton and Lee."

"No, I'm going to fire those two chaps. Harvard men aren't worth a damn. I tell you it's you, Gretchen. What did you say happened to Lee and Braxton?"

"Lexington and Concord."

"Forget Braxton and Lee, Gretchen. It's you I care about."

"Shall I take that down?"

"Please yourself. I only want you to be happy, Gretchen. Give me your hand."

"I can't take it down and give you my hand."

"Why not?"

"You can't have me make love to you and work at the same time."

"Why not?"

"You can't, that's all."

"You can't, that's all," Poxe said, mimicking Gretchen. "Do you need both hands to write?"

"Yes."

"Why?"

"I do, that's all."

"Women. I will never understand women, Gretchen. But," he said in a lower tone, "we can't let words like this stand between us." He moved his hand away from the *Pilgrim's Progress* and onto her knee. "When we are together, when you are close, I feel a heat, a vibration, a kind of electricity."

"What is electricity?"

"Something Franklin is working on," Poxe said, moving his hand up her thigh. "Franklin doesn't give a damn about our newspaper any more. He's got this kite and key and he gets electricity from the clouds or some such rubbish, but it's you I care about, Gretchen."

"I don't think much of your idea."

"What idea?"

"Making me Miss Boston Massacre of Seventeen seventy-five."

"It was just a circulation gambit, Gretchen. It's you I really care about."

"You already said that," Gretchen said abruptly, putting down her copybook. "The readers won't want to hear about it again."

"It's you I love, Gretchen."

"The readers won't want to hear about it."

"What about tonight?"

"Tonight we have got to get out a newspaper."

"Nothing is happening in the Colonies."

"There's the trouble at Lexington and Concord."

"There is no story in Lexington and Concord, Gretchen. I have a nose for the news. Tonight there's only you and me."

"You and I," Gretchen said, writing.

"Yes. The Revolution will blow over but we will still have our love."

"What about Mrs. Poxe?"

"What about her?" Poxe said, his hand at Gretchen's breast. "Must you bring my personal life into this? Remember there is a Revolution on."

There was a rattling at the door, the entrance from Knox's bookstore, then much pandemonium and shouting and much Christian wailing, "Goddamn the British, they'll pay for this!"

"Don't answer," Poxe said. "Be quiet. It's a trick."

Now the back door crashed open and in ran Young Wild Tom with torn and bloodied clothing. He stood stock still in front of Poxe's desk and announced, "Braxton and Lee are dead! Both shot through the heart by the British on the North Bridge! The British captured me and think they are using me as a double agent. But this be true: Braxton and Lee are as dead as mackerel."

"We must maintain our calm," Hieronymus Poxe said, quietly removing himself from Gretchen. "If what this young man says is true—"

"It is true, Master Poxe," Young Wild Tom said. "To help out I have been firing at the British all day from behind every fence I could find. Then I saw Braxton and Lee strolling across the North Bridge as disinterested as you please and I held my fire but the British whaled away at them. They got them both through the heart and the liver and the lights and every which way. They are both as dead as mackerel."

"Don't interrupt me, boy," Poxe said to Young Wild Tom.

47

THE
LONG
NAKED
DESCENT
INTO
BOSTON

48

THE
LONG
NAKED
DESCENT
INTO
BOSTON

"Now if what Young Wild Tom says is true, then Braxton and Lee are as dead as mackerel. And *The New Boston Times* has lost half its staff in one volley, but it could be a trick. Never trust a Harvard man. Now, Young Wild Tom, I want you to gallop back to Lexington and check this story out. No hearsay, no second-hand evidence. I want those men brought back dead or alive. If they say their bodies fell in the water, laugh at them. I never met a Harvard man who wasn't a liar."

"But master," Young Wild Tom said, "if they're dead?"

"It could be a trick, Young Wild Tom," Poxe said. "Don't sob, Gretchen, we still have each other. Young Wild Tom," he commanded, "get back there and get to the bottom of this. There will be a fine bonus in it for you if you smell something fishy—and blow your nose. You're no credit to *The New Boston Times*. The whole lot are no credit. What do you suppose Braxton and Lee were doing on the North Bridge? There could be a story there. Be off," he said to Young Wild Tom, "and look alive. That's a good boy, Young Wild Tom." When Young Wild Tom was gone, Poxe said to Gretchen, "If Braxton and Lee are deceiving me, I have Young Wild Tom for replacement, and if a woman spurns me, she, too, can be replaced."

"By Young Wild Tom?"

"Nothing is impossible, Gretchen. On *The New Boston Times* everything is possible. Will you take that down? I believe I can work it into an editorial on the problems of the war. I wonder what's up with Braxton and Lee now. Do you believe in a hell? Sit closer. Or a heaven? We must believe in ourselves, Gretchen, and in our love and in our destiny in this time of darkness and peril. Will you take that down? Set it up in type and sweep the floor, polish the press, and sit closer. The Franklin saying we will use today is 'Small strokes fell great oaks,' or 'We must all hang together or we shall hang separately.' Move closer, Gretchen, and we will observe a minute's silence for Braxton and Lee."

seven

Sam Adams was getting dressed upstairs at Clark's house in Lexington, together with Parson Clark's aunt and Abigail Quincy. They had all slept in the same bed. This was not licentious. Nor was it an economy. Nor was it a shortage of beds. Nor was it a concession made by Parson Clark to Adams because Adams would be hung by the British on the morrow. Parson Clark knew Adams had no intention of throwing his life away for a mere ideal. Adams was permitted to sleep with Clark's aunt and his own sweetheart because before the Revolution "values were different in America," Poxe wrote later. It was not until after the Revolution, Poxe recalled in a now "infamous, wicked" editorial, that the crackdown on sex came on like thunder. The bookstore was closed. Dilsie's column was cleaned up. The former Sunday section devoted entirely to sex with illustrations by Lee was soon dedicated to huge idiots playing cricket, then something called football in which men chased men on an open field in peasant brute simplemindedness instead of running screeching over a sheeted bed as in days of yore in aristocratic gambol and delight to wake the neighbors in the night. Poxe was proud as flesh of his editorial. But it finished him. The manly art of sport between consenting adults was in. Sex was out. But even now, as Adams buckled his fustian and pulled up his jerkin on the eve of Lexington, there were already gathering clouds of the approaching Puritan Protestant Ethic as Aunt Mildred twinkled out, back to her own room, and Abigail Quincy pulled up sanctimoniously on her drawers and listened to the shooting on the North Bridge and said, "Sam, this Revolution means the end of freedom as we know it."

"By Christ, I promise you on my bare bodkin, Abigail,"

50

THE
LONG
NAKED
DESCENT
INTO
BOSTON

Adams said, setting down his tortoise-shell and silver comb that he carried about with him in his fustian belt like a pistol, "I promise, dear Abby, that what's going on out there on the bridge between consenting adults in the privacy of war will never interfere with what we do here in the public domain of our own bedroom."

"Say that again, Sam."

"You're emotionally disturbed, dear Abby. After the war things will return to normal and we can return to our old perversions."

"I'll believe it, dear Sam, when it happens. I do not know, dear Sam," she said solemnly as though pronouncing the death of a generation, an old and hallowed way of life, "whether any of us living will ever again see the day when men—to quote Francine Wilkes of the *Times*—'would rather fuck than fight.' " And now dear Abby touched the white counterpane to a falling tear before the tears came in a gush over a heaving bosom. "Oh Sam, oh Sam, the Colonial Puritans are going to make it all dirty, like their war. There will be no more innocence. Sex will be all shame and disgust. Fresh babes and meek children will be lied to. Mendacity will rule in the guise of the people. God will flee—oh Sam, oh Sam, what will happen to us older people once decency and sex are no more and vicious upright youth hold sway?"

"Abby," said Sam, who would rather face a musket than a crying woman. "Dear Abby," he said, flustered and putting his tortoise comb in the wrong pocket, "I assure you that as long as there are people like Braxton and Lee, the old sex customs will never disappear. Not entirely."

"Where are Braxton and Lee now, dear Sam?"

"Dead."

"I told you so," Abby said.

"But it's only a rumor. You can't kill Braxton and Lee. We've tried. I mean, they're not reliable. They're camp followers to both armies. They don't want to fight for either side. No one knows where *The New Boston Times* stands—even Poxe. Poxe won't even take a bribe to help him make up his own mind."

"Then there's still hope," Abby said. "Hold me, Sam. Hold me, Sam."

"I've been holding you all night, Abby. Someone's got to start the Revolution."

"I thought all revolutionary wars started over Manifest Destiny and things like that."

"You've been reading history books again, Abby. History books are written to justify man's stupidity to women and confound the young. I go, dear Abby, because I go. In Latin, *Me voy porqué me voy*. That is all man knows and all ye need to know. Dear Abby," Adams said, grasping his tortoise and silver comb shaped like a scimitar and sticking from his fustian like a sword, "dear Abby, I love you."

"Say it again, Sam."

But Sam Adams had already gone to the Revolution.

Downstairs, Adams was surprised to see Braxton and Lee awake, alive, and well in Lexington. When he was introduced he said, "I thought you were dead." His tone showed a trace of disappointment. But he glossed over this for now. He would get back to their deaths later. "Now," he said, "I want all the Minutemen to crowd in the Common and when the British arrive I want every man jack to start pushing. That should provoke the King's men to blast away at women and children and sundry others. Lee and Braxton, I want you both to be there and give an honest report of the British massacre at Lexington. If that doesn't start a war, our cause is hopeless and liberty and freedom will be flags in the dust. If we don't get the war off the ground this morning, your *New Boston Times* is dead. The Revolution has been postponed twice. This time the Revolution may be canceled. However, I want you to put your newspaper business aside for a while and warn the Concord Chamber of Commerce that the war will go exclusively to Lexington unless Concord shows more interest. And all their future tourist business will be shot to hell. I'll see to that. Concord will become a ghost town. Dilsie and Francine, I want you two women to witness the massacre. Keep up front. Lee will sketch you. Braxton will write something like WOMEN STAND IN HORROR AND AGHAST. BARE THEIR BREASTS TO THE MUSKETRY TO DECOY BRITISH FIRE AWAY FROM THEIR TINY TOTS. MUCH PANDEMONIUM. WOMEN BLACK AND WHITE STAND

52

THE
LONG
NAKED
DESCENT
INTO
BOSTON

TOGETHER FOR THE OLD GLORY RED WHITE AND BLUE. LONG MAY IT WAVE. 'STEADY, STEADY,' THE BLACK DILSIE HEARD TO WHISPER BY THIS REPORTER TO HER STAUNCH FRIEND FRANCINE. 'DON'T FIRE TILL YOU SEE THE WHITES OF THEIR ASS.'

"Clean it up, Braxton," Adams said, touching the hope of *The New Boston Times.* "Clean it up and have a go at it. I want the rest of you to get down on the Common and start shoving."

"I ain't going no place," Dilsie said, "lessen I see some point to the shoving. The King ain't done my peoples no harm."

"Yes, Dilsie," Francine said in her upper-class Yale accent. "The war is no skin off your ass."

"I'll quote that," Braxton said, "and see if Poxey kills it."

"Get cracking, everybody," Samuel Adams said, "and everyone have a good Revolution."

eight

Lord Percy was already on his way to save the day for the King. To restore order to the rabble. To collect a token tax. After all, there must be only a few terrorists and they did not represent the thinking of the Colonies. If the Colonialists thought. If the Colonials do not think, what do they do with themselves in this Godforsaken country called America? Lord Percy wondered in surmise. It will be a historical shame but my name will be known for fighting these poor souls—Colonial rustics who know not the proper evolutions of the drill, who have not uniforms, who have not courage because they fight hiding behind stone fences, who have not respect for British flag or King or country, who have not a good wine or a fair lady, who, sodden with rum, slump from stone hedge to stone fence, shooting down their betters. For what? Independence. Independence to be ruled by the mob. No King's protection for the weak. No wine, no women, no song. And for this the Colonials are willing to pledge their lives, their honor, and their fortune—their lives are boring, their honor debatable, and their fortunes nil. So they take a shot at me, Lord Percy thought, to relieve their boredom, recapture their honor, and announce their poverty of mind.

"Stop mumbling, Lord Percy," Madame de Tocqueville said. Madame Annette de Tocqueville was marching in the vanguard with General Percy, all flags flying toward the doom of Lexington.

"Look smart, Lord Percy," Annette said. "History is watching you."

"My gout is acting up," Lord Percy said.

"And stop mumbling against the Colonials. You must, my Lord, live among these clods as I have to appreciate their good

54

THE
LONG
NAKED
DESCENT
INTO
BOSTON

points. I have a son who will come to this country and remark their good points. I have requested him to do this."

"Madame de Tocqueville," Lord Percy said, "I can appreciate in the genius of your youth that glows beside me that you are someone's daughter, but never someone's mother."

"It is true, my Lord Percy, and it is also true you'd like my son. You must suffer the Colonies, you must live among these countrymen as I have to appreciate their points."

"Madame, I may well die here, but never live here."

With pipers piping, drums drumming, flags flying, Lord Percy stumbling, Madame de Tocqueville swaying, the most dreadful power of the British Empire swept down upon the small band of farmers that stood outside Buckman's Tavern in Lexington, armed to the teeth.

"Keep your powder dry, men," Adams said. "Those who wish to go inside Buckman's and wet their whistles may."

Lord Percy and Madame de Tocqueville had mounted their horses now for battle, or whatever the rustics had in mind. A magnificent array of King's men accoutered in gold and blue and buff-silvered bayonets and bejeweled shako headdress, star sapphire on the buckle, diamonds on the breast, curses not loud but deep on their lips, a touch of perfume on the lobe of each ear—these were all the King's men that could be mustered this foggy Boston morning. And a fine lot they were, too!

Adams looked over his seedy Patriot bunch wandering half-crocked in and out of Buckman's.

"But they're dedicated Minutemen," Colonel Conant said.

"What?" Adams said.

"Dedicated."

"They look a bit drunk to me," Adams said.

Lord Percy's army was proceeding as planned. And as if that were not bad enough, they had forgot the cannonballs as well.

"We will make do," Lord Percy said. "Any general can win with cannon. How long has it been since a general has won without cannon? At least without balls."

"Never, General."

"You're quite right. Have someone go back and fetch some. On the double. The nice thing about being a general is everyone does what they're told. It's much better than being married, wherein everything is hit or miss."

"What, sir?"

"I said this is better than being married."

"You're quite right, sir. But in this country no one is married. Everyone, I hear, does as they please."

"Well, we'll fix that," Lord Percy said. "It needs looking into."

"It does. You're quite right, Lord Percy. It does."

Lord Percy had not only carefully arranged the logistics and supply of the campaign—witness the forgotten cannonballs—but had, to his credit, remembered to bring all sorts of things ordinary people would forget. Like Madame de Tocqueville. Ordinary people would think that a beautiful woman such as the likes of Madame de Tocqueville would be an albatross around a soldier's neck. None would think of her as the missing cog; that is why there are so many ordinary people and so few generals.

"Did the general say something?"

"No, he didn't," Lord Percy said. "Did the cannonballs arrive yet?"

"No."

"No, what?"

"No, Your Worship."

"We will make do," Lord Percy said, flashing his marshal's baton.

"Did you flash your marshal's baton, sir?"

"Yes, I want to know if Young Wild Tom has returned yet."

"I didn't know he'd gone."

"Yes, I sent him—he's one of their spies—to report to the Boston newspaper, the *Times,* that we had killed both their correspondents on the North Bridge."

"Why, sir?"

"So that there would be an outrage in the Colonies after their morning editorial. Then the Patriots will be able to raise sufficient money for uniforms."

"Clever, clever, clever, sir."

"Not clever by half, Lieutenant McNaughton. I see so far all the enemy we have met are accoutered in overalls."

"Give them time to nip home and change, sir."

55
THE
LONG
NAKED
DESCENT
INTO
BOSTON

56
THE
LONG
NAKED
DESCENT
INTO
BOSTON

"Time, my dear Lieutenant McNaughton, is what a general cannot give."

"Well said, Lord Percy. Well said."

"You may fire at will, Lieutenant McNaughton."

"That's only two civilians crossing the North Bridge, sir."

"Fire anyway," General Percy said. "It's practice what does it."

"As you please, Your Excellency. As you please."

Lee and Braxton were moving in and out of Buckman's Tavern with the Minutemen and talking about going down to the North Bridge and having a look-see for the British. Dilsie and Francine were more popular with the Minutemen than the Revolution. No one was aware the British were close. A young lady by the name of Constance Ayers Denay had thoughtfully gone up to a second-story bedroom to have a look-see for the enemy. She raised the guillotine window and stuck her head out. The window came down on her neck and she was stuck and she saw the British and said, "Shoot if you must the old gray flag but spare my head," she said.

Braxton and Lee wandered over the old North Bridge. Drunk as lords.

"Did you hear something?"

"No."

"Something like 'spare my head she said.' "

"No."

"We have had too much to drink."

"Yes."

"Did you hear that shot?"

"By the rude bridge that arched the flood, the shot heard round the world."

"Then the Minutemen started it."

"Yes."

"What was that?"

"The British have ended it."

"Are you hurt?"

"I think so."

"Can you swim?"

"I'm swimming."

"We have met the enemy," Braxton said, "and it is rum."

"When I claimed yesterday," Lord Percy said, "that those two men were dead, they were as good as dead. Jolly good, well done, Lord Percy, if I must say so myself."

"My dear Lord Percy, on the morrow the whole world will sing your praises," Madame de Tocqueville said. "It is not necessary to toot your own horn."

"Toot my own horn is capital phrasing, Madame de Tocqueville."

"And do we have a hung jury, as you promised, of those rustics who defamed my honor?"

"Yes, my dear."

"Good. The dirty bastards," Madame de Tocqueville said.

Braxton and Lee were making pretty red circles in the water and looked up at the pure New England sky, then at the approaching British, then at the collection of Boston Patriots and local Minutemen that milled around the rude bridge that arched the flood, then looked up at the second story of Buckman's where poor Miss Constance Ayers Denay's spared or spare head was still stuck out the window.

"We must save the girl's head, she said," Lee said.

"After we finish dying."

"Yes."

57

THE
LONG
NAKED
DESCENT
INTO
BOSTON

nine

"I have not only lost my two favorite correspondents for *The New Boston Times,*" Poxe told the visitor, "but my only correspondents, my finest correspondents, my—and I say this without hesitation—my Harvard friends, my friends' friends, my only friends. I hope that our rejection of your manuscript, sir, will not leave you in a doldrum but will be an inspiration to your life, your happiness, and your well-being. I can see that you are made of stern stuff, that this rejection will inspire you to better writing. You are young; you have a long life ahead of you."

Nathan Hale stared at his rejected manuscript, then at the editors Brown, Knox, and Hieronymus Poxe.

"I hope so," Nathan Hale said.

"Are you Jewish, Nathan?"

"My only regret is that I am not Jewish," Nathan Hale said.

"Well said," Brown said.

"Do you have any other regrets, Mr. Hale?" Knox said.

"Not at the moment," Hale said.

"What about your rejected manuscript?"

"I can live with that," Hale said.

"Well said," Brown said. "I wish my other writers could have that same rum attitude. These are hard times for publishers, what with the paper shortage—"

"The high price of paper," Knox said.

"High wages," Brown said. "Hard times. The first thing people do is cut back on their purchase of books."

"We'll have to raise the price of books again," Poxe said.

"These are hard times," Brown said. "But I'm sure the publishing business will pick up—in time."

George Brown and Robert Brown had been partners. George Brown—Big Brown—had been killed by an irate writer, but the smaller brother, Robert Brown—Little Brown—went right ahead with the business and had just bought out Henry Knox, who was off to the Revolution. Knox's bookstore and Poxe's *New Boston Times* had a joint book-publishing venture. Little Brown had placed several copies of William Shakespeare's complete works on his chair so he sat as high as the rest.

"Yes, Nathan," Little Brown said, "I am sure everything will come out in the wash."

"Well said," Poxe said. "Well said. I can see why you're in publishing, Little Brown," Poxe said.

"I'm in publishing," Brown said, "to make a bit of money, and I'm afraid, Nathan, your book doesn't cut the mustard. I like your title, *The Successful Espionage Agent*. That's positive. But after reading the book, you seem to be green at the business."

"Yes, I regret that," Hale said.

"This reads like your Yale doctoral thesis."

"It is."

"Get some experience, Nathan," Little Brown said, "and when you get the hang of it, come and see us."

"Don't write us," Poxe said. "We'll write you."

"Shall I write this down?" Gretchen said.

"Yes," Poxe said. "I was wondering, Gretchen, whether you could find time to show Nathan the town. He must be down in the dumps. There's always a lot going on in Boston, Nathan, and with the British out of town it shouldn't be too difficult to get reservations. I'll put Gretchen on the swindle sheet. Are you game, Nathan?"

"I regret—"

"No, you won't regret it, Nathan. Gretchen's a firecracker."

"I feel I should be doing something for the war effort," Nathan Hale said.

"You mean collecting scrap metal, things like that? Liberty bonds? For which side, Nathan?"

"The Boston Patriots."

59
THE
LONG
NAKED
DESCENT
INTO
BOSTON

60

THE
LONG
NAKED
DESCENT
INTO
BOSTON

"Not spying, I hope."

"Yes."

"Then I might have a job for you, Nathan. I want you to trot up to Lexington and find out what happened to Braxton and Lee. They claim they're dead but I think it's an angle to get a raise in pay. Or why don't you come up in the balloon over Concord with me to cover the Revolution, and you can practice spying for a rewrite on your book. I hope you didn't get your hopes up, Gretchen, about a night out on the town."

"I never get my hopes up," Gretchen said.

"Let's not be bitter, Gretchen," Poxe said. "Let's all try to be one happy family. You can join us in the balloon."

Poxe, Knox, Little Brown, Gretchen, and Nathan Hale sat quietly on this eve of the Revolution. Gretchen wanted to get out a newspaper, Brown to find a book, Hale a profession, Poxe a mistress, Knox a war. When war came—and God save the King it must come—all their problems would be solved. There would be prosperity and peace and happiness. The young would die bravely, the old would get rich steadily. The paper would do well. The publishing business would prosper. Hale would find a profession, Poxe a mistress, Knox a war.

"What, then, gentlemen, is the problem?" Poxe wanted to know. "No problem, gentlemen, excepting lack of patriotism and shortage of uniforms. Nothing that a few slam-bang editorials will not solve. We in the writing profession can be justly proud of our part in saving our liberty and freedom and pursuit of happiness, et cetera. Oh, that I was young again, could take the field again. Run race with death again. Where was I? Gretchen, help me."

"Run race with death again," she said.

"Yes," Poxe said, recovering himself and staring around at all the stern Patriots in solemn conclave. Then he looked out the window to the good ol' boys of Boston scurrying about happily to find a pitchfork, a knife, an axe to kill. With regret.

"Yes, gentlemen, this conference is over." He gestured them out. "Have a good Revolution."

General Lord Percy was bearing down in full panoply of war with light flankers flying to right and to left and a solid center of King's Heavy Grenadiers marching straight ahead, sweeping all before toward Lexington, toward where the embattled farmers stood at the rude bridge that arched the flood, waiting the shot heard round the world. The embattled farmers moved in and out of Buckman's Tavern, taking the shot before the shot heard round the world.

"A man needs," Young Wild Tom said, "a man needs a drink, a good shot before he can face shot and shell. Can you see anyone facing the British sober? Can you see the British? Can you see the British charging us sober? Can you see?" he said, embracing the King of Spain and the Emperor of China on the steps of Buckman's Tavern amidst the swarm of soldiery. "Can you see, comrades, fellow Patriots," Young Wild Tom said, "war is not hell, it is al-co-hol. Unfortunate. We would like to win some other way. Sober. Hi, fellows! Courage. Steady. Steady. Hi, fellows. Oh my Lord," he said, bowing to Adams, and "Oh oh, my Lord," he said, bowing to Hancock. "Hello up there," he waved to the woman in the window.

"Colonel Conant," Hancock said, "get these men out of the tavern and onto the green before the British get here or there'll be no Revolution, I promise you that."

"Hi, fellows," Young Wild Tom said. "If you don't get on the green and behave like proper Minutemen, there'll be no Revolution and no supper either, I promise you that."

Hancock hauled off and gave the whippersnapper Young Wild Tom a cuff alongside the lug that sent Young Wild Tom sprawling on the green.

Young Wild Tom got up a bit sober now and decided he might be on the wrong side of the bridge. The Minutemen were a rum lot, his own kind of people. My kind of people, he thought. There might be a song there. But for now he might join the other side. He had already taken a message to Boston for the other side. Braxton and Lee were dead or were not dead, that was what he was supposed to find out. He would report to Lord Percy. He got up from the green where the Minutemen were trying to assemble in orderly chaos under Colonel Conant, dusted off his jerkin and buskin, placed his torn tricornered hat on his head, and thought himself a pretty sight to present to Lord Percy. His Worship himself. Young Wild Tom made his way toward the bridge amidst the spring beauty of the dark forests of Lexington, the bright

61
THE
LONG
NAKED
DESCENT
INTO
BOSTON

62

THE
LONG
NAKED
DESCENT
INTO
BOSTON

insects buzzing, the thrush singing to Lord Percy's distant marching band.

Crossing the bridge, he hollered to the distant figures down, far down the river in midstream that might be the bodies of Braxton and Lee, "Hi, fellows."

As Young Wild Tom approached Lord Percy's army, he had fewer regrets about leaving the Minutemen, his kind of people, my folk. Just fellows. "Hi, fellows." Fewer regrets for his loyal lack because Lord Percy, the British Army, as it touched in sight over yon hill, dazzled the world with the sheer power of the beauty of its uniforms alone, to say nothing of its smart formation, its sounding brass, its polished black and white horses, its beautiful black servants and white serving damsels. But mostly what made Young Wild Tom's heart leap was the amount of money behind all this. Young Wild Tom came from poor but deserving yeomanry. It is very easy for us now that the Revolution is over to say that had we been Young Wild Tom we would have fought for the right always. But you don't know, do you? No one knows. It is the moiety of humankind never to know. Ye are born, ye fornicate, and ye die, and nature hath no further interest. We become slogans. We go to our damp graves knowing everything and nothing.

But Young Wild Tom believed in something now—the power of the beauty. The British flag. The Union Jack. Flung over an empire the size of the world. This Cross of Saint George, this banner of salvation, this hope, this righteous flag, this England. Quick-step, men, quick-step. One flag, one union, one country indivisible, with liberty and justice for all. Quick-step. God save our gracious King. God save our noble King. God save our King. Quick-step.

As Young Wild Tom approached the array of might and beauty of the British Empire upon which the gods never set, he quavered before it all and wished to his soul he had taken another tot of rum with the Minutemen and looked down at his own tattered Colonial duds and up at the big Grenadiers' uniforms all spit and polish and thought himself a sorry sight to set before the King.

"Young Wild Tom," Madame de Tocqueville said, "you are a pretty sight to confer with His Excellency, Lord Percy." Madame de Tocqueville licked down Young Wild Tom's shock of hair with her wetted palm, buttoned his jerkin, dusted his buskin, and straightened his three-cornered hat and asked whether he had to wear his hair that long simply because all the Colonials did, gave Young Wild Tom a reassuring pat on the behind, and told him to bow to Lord Percy.

"Young Wild Tom," Lord Percy said, "I have another mission for you. Take this message to Colonel Conant, Hancock, Adams, or whoever's in charge. If you lose the message, as seems to be your wont, then tell who's in charge we do not want a war. It would ruin my supper."

"Lord Percy is joking," Madame de Tocqueville said. "Lord Percy, this is no time for levity."

"Tell them," Lord Percy said, "that this has gone quite far enough. Tell them we could whip them to a frazzle but we are willing to retire to Boston until we can straighten this thing out."

"Don't tell them you can whip them to a frazzle," Madame de Tocqueville said. "That will incite them. And don't tell them you will retire to Boston without a quid pro quo. That way you will lose face and credibility."

"I don't want to bore them, my dear. What do you suggest? You're right. We simply can't turn tail and run, and neither can we insult the chaps. For a plugged shilling I'd be willing to forget the whole thing, but here I am with this army the middle class has bought and paid for, and the newspapers expect me to restore law and order to the Colonies and everything. It could be embarrassing. Young Wild Tom," Lord Percy said, recovering his command voice and military demeanor, "tell the Revolutionists there is nothing to fight about. Tell them this calls for clear heads. Tell them no one has been killed yet, excepting two correspondents—I hope that poor woman at the window was spared—tell them what paper the dead correspondents were from—that might help. Look alive, Young Wild Tom. Tell who's in charge that we both still have our lives and our honor to cherish for our children and our children's children and generations yet unborn, but a slip here on the other hand might—"

"Cut it right there," Madame de Tocqueville said. "That was brilliant, my Lord Percy. Brilliant. I did not know you had it in you."

63
THE
LONG
NAKED
DESCENT
INTO
BOSTON

64

THE
LONG
NAKED
DESCENT
INTO
BOSTON

"Now be off, Young Wild Tom," Lord Percy said. "Look alive. For you soon may be dead."

John Hancock was the wealthiest man in the Colonies. Samuel Adams may have been the poorest. Adams on the eve of the Revolution was about to go to jail for "defalcation," which means stealing the tax money. Sam was the cousin of John Adams, who was honest. Sam was not dishonest but "careless" with other people's money. John Hancock was about to go to jail for "smuggling." The Revolution interested Hancock because he wanted to found a new aristocracy in America based not on royalty but on money. He had arrived at his position as Representative-Elect to the Second Continental Congress by "gifts of money" and an ability to draw his signature beautifully, which attracted the rustics for miles around. These were harsh judgments, Paul Revere knew. Based on nothing but the evidence. But Revere was in no mood when he entered Buckman's Tavern to be fair. Paul had been preempted all along the route. Braxton and Lee. If Hancock and Adams did not know of this, they should have known. I ride my ass off and it's not the credit I want for the ride, it's that if we win the war, I'll read like a damn fool, and if we lose the war, I'll read like a damner fool. If we break even, I don't know what will happen.

"Paul," Hancock said across the rough table at Buckman's, "I know how you feel. I'd like to make you a gift. How would one hundred pounds hit you?" Paul was silent. "I know you have nine children—"

"Ten," Adams said.

"Paul, this is a gift," John said. "I realize with all your riding you are bound to be short. I like to help my friends. What do you say?"

"He'll take it," Adams said.

"Let him speak for himself."

"He can't," Adams said. "Paul has lost his voice."

Revere shook his head, meaning that he would not take the money, then he made Indian sign language with his hands that seemed to be getting off the subject.

"I don't understand Indian sign language," Hancock said.

"Paul has delivered many messages to the Indians," Adams

said, "and he speaks sign language fluently. The only other person I know in the Colonies who speaks Indian sign language fluently is Dilsie Firstchild, a free black. She comes from Punkhatasset and used to hunt Indians on her weekends off with her blunderbuss. She should be here someplace. She works for *The New Boston Times* now. They are covering this. Send one of your minions, John, and see if you can dig her up."

Hancock took out his purse, found a brass farthing, gave it to a Minuteman, and in sixty seconds Dilsie appeared with blunderbuss and Francine.

"What do you wants?" Dilsie said.

"We understand you speak sign language. That you at one time hunted Indians with the blunderbuss on your weekends off."

"You got it wrong," Dilsie said.

"Ass backwards," Francine said.

"I hunted *with* the Indians on my weekends off. We used to hunts white people."

"Nevertheless you speak sign?"

"Yes."

"What is Revere saying?"

Dilsie watched Revere, then said, "One if by land, two if by sea, and I on the opposite shore will be."

"Tell him we know that," Hancock said.

"Ask him if he enjoyed the trip," Adams said.

It took four Minutemen to hold Revere down. The rest of the Minutemen assembled on the green under Colonel Conant. Adams and Hancock inspected the men, looking for faults in their gear and their military bearing. There was very little gear and no military bearing, but there was dedication and fire in their eyes.

"The gear and military bearing will come in time," Adams told Colonel Conant. "What have we here?"

"This is the King of Spain," Doctor Neat said, "and the smart chap alongside him is the Emperor of China."

"And fine lads they look," Adams said, taking the Spanish King's musket as it was presented to him and looking down the bore for flies. He presented it back and took the Emperor of China's musket, inspected the lock and flint, touched the pan for dust, and said, "We're proud of you lads. If all the Minutemen are made of such stuff, the day is ours." Then Adams told Colonel

65
THE
LONG
NAKED
DESCENT
INTO
BOSTON

66

THE
LONG
NAKED
DESCENT
INTO
BOSTON

Conant that Hancock and himself would have to nip off before the fracas because he felt a headache coming on and Hancock's stomach was acting up. "But we are with you in our heart of hearts, Colonel Conant, on this day of days. You don't have an aspirin? I see the British are approaching and they look out of humor. We are not leaving you in the lurch, I hope, Colonel Conant. We are not leaving you because so many good ol' boys here seem ready to throw their lives away for a tot of rum and a rousing huzzah against the King, but someone must go posthaste to Philadelphia and sign papers for independence, write a constitution, raise an army, find a general—all sorts of things good ol' boys don't realize must be done in starting a new country without any experience. It will take us a while to get the hang of it. Meanwhile you do your best to get things started here and we will arrange things in Philadelphia. The Constitution, the Declaration of Independence, the whole ball of wax. How does that hit you?"

"All right, I guess," Colonel Conant said.

"Dilsie and Francine, I'm sure there's a story here for you. If you're ever in Philadelphia, be sure and look us up. Toodle-doo."

"Toodle-doo," John Hancock said.

Dilsie and Francine thought it must be about time to see what drunken damn foolishness Lee and Braxton had gotten into this time. They looked up the streets to see if they had fallen in the gutter. Then they looked up and down the stream to see if they had fallen in the river. Then they saw the British poised on the opposite bank and then they saw Young Wild Tom crossing the bridge with the message and then they saw Young Wild Tom proudly present the message to Colonel Conant.

"What have we here, Young Wild Tom?" Colonel Conant said. "No talk of peace, I hope, at this stage of the game." Colonel Conant broke Lord Percy's royal red wax seal, unfurled the pink paper, turned it right-side up then right-side down, stared at it from all angles, held it up to the dark, then to the light, and finally said, "I have forgot my glasses. Anyone here that can read?" The Minutemen looked at each other, fingered their muskets, stroked their knives, admired the view, swore strange oaths. Some jigged, some could play a tune, follow a plow, attend some class at Harvard—but none could read or would confess to being able to read in front of this rum lot.

"I will read it, Colonel Conant," Abigail Quincy said.

"Thank you, Abby."

"Lord Percy wants to get off the hook—"

"But honor would suggest—"

"Shut up and let her finish," Francine said.

"That you lay down your arms."

"And kiss the King's ass," Francine said.

"Lord Percy says there is nothing between us that could not be settled over a good cup of tea."

"That puts a different light on the matter," Colonel Conant said.

"No it doesn't," Dilsie said. "It could be a trick. Lord Percy is a tricker."

"You're right," Colonel Conant said. "That puts a different light on the matter."

"Lord Percy requests that you turn over Hancock and Adams for divers crimes against ye law and order—"

"But," Colonel Conant said, "John and Sam have already toodle-dood. They've already flown the coop to write the Constitution, they said, and the Declaration of Independence, too, wasn't it? I don't remember how they said it, that is, in which order their priorities were placed. Has anyone seen my glasses?"

"Your glasses wouldn't help," Dilsie said. "They didn't write anything. You've got to get hold of yourself, Colonel Conant. The British are coming. Adams and Hancock have both toodle-dood off to Philadelphia and left us here at Lexington holding the bag."

"That puts a different light on the matter," Colonel Conant said.

"Lord Percy said," Abigail continued, "that if you have further questions concerning your surrender, to consult the young whippersnapper bearing this message, Young Wild Tom. Young Wild Tom is a bright head and is hereby granted leave to act as my *envoi du Roi.*"

"The last sounds like Madame de Tocqueville, but I'd buy it, Colonel," Abigail said, staring at a gang of Minutemen lolling on the green. "You have no options."

"No. We came all the way from Boston," Dilsie said, "for the Revolution. There should at least be a show of something for the paper. Lee is supposed to sketch it, Braxton to report it, and I

67
THE
LONG
NAKED
DESCENT
INTO
BOSTON

68

THE
LONG
NAKED
DESCENT
INTO
BOSTON

supply the local color, Francine the gumbo language."

"Jesus Christ, Colonel," Francine said, "you mean there's not going to be a goddamn war?"

"Shut your foul mouth!" Abigail said. "Camp follower."

"Who slept with Sam last night?"

"War bitch! Sam and I were discussing the Declaration of Independence thing. That's something a camp follower wouldn't understand."

"That's enough," Colonel Conant said. "There will be no Revolution until you people learn to behave yourselves. Now that's final." Colonel Conant turned to Young Wild Tom. "Now what do you have to say for yourself, Young Wild Tom, and be quick about it."

Young Wild Tom wiped the snot off his nose with the sleeve of his already green jerkin, struck his tricornered hat at a gentlemanly angle, and snapped to attention. "There were promises made, sir, and promises to be kept. Remember, sir, the Declaration of Independence has probably already been knocked out—"

"No it hasn't," a Minuteman said.

"And they're working on the Constitution, this I know—"

"No they're not."

"Let Young Wild Tom finish," Colonel Conant said.

"What is honor, sir?"

"I forgot my glasses, Young Wild Tom."

"Honor, sir, is doing in our heart of hearts what we know to be right, even what common sense says to be wrong. Honor, sir, is that last full measure of devotion that a soldier gives when he lays down his life for his country."

"But we don't have a country yet, Young Wild Tom."

"Honor is that courage that allows a rough rude farmer to stand up to the British Army. And say no."

"No what, Tom?"

"No sir, sir."

"I mean no *to* what, Young Wild Tom. What you are saying is interesting. No to what, Young Wild Tom?"

"No to liberty and justice for all. I mean, yes to liberty and justice for all."

"Make up your mind, Tom."

"It's yes, sir. Honor is that which talks quietly to a man's heart when the clang of shame and dishonor hammers at a man's head. Honor, sir, is—"

"You're not making any common sense. What is your last name, Young Wild Tom?"

"Paine, sir."

"But I suppose, gentlemen," Colonel Conant said, turning to the rustics, "we have no alternative but to stand and fight the British."

"It's about time," Dilsie said.

"The ayes have it," Colonel Conant said. "And may history so record."

"Now charge," Lord Percy said, "but no man fire a shot."

"Stand where you are, men," Colonel Conant said, "and knock them on the beano. Be as rude as mice. The British, the King's men, can stand up to a volley, but they will never tolerate rudeness. Rudeness should provoke a fight."

"What are you writing down?" Lee said to Braxton.

"History."

"But how do you know Percy said 'Charge' and Conant said 'Stand and be rude'?"

"History is anyone's guess, Lee. Mine will be better than most. I was here."

"History will say differently."

"Goddamn it, I was here."

"Lee, I've staunched the flow of blood."

"Do you have to say 'staunched the flow of blood'—all those clichés. Write 'stopped the blood.' "

"Poxey likes words like 'staunched,' 'beckons,' and 'behooves.' Here come Dilsie and Francine. Lay low so they can't see us."

Braxton wrote, "It behooves us here at the beginning of the war to note that history beckons."

"What's that shit you're writing?" Francine said.

"You know, Francine," Braxton said, "Poxey plans to send up a balloon with a sign on it, THE NEW BOSTON TIMES. He spends money for things like that rather than pay his correspondents a living wage—he gets what he pays for."

"You're bleeding."

69

THE
LONG
NAKED
DESCENT
INTO
BOSTON

70

THE
LONG
NAKED
DESCENT
INTO
BOSTON

"He was, but he has staunched the flow of blood," Lee said. "I've made a sketch of him dying at Lexington—THOSE WHO PERISHED."

"You're both damn fine correspondents. Look at the job you did on the French and Indian Wars. Poxey has destroyed your self-confidence."

"Poxey has made Gretchen Miss Boston Massacre," Lee said.

"You both have got it in you, boys. Don't let Poxey get you down. Watch what's going on down there. You can do a bang-up job on this war. The world, Braxton and Lee," Francine said, "will little note nor long remember what they did here, but will never forget what you said they did here."

ten

It is true, Poxe thought, that no two people can watch the same event and come up with the same version of what happened. It is a common thought on Boston Common that the truth lies somewhere in between. Between what? The truth is what a newspaper says is truth. If one newspaper says one thing and another another, does that mean the truth lies somewhere between Hong Kong and Singapore or between Venus and Saturn? Saying people start a war is like saying a bonfire starts itself. It takes a newspaper to start a bonfire and a newspaper to start a war. It is commonly said that the common people will die for what they believe. No, they will die for what the newspaper does not believe. Wars are not fought for God and country but for *The Boston Globe* and *The New Boston Times.*

Waiting in the waiting room of *The New Boston Times,* which was in fact the Little Brown Book Shoppe, was Benedict Arnold himself, as big as life and by his own reckoning twice as important.

"I do not like, sir," Brown said to Arnold, *"The New Boston Times* using my shoppe as a waiting room. Important writers come and go, and so perchance do some respectable persons. What I am saying, sir, and I hope without offense, is that you may be occupying the space of a cash customer. Even in these hard times we have been known to sell a book, sell a book, sell a book," he mumbled and he tried to kick the cat. "Do you believe,

72

THE
LONG
NAKED
DESCENT
INTO
BOSTON

sir, Henry Knox sold me a dying turkey? I didn't catch your name."

"Arnold."

"And has the cat got your tongue, sir?" Brown asked rhetorically and with a bite and followed the poor tortoise-shell cat Knox had left along with unpaid bills and Bibles on consignment—followed the shuffling elderly and rheumatic tortoise-shell around the mile-high stacks of unsold best sellers that climbed to heaven and back (one bore the title *To Heaven and Back*), around the mile-high stacks that threatened to kill them all in the next earthquake or Revolution. "There is no humor in this," Brown said, but he was unable to catch the cat and kick it.

"Do you have a book, sir," Arnold said, "entitled *To Heaven and Back*?"

"I certainly do, sir," Brown said, shaking and becoming red, then blue with rage.

"No offense, sir," Arnold said. "I was merely trying to pass the time of day."

"You, sir, are a scoundrel and a popinjay," Brown said.

"I am, sir," Arnold said, "the Assistant Professor of Ethics at Yale University."

"And where be that, sir?"

"New Haven."

"And where be that, sir?"

"Connecticut."

"Connecticut and university are a contradiction in terms, but I will let it pass," Brown said, philosophizing and mellowing, pleased at his wit. "Assistant Professors have been known to buy books."

"They have, sir."

"Something cut to the style," Brown said, "with a touch of blue, wide lapels, and pinched in at the back."

"Indeed, sir, to the style."

"How does the Bible hit you?"

"To the turn, sir, to the turn."

"Christmas wrap?"

"If there be no charge."

"No charge to you, sir. Ethics, Connecticut, Yale, Assistant Professor. Cash or credit?"

"Credit."

"Ethics, Connecticut, Yale, Assistant Professor. What more could one ask? Hop to it," Brown said to the cat. "We have a customer. Could I interest you in something on West Point, sir? Plans, maps, forty-nine colored illustrations, to the style. Christmas wrap."

"Not today, sir," Arnold said.

"What we have here truly, Gretchen, is a Benedict Arnold waiting in our waiting room. I don't know why Brown complains. People have been known to buy a book. Knox never complained. Knox's going to war was simply an excuse to unload the business. Think so? Arnold. Yes. He wants a job. Comes with highest Yale recommendations. Why doesn't he join the army? It's expanding. There could be a great future there. Has personal recommendation from Francine's father. Father believes Francine prospering here. No one is prospering here. Show Arnold in, Gretchen.

"Mr. Arnold, sit down. I was just telling Gretchen no one is prospering here, but it's a good chance to get in on the ground floor of the newspaper business. I now have the two top reporters in the country, Braxton and Lee, who may have already given their life for the cause—the newspaper cause. What I plan to do is work this business up to the point where there are no salaries—no one but women working. I've got Dilsie and Francine out now as stringers with Braxton and Lee, learning the trade."

"Learning to drink," Gretchen said.

"Are you acquainted with the fact, sir," Poxe said, "that our salaries are modest?"

"To what degree of modesty?"

"I have the modesty, sir, to offer nothing but the opportunity to get in on the ground floor of *The New Boston Times*."

"I prefer heights," Arnold said, "and my Peggy, diamonds. I'm afraid the twain shall never meet."

"Do you really mean 'twain'—not 'train'? You do not lisp, my dear Arnold?"

"I meant 'twain.' I do not lisp, sir, on my honor. No one at

73

THE
LONG
NAKED
DESCENT
INTO
BOSTON

74

THE
LONG
NAKED
DESCENT
INTO
BOSTON

Yale lisps, sir. When we say 'twain' we mean 'twain.' ''

"Then say 'train.' ''

"Twain," Arnold said.

"Although there is not a spot for you here on the ground floor of *The New Boston Times,* my dear Arnold, I am sure there is a spot for you in the army. Our principle here at the *Times* is to pay small salaries, and our prejudice is to hire no one who lisps. But my understanding is the army is scraping the bottom of the barrel, and right now you have your choice of armies—the Boston Patriots or the British. The Patriots are dedicated and the British have uniforms. It's six of one and half a dozen of the other. If I were a betting man I'd take the Patriots."

"Why, sir?"

"The odds at Lloyds are against the Patriots sixteen to one. These are good odds, Arnold."

"No uniforms."

"They'll get uniforms, Arnold. Our paper is working on uniforms."

"The Patriots have no experience."

"They're getting it today at Lexington and Concord."

"A twin bill?"

"Yes."

"The Patriots should start easier."

"I warned Adams the Patriots are green, but he had to jump in. You don't get experience, he said, by watching the British drill. Yes, Lord Percy will gobble the Colonials up today. I've got Braxton and Lee covering the Patriots. If the Patriots show good the first outing, the paper will back the Revolution hook, line, and sinker. I've promised that."

"War is not a game," Gretchen said.

"War is man's business, Gretchen."

"War is not a business."

"If war is not a game and not a business, then what in God's name is it? I wish women would stay out of these things."

"In a war people get killed," Gretchen said.

Poxe and Arnold stared at each other and wondered about women.

"She may have a point," Arnold said.

"It doesn't make any difference whether Gretchen has a point.

Both sides are already in this thing up to our ears. If we withdraw now, we'll lose face and credibility all over the world. I've already got the uniform campaign for the Patriots going full blast and I've rented a balloon from Cambridge Balloons to get the war off the ground."

"That blows the budget," Gretchen said. "I scrape and save and go without lunches or carry hot-cross buns in a paper bag to work. I haven't had a new dress since the Boston Tea Party or a pair of shoes since the Boston Massacre, and Poxey, you go out and blow the budget on a goddamn balloon to get your stupid Revolution off the ground. How much was it?"

"Thirty pounds."

"My God, we could have bought a new set of type. Our readers now think we're printing the *Times* in Chinese."

"Our Chinese readers haven't complained. Gretchen, I apologize. The balloon seemed like a good idea at the time."

"So did the war."

"I know, Gretchen, but in for a penny, in for a pound."

"But that's not what makes the world go round. I'm sick and fed up to here with you goddamn men starting a war every ten minutes."

"I know, Gretchen, I know," Poxe said, leaning over his good belly and touching her. "I'll make it up to you, Gretchen, I swear I'll make it up to you. Isn't there something left in petty cash?"

"No, Braxton and Lee took all the petty cash for the horse rentals."

"Couldn't they have put the horses on the cuff, Gretchen, if they had their wits about them? You know what dumbos Lee and Braxton are. You should have told them to charge the horses."

"Charge the horses to what? Everyone in Boston is wise to the *Times*."

"Oh dear. What about our cash flow?"

"There is no cash flow. What do you think the *Times* is, the Charlestown River? Poxe," she said, standing up and throwing down her memo pad and flinging her plumed feather quill pen at Arnold and sweeping all the papers off the desk and emptying the wastebasket over Poxe's head, "what do you think I am, a free-loading ninny? I am a woman and I have my rights and if you want to know what your war is all about—male stupidity, that's

75

THE
LONG
NAKED
DESCENT
INTO
BOSTON

76

THE
LONG
NAKED
DESCENT
INTO
BOSTON

what your war is about. Go up in your hot-air balloon—buy your pretty tin soldier uniforms while I work my fingers to the nubbin and carry my lunch in a paper bag so you can support your female harridans with silk dresses and pomander balls to hide their stink in great homes on Water Street while I have to sleep in a shithouse in the same bed with four other trusted employees so you can afford to spend thirty pounds on a hot-air balloon. I quit, Poxey," and she was gone.

Her plumed feather quill pen she had shot at Arnold still sailed round above the printing press.

"That's a woman for you, Arnold."

"Yes."

"All logic and no understanding."

"Yes."

"Women have the wit to quit but not the patience to make it stick."

"Yes."

"Women are good for only one thing, Arnold."

"Yes."

"Women's undoing is their curiosity."

"Yes."

"They always come back to find out what mess the men are up to now."

"Yes."

"And clean it up and get things tidied up again for the next war."

"Yes."

"But that's the way the world bounces."

"Yes."

"Arnold, I have no harridans in silk dress and pomander balls on Water Street to hide their stink. I wish to God I did. I can't afford it. These are hard times."

"Yes."

"That's the way a woman's imagination works."

"Yes."

"Does your Peggy want silk dress and pomander balls?"

"Yes."

"That could be the death of you, Arnold."

"Yes."

"Arnold, I apologize for washing our linen in public but you know how women are."

"Yes."

"Now that Gretchen has quit, do you mind if I bounce a few ideas off you?"

"Yes."

"Well, bear with me"—her feather pen just floated onto the printing press—"Arnold, you must have known Nathan Hale at Yale. Is he Jewish?"

"No."

"What you say will be held in the strictest confidence. Has Nathan always had this inferiority complex? Has he always regretted things?"

"Yes."

"Poor boy, but I've given him a second chance. I have always been partial to Jews. I have sent him on to Lexington to spy things out for me, then we will go up in the balloon to have a look-see. He turned down a night on the town with Gretchen with all expenses paid. Do you suppose that is why Gretchen is in such a huff?"

"Yes."

"And what do you think of Young Wild Tom Paine? I've been dwelling on the idea of putting him on the payroll. Of course I mean payroll in the figurative sense. I hope Young Wild Tom understands that." Poxe picked the wastebasket off his head, gathered the papers from the floor, caught the feather pen that had floated off the printing press when Arnold sneezed, got the memo book, and poised the pen. "Now where were we? I was asking you what you think of Young Wild Tom Paine. Does he have the mustard, the flair, the gift of gab combined with enough common sense to get our Revolution off the ground—in short, sir, is there a place for Young Wild Tom Paine on *The New Boston Times*?"

77

THE
LONG
NAKED
DESCENT
INTO
BOSTON

eleven

Revere, Tom Paine, Benedict Arnold, and Nathan Hale were hammering to find a place in history. No. Tom Paine wanted a place on *The New Boston Times*. So did Benedict Arnold. So did Hale. But times be hard. Rivers wild. Oceans deep. Time insouciant, fickle, capricious, arcane. There was no place on *The New Boston Times* for such as our young heroes. So they found a place in history. Happiness for them under Poxe's warm wing and sibylline eye and real world would be replaced by the escape, the platitudes and the drumbeat, the metronome of history. What might have been a life would be a death in the mud of Lexington or on a library shelf in Perth Amboy, New Jersey, Grand Rapids, Michigan, Council Bluffs, Iowa—impotent and without balls or blood beneath the virginal stare of the censors in Conshohocken, Pennsylvania. No warm bed of Dilsie, Gretchen, and Francine, but the joining of the dead in the cold fiction called history—but some can be rescued, Braxton thought, writing. Some restored to life, some blessed with balls, others made whole again, depending on Poxe's budget, Dilsie's warmth, and Francine's vocabulary.

"And my art," Lee said, sketching.

"What in the fuck has happened to the war?" Francine said.

"Patience, my dear Francine," Braxton said. "Time and war wait for everyman. They're all down there on the Lexington green now. In a few minutes they'll be going at it hammer and tong."

"What will the Revolution be about?" Dilsie said.

"Taxes."

"I ain't never paid no taxes." Dilsie said.

"That's what the war's about."

"I ain't going to pay no taxes no matter who gets in," Dilsie said.

"We will have another Revolution about that," Braxton said. "Then there's freedom and liberty." Braxton watched the two sides below maneuvering for position.

"I got plenty of freedom and liberty now," Dilsie said.

"But other blacks haven't. With your wit and good looks and a kind master who gave you your freedom after you threatened his life with a blunderbuss, you're a special case, Dilsie. Other blacks are in durance vile."

"Blacks going to be in durance vile no matter which side gets in," Dilsie said, "lessen they get a blunderbuss. And learn how to use it."

"Then there's the pursuit of happiness," Lee said, sketching the armies below at each other's throats. "And a living wage."

"Poxey ain't going to pay a living wage no matter what side gets in," Dilsie said.

"And then there's women's rights," Braxton said, desperate. "Equal pay for equal work. Something like that."

"Kiss my sweet ass," Francine said, "if that's what these men are fighting for."

"Temper, temper."

"Kiss my sweet ass," Francine said.

"This is a hallowed day," Braxton said.

"Kiss my sweet ass if it is," Francine said.

Lee put down his sketch pad and charcoal pencil with impatience. "You two girls—"

"Women."

"You two women are determined to stop this Revolution, aren't you?"

"Francine's right," Dilsie said.

"About what?"

"Kiss my sweet ass," Dilsie said. "What in the hell do you thinks we get out of this? The privilege to follows you two great artists around. The gentlemen of the Press, the boy heroes of the Revolution. We ain't gets no bylines. All we gets is to take Poxey's shit. Camp followers, that's all we is."

79
THE
LONG
NAKED
DESCENT
INTO
BOSTON

80

THE
LONG
NAKED
DESCENT
INTO
BOSTON

"Dilsie," Lee said, "Poxey plans to give you a daily column. Advice to the lonely soldier—'Dear Dilsie'—something like that."

"That will be the day," Dilsie said.

"And you both get to sleep with us," Braxton said.

"Big event!" Francine said, jumping up. "We get to sleep with the boy heroes of the Revolution. Big event! Lucky, lucky, lucky girls. Lucky day. Sad night."

"We're not that bad," Lee said.

"They tries, Francine," Dilsie said. "You got to give them credit. They tries."

"Lucky girls," Francine said. "Lucky, lucky, lucky girls." She sat down again.

Lee picked up his sketch pad again. Something was afoot on the darkling greensward below. History. Ignorant armies clash by day. Up here all was peace. Excepting the usual war. Women. Women demand a continual war. Women have no objection to war if it is continuous. Men prefer supervised intervals of peace. This is the only known difference between men and women. Excepting women's biological need to cuff young gentlemen about the ears in sudden unprovoked affray, swear unladylike oaths, and kick young farmers between the you-know-where. Otherwise, women be gentle as lambs and twice as sweet. Sugar and spice and everything nice.

Meanwhile, in the phony war below on the Lexington greensward the armies glared at each other, jangled their spears, beat their drums, stamped their boots, scattered their rage, cursed the good King, and threw rocks at the woman in the window—while Nathan spied, Arnold hid, Paine exhorted, and Poxe asked for more copy.

"Wait a minute," Francine said. "Get hold of yourself, Braxton. You know that Poxey is not going to buy that kind of writing. Someone has got to take care of you, Braxton. I guess I'm elected."

"What does Poxey want?"

"Objective reporting."

"What's that?"

"Lie a little," Dilsie said.

"Let's get closer to the fighting," Lee said, getting up. "I can't get a good sketch here."

"Where can you get a good sketch?" Dilsie said.

"Lay off the boys, Dilsie," Francine said.

"It don't make me no never mind where they goes," Dilsie said. "This poor nigger has to follow the boy heroes of the Revolution wherever they goes."

"Give the boys some peace, Dilsey," Francine said. "Let's go and have a better look-see. And give the boys some peace."

81

THE
LONG
NAKED
DESCENT
INTO
BOSTON

twelve

When Lord Percy had ordered Britain's finest to charge without firing a shot, to load their guns with powder but no ball, he was sensitive to the fact that there would be a royal inquiry into the death of a King's subject. The King did not have so many subjects that he could afford to have some subjects killed off like sitting ducks. Each subject was dear to the King. The good King shed a tear for each subject lost, strayed, stolen, or shot dead in the distant Colonies by Lord Percy. It made no difference whether the subjects were killed accidentally or on purpose by Lord Percy's men; whether the subject was a country bumpkin or to the manor born, the good King wanted each subject to be present or accounted for. The noble King had been anointed and appointed by God. So God was up to His ears in this thing, too. Lord Percy was sensitive to the whole ball of wax. That is why he had ordered ball but no powder.

"What was it," Lord Percy said, "powder and no ball or ball and no powder? Or a little bit of both?"

"A little bit of both, sir," Colonel Coudray said, riding up, "but not enough to kill, only enough powder and ball to make a dent."

"That was clever of me," Lord Percy said. "How will that sound at the inquiry?"

"Considering, sir, what my spies say, Hancock and Adams have prompted the Minutemen to push and shove us when we arrive at the green."

"What for?"

"Justice and liberty."

"Justice and liberty were never born in anarchy and rudeness, in pushing and shoving, Colonel Coudray. I don't want to sound like an old fossil, a law and order man. I realize the Colonials have justifiable complaints."

"What justifiable complaint?"

"They live so far from England."

"There's nothing we can do to redress that, sir."

"Quite."

"Being so far from England gives people queer ideas, even the best of people."

"Quite."

"It's amazing what this simple geological phenomenon will do to a young man's imagination. It seems to have no effect at all upon elderly people. Nothing to do with sex. It seems to affect both sexes the same—being such a great distance from England."

"Quite. But I apologize, Colonel Coudray. I'm not being scientific. What we should do is set up control groups with a double blind—that is, set up different groups at different distances from England, but none knowing how far they are from England, then asking each control group what it thinks about liberty and justice."

"Capital."

"I believe the answers would surprise Parliament. I believe the further the control group would be from England, the wilder would be the imagination. By the time you get to Lexington, I would defy anyone to make head or tail of what the group was saying."

"You cannot anticipate the answer to an experiment before the experiment, sir. It's not quite being fair."

"I know, I apologize, Colonel Coudray. What were we about?"

"You have already given the order to charge, sir."

"Then let's be on our way and have done with it," Lord Percy said. "What we do here today will not only reflect our integrity but our honor to boot. Does every man jack understand that? Death before dishonor? That our good and noble King sees all, feels all, watches all, that even in a heavy overcoat or if it's

83

THE
LONG
NAKED
DESCENT
INTO
BOSTON

84

THE
LONG
NAKED
DESCENT
INTO
BOSTON

raining cats and dogs, nothing, nothing, no matter how small a slip or how great the distance from England, nothing is hidden from his worshipful eyes. Have you got that?"

"Quite."

"Then consider that the order of the day, Colonel Coudray."

There were only two subjects permitted to be discussed at Buckman's Tavern—religion and politics. Lee sketched, watching out the door across Bedford Road to the Lexington Common where the Minutemen stood or moved about in smart drill, piling into each other and keeping their powder dry.

"Chaps," Colonel Conant said, "we must learn the evolutions of the drill before the British get here."

"The British will be upon us in a trice, sir."

"Steady does it, men," Colonel Conant said. "I want you all to practice pushing and shoving and mumbling strange oaths and shouting loud slogans."

"Such as, sir?"

"Death before dishonor."

"What about 'Don't tread on me,' sir?"

"Oh, that's a good one, lad, a very good one, and it so does fit the occasion to a tee. Your name, lad?"

"Paine, sir."

"I've heard of your slogans, Paine. Some are priceless. Some are tuppence the sheet, some are so-so, and some are not worth a tinker's dam or the powder to blow them up."

"I'm sorry, sir."

"Don't be sorry, lad. Just put your mind to it. If this war is to be won, it will be won by slogans or not won at all. It certainly will never be won by this sorry lot," the colonel said, staring at his men.

"They are dedicated, sir, and they will have uniforms in the morning."

"And who be you, sir?"

"Henry Knox, sir."

"Not the same Henry Knox who has the bookstore between the Rose and Crown and *The New Boston Times*?"

"The same, sir."

"How is Poxey, Francine, the whole gang?"

"The same, sir."

"That's a pity. And what brings you to the Revolution?"

"I am Captain of Cannon—"

"And where are the cannon?"

Knox looked around. "There be none, sir."

"Then fetch some—but not now. Stand fast. I think I see the British coming or am I seeing things? Have you a spyglass?"

"I have, but I loaned it to Nathan."

"Not Nathan of Yale?"

"The same, sir."

"Well, he is getting up in the world. Stand fast, Knox. When and if the British arrive, pretend not to notice. That should cut them down a peg."

"Are you getting this?" Dilsie said to Braxton.

"Yes."

"Can Poxey use it?"

"I don't know, Dilsie."

"I can spring for a Flip," Dilsie said. "I hit Poxey for a pound note."

"Don't pay cash, Dilsie. Charge it to the *Times*."

"I've tried that. No dice."

"Then buy Flips all around and get a receipt from Buckman for oats. Put it on the expenses tab."

"Poxey's wise to that. We've charged enough phony oats to sink Boston."

"Give it another go, Dilsie."

"All right," Dilsie said. "Flips all around."

"I'm sorry," Buckman said. "No credit till after the battle. That's our policy. You give a soldier credit and he goes out and gets himself killed to beat you out of it. I can't finance the war."

"Try."

"No," Buckman said. "No credit to soldiers."

"We're not soldiers."

"How do I know that? No one has uniforms yet. When uniforms are issued, I'll know where I stand. Even if you're not soldiers—and I suspect some of you are—but even if you're not, you could get killed in a crossfire. It happens all the time."

"I've got a pound note," Dilsie said, flashing it.

"My God," Buckman said, taking it. "I haven't seen a real one

85

THE
LONG
NAKED
DESCENT
INTO
BOSTON

86

THE
LONG
NAKED
DESCENT
INTO
BOSTON

of these since the Boston Tea Party." And he squeezed Dilsie to himself like a lost black orange.

"And give me a receipt for oats," Dilsie said.

"In a trice," Buckman said, and a cannon went off. "That's only the British trying to scare us," Buckman said and he busied himself making the Flips all around.

A Rum Flip was made with the help of Doctor Neat because he was damn good at it and all his patients had left for the war. Which was fortunate because Colonel Conant arrived at the tavern door and said that "You're wanted at the barricades, Buckman."

Buckman dropped everything and Doctor Neat poured five quarts of beer into a stone pot that swung from the iron rod over the open fire; next he beat seven yolks of eggs with a whisk in a tin bowl; then he stirred this slowly into the hot beer, then a dram of molasses, then a pinch of salt followed by eight gills of New England rum. The eggs and molasses and rum were stirred slowly so as not to curdle, then the whites of eggs were warmed separately before being poured in the pot, then nine gills of rum were added to cap it off, then twelve gills of rum added hurriedly because Buckman might come back. Then all this was set before the guests in warmed pewter tankards and the guests smacked their lips to the roar of artillery—had Knox come up with a cannon?

As Buckman had suspected, it was only a warning shot by the British, fired over the bow of the Minutemen to get them to stop what they were doing and pay attention to the King.

The Minutemen were occupied pulling cartridges out of their cartouche boxes, biting off the ends, then tapping powder into the pan before pouring the rest of the powder, then the ball, down the barrel of the musket, then tamping it all down with a ramrod. All this while everyone in the world is shooting at you. You would have thought that no one would have survived loading a musket. But the salvation of the gun loader was that the other side was doing the same thing. There was always a time-out while both sides loaded their guns. Sometimes spectators would wait for hours for the armies to load their guns. Sometimes spectators would leave the field, bored with the lack of action. Both Lord Percy, who represented our great and noble King, and Colonel

Conant, who represented "the misguided peasant," were brothers in this conviction—that the spectator was feckless, that spectators knew more of wars than generals, that spectators ended up supporting the opposite side, that spectators became drunk with power and possessed infant children who could perform better than those soldiers in the field. Both knew that a spectator gains his wisdom in a grog shoppe and from such fountains of learning as *The New Boston Times.*

Lord Percy strode his troops onto Lexington Green. The Minutemen stood fast.

"Where oh where are Hancock and Adams?" Lord Percy asked the rustics with politeness.

"Philadelphia."

"Why?"

"Independence—"

"There be no such thing as independence, Colonel. We are all dependent on one another. Now you've all had entirely too much to drink. I suggest you go home and sleep it off. Don't do anything rash like declaring your independence until you've thought it over. Drunken riders can be dangerous, so drive home slowly. I assure you your good-hearted King will grant you all amnesty for your helter-skelter impudence. That's more than your new masters would grant you. Independence!" Lord Percy shouted, staring at Colonel Coudray and Madame de Tocqueville. "We would all like to declare our independence and have a tavern binge, curse God and King and insult our betters, declare our independence from our cares, our wives and sweethearts and other problems. Not milk the cows, not mow the hay, not shovel the shit—*excusez-moi*, Madame de Tocqueville."

"*Continuez,* Lord Percy."

"Where was I—?"

"Shoveling shit," Colonel Conant said.

"No, I already said that. Something else you had in mind?"

"Independence."

"Yes, do you intend to give the blacks their freedom? Women? Give the land back you stole from the Indians?"

"No."

"Then what, may I ask, my good Colonel Conant, excepting your slogans, is your Revolution about?"

87

THE
LONG
NAKED
DESCENT
INTO
BOSTON

88

THE
LONG
NAKED
DESCENT
INTO
BOSTON

"Hancock and Adams have left for Philadelphia, sir. That is their area of competence. Their kind of questions. I believe you are trying to confuse us, sir."

"I am not confused, sir," Young Wild Tom Paine said. "I think I speak for all when I say I would rather spend a whole life on my knees than stand this one day for justice."

"My God, Tom," Lord Percy said. "You mean just the opposite. You mean I would rather spend this one day on my feet for justice than the rest of my life under tyranny on my knees."

"Thank you, sir, that's what I meant."

"My God," Lord Percy said. "You don't even know your own slogans properly. Hancock and Adams have abandoned you here at Lexington and are staying at a comfortable hotel in Philadelphia, thinking up more slogans you won't remember and writing a lot of balderdash to bore lads and lasses in history classes rather than pay the taxes they owe. Now why don't we all sober up, let bygones be bygones, and go to the parson's cottage and have a nice cup of tea?"

"Don't tread on me," Tom Paine said. "Death before dishonor. It is better to have self-government than good government. I do not choose to accept this crown of thorns—"

"You may have a point," Lord Percy said. "What does Colonel Coudray think?"

"Some of their slogans express excellent sentiments," Colonel Coudray said. "Worth dying for if they were touched up a bit."

"Good," Lord Percy said. "Then we have no real quarrel. The Revolution is only a question of semantics. We had best toddle back to Boston, then England. If you will join me, Madame de Tocqueville." Lord Percy raised his marshal's baton. "I will weep for joy to set my foot in England once again. That sceptered isle. That England. That jewel set in a silvered sea, proof against invasion and the hand of war—"

A spectator threw a rock, another a tomato and a ripe potato, another a small pig and a dead rabbit, another a Bible, another a plugged hat. A peasant swung and a Redcoat swung back. Of such stuff are Revolutions started—a stolen speech, a good tomato and a ripe potato, an innocent pig and a dead rabbit. Boredom at Buckman's Tavern. A shot was fired.

"Who fired first?" Lord Percy shouted.

"You did!"

"No, you did!"

Now everybody fired second.

"This," General Lord Percy said, "has turned into a Revolution, Colonel Coudray. No place for the likes of us. Those people are out of uniform. This is something for the courts. Shooting at the King's men. You have witnessed it, Colonel Coudray. Will you join me in a retreat?"

"I will, sir."

"Then let's get the hell out of here," Lord Percy said.

"Look at the balloon up there," Braxton said.

"Where?" Dilsie said.

"Look over Concord," Lee said. "Poxey should have held his balloon trip up until after the Revolution. You can always have a war, and anyone can get in the Revolution by sticking his ass out the window, but very few people get a chance to go up in a balloon. If Poxey had put the balloon off until after the Revolution he could have sold a lot of papers with it. Now people will be angry with him for changing the subject."

"Where is the balloon now?" Dilsie said.

"It has disappeared."

"Yes."

"Poor Poxey."

"Yes."

"Do you suppose Gretchen is with him?"

"Yes."

But the balloon had not disappeared. People wrongly suspect that because they can no longer see a balloon, a balloon has disappeared, but a balloon never disappears. It may crash to earth, killing all of the inhabitants of the balloon basket, or it may shoot up high into the very heavens so that the inhabitants of the balloon basket, the "aeronauts" Poxey called them, can talk with angels, but a balloon never disappears. Certainly if an angel can see a balloon, it has not disappeared.

In Poxe's case, fortunately for those who loved the old son-of-a-bitch, the balloon had not crashed into Concord, killing

89
THE
LONG
NAKED
DESCENT
INTO
BOSTON

90

THE
LONG
NAKED
DESCENT
INTO
BOSTON

all aboard, but had decided to shoot up into the nether world, not high enough for the angels but maybe a fallen angel, high enough to escape the "idiots" fighting below and not be caught in the crossfire—I say the balloon decided because you have no control over what a balloon does. It was once thought as recently as 1765 when Montgolfier began experimenting with balloons in Paris, France, that balloons were subject to the whim of the winds, that they would go where the winds happened to think they should go. This was unscientifically presupposing that winds had a mind of their own. Now in 1775, science knew better. It was clear to the scientific community after repeated testing that winds clearly had no mind, their own or anybody else's. And all the scientists wondered how they could have been such *dummkopfs* to believe that the wind had a mind. Then it must be that a *balloon* has a mind. This is called scientific deduction. That is how science works. It shows how smart scientists are. Particularly at Harvard.

Poxe was not interested in science for the nonce. He was interested in getting the balloon down without breaking all their heads. He had Nathan along for ballast, still in his green pants and holding Knox's telescope. Gretchen was along to feed the fire and take notes. Poxe was along to pilot the thing. Very little was known about balloons in '75, so Poxe knew as much as anyone. At Cambridge Balloons, a company formed by Harvard whiz kids, a go-go team of young geniuses, they had carefully informed Poxe about how to get the balloon up, but told him nothing at all about how to get it down—the balloon itself would take care of that, they said.

Gretchen was feeding more damp straw into the fire beneath the canopy of the balloon and that is why the balloon was bent heavenward. When Gretchen heard the helter-skelter and bang of the fighting below, she began to feed the fire faster.

"Enough, Gretchen, enough," Poxe said. "Below has already disappeared."

Of course below had not *disappeared*, which was very obvious to anyone in the Revolution. Those in the Revolution below had no more disappeared than those in the balloon above. Both illusions are laymen's misapprehensions of natural phenomena, such as flying saucers were to become in '78.

"I am not interested in your scientific explanation, Nathan," Poxe said. "I am only interested in getting this damn thing down."

"I regret, sire," Nathan said, "if I said anything that—"

"Oh hell," Poxe said.

"—discommodes you, sire, but the scientific community at Harvard will—"

"Oh hell," Poxe said. "Gretchen, stop feeding the fire."

"The last time I stopped feeding the fire," Gretchen said, "we hit the ground and bounced twice, scattering fire and notes."

"Make a note of that, Gretchen," Poxe said. "Nathan is right. It's important that this expedition be kept track of. If we perish in crashing or in flame or both, it's important for future air travelers to know how we accomplished this so they will not make the same mistake. So there will be no fear of flying. Put your notes in the black box where they can be safe and easily found in the wreckage. What do you see in your spyglass, Nathan? Who is winning below?"

"I regret to say they are."

"Who is 'they'?"

"The British."

"Are they still popping away?"

"Yes."

"And are the Patriots popping back?"

"Yes."

"Do the Patriots have uniforms yet?"

"No."

"Make a note of that, Gretchen. No uniforms. Difficult now to tell who is who. It may soon become impossible."

"I cannot feed the fire and keep us aloft and take notes at one and the same time," Gretchen said.

"That's a woman for you, Nathan," Poxe said. "Then stop feeding the fire, Gretchen. We are already in the heavens; there is nothing going on up here in the heavens that would interest the heathen readers of *The New Boston Times*. Although our readers are not a bunch of nincompoops, they are more interested in the price of corn than in what God is up to. I have discovered, Nathan, that a balloon has free will. Even if a balloon does not have complete free will, it must act as though it does. It cannot

91
THE
LONG
NAKED
DESCENT
INTO
BOSTON

92

THE
LONG
NAKED
DESCENT
INTO
BOSTON

transfer its responsibility to God and remain a free balloon. Now, I have a thought, Nathan, that has nothing to do with balloons. You must always try to speak the truth to power. This is extremely difficult in the academic community and perhaps impossible in the newspaper business, but it's a goal to shoot at. Another thought while up in a balloon—women, like any conquered people, are not interested in our Revolution but are more interested in—are we going down or up?"

"Down."

"Good girl, Gretchen," Poxe said. "Women have at last stopped feeding the fire of disharmony and discontent. The world is making progress. Nathan, you can put your green pantaloons on it, and don't say 'I regret' or I'll bop you on the kisser with Knox's spyglass. I'm in control of this contraption and if the balloon has ideas of its own, I'll deflate it with a pinprick. I am not the sole owner, publisher, and editor of *The New Boston Times* for naught. If I say things are up, they're up; if down, they're down."

"What is your wish now, sire?"

"Up."

"No, it's down. We've run out of straw."

"Oh my God," Poxe said. "We are about to crash. Quick, Nathan, your green pantaloons."

"My only regret, sire—"

"Yes, Nathan?"

"—is I have no underwear."

"Pay Gretchen no heed. She sleeps five in a bed."

"All girls or all boys?"

"Mixed."

"You may have my pants, sire."

"Thanks, Nathan. You're a brick."

But Nathan's pants would not hold up the balloon very long. All of the aeronauts were sensitive to this and an air of gloom descended upon those in the balloon basket beneath the red, white, and blue balloon that said, THE NEW BOSTON TIMES. SUBSCRIBE NOW AT OUR ESPECIAL PRE-REVOLUTION RATES.

thirteen

The British, according to Madame de Tocqueville, had lost their savoir-faire and were knocking the rustics about between Lexington and Concord. When an army has brand-new uniforms, as the British did, and knows all the evolutions of the drill, as the British did—"It is embarrassing to lose," Lord Percy said. "The Patriots were trying to make a mark for themselves. They know the people of New England will never back a loser. After having shot at nothing but rabbits, squirrels, chipmunks, and groundhogs their whole lives, it is sport to kill a soldier. Take the head to the taxidermist in Medford, have it mounted on an oak panel, and hang it next to the portrait of Grandpa Frick."

"Never that, my Lord Percy."

"And why not, my dear?" Lord Percy said. "Americans do live such a great distance from all of the civilizing influences. If I was a young lad full of piss and vinegar and lived so far from London and under the influence of drugs to conceal my low breeding from myself, who knows? My drug, Madame de Tocqueville, is the wine of victory. I have drunk of the cup many times and I shall taste of it again before this day is done."

"Well phrased, my Lord Percy, and who be the band of jackdaws that follow our baggage train?" Colonel Coudray asked.

"Whores and pimps, beggars, card sharks, loan sharks, cut-purses, liars, thieves, murderers, bigamists, stigmatists, kindly curious elderly gentlemen out for a walk, unemployed actors,

94

THE
LONG
NAKED
DESCENT
INTO
BOSTON

ladies to do the laundry, ex-acrobats, over-the-hill boxers, retired bisexuals, children of all shapes and sizes, dogs and cats, small goats, flags of all nations, troops of politicians, bands of pirates, Eskimos, cannibals, jugglers, miniature poodles, comets, elephants, three blind mice, two sets of Siamese twins, a whole world of young girls, a gaggle of geese, and between Antwerp and Chartres after the Battle of Agincourt some leftover Roquefort cheese, all and always followed by the Ladies and Gentlemen of the Press.

"Those are the usual camp followers, Colonel Coudray, and here in the Colonies I don't expect a different mix," Lord Percy said. "Do you?"

"I don't like the cut of their jib."

"Generals cannot be choosers, Colonel Coudray."

"May I have reason to expect, sire, a generalship from this mess?"

"If my plans do not go awry, you might. Without getting your hopes too high, or as the old soldier said, too many ribbons up your ass and too many bayonets down your throat, you might entertain expectations of a dukedom."

"No, sire!"

"Why not?" Lord Percy said. "Anything can happen in this day and age. I hear the King is balmy."

"Not King George the Third?"

"Yes, I hear he's got a few screws loose," Lord Percy said. "Up here in the noggin," Lord Percy said, touching his baton to his head already crowned with the badge of the King's General in the field. "Now why don't you trot off and get the bastard who just fired at us from behind that stone wall."

"Is this war, sire?"

"If it isn't, then my name is Roger Mud."

"As you wish, sire."

"I don't wish my name to be Roger Mud. Get that nut behind the stone wall."

"Right away, sire."

"Before you trot off, Colonel Coudray, are there any dispatches from the rear?"

"Just some Christmas cards."

"Let me see them," Madame de Tocqueville said. "Just as I thought," she said from behind her outdoor lorgnette. "Notes from that vixen in Boston, Mrs. Loring. In the future, Colonel Coudray," Madame de Tocqueville said, "I want all of the dispatches from the rear delivered directly to me. Lord Percy has forgot his glasses anyway. The War Office will understand. Lord Percy is getting old. A touch of the palsy. And his dangle dripples at bedtime—all off the record, of course." She looked around. "Now be off, Colonel Coudray. That last bullet just missed my horse's ass."

"I felt no bullet whistle close to me," Lord Percy said.

"Not you," Madame de Tocqueville said. "I was just referring to the general pandemonium."

"And a fine general he is, too. We are fortunate he is on our side," Lord Percy said. "Do you appreciate my wit, my dear?"

"Your body more, my Lord Percy."

"Enough of that," Lord Percy said. "Remember I still be British."

"And I like the cut of your jib."

"Thank you, my dear. And I like you and an old-fashioned war. I am gifted with both. The gods are kind. There be nothing like an old-fashioned war to buck you up on a rainy day. Don't stand there like a bump on a log, Colonel Coudray. Get that bastard firing from behind the stone wall as I bid."

"And as I bid, too," Madame de Tocqueville said.

"And give me that Christmas card, my dear," Lord Percy said, taking it. "I be still in charge here."

"Spoken like a British soldier," she said.

"And kiss me, you French fool," Lord Percy said.

And there and before the Battle of Lexington and Concord, they kissed.

"You can't say, Braxton," Dilsie said, " 'And there and before the Battle of Lexington and Concord, they kissed.' Nobody but nobody is going to write that kind of bungaloo as long as I am copy editor of the *Times*. 'Before the Battle of Lexington and Concord they kissed' ain't going to get by me."

"You take the phrase out of context, Dilsie."

95

THE
LONG
NAKED
DESCENT
INTO
BOSTON

96

THE
LONG
NAKED
DESCENT
INTO
BOSTON

"You know Poxey don't want no context. He wants bang bang bang, shit shit shit. Context is for the *Globe* and them dull papers. We are keyed to the people."

"I'll put my dispatches directly to Poxey when he gets down," Braxton said.

"It is no skins off my ass," Dilsie said. "You does what you want. I know where I stands. Poxey slipped me a pound note."

"Braxton and myself," Lee said, "are thinking of leaving for the *Globe.*"

"Don't do that, honeys," Dilsie said. "I like the way Lee draws them pictures. I'll see that Poxey slips pound notes all around when he gets down. Otherwise we'll all quit to the *Globe.* You game, Francine?"

"You can bet your sweet ass I'm game," Francine said.

"What do you see, Nathan?"

"Nothing but general pandemonium, sire."

"Braxton will make a bad joke out of that one," Poxe said. "I made the mistake, against my principles, of slipping Dilsie a pound note. Women talk. As soon as it gets around, they'll all be gibbering for money. The blackmail will start as soon as we get down. How long will this thing stay up, Nathan?"

"You're the expert, sire. I don't know how long a pair of pants will hold us."

"They told me at Cambridge Balloons that everyone is green at this game, so your guess is as good as anyone's, Nathan."

"Fifteen minutes," Nathan said, still spying through his spyglass. "Give or take a few."

"Nathan, you've got the telescope reversed."

"I thought those soldiers looked small," Nathan said.

"Gretchen," Poxe said, "have you got a pinafore you can spare beneath all those furbelows?"

"I'm not going to sail naked back to earth," Gretchen said. "What about burning your notes?"

"I thought we lost those when we bounced."

"We've still got plenty," Gretchen said.

"I plan to save those for a true history of the Revolution, Gretchen, that I plan to write and Brown to publish."

"Everyone is planning a true history of the Revolution."

"But I own the only press in town, along with the Fidelity First Mortgage and a small piece hugged to his bosom by Franklin to make sure his sayings get to see the light of print."

"I rather like Franklin's sayings," Nathan said, still spying down—now the spyglass was turned properly.

"Franklin is a small bore," Poxe said, "although if you get to know him well, after a while he becomes a big bore."

"I hear he does well with the women," Nathan said.

"What do you think, Gretchen?"

"When he took me to the Boston Chophouse," Gretchen said, "he sprang for two of the biggest chops and a frog salad, but he cut me off without dessert. He said a penny saved is a penny earned."

"Did we use that saying?" Poxe said.

"I'm afraid we did, in ten editions," Gretchen said, pulling off her pinafore and feeding the fires of discontent.

"I appreciate your pinafore, Gretchen. I'll make it up to you."

And they went higher and higher.

"I regret," Nathan said, turning his spyglass round and round, "I regret to say that the British are taking a shellacking. They will be lucky to get a man out of Concord alive."

"And why do you regret the British taking a beating?"

"Because they will go back to England next week and the Revolution will be over before I have gotten a chance."

"I cannot believe, Nathan, that General Gage will leave *The New Boston Times* holding the bag. I promise you, Nathan, the British will not go home as long as Mrs. Loring is free."

"You mean as long as Mrs. Loring doesn't charge?"

"Available, Nathan."

"It's regrettable, sire," Nathan said, holding his telescope like a flute he was about to play, "but I understand Mrs. Gage is arriving on the next boat."

"General Gage is not a British general for naught, Nathan. He will put her ship in quarantine. How goes the Revolution, Nathan?"

"The British have started back from Concord."

"And the camp followers?"

97

THE
LONG
NAKED
DESCENT
INTO
BOSTON

98

THE
LONG
NAKED
DESCENT
INTO
BOSTON

"Right behind."

"Will they all make it?"

"No, Lord Percy has got himself in a box."

"And General Gage will get him out. Give Gretchen your shirt, Nathan, for the fire."

fourteen

General Gage was gravely concerned and sitting in his drawing room with a glass of hock across from Mrs. Loring, who was working on a crazy quilt. The two black slaves, Pomfret and Pomeroy, were standing at the wall map of New England, trying to figure out by moving about red pins how to get the British out of the bind.

"I am very concerned, pet," General Gage said, staring vacantly at the New England road map. "We cannot keep Mrs. Gage in quarantine forever—then there's the Revolution. Why do you suppose the Patriots chose this occasion to embarrass me?"

"Will you come here?" Ali Pomfret said from the road map.

"No, I will not come there," Gage said. "I have stared at that road map until I am blue in the face. I have moved those red pins about until the map is in shreds. No, I will not come there. Lord Percy got himself into this mess and he can get himself out. And it's not your job, Pomfret and Pomeroy, to help out, although I do appreciate your efforts."

"We believe, sir," Pomeroy said from the map, "there is a possibility for a good play fake here. If Lord Percy will move his flankers in the direction of Roxbury, the Patriots will have to shift above Newbury to intercept. Then Percy can move his main force across Charlestown Neck and be home free."

"Why didn't I think of that?" General Gage said.

100

THE
LONG
NAKED
DESCENT
INTO
BOSTON

"Because, pet," Mrs. Loring said, shifting the stitch on her crazy quilt, "because, pet, you have been drinking steadily since our Lord Percy got in a bind. It is as though," Mrs. Loring said, picking up a blue ball of yarn, "it is as though you either wanted Lord Percy to fail or you wish the war to last out of good sportsmanship. You want the Patriots to get off to a good start. You believe they suffer from a lack of uniforms, which gives you an unfair advantage."

"Quite," Gage said. "But none of those facts can excuse my not thinking of that play fake. You would think that if all you said was true, I would be unable as a British major general to resist the temptation to win."

"You have always resisted that temptation, pet. Long, long before I knew you."

"Quite," Gage said. "But this is too good to miss. Pomeroy and Pomfret, are you busy at the nonce?"

"No, General," they both said, looking away from the map.

"Then why don't you both nip up to Concord in the night, when you will both probably be undetected, and give your escape maneuver to Percy."

The blacks looked at each other, questioning.

"You haven't been drinking?" Gage asked.

"Some," Pomfret said. "Enough to keen us up."

"But not enough to make the trip to Concord?"

"Not quite," Pomeroy said.

"Then have another gill and be off. Pet, what are you up to now?"

"Writing my Christmas cards."

"In April?"

"It is," Mrs. Loring said, "the perfect method of getting information through the lines. The Patriots are always sensitive to the fact that the mail is late, and they still believe in Santa Claus."

"Quite," Gage said. "Why didn't I think of that? Don't tell me. Both these chaps, Pomfret and Pomeroy, have been drinking but their minds still seem on the uptake."

"You had more to drink than we did," Pomfret said.

"Stop, everybody, making excuses for me," Gage said. "I used to be a two-bottle man."

"You had three, pet," Mrs. Loring said.

"Is that a fact?" Gage said to Pomfret and Pomeroy.

"That's a fact."

"And is Mrs. Gage still in quarantine?"

"That's a fact."

"Then I still appear to be in control of things. You know I think I'll allow Percy to stay in that box he got himself into."

"Do you like this Christmas card, pet?"

"Quite," Gage said. "On the other hand, I could ride to Percy's relief as a heroic deed and be mentioned in the dispatches. But that is more insult to Lord Percy's generalship than I ever intended."

"You will never be mentioned in the dispatches if *The New Boston Times* has anything to say, pet," Mrs. Loring said from her Christmas cards. "The *Times* has a good deal to say about your sex life but hardly mentions your military prowess."

"Quite."

"All of the *Times* staff have it in for you, pet," Mrs. Loring said, "from Poxe to Braxton and Lee, to Dilsie, Gretchen, and Francine."

"I did not realize," Gage said, "that the paper was that large."

"Half of them are up in a balloon."

"Good," Gage said. "Where are the other half?"

"Following the British with the other camp followers."

"How do you know all this?"

"Christmas cards," Mrs. Loring said.

A heavy hand was laid on General Gage's shoulder.

"And who be you, sir?" Gage said.

"An emissary from Mrs. Gage. If her quarantine is not lifted forthwith, she will have her captain fire a broadside at Boston."

The British at Concord were doing the King proud. They had scattered the Rebels for miles around. The odds in the gaming houses in Boston had gone from two to one the British to win to five to one the British to win. But the odds still were eight to five against any battle leading to a general war against the King. If there came a Revolution, the odds were fifteen to one for the British to win in three months. And this was all Colonial money. The British found it vulgar to bet for or against the King's men—sacrilegious.

101
THE
LONG
NAKED
DESCENT
INTO
BOSTON

102

THE
LONG
NAKED
DESCENT
INTO
BOSTON

As Poxe had mentioned in his daily editorials, the problem facing the Rebels was a language problem. The Rebels from Virginia would not be able to understand the accent of the people from New Jersey, the Pennsylvania people could not understand the New Yorkers, the New Yorkers could not make head or tail of what the Rhode Islanders were saying, or people from Maryland or Maine. The North Carolinians had no contact at all with the outside world through language, and no one on earth could understand what the New Englanders were trying to say. Surprisingly, Poxe concluded, they were all trying to speak English. But an Englishman would never have guessed it. The *Globe* blamed Harvard University. Poxe blamed the *Globe.* Jackson of the *Globe* said, quoting Francine's father, "The universities are senility in search of a sinecure." Poxe warned Francine not to feed the opposition. Poxe said finally that some way would be found for the Colonies to speak to each other. Esperanto. Then again, although the spoken word was peculiar to each Colony, the written word bore a strange resemblance. Even now in London, a Doctor Johnson was working on a universal dictionary of English words that might make it possible for the Colonies to win the war. This fact kept the odds against the Colonies from skyrocketing to a hundred to one. This fact, and the fact of Mrs. Loring and the fact of General Gage and the fact of Lord Percy and the fact of Madame de Tocqueville and the fact that the Patriots would get uniforms, kept the odds against the Colonials within reasonable limits so that a man could make a bet without feeling like an idiot—or without thinking he had a lead-pipe cinch.

Now the British at Concord were making any kind of bet silly. They not only were scattering the good ol' boys with mighty blast from cannon and musket, but also were burning everything the Colonials had stored to make war against their King. Powder and ball were dumped into the Mystic River. The saltpeter dissolved into the swamp. The rum kegs split in twain so all the streets ran white with foam. The beer barrels were bounced till they burst, causing all the rivers to rise. The casks of wine were allowed to float down the Charles River with the British hope that they could be recovered in Boston. Condoms to wear and silk stockings to give were burned alive, so that all things concerning the Colonists' ability to make war from this day forth were fast becoming nil. So be it. Victory for the King. Back to England. All aboard. Quick-step.

But one thing had been overlooked this day in Concord and in the gaming houses of Boston. The hardihood of the native American soldier. His ability to live in the brush. His stamina to stand up under no uniforms, and not only to endure but to prevail with inept slogans. Not only could he survive with no booze, food, or fornication, but he could seemingly prosper. There was something happening this day in Concord that must give the British pause. Why not call the war off now that the hardihood and rectitude of the American soldier had been discovered? He was tough as nails. Resolute as a rock. Straight as an arrow. Honest. Forthright. Determined and dedicated. And knew how to fire from behind a stone wall. God was on both sides. No help there. But Lord Percy did conceive from one quarter where help might come from—not Madame de Tocqueville or Mrs. Loring but, you guessed it, Mrs. Gage. If Mrs. Gage could fight her way into Boston, certainly the general would have an excuse to take to the country—to escape Mrs. Gage in the guise of coming to Percy's relief.

The Patriots had Concord surrounded—there was no way out. The camp followers, all of them, were caught between the fire lines. This happens all the time in war and it makes almost no one happy. Yes, it makes the whores happy—they can go both ways; and it makes the entertainers happy—the jugglers, the adagio dancers, the trained dog acts, the fire eaters, the small traveling circus. All these camp followers caught in the crossfire are not too unhappy because they can support both sides at the same time and avoid the stigma of showing favoritism to either group. But they can get plinked in the ko-ko or get a cold steel bayonet up their ass if they are not quick in the night, but jugglers are quick and so are adagio dancers and small elephants. Newspaper reporters are fortunate, too, between the lines because they can cover both sides. To both sides newspaper reporters are the enemy. Why not? The reporters are the referees. The umpires. They tell the world who won. Who lost. And who ran away. They reveal the truth that both sides won, both lost, both ran away. That is ye war for you, since the Battle of Thermopylae. When a

103
THE
LONG
NAKED
DESCENT
INTO
BOSTON

104

THE
LONG
NAKED
DESCENT
INTO
BOSTON

war starts, all are losers. Tell the dead ye won. Then run.

Lee was sketching the battle from his horse to go with Braxton's copy. Francine and Dilsie were writing notes to both sides and sticking them on thorn of huckle and blackberry bush and pinning notes to maple and larch and rose that read, GO HOME. YOU ARE LATE FOR SUPPER. WHO IS MILKING THE COW? IS YOUR DAUGHTER SAFE? GENERAL GAGE IS SAFE IN BED WITH MRS. LORING—HANCOCK AND ADAMS ARE LIVING IT UP AT THE WILLIAM PENN IN PHILLY—BETTER DISHONOR THAN DEATH— BETTER A LIFETIME ON YOUR KNEES THAN TO STAND UP AND GET YOUR ONE AND ONLY KO-KO BLOWN TO BITS—BETTER TO PROVE YOUR MANHOOD IN BED THAN TO TRY TO PROVE YOUR MANHOOD BY BLOWING OSCAR DOE TO BITS AND PIECES SO THAT HIS MOTHER CAN'T STICK HIM TOGETHER AGAIN—OR HAVE YOU TRIED THE BED BIT AND FAILED?

"That's not a note to stop the war, Dilsie," Francine said.

They both looked out at all the notes they had strewn on huckle and blackberry bush for all the soldiers to read.

"I never met a dead person that was reasonable happy," Dilsie said, "lessen it was that parson's son."

"Then there are my father's colleagues at Yale," Francine said. "They have been dead but happy with tenure lo these many years."

"You never did meet a happy dead soldier though?"

"You're fucking well told I haven't, Dilsie."

"I likes the way you put it," Dilsie said. "I will try to work that into my column."

"Do you really think, Dilsie, Poxey will give a woman, any woman, a column even in this late day and age?"

"I think so, yes," Dilsie said, touching her blunderbuss.

Lee and Braxton decided to remove themselves from all this antiwar talk. Antiwar talk was not the temper of the times. If you work for a newspaper during a war it is best to be *for* the war. It doesn't make any difference which side you are on so long as you are for the war. A newspaper cannot survive being against a war. Many have tried; all have failed. At the Harvard School of Journalism, Braxton and Lee were taught this—they were not taught much else. Harvard told them ye need to know nothing more. Harvard discovered very early in its establishment that if you cram too much into a young man's head, it will all spill out the top. So it was Latin and Greek and support the war. Particularly, and this was underlined, if it's a *Revolution*. Lee was discouraged in his artwork at Harvard. The Professor of Fine Arts on the first day of class announced that with the splendid vistas from every window, art was not necessary in America, and if anyone had any different ideas they could go back where they came from. Any small amount of art that was needed could be brought over from Europe. Art is the first step down the short road to degeneracy of the moral fiber of any given country. Art is habit-forming. Art has a bad effect upon the left lobe of the brain. Art leads to strange drugs. The artist, if not stopped right now, will soon be painting frontal views of naked people. And what kind of a country do you have then? A country of perverts. That's what the Revolution is all about. Art should only be permitted between consenting adults. In the nighttime. Behind locked doors. Art was first discovered in the Dordogne Caves of southern France and should have been left there, the Professor of Fine Arts at Harvard said. Art should be a felony and not a misdemeanor. If you learn nothing more at Harvard, my young idiots, remember this: Art has its place, but its place is not America.

"Where, then, is art's place, Your Worship?"

"Try France, Spain, Italy. Degenerate places like those."

"Thank you, Your Worship."

"Don't thank me. I get paid to do this," the professor said.

"But Your Eminence has gone far beyond the call of duty to warn us country rustics about the pitfalls of art."

"Knock it off, Lee," the Full Professor of Fine Arts at Harvard said. "Flattery will get you nothing but straight A's."

"Can we doodle in class, sir?"

"You can do anything you damn please in class," the professor said, "so long as you don't bother me. You can jerk off if you want."

"Can we jerk off in Harvard Yard, sir?"

"The correct pronunciation, young man, is Hahvid Yahd. No, you can't jerk off in Hahvid Yahd—it frightens the horses." The professor pronounced horses "hahses." "We will need all the

105
THE
LONG
NAKED
DESCENT
INTO
BOSTON

106

THE
LONG
NAKED
DESCENT
INTO
BOSTON

hahses we can lay our hands on for the Revolution. But find some quiet place to jerk off after you have nailed down your Latin and Greek. There is nothing else to do at Hahvid. At least it was true"—the professor rubbed his rum red nose in recollection— "at least it was true when I graduated from this dump in sixty-five."

"Then Your Highness does not think much of his alma mater."

"That's the problem, Lee. I think too damn much about Hahvid. I'd think a hell of a lot better of it if they got some women around here. How would you feel staring into all those male faces right after breakfast? Before you've had a stiff drink."

"I hear, sir, Harvard is considering allowing some token women to attend."

"Never!" the professor said. "And if they did, women would never fall for it. Women can see right through Hahvid all the way from the coast of Maine. Women would never waste their time in this dump. Women could teach Hahvid a thing or two, but not the other way round."

"They could force women into Harvard or they could make women think they're missing something."

"But what if they won't come?"

"They'll come or we'll beat the bejesus out of them," the professor said. "Put them all in stocks. Now what did we learn in class today?"

"Never argue against a war. That kind of action can be remiss and get you in deep trouble. To quote you directly, sir, fly with the flock. Even if you lose, you will have the joy of flying."

"Particularly in a Revolution."

"Yes, sir."

"You will go far, Lee. I hear there's an opening on the *Times*. Take it. These are hard times, Lee, particularly for a Hahvid graduate. Boston is wise to Hahvid. Tell Poxey hello for me. Tell him I still think he's a son-of-a-bitch."

"Yes, sir."

"Braxton."

"Yes, sir?"

"You, too. Now the rest of you galoots get out of here," Professor Tydings, the Full Professor of Fine Arts at Harvard, said, "and give me some peace before the fighting starts. This class is dismissed—have a good Revolution."

"Do you know what, Lee?" Braxton said.

"No I don't know what," Lee said between dodging cannon-balls.

"On that last incoming cannonball I thought I was dead and my whole life passed in front of me—everything except my stay at Harvard."

"Hahvid."

"Yes."

"Someone is trying to tell you something, Braxton."

"Yes. It may be that it's because I just saw Professor Tydings out there on the battlefield."

"On whose side?"

"He can't seem to make up his mind. He seems to be shooting at random."

"I am not going to say Random is a nice guy and deserves better treatment. I will say that Professor Tydings will in time find the right side and I wish him well. At this point he is still sticking to his ideals, that it's not the side that's important, it's the Revolution that's important. Can you get a story out of this Concord brouhaha, Braxton?"

"I can get a story if you can get a picture."

"What do you think of this picture?" Lee said, handing it over.

Braxton held the picture up to the bullets. "I can't make head or tail of this, Lee. Which side is up?"

"This side is up," Lee said, reversing the picture.

"Then that paints a different picture," Braxton said. "Who are the lads over here by the bridge with the bayonets sticking out of them?"

"That's us."

"Who is us?"

"The Patriots."

"I didn't know Poxey had taken sides."

"He has."

"I didn't know he was a new man."

"He is."

107

THE
LONG
NAKED
DESCENT
INTO
BOSTON

108

THE
LONG
NAKED
DESCENT
INTO
BOSTON

"Who are these women and children in front of the tavern being bashed on the head by the British?"

"That's still us."

"I didn't see any of that."

"You don't have the artistry I have, Braxton."

"And what's all this over here?"

"That's the British running pell-mell."

"And what's all this red over here?"

"That's the setting sun."

"You're very good at sunscapes, Lee."

"Thank you."

"Did you ever give a thought to sticking to straight land-scapes?"

"That's what Poxey keeps saying."

"I hear he's going to make Gretchen Miss Lexington and Concord."

"Yes."

"Lee, what the Revolution needs is someone sensible involved in it. I cannot believe that war is like this."

"Things your mother never told you."

"I'm sure things will straighten out in time. We've got to give both sides a chance. The war only started today. The Patriots are green at it and the British are in a strange country. That accounts for a lot. I'm sure in time it will settle down to a real war."

"What's a real war?"

"What we read about."

"Braxton, you've been had."

"You mean this is it?"

"I'm afraid so, Braxton."

"But people don't behave like this in civilian life."

"They do, Braxton, they do. It's just that they go unobserved; they live behind closed doors. War gets them out in the open. Where they can shoot and be shot."

"Will you two girls come up here," Braxton said.

"We not girls," Dilsie said. "We women."

"Come up here anyway," Lee said. "The war has taken a turn for the worse. There is not a British soldier that will get back to Boston alive."

fifteen

The two slaves Pomfret and Pomeroy had already left the headquarters of General Gage and Mrs. Loring with the plan that could save Lord Percy, Madame de Tocqueville, and all the King's men from the Patriot trap closing in around them at Concord. Pomfret and Pomeroy first stopped their horses at the Queen Apothecary's on State Street to pick up a newspaper to find out which roads to Concord were held by the Rebel troops. The pharmacist, a Doctor Glanders, a jolly-well-met Tory of fun and games and high-priced drugs, was today somber and saddened. His usual banter and jest about the pathetic Rebels was not forthcoming as he said, "My dear Pomfret and my dear Pomeroy, all goes worse than I have power to tell."

"Try," Pomfret said.

"The King's men are surrounded by the Rebels at Concord."

"These things happen," Pomeroy said.

"But today was supposed to be a gay day—the start of the war—and now this," Doctor Glanders said, packing away his higher-priced herbs to hide his tears.

"I understand," Pomeroy said, "that the 'h' in herbs is silent. It is true in Newark."

"It's true in Boston, too," Doctor Glanders said, "but the war will ruin everything. People will come trooping into Boston

110

THE
LONG
NAKED
DESCENT
INTO
BOSTON
higgledy-piggledy, destroying everything, including the King's English. I warned Gage and Mrs. Loring against an expedition to Concord at this time of year, but they listened not."

"We can promise you that all is not lost, sir."

"Do you two gentlemen have intelligence that I do not?" Doctor Glanders said, adjusting his spectacles so as not to miss anything, and mentally raising the price of his Sedlitz powders. "What be your intelligence, sirs?"

"We ride to Concord with a plan to extricate Lord Percy. He will feint toward Roxbury, then swing to Medford, leaving the Rebel army on Harvard Road while the King's men escape across the Charlestown Neck and into Boston."

Doctor Glanders dropped a box of condoms in his joy. "My God," the doctor said, jumping up and down, "Gage and Mrs. Loring have life in them yet. This is the best news I've heard since the Coronation. Be off with you, messieurs, and take this box of condoms as a token of my esteem, and take these peppermint sticks and these licorice whips and these orange-flavored cough drops, and this throat syrup is pure opium. Take that, and this rubbing alcohol is good for your horses and this cocaine is good for your spleen. Sniff it," he said. He held the vial up to Pomfret's nose. "Sniff," he said.

"That's real good," Pomfret said.

"There's more where that came from," the good doctor said, ushering them through the door.

When Pomfret and Pomeroy got on their horses, they had not yet got rid of Doctor Glanders. Doctor Glanders was determined to fill their saddlebags full of all sorts of medicaments for the embattled King's men. There were packets of fruit, bouquets of flowers, apothecary jars filled with chocolates and boiled sweets, brandies, corn plasters for the feet and hot mustard plasters for the chest, Glanders' Little Liver Pills for the liver and Glanders' Large Kidney Pills for the kidneys. For those shot in the head there were head patches; for those shot in the heart there was heart balm; for those in the rear, ass patches. There were winding sheets to bury the dead and crutches to help the lame and stretchers to carry the wounded, medals and laurels for the heroes and get-well cards for the dying and consolation cards for the dead.

"Have I forgotten something?" Doctor Glanders said.

"You have forgotten us," Pomfret said.

Doctor Glanders kissed them both and wished them a safe journey, helped them tie the crutches and the stretchers to the saddle thongs, and pointed to the road to Concord before retiring to his apothecary shoppe to raise the price of everything for the Revolution.

Pomfret and Pomeroy galloped off and got as far as the Rose and Crown before they decided they needed something for the road. *The New Boston Times* and Little Brown Adult Book Shoppe and Publishing were shuttered because most had left for the Battle of Lexington. Little Brown was helping out, tending bar at the Rose and Crown. He had put thick boards in back of the bar to stand on the boards so he could see over the top of the bar.

"What will you have, gentlemen?"

Pomeroy and Pomfret decided on Rum Flips. "If they won't take too long," Pomeroy said.

"Lexington or Concord?"

"Concord."

"I have nothing against the English," Brown said to the two blacks. "Some of my best friends are British."

"We be in a hurry," Pomeroy said.

"I don't know how to make a Rum Flip," Brown said. "Anyway, during the battle we're not serving any mixed drinks."

"What about a gin and peppermint?" Pomeroy said.

"If there's anything that gives a man's balls a lift, it's rum and maple syrup."

"All right."

"You know," Little Brown said, mixing the drinks and then shaking them in a silver Revere shaker, "this drink is called a Colonial Big Sweet Mama Shake-up. Now see how you gentlemen like that," he said, pouring them the drinks and watching them throw their heads back and pour them down the hatch. Pomfret and Pomeroy were dressed in bright silver buckles on red boots; gold, silver, and blue livery costumes with white wigs. When they poured their Colonial Big Sweet Mama Shake-ups down the gullet with thrown-back heads, they had to hold onto their white wigs, which were only secured with stick-em from Glanders.

111
THE
LONG
NAKED
DESCENT
INTO
BOSTON

112

THE
LONG
NAKED
DESCENT
INTO
BOSTON

"Did that hit the spot?" Brown said.

"Let's have another Colonial Big Sweet Mama Shake-up," Pomfret said.

"Who's winning the Revolution?" Brown said.

"Big Sweet Mama Shake-up," Pomeroy said.

"You know, I have nothing against war," Brown said while mixing the drinks. "Some of my best friends are soldiers. But they picked a helluva time to start this one. I see a continuous war in this country. After the British we will fight among ourselves, a civil war, then we will fight the Indians, then when we are bored we will go to a foreign country to fight. That's because this country starting today will be founded on war."

"You sound like a bartender," Pomfret said.

"I'm learning," Brown said. "Another consequence of war is that Americans, like dark cave salamanders, will lose their eyes because there is no need for sight in a country of perpetual darkness."

"I'll write that down. You are learning how to tend bar fast," Pomeroy said.

"I try," Brown said. "Have you heard that between battles during the Revolution, Poxe plans to sell rides in his balloon?"

"No, we hadn't heard," Pomeroy said.

"He's even dwelling on the idea of trips over the battlefield."

"No, we hadn't heard that," Pomeroy said.

"I don't know where we've been all this time," Pomfret said.

"You've been working with General Gage, I understand from reading the *Times*."

"Yes, we have just concocted a plan to get the British out of a trap."

"That should keep the war going for a while," Brown said, pouring the drinks. "What plans do you gentlemen have for yourselves after the Revolution?"

"If the British win, we will be freed. If the Americans win, we will probably remain slaves till the cows come home."

"It's tough all over," Brown said, pouring himself a drink from the pitcher of Big Sweet Mama Shake-ups and touching glasses with Pomeroy and Pomfret. "Cheers," he said.

Brown left to wait on some dull Tories, but came back in a trice.

"I have an idea," he said, "that after the war, air travel will be the big thing—a man could do worse than buy stock in a good solid balloon company. Let's say a man or a woman wants to go from Boston to New York. I don't know why, but let's say they do. In a balloon they could be there in a trice."

"Right now we best get to the Revolution," Pomeroy said.

"Finish up first," Brown said. "While I'm on the subject, with the high price of fuel in Boston today, a man could make a fortune in a horseshit fuel factory. Horseshit is scattered all over Boston, free for the taking. Do you know what the fuel trusts are selling wood for today?"

"No."

"Two pounds a cord. They claim the Indians are charging them three pounds a barrel. The Indians have a stranglehold on our economy."

"No."

"Yes, but a man with imagination who gets in on the ground floor of horseshit could make a fortune during this fuel shortage. There's a good future in horseshit."

"You said before," Pomeroy said, "that air travel, balloons, were the future. That would eliminate the horses that make the horseshit. In order for there to be any future in horseshit you must, as I see it, have horses. If everybody is traveling by air, there will be no horses to make horseshit. No one, not even John Hancock, could afford to keep horses for the sale of shit alone."

"There will always be short distances between balloon pads," the bartender Brown said, "that must be traversed by horse. But if a man wanted to be safe he could put half his money in balloons and the other half in horseshit. That way he could not lose whichever way the ball bounced. It seems to me he'd still have the world by the balls. Will you gentlemen have another round of Colonial Big Sweet Mama Shake-ups or are you three sheets to the wind already?"

"It's always good to have another sheet to the wind," Pomfret said, "and ask those Tories if they will join us."

"Delighted," the big Tory on the end with a small blue nose and wide purple velvet lapels said. "We could not help overhearing your conversation. Wilberforce here is already in balloons and I'm in horseshit. And what may you be in, sir?"

113
THE
LONG
NAKED
DESCENT
INTO
BOSTON

114

THE
LONG
NAKED
DESCENT
INTO
BOSTON

"Books," Brown said.

"That is a pity. And you two gentlemen?"

"Slaves."

"People do pick the strangest occupations," the Tory said, "but it all goes to show it's still a free country. We are having a party at my place this evening. Are you gentlemen engaged? Do you have any plans for the evening or are you loaded up?"

"We are booked to go to Concord," Pomfret said.

"On the Concord Stage?"

"On Gage's horses."

"Nothing serious, I hope."

"We carry a plan to allow what's left of the King's men to escape."

All the Tories clapped each other on the back and said it was capital and that they were from the Harvard School of Business and that Pomfret and Pomeroy must drop by on their way back and have a nightcap. With that, the Tories staggered out and Pomeroy and Pomfret adjusted their wigs as it was getting late and they must be off, too.

"By the bye," Pomfret said to Little Brown, "here is a box of condoms for you. Doctor Glanders gave us extras for the King's men."

"Thank you very much," Brown said. "I do appreciate that. I haven't used one of these for a dog's age. That accounts for my large family, I suppose. What are they made of, do you reckon?"

"Half are India rubber and half are sheep's intestines," Pomfret said. "So please yourself."

"That is intriguing," Brown said. "Sheep's intestines? What will they think of next? Do you suppose sheep are the coming thing? Maybe we should buy some stock in sheep? That was supposed to be a joke."

"Yes," Pomfret said.

"Are you sure you don't want one more Big Sweet Mama Shake-up for the road?"

"No, the road has had plenty," Pomeroy said, and they quit the Rose and Crown, fell on their horses, and were off to Concord to save the day.

"Or night," Pomfret thought out loud. "These Colonial Big Sweet Mama Shake-ups sure do get to you. Do you remember what Little Brown said—that in a world at perpetual war we will in time lose our eyes because there's no need for sight in the darkness of evil?"

"Yes."

"Is that a metaphor?"

"No, it is the truth, Pomeroy," Pomfret said.

"And will Dilsie get her column like she says?"

"That is a metaphor."

"And when we are freed if the British win, will we become wage slaves like the poor whites?"

"That is the truth."

"Then why are we helping the British?"

"Because the British are in dire straits and Mrs. Loring asked us to."

"I would rather be in Dire Straits than in Concord or working for wages," Pomeroy said. "But Mrs. Loring gets what Mrs. Loring wants—that is all that is certain in war."

Their two horses trotted through the streets of Boston. Boston was full of shit. That is, the streets of White Bread Alley, Milk, King, Pie Alley, Moon, Cow Lane, Water, Bath, were thick with the droppings of pig, chicken, cow, and the common people. Pomfret and Pomeroy did not think themselves above the common people, but it was impossible not to feel themselves above the lower classes—Pomfret and Pomeroy lived in a mansion fit for a queen, dressed in costumes befitting a prince, rode the finest horses, ate the best food, drank French wines, used Italian perfume, read the latest books, and were in the position now, along with Mrs. Loring, to defeat the Revolution. There was one hitch. Madame de Tocqueville had ideas of her own on how the Rebels should be punished.

In the outskirts of Boston the common people touched their hats to Pomfret and Pomeroy. They were probably all Tories—the Patriots were all out whaling away at the British between Concord and Lexington. It is a common supposition that the Rebels had a monopoly on poverty and that all the Tories in the American Colonies were rich—this is a historical blunder, as for Pomfret and Pomeroy it was plain to see. Some of the Tories were young whippersnappers with holes in their jerkins and ass patches on their pantaloons. The middle-aged Tories sometimes

115
THE
LONG
NAKED
DESCENT
INTO
BOSTON

116
THE
LONG
NAKED
DESCENT
INTO
BOSTON

had a missing shoe, and many older Tories a case of clap they could not afford to have fixed. So much for the idea that common people are not common regardless of race, creed, or politics.

Pomeroy leaned down now from his brightly caparisoned horse to question an elderly Tory who was both clapped and ear-trumpeted. Pomeroy wanted to know if the gates of Boston at the Boston Neck were closed.

The elderly Tory had a multiplex Franklin trumpet, that is, one you could hear through or see through or use as a megaphone, depending on which way you pointed it or which of the human orifices you stuck it into. You could even stick it up your ass and make thunderous fart explosions to scare the enemy or announce your arrival to friends.

"I don't know," the Tory said, using the multiplex Franklin ear trumpet as a megaphone. "Since the clap quarantine the British have the North Gates closed tighter than a drum."

Another Tory citizen came up, holding a fishing pole, and wanted to know what the hell was going on. He said the shooting had scared the fish and he also wanted to know, examining a new lure, who was going to clean up all the shit in Boston. "It's getting so," he said, "that a fellow can't stop to think any more without sinking up to his knees. It's women's responsibility to organize and clean up the town while the boys are at war, don't you think? I am an out-and-out Tory because without law and order Boston will become so full of shit it will float away. Then, if you can't trust the government, who can you trust?"

At the North Gate, the King's guard told Pomfret and Pomeroy that the clap quarantine had been lifted since a royal committee had discovered there was more clap in Boston than Connecticut. "Which is a fine kettle of fish, Pomeroy—don't you think? But a new quarantine has been enforced against Rebels sortying into the country and spreading rumors about the good General Gage's sex life and Lord Percy's friend Madame de Tocqueville, all to make us British a bunch of degenerates with too much lead in our peckers to fight. It is an unsportsmanlike, rude, unseemly way to spread calumny and start a Revolution by making our wise and compassionate King a ninny and knucklehead whilst you and I know better, don't we?"

Pomfret and Pomeroy showed the King's guard their papers.

The King's men touched the crutches and stretchers and felt of the bulging sleek saddlebags in the manner they would feel a woman's thigh and pinched them as they would a woman's ass and said, "What have we got here?"

"Medicaments and sundry items to succor the King's troops," Pomeroy said, "through the generosity of Doctor Glanders."

The Captain of the King's Guard was examining the papers and plans for Lord Percy's retreat.

"This looks like Mrs. Loring's handwriting," the King's captain said.

"It is her writing, but it was General Gage's idea," Pomeroy said.

"I'll believe it when I see it," the King's captain said. "You would be wise," the captain said, "to hand these plans to Madame de Tocqueville first. That way she will think it her plan and not try to talk Lord Percy into coming back the same way the King's men went out. The way they went out is full of misguided rustics shooting at anything that moves. By the bye," the King's captain said, "why are you two on our side?" He tapped the war plan against the Belgian lace on his wrist, waiting for an answer. Like any good soldier he was suspicious of anything with two legs that moved. "Is it, sirs, the pay? The uniform? Expanding consciousness? The weather? The exercising of freedom of choice? Or just for the hell of it? I'll join the first side that comes along? Perhaps the feeling that we should give the King another chance? Or like so many chaps, the idea of not jumping from the frying pan into the fire? Or did you wake this morning born again?"

"No," Pomeroy said, "we just wanted to help out Mrs. Loring."

"Good," the captain said. "You may pass. If you had bought any of my idiot excuses for joining the King's men, I would have clapped you in durance vile. The idea of being born again I find preposterous, don't you? I don't believe in reincarnation, do you?"

"No."

"Then pass, gentlemen, please pass."

At the Charles River, Pomfret and Pomeroy met another fisherman, not a fisher after men but a fisher after fish with artificial flies, and he complained that the shooting was keeping

117
THE
LONG
NAKED
DESCENT
INTO
BOSTON

118

THE
LONG
NAKED
DESCENT
INTO
BOSTON

the sturgeon from rising to the Royal Coachman or any fly he tried. There would be no caviar on the table tonight. He also volunteered that if the people in Massachusetts kept allowing their shit to flow into the Charles, there would soon be no run of sturgeon at all and the people of New England would have to learn to get by with shit or starve irregardless of who won the war.

"Regardless is correct," Pomfret said. "Irregardless is just another word that murders the King's English."

"I don't want to change the subject," the fly fisherman said, "but did you see the extraterrestrial object in the sky over Boston?"

"No."

"I believe it is an extraterrestrial object," the fly fisherman said. "A vehicle from outer space. Do you believe we could be visited by creatures from outer space—that it's mere vanity, earthophilia, to believe we are the only intelligent life in the universe?"

"No."

"Why?"

"Because you saw Poxe's balloon and he's no more intelligent life than the rest of us."

"Do you believe we can get closer to God by going up in a balloon?"

"We don't know," Pomeroy said. "Anything is a fair supposition. At this point all we can say is we don't know. I understand Poxe is doing a paper on it. But the literature now is meager. All we can do is see how Poxe's paper turns out. It may be we will have to go in the opposite direction to find God. Poxe may be off on a wild goose chase."

"But Poxe is not just theorizing, he's actually going up in a balloon to have a good look-see and draw his conclusions from facts. I suppose the problem is we don't know exactly what God looks like and neither does Poxe, despite all his blowing off."

"That's true, but Poxe will find out."

"No crap? Did it ever occur to you what life will be like in the Colonies without caviar when there are no more sturgeon running in the Charles?"

sixteen

From Boston to Concord by way of Roxbury it was twenty-two miles. From Boston to Lexington by way of Harvard College it was sixteen miles and it still is. Pomfret and Pomeroy were farting explosively from their Colonial Sweet Mama Shake-ups, so much so that the rustics along the route must have thought the horses were fired and propelled by giant farts that scurried them on to Lexington.

At the Yerkes Observatory outside of Harvard College, an elderly gentleman astronomer by the name of Yerkes with a decided academic limp had already set up his telescope under a red blooming plum tree and was focusing in on the girls of Cambridge. When he heard Pomfret and Pomeroy coming, he switched the scope to Jupiter and Mars. His students had all fled to the war at the first excuse. Yerkes was a lonely astronomer when he waved down Pomfret and Pomeroy from his astronomical site under the red blooming plum tree. The Revolution began April the 19th, 1775, a perfect time and a good year for the wild plum. It was also the time when Mars would make its closest approach to earth till the twentieth century, and that is why Doctor Yerkes was out bright and early under the plum tree on

120

THE
LONG
NAKED
DESCENT
INTO
BOSTON

the road to Lexington and why he was not for long put off by the girls of Cambridge.

"According to *The New Boston Times* and Benjamin Franklin, haste makes waste, gentlemen," Yerkes said as the boys of war rode up. "Stop and talk."

"We can't dilly-dally now," Pomfret said.

"Mars will never come this close again in our time," Yerkes said. "You know there is a misconception abroad about Mars that pseudoscientists encourage, that Mars is peopled by little green men who live on canals. We know now that these Martian people are big and that in all probability they are a mixture of all colors, and if you mix all colors you get a mess, so in all probability Mars is peopled by a big mess."

"We can't dilly-dally now," Pomeroy said.

"Did you see the balloon?" Yerkes said. "In a few years, when we get a bigger hot-air balloon and a bigger fire under it, we will be able to fly to Mars and I promise you we will not bring back little green men, we will bring back big men, or I am not the head of the Harvard Astronomical Observatory. People think we spend all of our time at the giant nine-foot telescope looking for girls in Greenwich. We do not, sir. We do not. As a matter of curiosity, sir, what is all that in your saddlebags?"

"Medicaments for the beleaguered British," Pomfret said. "As a matter of concern, can you look through that telescope and tell me where Lord Percy and the King's men are now?"

"No, because the earth is round and Lord Percy has long since disappeared over the curvature. The taxpayers believe, due to a bad Press, that we at Harvard College do not know our ass from a hole in the ground. This has proved not to be the case. We at Harvard know the earth to be—and hold on to your hats, gentlemen—the earth to be square. The earth appears to be ovaloid, and for the nonce it may be, but the world has been knocked about and Professor Velekicher assures me that in a few millennia it will return to its normal shape and the universe will fit together again. Round objects do not fit together, so the earth cannot be round for long. Can you imagine a universe that does not fit together? Now be off to your stupid Revolution, knock the earth about some more, and Professor Velekicher and myself will put it together again. Don't dilly-dally here. I have work to do.

Mars will never pass this close to earth again in your lifetime or your daughter's lifetime. Would either of you two black gentlemen want your daughter to marry a Harvard professor? With tenure? With an income of ten thousand pounds a year? With an estate in Martha's Vineyard? Get the hell out of here if you can't make up your own mind. I can't make it up for you. You are both like my goddamn students, and as far as I am concerned, you can all take a flying fuck for yourselves. What we need at Harvard is more money for pure research. Otherwise there is, gentlemen—and I am not being an alarmist—there is the strong possibility," he said, staring at Mars, "that we will never get the goddamn universe to fit together again, and don't you say that that is no skin off my ass, because you get what you see through my telescope and right now the picture is trouble." Then Yerkes said, smiling at Mars, "Tell Lord Percy for me Jupiter is in its zenith and Pluto is ascending. If he is a Leo or Aquarius, he cannot lose." Professor Yerkes placed his hand over the eyepiece and hung his head in thought. "Lord Percy will carry the day," he said.

Pomfret and Pomeroy farted off in the direction of Medford.

"With Harvard's reputation," Pomfret said, "I cannot believe we are meeting the cream of the crop."

"Any school," Pomeroy said, "needs time to work out the kinks."

"How long do you give Harvard?"

"A thousand years, give or take a hundred," Pomeroy said.

At Alewife Brook, before Medford, the Concord road took a dangerous sharp left, as it still does, and the horses bumped each other, smashing some medicaments, but there were still plenty more on the outside of each horse. The apothecary Doctor Glanders, being a man of care and knowledge of this sharp left turn before Medford and knowing Gage's horses to be rambunctious, had packed duplicate drugs on the nigh side of each beast—that's what he had called them, devil-may-care beasts. And Pomfret recalled now Doctor Glanders giving the horses a kick as Pomfret and Pomeroy cantered off to the Rose and Crown.

As they crossed the Mystic River—by the lower bridge to avoid Medford and save two miles—Pomfret and Pomeroy kept

121

THE
LONG
NAKED
DESCENT
INTO
BOSTON

122

THE
LONG
NAKED
DESCENT
INTO
BOSTON

meeting troops of Minutemen hours late. The Minutemen appeared dedicated. Some swore strange oaths. Some wore their pantaloons backwards to show their defiance of the King's men. Or perhaps, Pomfret thought, to confuse the Royal Grenadiers into wondering whether the Minutemen were advancing or retreating or whether their movement was sideways or backwards, grade or retrograde, or simply lost. The Minutemen were puzzled by the appearance of Pomfret and Pomeroy. Some doffed their tricorn hats. Some loaded their muskets and blazed away at them, but it took a Minuteman fifteen minutes to load the damn thing at this stage of the Revolution. Later, things would pick up; now there were too many flashes in the pan, to their captain's horror and to the Minutemen's humiliation after spending fifteen minutes loading the damn things. By that time Pomfret and Pomeroy were many leagues toward Concord and could see the distant pan flash followed by strange oaths that might possibly be heard as far distant as Saratoga. But there were always fresh crowds of Minutemen for Pomfret and Pomeroy to surprise with their gay and gaudy accouterments and the aplomb and panache with which they sat their mounts. The scene between Concord and Boston this day of April 19, 1775, was a dish to set before the King. Chaos, confusion, and consternation; farmers and farm hands piled into each other as they dashed in and out of the same barn. They handed each other pitchforks in exchange for information as to the whereabouts of the war. Lanterns were being hung in broad daylight to attract attention to the wrong road. One rustic crashed into Pomfret's horse, grabbed the stirrup, and said, "My God, sir, if you know where be the Revolution, lead me to it."

"Follow us," Pomfret said.

Soon they had a good following. At Menotomy it had been a platoon. At the second crossing of the Mystic River—the river looped before Lexington—they were leading a company, then a battalion, regiment, division, corps, and finally a small army straight into the jaws of Lord Percy. War is strange. If you have never been to a war, you have not only missed the wound that will not bind but the insanity of command, the waiting, the hunger, the boredom, the wrong route taken, the wrong commander followed, the wrong cause fought for, the end of truth, the beginning of ignorance, the only weapon humor, the only victor the woman who called herself courage, hope, patriotism, flag, honor, country, the mistress of Lord Percy, that lady in waiting to every soldier, that keen-eyed bitch, the only loyal camp follower and comforter to the dying—death.

"Wow!" Dilsie said.
"Yes," Braxton said. "Wait and see what Lord Percy will do now that his left flank is piteously exposed. He has tried to anchor it in that motte of woods in back of Harrod's house, but he cannot hold it with only a line of skirmishers. Percy has strengthened his center at the expense of holding only one company in reserve. His left flank has all the power; it's as though he wants to tempt the Patriots to hit him in the center, then fall back to Keely's Brook and envelop the attackers with his left flank. He will have the advantage of attacking in smooth terrain and it's downhill most of the distance. Percy's hope is that the Patriots will not be able to detect—because of Harrod's Wood—that his right flank has been robbed to strengthen his enveloping movement. Percy's bet is that no competent commander will attack into a blind spot that may be secretly strong. Notice that Percy has moved all of his flags and regimental banners into his center to bait the trap. He has built no fascine or ambuscade there, and the terrain— except for a slight rise—seems perfect for the enemy to drive through and get into Percy's secondary, which seems nonexist- ent, as though Percy had put all of his men into the front line, which to the untrained eye appears too extended and thin with no flankers. The Patriots cannot see Keely's Brook, which is Percy's fall-back position. Percy can hold at the brook, even spare some men to further strengthen his powerful left to fall upon the Patriots when they are committed to blitzing his center and are bogged down at Keely's Brook. Notice how quiet Percy keeps his strength on his strong left flank. There's no sign of movement there at all. Notice how noisy he makes his weakness in Harrod's Wood. Goddamn it, I didn't realize Percy had it in him. The son-of-a-bitch is a genius."
Madame de Tocqueville crossed Kelly's Brook on horse,

123
THE
LONG
NAKED
DESCENT
INTO
BOSTON

124

THE
LONG
NAKED
DESCENT
INTO
BOSTON

splashing the King's company held in reserve, and entered Harrod's Wood on the oblique, hollering as loud as she could muster her voice, "Give me a 'K,' give me an 'I,' give me an 'N,' give me a 'G.' " The troops gave her nothing. Madame de Tocqueville asked a particularly quiet soldier, "Who's in charge?"

"I be," Colonel Coudray said, riding up.

"Then shake your ass," Madame de Tocqueville said. "The idea is to suggest we are a thousand strong in this copse. If we can carry the day, future generations will stand on tiptoe to hear how we answered rebellion here in Concord. We must make our weak position here so loud they will not touch us here with a ten-foot pitchfork. Make the men cheer."

"Men!" Colonel Coudray hollered, standing upright in his stirrups. "Men, Lord Percy is dead!" he lied.

A cheer broke out in the ranks. Then much and many noises of troops packing their bags and bayonets for the long voyage home.

"Men!" Colonel Coudray hollered, still up in his stirrups, "the road back to Boston will be thick with Minutemen behind every fence if we don't polish them off here. Your loved ones in Boston will be raped. The money you saved for a rainy day will be stolen. Your King will be embarrassed, your honor questioned, your integrity doubted, your veteran's pensions held up in Parliament, and to cap it all off, what about history? Those of you who have been saving clippings will slink toward England knowing every woman knows. And what will Mommy think? Some of you will slink in through the back pantry, others will hop over the front hedge to brazen it out, but women are wise to those gambits. I got a letter from my sister only the other day in which she said—"

"Just tell them to make noise," Madame de Tocqueville said.

"If you make enough noise," Colonel Coudray hollered—in talking of his sister, whom he loved dearly, his voice had trailed off into an almost-whisper—"if you make enough noise, men, the enemy will shake in their boots and attack elsewhere."

Now they all made loud noises and the enemy, the Rebels, did indeed shake somewhat in their boots and looked to Pomfret and Pomeroy for leadership in this troubled time.

"We are not your leaders," Pomeroy told the Rebels. "It just so happened that we were coming down the pike the same time you were."

"But my Minutemen seem to have taken a shine to you both," Colonel Conant said, coming up on horse. "You have the only uniforms in the bunch, but it's not only that, it's your whole attitude of presence and command, your panache. I'll be honest with you. We Patriots are not a team now. Maybe later, but now we're just a bunch of pickup farmers with no practice sessions behind us at all. You will do as well as anyone to command, and with your uniforms, better than most. If we carry the day I promise I'll make it up to you. As I said, the Minutemen have taken a shine to you both and that's a very good start. I've studied war in Knox's bookstore and watched the British drill and picked up a few pointers. Now the way I see the tactical situation is this—Percy's plan of battle is clear. He has fake-staged a weakness in his center, hoping to draw us inward to Keely's Brook and get us bogged down there. He has moved his best troops to his left flank, where he's keeping them damn quiet for the attack on our rear. His weakness is that his right flank is very poorly anchored in Harrod's Wood. That's why he is making so much noise there to scare us off. My suggestion is to hit him with everything we've got at Harrod's Wood and try and keep our men moving until we roll up his center and pin them back against Keely's Brook, where we can cut them to pieces. We should keep two companies in reserve on the Medford Road to cut off their retreat. His strong left flank will be out of position and the best they can do will be to try and hightail it to Boston. That's where I come in. I've already ordered the farmers all the way to Cambridge to whale away at what's left of Percy's men from behind every fence. That is, to shoot at every target of opportunity. That will about do it—what do you two think?"

"We think you don't need us," Pomfret said.

"But honestly we do need you. Until we get better organized. You see, you can know all about war, but unless you have the symbols of war—uniforms, command, presence, panache, a white horse—it's difficult to make much headway."

"You learned that at Knox's bookstore?" Pomfret said.

125

THE
LONG
NAKED
DESCENT
INTO
BOSTON

126

THE
LONG
NAKED
DESCENT
INTO
BOSTON

"Yes."

"Did you have to buy the book or could you read enough of it standing up to get the drift?"

"Generally I could read enough standing up to get the drift."

"Since Knox sold out to Little Brown, reading standing up is not permitted."

"For a small man, Little Brown is tough," Colonel Conant said. "Fortunately, when the war started, I had read everything of import. I had gone about as far as you can go standing up."

"Pomeroy and myself," Pomfret said, "read all of Gage's library—'how to' books on war—and it is surprising how little Little Brown has about war at this time. We read as deeply as we could on the art in case there was a slave uprising."

"So you could lead the slaves?"

"So we could put the slave uprising down. We see wage slavery around the corner. A man can't make it out there at today's prices. Pomeroy and I feed poor whites every day at Gage's back door. They have the freedom to starve—to try to make a living on an unliving wage."

"Things are bound to pick up after the Revolution," Colonel Conant said. "Doesn't it make you feel strange being part of the Revolution? You, we, are actually here at Concord and Lexington. What we do here today will astonish generations till the end of man. Concord! Lexington! Lexington! Concord!" Colonel Conant said.

"Are you feeling all right, Colonel?" Pomfret said.

"Yes. Just normal stage fright," Colonel Conant said. "A good sign."

"Does everyone talk bullshit like this before a battle?"

"Yes. Just a normal fear of failure. A good sign. All of Shakespeare's people did it."

"What about Alexander the Great and Caesar's people?"

"Not so much," Colonel Conant said.

"If we do not get this battle on the road," Pomfret said, "there will be no Revolution."

"I've thought of that," Colonel Conant said. "What do you think of my plan of battle?"

"It's as good as any," Pomfret said.

"Except the part about our leading it," Pomeroy said. "We

shouldn't do anything hasty. We should maybe just talk it out. I know Lord Percy to be a reasonable person. I'm sure he is as confused about the Revolution as we are. He wants to do the right thing."

"Oh, shit," Colonel Conant said, waving his sword and turning away from Pomfret and Pomeroy and toward his Minute people. "Men, I want every man to realize what we do here today will affect the outcome of the Revolution. If we can get off to a good start, we can get the necessary momentum to carry us through to the big day. I am sensitive to the fact that you have no uniforms, but you will get uniforms, I promise you that. I am also sensitive to the fact that because of Knox's blundering you have no artillery, but I can promise you you will get artillery, and so it goes for all of the paraphernalia of war right down to the medicaments, which even now as I talk, Pomfret and Pomeroy have brought us a whole trunkful of, enough to sink a ship, and you will find this happening throughout the war. Noble thoughts attract noble deeds. But enough of this. Get your fat farmers' asses moving and strike a blow for liberty, for God and King and country. Oh, shit. Strike 'King.' Just get your fat farmers' asses moving and keep them moving. God bless.

"How was that?" Colonel Conant said to Pomfret and Pomeroy.

"Very good," Pomfret said.

"Particularly for a person doing it for the first time," Pomeroy said. "With no experience outside of a bookstore."

"Everyone has to start sometime," Colonel Conant said.

"True," Pomeroy and Pomfret agreed.

The line of Rebels advanced to the attack in back of the illustrious Pomeroy and the gorgeous Pomfret to the thunder and cry by the spectator cheering of ten hundred of the lower classes brought from Old Southie in Boston and as far as Bangor by chartered stage, two shillings sixpence the head, with a box lunch thrown in consisting of one apple, one ham hock, one-half quince in season, two Chinese fortune cookies, and a booklet of Franklin's sayings or Arnold on ethics or Tom Paine's slogans or in some boxes *The Successful Spy: The Art of Concealment* by Nathan Hale, soon to be published by Little Brown, Ltd. or Little

127

THE
LONG
NAKED
DESCENT
INTO
BOSTON

128

THE
LONG
NAKED
DESCENT
INTO
BOSTON

Brown Corporation, depending on who wins. Please do not litter. In case of disaster please return to your chartered stage.

"If this sounds like padding," Braxton said, "it's the kind of seeming small memorabilia that will intrigue the future historians."

"It don'ts mean shit to me," Dilsie said. "I don't hear no Irish lower classes from Southie cheering nothing. The only time they makes a big noise is when the British tries to bus the Indians to school."

"But I'm writing local color, Dilsie."

"It won't get by my rewrite desk."

"I'll draw a picture, Dilsie," Lee said.

"That will help," Dilsie said.

"My God," General Lord Percy said, "these Colonial people are attacking. What do we do now? They have performed none of the proper evolutions of the drill. They fired no cannon first to give us fair warning. It's a mob. I intend to enter a formal protest. Don't fire, Coudray, until you can see that they are behaving themselves."

"They are attacking, sire, into Harrod's Wood," Colonel Coudray said.

"That is our weak spot?"

"I believe so, sire."

"Then tell them to stop it. Tell them to start over again. My dear," he said to Madame de Tocqueville, "I believe I've gotten you into a pickle."

"And your genius, my dear love, will get us out."

"I believe my life is finished," Lord Percy said, looking at his watch, "and here it is only three-thirty. Colonel Coudray?"

"Yes, sire."

"The Rebels are advancing against our center. But as any man with my training and instinctive acumen can see, it is a feint, an amateur play fake. Notice that they have already exposed their fraud to the experienced eye by sending their flankers wide away from our weak side at the wood to cover their deception, but their entire left flank will be exposed when their main column veers. An amateur blunder if I ever saw one. Colonel Coudray, take command of our artillery on the left flank from Major Pitcairn.

Do not commence your cannonade until their main column is completely committed to the veer and their entire flank exposed. Enfilade them with your ten-, then your fifteen-pounders. Do not advance the Seventh Light Infantry Foot until your cavalry screen has made their first pass at their rear. The Seventh Lightfoot is to be reinforced by two companies of Grenadiers to give them penetration power on the initial contact. Hold the Twelfth and Seventeenth Fusilier Regiments in reserve. Most of these men are recent replacements without experience, but can be used for mopping up. Check personally that all bayonets are fixed, Colonel Coudray, and outside of your screening maneuver, make certain your main column does not overreact, does not commit until the cannonading has reduced their rank and file, until they begin to mill. Then hit hard. Good luck, Colonel Coudray, and may God be with you."

"Well done," Madame de Tocqueville said.

"Oh, shut up," Lord Percy said.

"Colonel Conant has committed," Braxton said. "There is no turning back now. The Americans are behaving like amateurs; this will be a disaster. Can you get a sketch of this, Lee?"

"Yes."

They were sitting on the roof of Harrod's barn. Francine and Dilsie were down in the haymow.

Shots began to hit into the barn. Old Harrod's barn was faded and paintless. Harrod was too poor to paint and too proud to whitewash. Although the men seemed to have difficulty hitting each other, they had no problem hitting the broad side of a barn.

On the roof of Harrod's barn just outside of Concord on April 19, 1775, there was no better place to see this war. I do not believe that in any war or any history was there a better vantage point, and yet even those up here disagreed as to what happened. Even as to who won. After most battles there is the euphoria on both sides of feeling they have won. Then after licking their wounds and counting their dead comes the sneaking suspicion that they lost. Both sides. And both sides are right. How can both sides lose? They can. And do. And come back to try it another day. And lose again. Both sides. We all know that the enemy always loses. But who is the enemy? In this case the enemy are those

129
THE
LONG
NAKED
DESCENT
INTO
BOSTON

130

THE
LONG
NAKED
DESCENT
INTO
BOSTON

who kill the soldiers who represent the government. The enemy is us, Braxton thought. Then again you cannot sell papers by calling yourself the enemy.

"Write it down, Braxton," Lee said. "Write it all down."

"No one wants to know what happened here, Lee. What they want to read is, GLORIOUS VICTORY. ENEMY IN FULL FLIGHT. ENEMY ORGY OF RAPE REVEALED BY THIS REPORTER. LORD PERCY INDICATED AFTER BATTLE WAR WILL BE DUCK SOUP. ENEMY TO GET COMEUPPANCE. AMERICANS WILL PAY BACK TAXES. BRITISH TROOPS TO LAND LONDON 11:45 P.M. DELIGHTED FEMALES CRUSH TOMMIES. PANDEMONIUM REIGNS. DELIGHTED KING MAY ABDI-CATE. INDICATED HE MAY CASTRATE HIMSELF IN HAPPINESS. 92 BILLION POUNDS NEEDED FOR DEFENSE.

"COLONEL CONANT INDICATED TO THIS REPORTER THAT THE PATRIOTS' OVERWHELMING VICTORY AT CONCORD WAS NOT SURPRISE TO HIM. INDICATES WE HAD BRITISH BY THE BALLS WHEN THEY TRIED TO HOLD HARROD'S WOOD WITH SHIT FOR SOLDIERS. INSIDE SOURCES WOULD BE HAPPY TO MEET BRITISH AGAIN ANY TIME, ANY PLACE, IF WEATHER GOOD. JOY ROCKS COLONIES. RELIABLE SOURCES REVEAL WAR ABOUT OVER. EVERY-THING BUT THE SHOUTING, A SOURCE CLOSE TO FRANKLIN WHO FLED TO PARIS INDICATES. 92 BILLION DOLLARS NEEDED FOR DEFENSE. It depends, Lee, on what paper you read, London or New York, but the ninety-two billion for defense will appear in both papers."

"Braxton, you're cynical."

"Which side says I'm cynical?"

"Both sides."

"I saw some dead boy soldiers."

"That will do it every time, but try to get something down on paper—the part about glorious victory is a good start."

"Lee, you're more cynical than I am. Where are the girls?"

"Below."

"In the hay, where everyone belongs. Fuck the war."

"Braxton, if the soldiers go to all the trouble to fight the war, the least we can do is take a few minutes to watch it. Particularly since that is what we are paid to do."

"All right, I'll give the Revolution thirty-five minutes."

"I'm sure they'll appreciate it, Braxton."

"That's all right," Braxton said, "but I'd sooner be down in the hay—there will always be another war. When my balls dry up, I can always be a reporter. Or a play critic. Or become the Governor of the State of Massachusetts. It will always be a free country for everyone with their balls dried up, no matter who wins."

"Braxton, for Christ's sake, write it down."

"What I just said?"

"No, something printable."

"The printable never interests me. I wonder why it interests other people? What is printed is what people with their balls dried up say is printable. I'm sorry I was rude to your war, Lee. I'll try to get with it."

"Thanks, Braxton. Do you like this picture?"

"You've got both sides losing."

"That's the way I see it, Braxton."

In the hay below, the mow below Braxton and Lee, Dilsie and Francine were peeking out to see where the hail of bullets was coming from. They could not believe there was that much lead in the Colonies. They could not believe there were that many soldiers who missed. In order to miss this much, both sides must have had a lot of practice. There must have been a prize for the best missers. Anyone who hit anything but the broad side of a barn was summarily reduced in rank. Anyone who hit anything at all twice in a row was hung. Otherwise, Francine thought, how could you develop all those expert missers? It had not been too long since the blunderbuss had been replaced by the musket in the Colonies. The blunderbuss only had to be pointed in the general direction of the person or other animal to be shot. The musket had to be aimed. Very few in the Colonies had gotten on to this trick yet. Dilsie was happy that she had hung onto her blunderbuss. Dilsie had only to lean out of the haymow, point the thing in the general direction, and kill most of the soldiers on both sides. The blunderbuss had been outlawed for this reason. It would shorten war. The blunderbuss was illegal. Dilsie would be arrested if she tried. She would be placed in durance vile for stopping the Revolution. So she durst not.

131
THE
LONG
NAKED
DESCENT
INTO
BOSTON

132

THE
LONG
NAKED
DESCENT
INTO
BOSTON

"I durst," Dilsie said to Francine. "I durst. I bet you two shillings I durst if I feel like it. I can do anything I damn well durst."

"The new idea, Dilsie," Francine said, "is not to behave like a man. That has been tried by men and it doesn't work. The idea is to add something new to the porridge."

"Like what—I sure like the smell of this hay—like what?"

"Like fucking the war," Francine said.

"What?"

"Get Lee and Braxton down here in the hay."

"I was," Dilsie said, "brought up conservative. A small town called Punkhatasset. Not that we didn't get in the hay. But it was never during a fight."

"You were always careful to separate the two?"

"Yes, Punkhatasset is conservative."

"Then why don't you go up top and keep Lee company and send Braxton down here in the hay. Tell him that like the women of Nineveh and Tyre during the Peloponnesian War and the girls in the bars of Lexington today, as soon as a battle starts, I get so scared I vibrate like a Colonial Big Sweet Mama Shake-up."

Dilsie crawled up into the crystal day of Concord. Oh, to see the world from the top of a barn in New England. Far, far, and very wide—the soft and deep green hills rolled on west toward the Indians. To the east stood the ships of Spain in Boston Bay. North the ice of Canada, cold as a whore's tit. South—the sweet song of the South—to the tune of love me gentle, love me true. Below, the dogs of war snapped and crackled and boomed at each other in mad affright—blood blotched the green.

"Ah, liberty," Braxton said. "What new and strange mischief have you found now?"

"Go below and get shut of this," Dilsie said to Braxton.

"Yes, before you take sides," Lee said. "If a reporter is not neutral, he can only be an interesting pain in the ass, of no value to the paper. Take this pint of rum, have a good roll in the hay, and make it back in time for the first edition."

"Yes," Braxton said, moving down through the cupola. "The battle is repeating itself. Get a good picture, Lee, and I'll take it from there."

Dilsie had lugged her blunderbuss up with her through the

cupola and placed it across her knees as she joined Lee sitting on the ridgepole. The roof was slate and slippery so you had to stick to the crest. The zinc cock weathervane on top of the cupola pointed the way the smoke of battle drifted. The bayonets below pointed the way to victory, defeat, glory, liberty and justice, King and country, and the boy who bought a farm. The hay beneath was as warm as rabbits.

"Not to change the subject," Lee said, "but is that a balloon up there or am I seeing things?"

"I saw it a bit ago," Dilsie said, "but it has shot up into the cloud now."

A man came up to the windward side of the barn now, dressed in corduroy, a WIN button in his lapel, and carrying a pitchfork. It was Old Man Harrod, who owned the farm.

"I'm going to have to ask you to get down from up there," he shouted up.

"We be from the Press."

"That don't make a damn. You didn't pay."

"Pay?"

"Yes, I've got to charge the spectators something to make both ends meet. This battle is costing me a lot in damages. I don't want to profit on the Revolution. I just want to get back what I put into this place."

"Charge the combatants."

"They won't pay damages. And the insurance companies call it an act of God or the fortunes of war. I checked with Hancock when I saw this coming. It was the same in the French and Indian Wars. Fight where it's convenient to fight—fuck the farmer. Leave him to clean up the mess. I don't like to charge you to watch the Revolution, but if the soldiers won't pay damages, who will?"

"How much?"

"How does seven and six hit you? You have the best seats."

"Seven shillings sixpence? That's scalping."

"There was some scalping during the French and Indian Wars. I got two pounds ten for a seat behind the corn crib, but I think now I'm being fair. I'm not charging you for the couple screwing in my hay. I'm trying to be fair, but we don't get a Revolution on this place every day. A farmer has to make it while he can. Corn

133

THE
LONG
NAKED
DESCENT
INTO
BOSTON

134

THE
LONG
NAKED
DESCENT
INTO
BOSTON

now is only two shillings the basket delivered in Boston. Barley at today's price, it doesn't pay to cut. If it wasn't for the Revolution, we'd all go broke."

"I only have two sovereigns and a crown. Do you have any change, Dilsie?"

"Just a pound note."

"Toss down the two sovereigns and I'll send up the dog with the change."

But the dog never came back with the change. Lee called him that son-of-a-bitch war profiteer. Dilsie said the dog might have died on the way from shock at Farmer Harrod's sudden honesty.

"Anyway, Lee, I think I see the balloon now."

"Do you know what, Dilsie? The Revolution is fading away to the east toward Medford."

"And just after we paid," Dilsie said.

"And do you know what, Dilsie? Before they quit the field the soldiers are taking a final potshot at us."

"Do you feel anything?" Dilsie said.

"No."

"I haven't been hit either," Dilsie said, "but at the start of any Revolution you have to make allowances for poor shooting. Why don't you get a picture of their mutual retreat and I'll write a poem to back it. Something for the Sunday second section about how the embattled farmer charged us seven shillings sixpence, then stood on the rude bridge at Concord and fired the shot heard round the world—he was so happy to be rich."

seventeen

"More straw, Gretchen."

"There is none."

"More clothes."

"There are none."

"Take my pants," Poxe said.

That was the end of it. Now there was nothing but the long naked descent to Boston.

"I would like to think," Poxe said, "that this—what our British friends would call unpleasantness at Concord and Lexington today—this misunderstanding will go no further. True, *The New Boston Times* has been pushing the Revolution. But everyone makes mistakes. Although I have never known a paper to admit one. The *Globe* made a mistake once and admitted it. I don't think they will ever recover from that. I plan an editorial in tomorrow morning's edition telling people the virtues of Revolution have been greatly exaggerated. The masthead will repeat Franklin's saying, 'There has never been a good war or a bad peace.' Franklin would like to dodge his statement now that he is banging the drums for war, but we will run it. Will you make a note of that, Gretchen?"

136

THE
LONG
NAKED
DESCENT
INTO
BOSTON

"No."

"Temper, temper."

"What am I doing," Gretchen said, "with my fear of flying, naked in a balloon over Boston?"

"A fair question," Nathan said.

"The unpleasure principle is involved," Poxe said. "The pleasure principle has been oversold. Everything important in this world has come about through unhappiness. Show me a happy man and I will show you a failure. The happy teacher is teaching hogwash. The happy explorer is probably lost. The happy politician is a fraud. The happy salesman is a thief. The happy housewife is a lie. Only through true unhappiness, the loneliness of despair, does anyone accomplish anything worth a tinker's damn. Then *Hamlet* is written. The *Mona Lisa* painted. The New World discovered. *The New Boston Times* born. The unpleasure principle is the secret, Gretchen."

"Christ, it's cold," she said.

"The unpleasure principle opens up the joy of flying. No one in their right mind would go up in a balloon," Poxe said, monitoring the distance down to the hard earth.

"No one but a member of *The New Boston Times*," Gretchen said.

"I regret that we may never live to tell the joy of flying," Nathan said.

"To the right of our aircraft," Poxe said to relieve the naked terror, "to the right of our aircraft is the River Charles. To the left, the Mystic. What appears to be on the surface darting fishes, are in fact drifting turds. You say the *Times* by itself cannot clean up the Charles. You say as long as people eat, people will of necessity shit. You say God's will. You say we are born, we eat, we shit, we die, and the Charles again flows unvexed to the sea. Not true. The Charles is vexed. The *Times* is vexed. You say—"

"Who says?"

"I'm sorry," Poxe said. "I am carried away by the joy of flying. Ahead of our aircraft," Poxe said, "somewhere under that smoke is the proud city of Boston. Somewhere to the left and hiding under the smoke is Breed's and Bunker Hill. Ahead of that, Dorchester and Noodles Island. In the bay the King's fleet—ready to pounce upon the unwary Patriot or ready to maintain some law and order, depending on your vision. The *Times* does not take sides. We are descending naked into Boston. Those of you who are leaving the aircraft in Boston—have a good Revolution and we want to thank you for traveling with the *Times*. Please do not leave your seats until the balloon has come to a complete stop. What do you think of my humor, Nathan?"

"Christ, it's cold," he said.

"The temperature in Boston is twenty-eight degrees," Poxe said, "and if you think that's warm for April in Massachusetts, wait until the fire of Revolution gets going. I have an idea, Nathan?"

Poxe always announced his editorial ideas in the form of a question. They usually occurred around the Franklin stove in the editorial room of the *Times*, which was also the only room of the *Times* at the time. Times were bad. Times were hard at the *Times*. Poxe also might get an idea at the Rose and Crown or Brown's Adult Book Shoppe or in a balloon. When an idea happened to Poxe he usually began to shake and turn red in the face and the minions would begin to scurry about, searching for plume and ink to catch each pearl of wisdom. Franklin was in the process of inventing a portable pen which he called the "fountain." This would mean, he said, that as a male moved about, as Poxe was prone to do, a female could follow him about with a portable plume fountain and catch every gem that fell or was pushed by Providence from his lips. After the fountain or ball—Franklin was working on a ball plume, too—no longer would the male and female be chained to a desk by the inkwell, but would be free to move about like birds. Some wanted to call the miracle plume "freedom for the male" or the "portable female." Francine wanted to bust Poxe in the noggin.

Franklin could not understand what women wanted. "My God, Poxe, if we could discover what women want, that would be the greatest discovery of all time. Bigger than the stove. Watt's steam engine. Johnson's dictionary. Electricity? I don't know. Man may never know. The eternal mystery. What women want. I give up," Franklin said. "What do you think, Poxe?"

"Well, it's not the portable ballpoint plume," Poxe said.

"I give up," Franklin said.

"My mind wanders," Poxe said to his fellow aeronauts sailing

137
THE
LONG
NAKED
DESCENT
INTO
BOSTON

138

THE
LONG
NAKED
DESCENT
INTO
BOSTON

naked over Massachusetts. The balloon was no longer descending into Boston because, as everyone knows, hot air rises.

"It does?" Gretchen said.

"Hot air rises" is not a smart-ass remark on the quality of the conversation in the balloon, but a scientific occurrence affecting this balloon, which had black stripes to catch and absorb the heat of the sun to make the balloon rise. The sun had just busted through near Boston, so the balloon went up, up, up, away from the Revolution below and closer to God. Because there was no longer any straw or clothing to burn, they were victims of the sun. They would go up and down according to whether the sun was breaking or entering the clouds. And they were sometimes lost. Once near Menotomy the balloon descended close to a Minuteman lurking behind a stone fence and Nathan hollered down, "Where are we?" and the man shouted back, "In a balloon!"

"That smart-ass son-of-a-bitch," Nathan said. "I regret that. I'm sorry, Gretchen."

"That's all right, I agree with you," Gretchen said.

Another time they shouted down the same question to an embattled farmer. The Patriot shouted back, "You are lost!"

"Sometimes I get a glimpse of why the British started the war," Poxe said.

"Did the British start the war?" Nathan said.

"We don't know," Poxe said, "and I haven't got the faintest idea how to get this damn balloon down."

Getting it down while the sun is up—that is the problem with the hot-air balloon. But the British below were in a sticky wicket, too. Pomfret and Pomeroy had at last arrived with the new British escape route plan to Boston and the medicaments from Doctor Glanders. But Lord Percy was as mad as hops for being left in the lurch. All he wanted to do was get back to Boston in peace. Everyone in the Colonies and kingdom come was shooting at his King's men along the road back. Why had Gage sent him on this fool's mission? Or was Mrs. Loring responsible? What had he, Lord Percy, ever done to deserve the Patriots' anger? Why couldn't we all have a quiet chat about this like civilized people? Love will find a way, Lord Percy thought. Whatever that means, Lord Percy thought. "Stop shooting, you bastards!" It must have been *The New Boston Times* who put them up to this. The ladies and gentlemen of that distinguished gang had joined his bunch on the retreat to Boston.

"And we British are not a bunch," Lord Percy said to Braxton. "We are still maintaining discipline in the ranks. We are still a force in being. Although I suppose your paper will call this a rout."

"Fie on your paper!" Madame de Tocqueville screamed at Braxton. "I hate you. I hate you. I hate everything about the Press. You are holding my Lord Percy up to public ridicule. You make the whole war a collection of damn fools. Have you no honor, sir? Have you no decency? Are you not, too, a member of the human race? My Lord Percy can bear no more and we are calling it quits."

"Don't be hasty, my dear," Lord Percy said. Then turning his horse to Braxton and speaking as quietly as the whistling bullets allowed, he said, "Madame de Tocqueville is out of sorts. You know how women are. She has had a hard day. We all have. There was that unpleasantness at Lexington and Concord and now this. I would suggest that you people, the Press, being in civilian clothes, have no need to join us here and be shot at. You can easily join the shooters and be safe and I will bear no ill will against you, considering the circumstance. I myself must show the flag and get my men back to Boston with what honor remains."

"If we be war correspondents," Dilsie said, "we prefers to remain in the thick."

"These are honorable words, madam," Lord Percy said, "and history will treat you kindly. I fear it will not do the same for me. Colonel Coudray, move up the Seventh Lightfoot to screen our right flank and keep the men moving."

Now there came over the fair countenance of our Lord Percy a beatific cast. All was lost. The Patriots had the British by the balls. And they would squeeze. The Patriots were fed on the stuff of Tom Paine. Righteousness. The fear of taxes. The joy of murder. They had the British trapped seven leagues from Boston crossing Alewife Brook, trying to get back to the protection of the big guns of their fleet. Lord Percy was angelic because he was involved in a disaster. Lord Percy's genius might have gone

139

THE
LONG
NAKED
DESCENT
INTO
BOSTON

140

THE
LONG
NAKED
DESCENT
INTO
BOSTON

unsung were it not for his blunder. Some of us will challenge God to see if we can get out whole again. Lord Percy was a mutation waiting for evolution to give him a niche to occupy. The Revolution did it. This battle. Gage's stupidity. Mrs. Loring's thoughtlessness. Women will frequently allow a man to hang himself, to walk into a minefield so that she might gain the satisfaction of showing the way out. It is not that man is woman's inferior; it is simply in the ways of war that men are lacking. They get too excited perhaps. Too eager. They lack the necessary patience of the female. The sangfroid. The killer instinct. In other pursuits such as sex or bowling on the green, men at times do remarkably well. Well enough that nature does not eliminate the male. Nature could do this at the drop of a hat. Give women a little of Doctor Glanders' green stuff. Then good-bye male. The male must perform some other unknown-at-this-time function in the scheme of life. The mystery. It may be the male is here simply to amuse women. Nature has her secrets, and why she evolved the male may never be known. Like the reason for the appendix or the male tits. It may be that nature was involved in evolving life on several planets at the same time and fucked up on earth. So the human male is nature's fuck-up.

"Oh, God, Braxton," Francine said. "Why do you write that junk?"

"To get my mind off the war," Braxton said.

"But you're paid to follow the Revolution."

"But not to be in it," Braxton said, "and that is what's happened."

"Shit," Francine said. "The Revolution will soon be over, and what are you going to tell your children you were doing at the Battle of Lexington and Concord—writing junk?"

"Writing something to go with Lee's pictures," Braxton said. "Don't take your hand away, Francine," Braxton said, unbuttoning his pants with one hand and holding hers with the other.

"Not here, not now," Francine said, and then she said, pushing back the blackberry brambles that pricked, "Not here, not now. What will history say?"

"Fuck history," Braxton said. "History is never interested in important things. History only wants to know—who won? What was the kill ratio? History is never interested in what really happened during a battle. At least historians aren't. That fact will save us, Francine. We will tell the children something to fit their generation—children make up their own history anyway. Children always see through the lie of the older generation. Move over."

"We can't do it here—now."

"Why not?"

"The blackberry thorns prick and a soldier might rush in here looking for cover."

"If he is British he will apologize."

So the two of them, Braxton and Francine, crept into the blackberry bush to escape the bee of bullets, the shuttershit of grapeshot, the death, the obscenity of battle to find life in a blackberry bush along the road to Boston.

Lord Percy was hung up trying to cross the Alewife Brook and beat his way backward home by cutting below Medford, then following the Mystic River, keeping the river on his left to protect his weak flank and hightailing for the Charlestown Neck to the sanctuary of the King's fleet, the skepticism of Gage, the condolences of Mrs. Loring. War is not hell—a hell into which angels sometimes fall. War is peace. That time in life when we are allowed to act out our fears against those we believe to be different and at the expense of everyone. This is something like, but not entirely like, what Lee and Dilsie were wondering about beneath a scattering of willow along the Alewife. Not wondering too much about anything, because the British under the wisdom of Colonel Coudray were enfilading the Alewife Bridge with grape by cannonading from Merriam's Hill, and the miniballs were taking down the willow.

The British must have the bridge. They would take it. The Patriots thought not. The Patriots think not much, Lord Percy mused. But enough to stop us if they had better leadership. They do not realize I am only feinting, that it is a play fake at this bridge, that my main force is already crossing the Alewife below the bend at Leslie's Ford. I could move in behind them and destroy them, but I must cross the Charlestown Neck in daylight

141
THE
LONG
NAKED
DESCENT
INTO
BOSTON

142

THE
LONG
NAKED
DESCENT
INTO
BOSTON

under the fleet's guns. Anyway I promised Madame de Tocqueville a night on the town. What's that balloon doing up there?

In Boston, Mrs. Loring took the note that the messenger
Pomfret handed her. It was in Madame de Tocqueville's handwriting but it sounded like Lord Percy. She read it, gave it some
thought, and handed it to General Gage.

The note read: "We have crossed the Alewife, stranding the
main force of the enemy in our rear. But heavy resistance is
building up along the Charlestown Road. Can you dispatch the
20th and the 14th Heavy Grenadiers by way of Leckmere's Point?
I will leave the 14th Lightfoot at the Menotomy cutoff as a delay-
ing operation. Make contact with them there. Then all withdraw
in strength across the Neck. It is beautiful in the country here at
this time of year. The foliage, particularly along the Mystic, is
beginning to sprout. Some columbine are already in bloom and
the willows are beginning to spin green, but I am forced to
cannonade some of it. So much for what is happening to me. I
hope things are going well for you in Boston. I don't want to
sound abrupt but I must buzz off. You can spare the 20th and the
14th Grenadiers, can't you? Why not? Do not bother to answer
this as we will be seeing each other soon. I am also looking
forward to seeing the 14th and 20th Grenadiers soon. Why not?
Give my love to Mrs. Loring and the kiddies."

"Kiddies?" Gage said, folding the note. "I didn't know."

"You knew about Mr. Loring. My husband, Lowell Cabot
Loring, the Dean of New England Poets?"

"Yes, a fine chap, a generous chap, an understanding chap."

"Well, there are kiddies."

"I trust they are well provided for."

"Yes, we are old-fashioned parents. We don't believe in the
modern point of view of coddling children. As soon as they reach
the age of reason, we will turn them loose in the wilderness. If
they want to make it to Canada or Yale or the army, it will be their
choice. We want nothing to do with them."

"Capital," Gage said. "But it sounds very modern."

"No, I believe it's old-fashioned," Mrs. Loring said. "I must
check."

"Now there's this uncomfortable business with Lord Percy,"

Gage said. "He does seem to have gotten himself into a bit of a mess. I promised to hold the night open for you, my dear, but this whole thing has come up suddenly. I thought Lord Percy was just out for a bit of a romp. I had expected him back before now. I wonder how the Fourteenth and the Twentieth will feel about leaving their warm barracks without notice. They must have, most of them anyway, made other plans for the evening."

"You are the general, pet."

"Yes." Gage stared at Pomfret. "What do you think? How are things up there?"

"Lots of shooting," Pomfret said.

"You've got to expect that in war," Gage said. "The younger generation believe war to be a romp. I expected better of Lord Percy, though. Pomfret, lots of shooting, you say?"

"Yes."

"These things happen. My attempt at humor seems to be failing."

"Yes, pet."

"Then all right, Percy can have the Twentieth and the Fourteenth. If the soldiers have made other plans for this evening, then to hell with their plans. These men took the King's shilling for fighting, not fornication. Right, lamb?"

"True, true, true, General," Mrs. Loring said, and Pomfret nodded in complete agreement. The Fourteenth and the Twentieth would have to change their plans. War is a problem that occurs and recurs out of the blue. Sometimes when you least expect it. As now. And every generation repeats it. As now.

143

THE
LONG
NAKED
DESCENT
INTO
BOSTON

eighteen

The betting in Boston was beginning to tilt again heavily toward the British. At the Betting Shoppe the rumor was rife that the Patriots had blown their chance to trap the British at the Alewife. That the British were home free. In the morning, there would be a few trials and a few hangings of the Rebels and everyone would go back to not paying their taxes and showing normal disrespect toward their betters. This is a problem that John Hancock and his like faced.

Samuel Adams and John Hancock were riding horse, passing through New Brunswick, New Jersey, on their way to Trenton, thence to Philadelphia to compose what they called an announcement or Declaration of Independence. What Sam Adams called the new and grand scheme before us.

"Not many hotels in America now, but I can see the day, Sam," Hancock said, "when there will be horse-tels all the way to Philadelphia."

"You are a man of vision, John."

"The problem," Hancock said, "will be seed capital. Where will the financing come from, when and if we break with

England? I can see prime interest rates climbing as high as five percent. Paper money. I believe some sort of tax shelter should be mentioned in the Declaration. Otherwise the lower classes could in theory tax the rich—rob the rich, the more successful, the more contributing out of existence. Now you have a rabble in arms. Tomorrow you have the rabble in power. No thinking man wants that. But we could have something for the rich like tax shelters or a tax depletion allowance on our slaves—our slaves don't get any younger, you know. And on our women, too. They don't get any younger either. Yes, that might do the trick. But no one seems to give a damn about the problems of the rich."

"John," Sam said, "that's for later. The Declaration will simply be a statement declaring our independence from the mother country. Something fancy in legalese that would stand up in court, like 'When in the course of human events it becomes necessary for a people to dissolve the political bonds which have connected them to another'—young Tom Jefferson can take it from there. Tom is very clever at phrases. I can see him President one day."

"President? What's that?"

"Well, we're not going to have a King."

"We're not?"

"No."

"Oh," Hancock said. "I'll have to think about that."

They rode through the smells of New Brunswick. There was no inn for the night.

"You mean," Hancock said, "that any Tom, Dick, and Harry with a gift of gab can take over the whole kit and kaboodle? Any one of those?" he said, pointing to the tatterdemain of New Brunswick, New Jersey.

"Yes."

"I don't like it, Sam."

"Don't you find it exciting? You'll never know what will come next out of the hat," Sam said.

"No, I don't like it, Sam."

"Every four years an election. It will be like a carnival," Sam said.

"I don't like it."

They were riding on Stacy Street. It was a wide street. The

145
THE
LONG
NAKED
DESCENT
INTO
BOSTON

146

THE
LONG
NAKED
DESCENT
INTO
BOSTON
only street paved in the Colony of New Jersey. Sam swung his horse in front of Hancock's mount.

"Oh, Jesus," Adams said. "Get off your high aristocratic ass, John. Give the common people a chance to make their own blunders, start their own wars, rob themselves for a change. Self-government is preferable to good government, or some such phrase that Paine will dig up. But it is not all tommyrot. There is something new cooking, John, if you would get off your high aristocratic ass and give it a chance."

"I don't like it one bit, Sam. I can't see myself putting my John Hancock to any such folderol as that."

"You will, John, you will," Sam said, "because it is much too late to turn back. What we started in Concord threw the shit in the wind—and freedom has begun its long naked descent into Boston."

"I don't like your language, Sam."

"I promise you, John, you'll like the Declaration of Independence. You'll have a hand in it. Jefferson is not a hog about things like this. You'll like Tom. He's wide open to suggestions."

"Too many cooks spoil the broth," Hancock said.

"Franklin keeps saying that. I wish Franklin would stop saying that. It's an antidemocratic statement, if he thought about it. Benjamin is a nice enough fellow, an honest straight shooter to be trusted, but he's getting old and he's stuck on his sayings and no one is about to stop him. Have you heard his latest saying?"

"No."

"It's on yesterday's masthead of *The New Boston Times.* 'Those that ask well, think well.' "

"What's that mean?"

"I don't know. Ask him when you see him. He'll be there in Philadelphia."

"Can't we stop over in New Brunswick, Sam?"

"No, New Brunswick is a shitty town."

"I don't like your language, Sam. Your cousin John doesn't speak like that."

"John is a horse's ass, a prig. He'll probably be President some day."

"What!"

"No. I'm only trying to scare you, John. Can't you take a joke?"

"Not about something as serious as that. I would like to stay over in New Brunswick, Sam."

"On to Philadelphia and independence," Samuel Adams said, turning his horse and leading the way down the cobblestones of Stacy Street, out of New Brunswick and on to Philadelphia by way of Trenton, followed by John Hancock, who rode well enough but was tired in the saddle and sick at heart.

Lord Percy was not fatigued in the saddle but was already bored with the war. There was this impudence of the mob on the road to Boston. You make allowances for anyone who has tax problems. Still, if the Colonials were clever by half, they would hire a sharp accountant and finish the year with a tax rebate.

"Still, by some miracle we British could still lose the war, Colonel Coudray," Lord Percy said. "But if we lose, we will lose with no blemish on our escutcheon."

"That's what I like about you, my Lord Percy," Colonel Coudray said, "you are a good loser."

"I've had a good deal of practice, Colonel Coudray. I went through the entire Seven Years' War and the Spanish Peninsula campaign without a single victory, even if I do say so myself. But the enemy never criticized my behavior. After the Battle of San Sebastian, the Spanish King gave me a medal. I pass it around the club. It causes comment. All favorable. 'Have you seen Lord Percy's thing?' All favorable. What was my thought?"

"My dear Lord Percy," Madame de Tocqueville said, "I don't want to interrupt your thought, but as you can see there is war here and now, and if I can comment, you are losing. Remember, you are my treasure, my reason for living, my thumpety thump, and I cannot sleep half the time because I lech for your body. I see you without hat or trousers but always on a horse. What does that dream mean?"

Lord Percy and his army were slowly descending into Boston through the Charlestown Neck. Note the blood-speckled horses under Lord Percy and Madame de Tocqueville in the vanguard, all the King's banners flying, all the King's men following, again in

147
THE
LONG
NAKED
DESCENT
INTO
BOSTON

148

THE
LONG
NAKED
DESCENT
INTO
BOSTON

smart formation and performing all the evolutions of the drill. The band picked up a martial tune and the cannon of Lord Howe's fleet sounded *boom boom boom.* The Patriots fled in disarray at such loud noises to build a ring round Boston to trap the British again and contemplate more mischief on the morrow.

Lord Percy raised his arm in signal to slow the troops for a proper entry into Boston. All flaps down, tail high, all flags flying, all drums drumming.

Madame de Tocqueville took her Lord Percy's bloodied hand and stroked the wrist gently. "My only hero. My life. You durst tear me apart, sire."

"I know," Lord Percy said. "I know. Bear up."

The camp followers pressed in closely behind through the gates of Boston, led by the stalwarts of *The New Boston Times.*

"There's a story here someplace," Braxton said.

"We just got to pry it out," Dilsie said. "You get any pictures, Lee? Did you see them cannon go *boom boom boom?*"

"I heard them. None of us saw them."

"Make a picture anyway," Dilsie said. "Did you get something for the women's page, Francine?"

"I didn't get shit," Francine said. "What with Braxton pawing me and the Patriots shooting at me, all I got was background stuff. Sex in the afternoon. That kind of unprintable stuff."

"No, that's good, that's good," Dilsie said. "Women eat that up. The *Globe* will carry their usual crap. PATRIOTS ZAP BRITISH IN OPENER. CLOSE SQUEAKER COULD BREED OVERCONFIDENCE IN NEXT FRAY. OUR FLAG STILL FLYING. All those clichés. The *Globe* will be careful not to mention what flag they mean so they won't lose no subscribers. Poxey is slam-bang kick-'em-up Charley, to hell with everything. Don't drop your lead story, Francine. Braxton, do a piece on that son-of-a-bitch farmer who charged for the show, and Lee, do one of your pretty pictures real good about the style old Percy had when he spread his wings to land in Boston."

"You're a good editor, Dilsie."

"I tries, the Lord knows I tries, I does my best," Dilsie said.

"When is Poxey coming down to earth?"

"Never, I hope," Dilsie said.

"Everyone should try to get back for the Declaration of Independence."

"The Declaration of Independence don't mean nothing to black peoples, women of any color, and Indian folks. That don't leave many peoples to celebrate freedom. That right, Francine?"

"We will go to the Rose and Crown anyway and have a Colonial Big Sweet Mama Shake-up," Francine said.

149
THE
LONG
NAKED
DESCENT
INTO
BOSTON

nineteen

As Sam Adams and John Hancock approached Trenton, New Jersey, they were from time to time and from village to village approached by Colonial British Loyalists telling them, "For Christ's sake, Hancock, don't sign anything until you sober up. Sam, you're an old friend of my father. He's dead now, but you know how he would feel about your pissing on the King."

"We're not going to piss on the King," Sam said.

"He will take it that way."

"I don't care how he takes it," Sam said.

"Who is going to be the General of the Continental Army?"

"Iz Putnam," Sam said.

"I hear George Washington is dressed for the part. He will take it hard."

"I don't care how he takes it," Sam said.

"My great-aunt is a cousin of the Washingtons by marriage. George is stubborn."

"I am stubborn, too," Sam said.

"You can bet your silver shoe buckles," John Hancock said,

"that George Washington will be General of the Continental Army over my dead body."

"George is a loser," Sam said. "He was with Braddock at that defeat, Fort Necessity at that defeat, Fort Duquesne at that defeat."

"Maybe George is due to win one."

"Over my dead body," John Hancock said.

"How are things in Boston?"

"We got the Revolution off the ground," Sam said.

"But can you win it?"

They allowed their horses to move in circles through the Loyalists, the peasants, and pottery workers who commuted by horse to Trenton. The smoke from the Trenton kilns hid the central part of New Jersey from the southern part of Pennsylvania. Boatmen boating down the Delaware could not see land until they got to the northern part of Florida.

"I said," the Trenton pottery worker said, "can you win it?"

"Not if you take that attitude," Sam said. "Not without positive thinking. When I was a young tyke and only in grade school, my teacher—and I will never forget this—she said, Sam—"

"We are not interested in what your teacher said to you when you were only a little tyke in grade school. We want to know—"

"She said think and grow rich," Sam said.

"What does that mean? Do you know how much I make now at the pottery after thirty-six years?"

"She didn't mean money," Sam said. "I think she meant a positive attitude toward the struggle of life. We never had any money in the cabin I grew up in unless we had just finished a good trade with the Indians. An Indian always dressed better than we did. It was always a great source of mortification to go to the log church with the seat out of your pants with all the girls looking on. I can tell you it wasn't all fun and games. All of the money is on my cousin John's side of the family and he is tighter than a pig's ass. He might make President someday," Sam said. "God bless him."

"Can you win?"

"Yes, we can win," Sam said, turning his horse toward Trenton away from the Tory potters but toward the more smoke

151

THE
LONG
NAKED
DESCENT
INTO
BOSTON

152

THE
LONG
NAKED
DESCENT
INTO
BOSTON

of the Tory potters' works. "But only by thinking positively," Sam said.

They rode in silence through the new Trenton Princess Jean Park housing development and the mobile homes pulled there by six horses. There were some eight-horse mobile double-wide homes in the better section.

"What I wonder about, Sam," John Hancock said, "and I don't know how this has struck you, but maybe we shouldn't talk about it."

"About what?"

"The fact that since we started our trip we haven't found anyone yet who's for independence. How wide would you say that double-wide mobile home is?"

"We haven't found anyone yet in New Jersey who's for independence because the New Jersey people are not independent people. They never will be. Notice how they always bunch up in groups. No dwelling can be more than two feet from the next. A Princeton researcher has called it spaceophobia. The need to grab your neighbor by the neck. The Indians like it because they can get all the scalps in one fell swoop. It cuts down on travel time. How wide is that mobile home? I would say twenty feet."

"But Sam, we didn't meet anyone in New York who was for independence."

"That's because we went through the city. The New York City people have tried all kinds of mayors but nothing works. They have petitioned the King to send a Prince to rule them and straighten things out. Prince Charles said he would like to visit but wouldn't want to live there. I don't understand how they got that double-wide mobile home down the road."

"But no one in Connecticut, Rhode Island, or any state we passed through was bananas for independence."

"I know, John, but when the Colonies get independence, they'll like it. I choose to think we are in a better position to judge what's best for the unwashed. What do they know about anything? Their only genuine objection is that after independence they can no longer make that shopping trip to London. They'll have to shop in New York and nobody likes that idea. Do you know what it costs for dinner and a show in New York now? And a lousy show, lousy dinner. Sometimes I don't blame them for not wanting independence."

"Watch it, Sam. You know and I know—even if no one else knows—you know and I know independence is a good idea. For one thing, it will cut back on the inflation and stop the business recession."

"Yes."

"Cut taxes."

"Yes."

"And not only here in New Jersey but everywhere in the Colonies it will give everyone the opportunity to have a mobile home of their own."

"You jest, John, out of bitterness at our lack of support. But I believe sincerely every man would like to have a mobile home of his own."

"But no one is stopping them now."

"We must act as though someone is, John. If we don't have an issue, it's difficult to have a Revolution. I think it was Julius Caesar who said that, and it's still true. Issues are important. Then there's freedom."

"From what?"

"We will think of something. These things take time to work out. It's generally best to have a war and then later in peace and quiet figure out what it was about."

"That makes sense."

"It doesn't make sense to the Colonists now, but it will after it's all over. John, shall we ask that twenty-foot-wide owner how he got the thing down the road?"

"How did you get that thing down the road?" John said. "And how far did you have to haul it?"

"From Jersey City," the man said. "They are manufactured there from mostly paper by Jerry O'Mahoney. He has a patent on the idea. They are not really mobile; notice the wheels have all been stolen. They will all be here two hundred years from now. It takes sixteen oxen to haul one. The oxen people, who are tied in with Jerry O'Mahoney, charge sixteen shillings a mile to haul a home."

"How do you stand on independence?"

"From what?"

153
THE
LONG
NAKED
DESCENT
INTO
BOSTON

154

THE
LONG
NAKED
DESCENT
INTO
BOSTON

"We don't want to put ideas in people's heads."

"From my wife?"

"Think again."

"Jerry O'Mahoney, who holds the second mortgage on this thing?"

"One more guess."

"I don't know," the man said. "We mobile home people don't have to pay any taxes on these things now. I guess I'm against independence."

"I promise you," John Hancock said, "that you mobile home people, as long as I have anything to say about it, will never have to pay taxes. As a matter of fact—"

"We'll give you a rebate," Sam said.

"Does independence mean any man will be free to marry any woman he wants and as many as he wants?"

"Independence means anything a person wants it to mean," Sam said. "That's what freedom is. Despite what *The Newark Evening News,* or for that matter *The New York Times* thinks it is."

"Well, I'm all for it, then," the man said. "When does it start?"

"As soon as we can get things organized," John Hancock said. "We are on our way to Philadelphia now to do just that and we will do it."

"If you think Trenton is a dead town," the man said, "wait till you hit Philadelphia. I heard they were thinking of moving the Independence Convention to Boston."

"No," John Hancock said. "The weather is so bad over Boston you can't even get a balloon down. If other people can stand Philadelphia for their whole lives, we can certainly take it for a few hours or for however long it takes to wrap this thing up. The times call for sacrifice upon the part of everyone. And I personally am willing to stay in Philadelphia until the cows come home."

"Not me," Sam said as they turned off the Garden City and hit the Princeton Turnpike. "Don't you think, John, we should soft-pedal this independence thing due to the poor response?"

"That man in the mobile home liked the idea. It's bound to catch on."

"But I don't think he quite knew what independence meant."

"None of us do, John. That's the whole point. These things are worked out as we go along. Why don't we just wait till we get to Philadelphia and then play it by ear."

"That's all right by me," John Hancock said, "as long as it is agreeable to everyone else."

At Princeton there was again no room at the inn. It seemed to all concerned that the Man Upstairs didn't give a tinker's damn whether the Declaration of Independence was signed or not.

"Certainly someone is trying to tell us something," Adams said.

"My ass is sore," Hancock said. "Maybe we'd better give up the whole idea of independence for now."

"No, I'm sure the manager can find us a bed in the manger."

"I don't want a bed in the manger," Hancock said. "I'm allergic to cows."

"Tut tut," Sam said. "As I said, the times call for sacrifice." He moved his horse toward the inn tavern, where the landlord was certain to be hiding. And as like as not, the landlord, a certain Howard Johnson, was a Tory, as was everyone at the time in the Colonies who owned a Holiday Inn and was thinking of building a horse-tel.

"Have you seen George Washington?"

"Yes, everyone has. Which one is he?"

"The man in the red and blue uniform who is not talking."

"You mean the one who is taller than the rest?"

"Yes."

"I think he should be the general."

"I think he thinks so, too."

"But he has never won a victory."

"But no one else has ever had a go at it."

"You have a good point."

Everybody who was nobody until now, including Hancock and Adams, had arrived in Philadelphia and taken over the State House. It was quickly agreed that due to the poor Press the idea of independence was getting, it was best to postpone independence for now and all meet right here again in a few months and

155
THE
LONG
NAKED
DESCENT
INTO
BOSTON

156

THE
LONG
NAKED
DESCENT
INTO
BOSTON

test the water again. Right now the idea was to get an army to Boston and get the war rolling so that the people finally wouldn't have any choice.

"I'm agreeable to that if everyone else is," John Hancock said.

"Have you seen George Washington?"

"Yes. Which one is he again?"

"The lean one in uniform who keeps pointing ahead."

"With a man like that, how can we lose?"

"Note his straight chin and his keen eye. I will bet on him any time of day. I cannot speak for the others, but he is my man, sight unseen."

"And when you get a look at him, you will be even more convinced."

"Do you think he objects to people staring?"

"Why should he? He has already agreed to serve with no pay. Just for expenses. Leadership is a long hard lonely road, but with all expenses paid it helps one to bear up."

"I think George Washington is a crackerjack."

"Me, too."

"I'd die for that man," an old man said.

"I will have to give it more thought," a youth of draft age said.

Anyway, the Convention was going great guns, even with independence tabled for now. Ad hoc committees were formed all over the place. Rump sessions were held without women. And things were sailing along as easy as chicken pie. The Press, or what in those days they called the Media, was not covering because there was a date conflict with the long balloon descent into Boston, which was a good reason for postponing independence for now until the war could get better Press coverage.

"I'd just as soon jump right in now."

"No, we better wait."

"It's agreeable to me if it's agreeable to everyone else."

"Oh shit," Adams said. "Try to think of some other saying."

Speaking of sayings, Benjamin Franklin had clammed up. He had become self-conscious about his sayings. Franklin had just gotten back from a trip to England with a new pair of glasses. His tax accountant had advised him to go slow on the sayings. They drew attention from the Internal Revenue Service. I know you think that a Revolution will stop the taxes, but you know and I know in our heart of hearts that nothing ever stopped taxes. So Franklin was somber at the Convention. Just sitting behind his new glasses and quietly taking over the whole show. Occasionally he would murmur approval of a saying by Patrick Henry, such as this at the luncheon: "As for me, give me a ham on rye," then after five minutes, Patrick's wise saying, "I haven't hit any ham yet." But for now, Franklin was willing to allow others to hog the show. Then, too, a saying here wouldn't bring him a brass farthing—save the sayings for the newspaper. Speaking of the newspaper, Franklin took off his new glasses and wondered what had happened to old Poxey—had he begun his long descent into Boston yet?

After ten days and ten nights the Convention was beginning to run out of gas. Everyone had said all they had to say three times and even the excitement of boredom was spent. George Washington, Samuel Adams observed, was not blowing his own horn. He was simply sitting there like a monument, waiting for people to remove their caps and bow. Wondering when his expenses would start. Wondering whether it was too late to get out of this. Wondering whether Martha had a point when she said, "Wear your winter underwear." Wondering what he would do with a bunch of ragtag misfits with no motivation other than beating the tax collector and getting out of marrying the girl next door. A loss at this time would not help his reputation. No army in the world would hire him then. Slogans were fine, but not much good against bayonets. These clowns have been talking for ten days now and ten nights about anointing me general, but have you noticed no one has done anything about it?

Franklin, ever perceptive, handed Washington his new glasses as Washington opened a message from Martha. It read: "Act nonchalant, George, as though you didn't give a tinker's damn about the generalship. I do not know whether we did the right thing in saying we would serve without salary. It sounds now as though we are too eager. To hell with it, I would just as soon go back to the farm anyway. I will abide by any decision I make, and I know you will go along as you always have. Your loving Marty."

George Washington handed back Franklin his glasses and

157
THE
LONG
NAKED
DESCENT
INTO
BOSTON

158

THE
LONG
NAKED
DESCENT
INTO
BOSTON

resumed his former pose as a granite monument. There's already talk about my being the father of my country. I wonder how that will sit with Marty. She is always one to prick my balloon. Which reminds me, that descent into Boston is overlong and taking a great deal of play from the happening here. What we need is more discipline and a sense of purpose. Franklin is getting old, and Martha's not getting any younger.

"Thanks for the loan of your glasses, Benjamin. Who's that blowing off steam?"

"Adams."

"Which one?"

"John."

"I think he wants to be President, don't you?"

"Yes."

"Who made your glasses?"

"I did."

"What with inventing electricity and the lightning rod and all those women, how do you find time?"

"Under the brow of every busy man there are bushels of time. When thee need help, go to a busy man."

"I'm sorry I asked," Washington said.

"And I didn't invent those women, George. For some un-understandable reason, women find me attractive."

"I don't understand it either," Washington said.

"It's not just my sayings."

"I hope not," Washington said.

"I can understand your being perturbed, George, having to sit here like a statue while they treat you like a mortal. These things take time. But I assure you everything will come out all right in the wash."

"I didn't ask for this job."

"And at the moment they're not going to give it to you. But always remember, no one else has a uniform."

"Knock it off, Benjamin."

"Just sit tight, George," Benjamin Franklin said, studying the next blowhard who was willing to lay down someone else's life for his own prejudices. I don't mean that, Franklin thought, but this session is getting trying.

Benjamin Franklin pounded with his gavel for law and order until his new octagonal handmade glasses shook.

"We will have no more of this nonsense," he said. "If the gentlemen will leave, the ladies are sure to follow." But there are no ladies at the Convention, Franklin thought. We must look into that little matter one of these centuries. "But," he said after the pounding of more gavel while his new glasses clattered to the floor, "we will clear out for now and get back to making the gentleman from Virginia—who I am proud to say is amongst us—the general of everything we can dig up on the morrow." Washington stood up and fled the hall in appropriate modesty among many huzzahs and a few wise-ass catcalls of "God save the King."

"I'm agreeable to it if everyone else is," John Hancock said.

"They're counting on you, Hancock, for the cash to make the war go."

"I know."

"Are you game?"

"If everyone else is."

Outside, after a session with the subteen autograph hunters, George asked Martha how it went. In your honest opinion?

"You have a lead-pipe cinch, George," Marty said.

159

THE
LONG
NAKED
DESCENT
INTO
BOSTON

twenty

But unbeknownst to Washington, Hancock, Franklin, Patrick Henry, and all ye brave, there was an unpleasantness occurring on the 17th day of June at Bunker Hill. All the King's horses and all the King's men had marched up the hill and bled down again. The King's horses and the King's men. Poxe thought, but it's not Bunker, it's Breed's Hill. The Patriots have fortified the wrong damn hill. Nathan, Gretchen, and Poxe were making the long naked descent into Boston again. But this was getting old hat to the Bostonians, who had seen this happen twice before, only to have the balloon catch an updraft or suffer a hot flash and disappear due west, climbing over the Patriots, who had not got uniforms yet, and the King's own darlings, who were decked out as pretty as a picture.

Francine was serving Colonial Big Sweet Mama Shake-ups again at the Rose and Crown, but only to the freeloaders from *The New Boston Times*. Little Brown had gone back to the Adult

Book Shoppe Henry Knox had stuck him with to pick up the latest gossip from the Rialto.

"Make my next one a Rum Flip," Braxton said.

"Don't you like my Colonial Sweet Mamas?"

"Brown makes them better."

"In the pig's ass he does," Francine said.

"Brown should stick to bartending," Lee said. "He's over his head in the book business. It's a shitty business anyway."

"The bar business or the book business?" Dilsie said.

"Any business," Lee said. "Take this business of soldiering. I can't understand why they're all out there kicking ass on each other."

"When they could be in here with a Colonial Big Sweet Mama Shake-up," Dilsie said. "That reminds me, we have got nobody in Philadelphia covering the Independence Convention."

"Brown said Revere came in with a dispatch saying they've given up the ghost on independence for now. People are having second thoughts. They would rather not pay taxes to the King with an excellent excuse than not pay taxes to their own ilk with no excuse at all. No taxation without representation is a good slogan."

"Yes, I like that," Dilsie said. "Poxey came up with that one last Shrove Tuesday when he was tanked up with elderberry wine. I said, 'Master Poxe'—I always calls him Master Poxe when he's got three sheets to the wind—'Master Poxe, you have got to write that down. I'll proof it and we can make the morning edition.' "

" 'I'm in no shape, Mistress Dilsie'—he always calls me Mistress Dilsie when he's feeling ineluctable—'Mistress Dilsie, I'm in no shape to write anything. Do we have any more elderberry wine?' "

"I said, 'No, you drinks too much, Master Poxe. Write it down. No taxation without representation. Attribute it to a source close to the Archbishop of Canterbury and blow it up to three paragraphs under a cartoon wood print by Lee showing the King eating little Colonial children and washing them down with elderberry wine filched from the Colonials.' "

" 'Mistress Dilsie, you have the makings of a great newspaperperson.' "

161
THE
LONG
NAKED
DESCENT
INTO
BOSTON

162

THE
LONG
NAKED
DESCENT
INTO
BOSTON

" 'Woman.'

" 'Newspaperwoman. When I die I want you to have the paper. Lock, stock, and barrel. Franklin's not as bad as he sounds. He'll give you the whole damn paper if you ask him. Franklin would like to devote all of his time to sayings anyway. Now that he is getting old and sees the end coming, he would like to be remembered for something more than "a stitch in time saves nine." Can you dig up another glass of elderberry, Mistress Dilsie?'

" ' So you wants to leave me the paper, Master Poxe?'

" 'Yes, Mistress Dilsie.'

" 'It's the elderberry talking.'

" 'You write this no representation without taxation thing for me, Dilsie, before Jackson of the *Globe* gets a hold of it. Sign your own name. That's a good girl.'

" 'Woman.'

" 'Woman.'

" 'I don't want those people from Southie tearing down my door.'

" 'You've got a blunderbuss.'

" 'I'll write it,' I told Poxey. We shook hands on that over the elderberry and kind of made history, you might say. That's how we got the kind of taxes we're going to get."

"Is Poxey still up in the balloon?"

"Yes."

"Poxey always said that despite the joy of flying, no two people from the *Times* were to go up at once. Too dangerous. An accident could wipe out the paper."

Paul Revere came in the Rose and Crown but he didn't order a drink. He sat near the hob next to the fire and acted disgusted with newspaper people. Mr. Revere was in a funk. His wife and children hardly recognized him. He seemed to spend all his time on the road. When he arrived in Boston from a far place, bringing strange news of exotic happenings, the people stared like posts and most walked away before he was halfway through the exciting news, and the others said, "What else is new?"

"How did things go in Philadelphia, Paul?" Braxton asked from the bar.

"I don't think you really care," Mr. Revere said.

"We do, and we appreciate what you are doing for the cause."

"I don't believe it. Do you know what happened on the Common after I broke my ass riding two hundred miles?"

"What, Paul?"

"When I made the announcement that independence was a dead duck, this joker said, 'What else is new?' I announced that a Virginian by the name of George Washington had the generalship all but wrapped up and some clown said, 'In that case it might be best to call off the war while we are still ahead.' "

"Paul, don't take it so hard. I enjoy your messages," Lee said. "How was the weather in Philadelphia?"

"Who cares?"

"I trust Martha was looking shipshape."

"How do you know about Martha?"

"The Washingtons were my neighbors in Virginia," Lee said. "She used to make candy."

"Yes, she looks shipshape," Paul Revere said, "but I didn't break my ass to report on Martha's health. You'd think people would take some interest in what is happening in the world."

There was a silence in the bar to commiserate with poor Revere. They had all known him well before he had gotten heavily committed to delivering announcements, when he was devoting himself to breeding ten kids and making excellent silver service in any time he had free. He had never advertised his silverware in the *Times*, but Poxe had been willing to let sleeping dogs lie. And said so in the paper, which further angered Revere.

"If you had been involved with a newspaper as long as we have, Paul, you would learn to accept the fact that people are not interested in any news except what their wives refuse to tell them. But at the present time in the Colonies, the daily newspaper is the only toilet paper available. They use it to wipe their asses with a vengeance to show their contempt for the Media."

"There are ladies present," Paul Revere said.

"We're not ladies," Francine said. "We're newspaperwomen. Anybody calls me a goddamn lady, I'll kick ass on him. I'm a Yale professor's daughter, I'm no goddamn lady."

"As you wish," Paul Revere said.

"I do like your silverware a lot though, Paul. You have a very real talent. Why don't you think about giving up having children

163

THE
LONG
NAKED
DESCENT
INTO
BOSTON

164

THE
LONG
NAKED
DESCENT
INTO
BOSTON

and delivering important messages and devote yourself full-time to the arts?"

"Because I don't care any more about anything," Paul said.

"Oh, Paul," Francine said, throwing down the bar rag on Dilsie's Rum Flip and coming up behind Revere at the hob and putting her arms around him. "My big strong night rider, the world's not coming to an end."

"Braxton and Lee," Paul said, "anticipated me at Lexington and Concord. I have been delivering messages for two years, and then when I get my chance to make a reputation, everything goes down the drain."

"As far as I am concerned," Lee said, "I will never mention it. You can have all the credit, Paul. If you blew the ride, it was not your fault. Then, as you say, it is not fair for you to ride for two years in vain."

"I will go along with that," Braxton said, "particularly the part about not riding in vain."

"Thank you, gentlemen," Paul Revere said, rising from the hob and throwing off Francine. "I guess I was getting paranoid. When you ride, when you bring important announcements for two years and no one pays attention, you can develop paranoia."

"What's paranoia mean?" Dilsie said. "The *Times* readers don't understand words like that. Can you give me another quote?"

"Disenchantment," Paul said.

"Still too big."

"Disillusionment."

"No."

"I have of late, but whyfor I know not, lost all my mirth, foregone all custom of exercise, and indeed it goes so heavily with my disposition that this goodly orb the earth seems to me a sterile promontory."

"That's better," Dilsie said, "but can you put that in two words?"

"Try 'pissed off,' " Francine said.

"You know, I just thought," Paul Revere said, "if I get the credit and if the British win the war, they will hang me for alerting the farmers at Lexington."

"That occurred to us, too," Braxton said.

twenty-one

Whilst Revolutionary War credits were being thrashed out in the Rose and Crown, Brown was arranging his best sellers alphabetically. The presses of *The New Boston Times* were silent. Poxe, Nathan, and Gretchen were out of reach and out of touch. The rustics under old Colonel Iz Putnam were digging into the wrong hill. It had been agreed in solemn conclave by the Patriot generals, Artemas Ward and Israel Putnam—who had not yet been fired because Washington had not yet arrived—to fortify Bunker Hill. It was a brilliant idea. Bunker Hill was 110 feet high. It commanded the Mystic and Charles rivers and the Charlestown Neck. You could even fire cannonballs into Old Southie if you felt like it. The only problem was the Patriots had dug into the wrong hill—Breed's—which was not high and not wide and commanded nothing but a girls' dormitory. Two hundred Connecticut men under Captain Knowlton marched over Bunker and onto Breed's Hill because a native Bostonian had told them, "Make a sharp right at the first whorehouse—you can't miss it."

166

THE
LONG
NAKED
DESCENT
INTO
BOSTON

When they got to the wrong hill, a young Connecticut lad wrote his mother: ". . . We entrenched and made a fort of about ten rod long and eight wide, with a breastwork of about eight more. We worked there undiscovered till about five in the morn, and then we saw our danger, being against eighty King's ships of the line and all Boston fortified against us. The danger we were in made us think there was treachery and that we were brought there to be all slain, and I must and will venture to say that there was treachery, oversight, or damn foolishness in the conduct of our officers."

But if you think the Patriots were blundering—there is a God, a Providence that protected the Patriots from themselves. Help arrived in the person of three brand-new British generals—Howe, Clinton, and Gentleman Johnny Burgoyne. The generals had arrived in Boston the morning of May 25, '75, much to the dismay of the British troops. The generals were not confined to quarantine as was Mrs. Gage, but were turned loose immediately on their own unsuspecting troops to devise a campaign to win the war in two shakes of a lamb's tail. Or as Gentleman Johnny said, "To make ourselves a little elbow room."

All the new British generals were pleasantly surprised on the morning of June 17th to wake up to the sight of the Patriots digging into the wrong hill. The British generals all marched over to General Gage's digs—Gage was still in charge—to advise him how to take advantage of this heaven-sent opportunity (God is an Englishman) to give the Patriots—all still out of uniform—a sound thrashing that they would not soon forget.

Gage said he would sleep on the idea of giving the Rebels a sound thrashing they would not soon forget. Actually he wanted to try the idea on Mrs. Loring, who was a late riser. Now, it seems ridiculous to consult a mere woman on war, but Gage knew from long experience that Mrs. Loring had her head screwed on carefully, and from equally long experience in the Seven Years' War on the European Continent that Clinton, Howe, and Burgoyne did not have their heads screwed on properly. They had turned a seven-week war into a seven-year war without half trying.

Both Pomfret and Pomeroy thought knocking the Rebels off Breed's Hill was a silly idea. "What does it prove?" Pomfret said.

"Even if you succeed," Pomeroy said, "you British will be right back where you started from."

"Why didn't you say that when all the other British generals were here?" Gage said.

"Because you didn't ask," Pomeroy said.

"Do you think it would be gauche of me to wake Mrs. Loring now?"

"It would not be gauche," Pomfret said, "but I think it might be best to let her get her sleep."

Nevertheless the two slaves and the general paced the veranda impatiently waiting for Mrs. Loring to shake a leg. They glanced occasionally at Breed's Hill toward the Patriots' mischief, and watched the civilian Bostonians assembling on all the high points of vantage for the coming show.

"If you feel you must do something," Pomfret said to Gage, "why don't you have the King's fleet fire at Breed's Hill and see what happens?"

"No sooner said than done."

The cannonading of the hill brought some cheering from the crowd. But there was some booing at this weak display.

"I would not take the booing personally," Pomfret said to Gage. "Those same fans who are booing you now will be cheering you tomorrow."

"Crowds are feckless," Pomeroy said. "It is always best to stick to the prearranged game plan worked out in the clear light of day rather than become victim of a thoughtless and ineluctable mob."

"I have often wondered what that word meant," Gage said.

"Its meaning is deep," Pomeroy said.

"And fraught with hidden danger," Pomfret said.

"I was afraid of that," Gage said. "Shall we give Mrs. Loring a poke?"

"Mrs. Loring has risen," Pomeroy said. "Even as we talk she is approaching by yon portico."

"What's all the noise, lovey?" she said. "Cannonading while I'm trying to sleep?"

"I'm sorry."

"Whose idea was it?"

"Pomfret's," Gage said.

167

THE
LONG
NAKED
DESCENT
INTO
BOSTON

168

THE
LONG
NAKED
DESCENT
INTO
BOSTON

"What's up?" Mrs. Loring said.

"The Rebels in the cloak of night dug into Breed's Hill."

"So let them," she said. "If that's what they want to do. If it gives them a feeling of accomplishment. The Rebels have had a tough time out there with nothing at all to do. Building forts gives them something to do that is utterly harmless, like building a snowman. Can't you see the Rebels are just trying to provoke their elders? The Rebels are behaving like children. Breed's Hill commands nothing. If they had their heads screwed on right they would have fortified Bunker Hill."

"Pomeroy said," Pomfret said, "that fortifying Bunker Hill was the Patriots' intention but they must have gotten turned around during the night. I've been lost up there myself."

"Then let the Rebels stay up there and freeze," Mrs. Loring said. "It is no concern of ours. They got themselves into this. Under absolutely no circumstances are we to attack the poor souls. I realize in their state they seem to be asking for it, but children behave like that. Don't let them provoke."

"But the new generals—"

"What new generals? Has Mrs. Gage arrived, too?"

"No, she is still in quarantine. Correct, Pomfret? No one has let Mrs. Gage out, have they?"

"No, I saw Mrs. Gage waving from out there on Noodles Island yesterday," Pomfret said.

"But the new generals were sent to help," Gage said. "Clinton, Howe, and Gentleman Johnny all insist that in order to save British credibility, and for our own honor and pride and in order to face our own fiz in the mirror, we must respond to the Patriots' impudence by marching up Bunker Hill and giving the Rebels what-for."

"It's Breed's Hill," Mrs. Loring said. "Don't make the same mistake the Rebels did. If it was Bunker Hill, I might go along. But Breed's Hill—who cares?"

"Burgoyne."

"Then let Gentleman Johnny march up," Mrs. Loring said. "I'll not sacrifice one of my darlings to that idiot."

"This is something," General Gage said, "that women just don't understand."

"What don't I understand?" Mrs. Loring said.

"The need to prove something."

"Prove what?"

General Gage looked to Pomfret and Pomeroy for help. But the two slaves, feeling that they were in a crossfire not of their own making, remained silent. Both their minds wandered back to Newark, New Jersey, in wonderment at why they had quit that place for this.

Gage fled the veranda and almost ran down Water Street, through the inflamed crowd, hoping to find the generals at the Rose and Crown.

At the Rose and Crown, Gage found all the generals led by Gentleman Johnny working out a plan.

"But I'm still in charge," Gage said.

"Although I am the rank by seniority," Howe said, "I am willing to let you run the show until I get over my sea legs and get the feel of the place. But I do think Johnny Burgoyne here has got a beaut of a plan, and if I were you, Gage, I'd give the plan a good going over. The crowd is getting impatient."

"I am not one to be moved by the mob," Gage said, rising to his new height, "but if Johnny has come up with a plan better than he had in the Seven Years' War, I am willing to give it a fair hearing, and if it shows that he has gotten his head screwed back on, I am, I promise you, more than willing to give it a go."

"Capital," Howe said. "Will you join us in a drink first?"

"I never drink before a battle," Gage said. "That's something I learned from the beating we took in the Seven Years' War."

"Have one for old times' sake," Clinton said.

"All right, just one," Gage said. "Now let me see the plan, Johnny. Mrs. Loring is not going to like this one little bit."

"What did you say?" Clinton said.

"I said, show me the plan to take Bunker Hill."

"Breed's."

"That's what I meant," Gage said, setting his Colonial Sweet Mama Shake-up on the corner of the topographical map.

"Let us get on with our plan to take the hill," Howe said.

"Which hill?"

"All of the hills."

"Hear, hear."

169
THE
LONG
NAKED
DESCENT
INTO
BOSTON

170

THE
LONG
NAKED
DESCENT
INTO
BOSTON

"Will you tone it down," Francine said, mopping up the spill from the Sweet Mamas. "Little Brown is trying to catch a nap. Little Brown and Paul Revere have both had a hard night."

"We didn't know."

"Now you do."

"We will be leaving in a nonce," General Burgoyne said.

"Don't run off, Johnny," Francine said.

"We will take the hill in twenty-two minutes. We must not tarry here," Burgoyne said, drawing his watch from his red waistcoat, then putting it back in its hole, "or my name is not General John Burgoyne and I never won the Seven Years' War, never wept for my King or slept with his mistress, never did anything that amounted to a tinker's damn. Back in a trice," he said, rising and clanking to the door with all the red-coated sword-swinging spur-rattling generals the King was trying to get rid of by shipping them off to the Colonies to a war that was hopeless from the start on both sides; a war that the King would have to hire the Germans to win (the King called the rent-a-soldiers Hessians so as not to offend Colonials of German extraction); a war the King had to do something strange to win because people who spoke English, regardless of which side they were on, had no common sense and the King thought them not worth the powder to blow them up. That's how the Germans got into it. The King was being accused of being bonkers, but Prince Charles of Wales said this was not true. That in point of fact, King George the Third—bless his little royal heart—was the only King around and maybe the lone Englishman who had his head screwed on properly. Prince Charles of Wales said he would put that in writing and swear to it under oath if he was not asked to testify to the King's sanity too early in the morning as he, Charles, His Nibs the Prince of Wales, was a late riser and enjoyed a chukker of polo before breakfast and could not think straight anyway before three cups of tea.

When all the King's generals were gone, Braxton wondered whether they should go along with them to the battle to get a story for the paper, or whether the whole thing would blow over when tempers cooled down in the cold light of day. "One thing is for certain," Braxton said. "The generals all could do worse than listen to Mrs. Loring."

Now the whistling of Mozart's Fourth Sonata entered the Rose and Crown. They all knew what that meant. It was Mr. Loring, Mrs. Loring's husband. Mr. Loring—the Dean of New England Poets, Lowell Cabot Loring—always whistled Mozart before entering to warn people to stop talking about him. It saved everyone the embarrassment of a confrontation. Like all Lowells, Loring was a poet, but that was not the only reason he did not object to his wife sleeping with generals. Brown, his editor, had told Loring, "Lowell, the reason your stuff will not sell is that you avoid confrontation in your work. I thought your stay in Martha's Vineyard had cured you of that, but apparently I was wrong. Your life carries over into your books and that's the problem. Why don't you go up to Gage and bop him on the beezer?"

"Fighting never settled anything."

"Tell that to King George. I've got to sell your books. People want confrontation. Show me a book without confrontation and I'll show you a clunker. You've got to have at least one killing in the first sonnet or you're dead. An editor learns the hard way. What advance did we spring for?"

"It was modest."

"I'm sure it was. Times are hard. You have got to remember Mrs. Loring's honor is at stake here, too, and you can become the laughing stock of Boston."

"That's better than being ignored," Mr. Loring said. "You said yourself that alienation was the problem of our time."

"Did I?"

What had not occurred to Little Brown, Braxton thought, was that some men, including Lowell, don't want to own a woman. Some men find this a poor wicket. Let her go out and seek her fortune and not tarry around the house till she becomes a big bore. She should have experiences. Get to know people. People in important jobs like General Gage. Mr. Loring could always whistle Mozart when entering strange places so no one would be embarrassed by being caught discussing Mrs. Loring.

Mr. Loring came in and sat next to the fire. When everyone had seen him he stopped whistling Mozart.

171
THE
LONG
NAKED
DESCENT
INTO
BOSTON

172

THE
LONG
NAKED
DESCENT
INTO
BOSTON

"How is the poetry going, Lowell?" Lee said.

"All right. How is your painting going?"

"All right."

"Do you think there will be a fracas up there on old Bunker's Hill today, Lee?"

"There could be. Braxton and I were just talking about whether or not to cover it."

"Is that what you were talking about?"

"Yes."

"Doesn't the paper have a stringer in Charlestown who can cover Bunker Hill?"

"No."

"Has Poxe gotten down yet?"

"No."

"Well, maybe he can cover the Revolution from up there in the balloon," Lowell Cabot Loring said, and he began to whistle Mozart again when he saw a stranger enter.

But the stranger was only a stranger to truth. The stranger was Scoop Jackson of the *Globe*.

"Hi, Scoop," Francine said.

Scoop was not talking.

"How does the *Globe* stand on the Revolution, Scoop?" Braxton said.

Nothing.

"They tell me, Scoop, that you have a personal tie-in with Cambridge Balloons," Lee said. "That you are going to sell balloons to the army—which army?"

Nothing.

"Scoop, if everything else fails, you can always run for dogcatcher," Francine said.

Harry Hurtz of Hurtz's Rent-a-Horse came in and sat with Scoop. Jackson and Hurtz discussed the rental business and the balloon business. Jackson seemed to have lost interest in the Revolution—it wasn't selling any papers or balloons or getting him elected to anything.

Harry Hurtz was in the process of expanding his rental business. Why should a country have to own military equipment? Guns are used maybe once every four years. Why shouldn't every country rent the guns? Take this Revolution—the Revolutionists are at a terrific disadvantage. Where are they going to get the money to buy guns? They could afford to rent but not buy. Even the British, if they thought about it, Harry Hurtz said, would rather rent than buy. After the Revolution, neither side would have any use for guns. Harry Hurtz could rent them to the next Revolution.

"What do you think, Scoop?"

"Would you be interested in buying some balloons?" Jackson said.

Little Brown came into the bar with the latest edition of Paine, a paperback that would sell for sixpence. "I don't like to hear this talk about selling the army balloons," Brown said, looking at Harry and Scoop. "It sounds like the start of a secret military-industrial hookup. I don't think this is any way to start a country."

"There's nothing secret," Harry said. "We're blabbing it all over the place. Right, Lowell?"

"Yes."

"Wouldn't you rather, Brown," Harry said, "rent a war than get stuck with all that junk? What are the Americans going to do with all that junk after the Revolution?"

"Benedict Arnold was in the shoppe yesterday. He wants to found an academy at West Point."

"So how many guns will that take?" Harry said.

"We can always use them against the Indians," Brown said.

"That reminds me," Harry said. "I could rent some guns to the Indians."

"Then there's the South," Brown said. "It might be interesting to have a war between the North and the South that would sell some books."

"A war over what?"

"We will think of something," Brown said. "I have several writers who already have some ideas on the subject. A certain Mr. Pomeroy and a Mr. Pomfret were in the shoppe only this morning. They have a book idea that should start a civil war. They're going to call the book Uncle Tom's Something—Castle, Cottage—they haven't got it yet, but Pomfret and Pomeroy don't give up easily. I hope they're not preempted on the project as Revere was."

173
THE
LONG
NAKED
DESCENT
INTO
BOSTON

174

THE
LONG
NAKED
DESCENT
INTO
BOSTON

"To change the subject, what about a rent-a-book?" Harry said.

"What would we call the company?"

"Public Library."

"Why not?" Brown said, tapping *Common Sense* on the bar. "It might give our Revolution some meaning. But it might put the book dealers out of business." Brown went about his business of making a Colonial Big Sweet Mama Shake-up. "We don't want to give the Revolution *too much* meaning at this point in time, to take a posture in terms of killing the book business," Brown indicated.

Braxton wrote these newspaper clichés and all the while Lee sketched the whole shebang. Francine and Brown tended bar. Dilsie tried to get out a paper, whilst Poxe, Nathan, Gretchen, and God sailed naked over Boston.

"Another idea," Brown said. "When my brother Big Brown was alive he had an idea to save the book business from the slump, and I haven't given it up. Big Brown's idea was to make books edible. If you don't enjoy reading a book, you might enjoy eating it. With the stale food you get during a revolution, people complain all food tastes like paper. Now paper will taste like food. If it is a western, the book will taste like horse. If it is a mystery, it will taste mysterious. If it is a sex book, that's what it will taste like. The publishing house is not to be called Little Big Brown, but the edible books company would be called The Digest Reader."

"What does sex taste like, Brown?"

"Buy the book," Little Brown said.

Poxe, Nathan, Gretchen, and God still sailed naked over Boston—no longer because they could not get the damn thing down but because something heroic was afoot. A plan to save our country from the gaudy British below—the Red Menace.

"What is the Red Menace this time, Brown?"

"Finish reading the book," Little Brown said. "If you don't like it, eat it." Brown finished making the Sweet Mama, tasted it, and decided to drink it before the American Revolution was successful and a law of Prohibition was passed against drink and all and any pursuit of happiness in the publishing business.

"The British," Brown said, sipping the Sweet Mama, "can't be all bad."

Young Wild Tom entered, heard the remark, slammed the door, and said, "When in the course of human events it becomes necessary to—"

"Have a drink," Brown said.

175
THE
LONG
NAKED
DESCENT
INTO
BOSTON

twenty-two

"The Cambridge Balloon people," Poxe said, "with Jackson of the *Globe* probably behind it all, gave us plenty of dope on how to get this thing up but nary a sentence about how to get it down. Gravity doesn't work. The balloon is part black and catches too much sun. Today is the only sunny day Boston has had in the eighteenth century and it would be the day I picked to be up in a balloon."

"You could do an editorial," Nathan Hale said, putting aside his spyglass, "on the failure of gravity in a balloon and all the ramifications of this problem. I believe the theory of gravity is an excellent one even if it doesn't work. It's nice to put things down and have them stay down. Ho, ho," Nathan said, raising his glass to his good eye, "what have ye here? It looks like a war. Fancy that."

"Let me see," Poxe said. "Move over, Gretchen, so I can have a look. Does it embarrass you, Gretchen, our being naked?"

"Not at all," Gretchen said. "Have a look."

The young Patriots below were digging into the wrong hill, any hill in a storm, as though their lives depended on it. And they did. It is surprising that country bumpkins—that was their official name among the British—could perform any military functions at all since they couldn't speak French. Most military words, particularly on fortifications—sometimes confused by the layman as fornications—are French. The French apparently cannot fight or fornicate excepting behind a wall—so the rustics had to perform functions while not having the slightest idea what they meant. Lafayette, who spoke French, knew, but he had not shown up yet, so the Patriots went ahead anyway building French things like abatis, barbette, bastion, chevaux-de-frise (crossed logs studded with spikes), demilune, épaulement, fascine, flèche, ravelin, redan (it would take an expert to tell a redan from a ravelin, although the redan is most frequently smaller), redoubt, feu de joie (not a fortification but a gun salute that relieves boredom while building), piquet, rampart, tenaille, an up-in-the-air (not a French phrase, but it is that part of a fortification or exposed flank vulnerable to attack). Colonel Conant kept looking for up-in-the-airs and checking on the spirits of the men. They were surprisingly mostly atheists before the battle and then quickly became Protestants—Protestants against the war. Some, as luck would have it, were Protestants before the war even started; mostly Church of England, but the lower classes were amply represented in the battle by Presbyterians, Baptists, Seventh-Day Wonders, Mary Baker Greenberg's Church of Jewish Scientists, and Methodists. The minority groups were represented in this fight for freedom by three Indians, three blacks, three women, and a handful of Irishmen. When it looked like the Irish would get out of hand by refusing to fight beside blacks, Indians, and women, Colonel Conant sent for more rum. Over the protest of Doctor Neat, he detailed the King of Spain and the Emperor of China for the job.

"You are young and spry and seem to have your wits about you. Run in a moment to some of the stores of Charlestown and

177
THE
LONG
NAKED
DESCENT
INTO
BOSTON

178

THE
LONG
NAKED
DESCENT
INTO
BOSTON

fetch some rum. We can't have a war without the Irish, and we can't keep the Irish without rum."

"That is correct, sir," young O'Casey said. "I am willing to fight beside the blacks, the Indians—even the lasses—if I smell the blood of an Englishman and have my bit of rum."

But let the fetchers of rum for the Irish tell what happened next in their own words: "We threw down our implements of war and run as fast as we could and passed over the hill . . . down to Charlestown Neck and found there was a firing in that quarter. We heard the shot pass over our heads, which I afterwards understood were thrown from a floating battery in Mystic River and from the shipping on the Boston side of the Neck.

"We, however, immediately passed on and went into a store, but saw no one there. I stamped and called out to rally some person and a man answered us from the cellar below. I told him what we wanted, but he did not come up, nor did we see him at all. I again told him what we wanted and asked him why he stayed down cellar. He answered, 'To keep out of the way of the shot,' and then said, 'If you want anything in the store, take what you please.'

"I seized a brown, two-quart, earthen pitcher and drawed it partly full from a cask and found I had got wine. I threw that out and filled my pitcher with rum from another cask. Ben took a pail and filled it with water, and we hastened back onto the entrenchment on the hill, when we found our people in confusion and talking about retreating, but the Irish prevailed . . . our rum and water went very quick. It was very hot, but I saved my pitcher and kept it for sometime afterwards."

Which is not very interesting, but sometimes history is dull. What was interesting and concerned our Patriots deeply at the time was that the British were firing cannonballs at them from the men-of-war in the Mystic and the Charles—the *Lively*, the *Somerset*, the *Glasgow*, the *Symmetry*, the *Cerberus*, and the *Falcon*. The *Somerset* alone had sixty-eight guns, which will give you some idea of the music they made.

The battle had commenced. Soon it would be decided who would pay taxes to whom and why. No one knew at the time the war would last till hell and gone. How could they know? Harvard took in very few people, and the only other accesses to misinformation at the time were Yale, Princeton, Dartmouth, and the *Globe*. So who can blame the Colonists? If you were alive at the time with all of the excitement, you probably would have hooked up with one side or the other. If you like your central Franklin heating, a decent carriage, and three squares a day, and are easily bored with slogans, you probably would have gone Tory, like any good American who respected ye law and order.

"As I was saying," Braxton said, "and any future poet can quote me, the fat is already on the pyre. Look at Charlestown burn. The Patriots' latest feu de joie must have touched it off, or did the British start the burning on purpose?"

"The British started it on purpose. If this paper doesn't have a policy, you end up like the *Globe*. Our policy is that everything we do is good, everything the British do is bad. You've got to keep the policy simple."

"Else what's a paper for?"

"The simple-minded."

The girls of Boston were scurrying about from Boston Neck to Beacon Hill, seeking out their finest furbelows and flirting fans to climb to the highest heights at Copp's Hill and the two-storied buildings on Back Bay and Griffin's Wharf to see the biggest show on earth. Such was the pandemonium in Boston town on this morn of battle with cannons banging from the King's fleet, women screaming, dogs barking, the King's men performing evolutions of the drill. Flags of all nations appeared on the roofs, trumpets blasted, fifes tweedle-deed, drums drummed, people stopped fornication in midflight to follow the mob (some still unpantsed), horses ran helter-skelter, the price of everything shot up to the moon, children sold themselves in the street for a bag of candy, spies from both sides circulated among the crowd in pasted-on black whiskers, Brown sold out his entire editions of *How to Stick with a Bayonet, How to Perform the Evolutions of the Drill, How to Survive a Revolution, How to Survive When All About You Are Bonkers, How to Talk to a Tory, How to Comfort a Rebel, How to Make Your Own Uniform, or the Joys of Sewing. The Poetry of Peace*, which began, "Oh, oh, I durst seek not your sweet cur-ved tits to suck if stained with battle dust/Rather I go to secret bower by yon hill to weep for Heloise and Abelard," by

180

THE
LONG
NAKED
DESCENT
INTO
BOSTON

Lowell Cabot Loring, sold not one copy, although featured in the window. The confusion in the Boston streets was so panicky that the landlords forgot to collect the rent, whores to charge for their favors; young men in the prime of life, in the flower of their youth, dashed about joining both sides and farting in the fiz of their betters. Flowers from Jamaica sold for three shillings the bouquet, up from tuppence. But oranges from Iberia went begging. More memorabilia—the churches shut up shop, Lowell Cabot Loring was moved almost to suicide, and Gentleman Johnny Burgoyne was in fine fettle even though stationed to command an artillery unit on Copp's Hill that would see no close action.

Nathan, Gretchen, and Poxe still sailed above. Mrs. Gage was still in quarantine on Noodles Island. Mrs. Loring went back to bed in spite of all the noise. Pomfret and Pomeroy swore secret oaths against both sides. Colonel Conant on Breed's Hill rued the day he had been born. Benedict Arnold wondered how he could support Peggy in the manner to which women quickly become accustomed. Benjamin Franklin was inventing a steam car. Young Tom Jefferson was not sleeping it off with a mulatto. That was a canard invented by Jackson of the *Globe* to advance his own political fortunes. Wild Tom Paine was down in the dumps with a case of laryngitis. Hancock and Adams were still holing up in Philadelphia with a price on their heads. "We shall tarry in Philadelphia until we get an agreement we can live with." Which means a tax cut across the board, no wood rationing, no proper respect for our betters. No tea except at our prices. No more fooling around in church. No more porno from England.

"I'm sick of Adams's no mores," General Gage said. "Let's cut off his head."

"That would mean a trip to Philadelphia."

"All right," Gage said, "then let's write a proclamation of our own. What's good for the goose is good for the gander. Try this: I have watched the tree of liberty grow—the vilest reptiles that crawl upon the earth are concealed at its roots. The foulest birds of the air rest upon its branches."

"No," Burgoyne said. "Something more fitting to the occasion: Whereas the infatuated multitudes in America who have long suffered themselves to be conducted by certain well-known incendiaries and traitors in a fatal progression of crimes against the constitutional authority of the state have at length proceeded to avow rebellion, it only remains for those of us who are intrusted with the supreme rule for the punishment of the guilty as well as for the protection of the loyal, to prove that we do not bear the sword in vain."

"Capital," Gage said. "Now I will send Lord Howe up Breed's Hill with the Eleventh and the Twelfth Lightfoot. You cover the advance with artillery from Copp's Hill, but make not enough noise to disturb Mrs. Loring's rest. It should all be over in two shakes of the lamb's tail and everything in the Colonies will be right as rain again and we can all get back to the business of cheating the Indians out of what's left of the country. How does that hit you, Johnny?"

"Capital."

"I already said that. Let's get this show on the road," Gage said, collecting his marshal's baton and marching off in all directions. Burgoyne steadied Gage down Water Street and ensconced him on the top floor of the Rose and Crown, where he could get a good view of the whole shooting match.

On the bottom floor of the Rose and Crown, the life blood of the Media was being drained away by rum and scarlet women on this day of all days when history of great pith and moment was being made, when the heavens were all lit up with stars of fire and the hills glistened with dews of blood; the ladies and gentlemen of the Press were *non compos mentis* and some on the floor of the Rose and Crown were *E Pluribus Unum*.

The gentlemen from the *Gazette* and the *Globe* were plastered much earlier than usual—the *Gazette* and the *Globe* had a policy against hiring women. The papers' rationale was that women could not tolerate the language of the gentlemen of the Press, to which Francine said, "I don't know what the fuck the *Globe* means by that, do you?" Francine was out on the street now, taking a Poxe poll. Should the British go up Breed's Hill? Yes? No? Maybe? Don't know? Don't care? What is your attitude toward the whole shooting match? Are you bored by the Revolution? Mildly bored? Reasonably bored? Completely bored? Don't know? Would you flee to Canada if you had the chance? As far as Detroit? As far as Ticonderoga? Bangor? Stay put? The next

181

THE
LONG
NAKED
DESCENT
INTO
BOSTON

182

THE
LONG
NAKED
DESCENT
INTO
BOSTON

question was, Do you believe in independence at this point? Partial independence? Strings attached? No strings attached? Independence but not from the British? From the British? At this point, would rather not say? Would say? Care but don't know? Know but don't care?

The most frequent answers to these questions in the order they were given were:

Are you bored by the war?

"Yes."

Should the British march up Breed's Hill?

"Yes."

Would you flee to Canada if you had the chance?

"Yes."

Do you believe in independence at this point?

"Don't know."

From the British?

"Know but don't care."

If your carriage is approaching an intersection in the right lane at rush hour and there is a carriage full of drunks crossing that intersection with the right of way, do you signal a stop? Curse the drunks? Run full blast into them?

"Run full blast into them."

Francine had expected that on the streets of Boston, taking a poll would be like pulling teeth. But the people, particularly around Beacon Hill, piled all over her to give their opinions on everything.

At what time do you think sex should be discussed with your children? Before the Revolution? After the Revolution? Not at all?

"Not at all."

If your answer to the above was after the Revolution, leave this space blank. If before the Revolution, then should discussions of sex be limited to the genitals? Of course? Maybe? Know but would rather not say?

"Know but would rather not say."

What is your feeling about Hancock and Adams? Who? Hate them? Love them? Adore them? Would hang them? Would not hang them?

"Who?"

Francine was getting bored with interviewing civilians and thought that it would be of some historical interest, even if Poxe disapproved, to interview the British soldiers before they went up the hill.

Most of the British soldiers on the Boston Common were smartly performing the correct evolutions of the drill, much to the delight of the Tories, who cheered every bit of choreography in the book and some the soldiers created on the spot. The Tory cheering section was a Boston symphony in itself; the world will never see their like again. The civilian Patriots, on the other hand, could see nothing happening that would help the cause. It might mean the end. The British soldier ballet was so impressive, so breathtaking, Patriots' hearts sank to their boots so that they appeared to be standing in mud. And all Patriots wondered how even the bravest of the brave on yon hill could stand up to this royal ballet at the opening day of their American tour. Maybe it would be best to call it off until the Patriots had more practice at the evolutions of the drill.

The British were busy going to war, not only performing the drill but packing their bags with all sorts of things. A change of clean underwear. Four pairs of socks. Smoke sunglasses. A book. A map. Playing cards. Writing supplies. An astrology chart. A pet cat. Dear John letters. And some ammunition thrown in for luck. Not that each soldier carried all these things, Francine observed, but they were divided up among the whole lot. The British, having had much training in the Seven Years' War, knew what to take and what not to take. The Patriots were always at sixes and sevens as to what to take and what not to take, discarding a pitchfork here and a bowling ball there (a bowling ball can be used in a cannon and a pitchfork comes in handy during a retreat). The British knew all these things and they knew that that is all ye need to know about a war. The Patriots would learn, Francine thought, at the expense of much time and sorrow and several bullets up their ass.

I am making no hay here, Francine thought. The soldiers refuse to be quoted directly and I'm fed up with "sources close to the corporal revealed to this reporter" and all that "indicated to this reporter" lying bullshit. I think I will cross the bay and find out if the Patriots have anything to say of historical interest. I can

183

THE
LONG
NAKED
DESCENT
INTO
BOSTON

184

THE
LONG
NAKED
DESCENT
INTO
BOSTON

hear my grandchildren say, "Grandma Francine, don't tell us any more about the goddamn war for independence. Tell us again about the time you were a whore in New Haven." My father only taught at Yale, but the young find that dull—so maybe I will pep it up a bit, throw in a few lies about how I made thirty shillings in four minutes and discovered a new way of life. Plain·ordinary people like you and me might be interested to know what people thought about just before they got their ass blown off in this Revolution. For a cause. For no cause. Those are the saddies that history always skips and I will try and nail down, Francine thought. That and those others who happened to be in Cambridge today and just went along for the ride and are the first to admit it.

Francine went back to the Rose and Crown to borrow that pound note from Dilsie to bribe the Tory spy boatman who was running a ferry to Charlestown—"to a place where you can see the Revolution as clear as day"—but Dilsie said no.

"Shake your ass for the boatman," Dilsie said back at the Rose and Crown. "Don't give him no money, just roll your tits. I know that Tory spy. Tell him you're a friend of Dilsie and he'll take you to Paris, France, but don't give that Tory son-of-a-bitch no money and don't tell him you work for *The New Boston Times.* He'll want an arm and a leg, the spying bastard."

So Francine left without money, but Dilsie's fame had preceded her and the Tory spy broke his ass to get Francine across the bay in time for the Revolution.

twenty-three

It was a glorious day on Charlestown Peninsula, June 17, 1775. The crocus were in bloom, and the iris and King George Rose that Bunker and Old Breed had planted were running wild all over the place. So it was as though God had decorated the arena with all the flair and color in His power to make this a day to celebrate, mourn, and remember.

Francine ran into a gang of Minutemen from Waterbury, Connecticut, who were lost near Breed's brick kiln on the main road to the Neck.

"We're not exactly lost," their leader said. "We're just getting out while the getting is good. No one dug in on Bunker; they're all over on Breed's Hill with a bunch of officers who've got shit for brains."

"Well, it takes time for the Patriots to get things straightened out," Francine said. "All the officers are new at this game."

186

THE
LONG
NAKED
DESCENT
INTO
BOSTON

"We found that out," their leader said.

"Maybe she's got a point, though," a corporal said. "We didn't give the officers much of a chance. Maybe when the battle starts, they will fight like lions."

"I would want good odds," their leader said.

"Old General Iz Putnam looked like he knew his ass from a hole in the ground."

"He didn't to me," the leader said.

"Well, there's nothing to do in Roxbury," the corporal said, "and we told all the girls we were going off to a war for freedom. What are we going to tell them now? And your mothers. You know how the women cried. I don't have to tell you, Sergeant; you were there."

"All right," the sergeant said. "Who wants to fuck and who wants to fight?"

"You know there is no fucking in Roxbury, Sergeant. I don't have to tell you that—you were there."

"All right," the sergeant said, blowing into his musket powder pan to clear it. "Who wants to fight under officers who got shit for brains?"

"I object to the phrasing of the question," a young man with a Yale accent said.

"All right, who wants to go back to Roxbury?"

The vote showed nobody wanted to go back to Roxbury.

"All right," the sergeant said, "but don't say I didn't warn you." And they all wandered off to Breed's Hill with Francine bringing up the rear.

"You can see," another private from Yale told Francine, "I am Stover of Yale. The man who objected to the phrasing of the question is Buckley of Yale. You can see on what unhistorical arguments wars are fought. If Roxbury had been a viable alternative, if there were interesting and/or fuckable people in Roxbury or even a good restaurant, there would have been no war today and possibly and/or tomorrow. So we would still be a part of England a thousand years from now if New England were not such a bore, so unbearably dull. Most of us fighting would settle for a small piece of ass or a good card game as a viable alternative to killing each other, but New England will not supply this and never will. And by the time all the boys discover this they will have had their fun and won the Revolution and it will then be too late. I don't think Old England will ever take New England back, do you?"

"No, and I expected Yale men to talk on a more elevated plane," Francine said. "Has my father had no influence on the school at all? But go ahead with your problem."

"There will be no second chance. We will have to put up with New England forever and ever with no help at all from the British. They will say, 'You made your bed, now sleep in it.' All we can answer is that independence sounded like a good idea at the time. A viable alternative," young Stover of Yale said.

"Buck up, Buckley," Francine said.

"No, I'm Stover of Yale. That shithead back there is Buckley."

"Well, anyway, I think that after the war you will realize, Stover, you did not die in vain or something."

"I do not plan to die in vain or something," Stover of Yale said. "I plan to duck off at the next crossroads and hightail it for Canada. Why do you think I joined you in the rear?"

"Don't be obscene," Francine said. "You didn't join me in the rear. We are simply walking to the war together. We met quite by chance and you decided to desert. Do you think whoever wins will grant amnesty to deserters after the Revolution?"

"Oh God, I hope not," the Yale man said. "You know, I never thought of amnesty happening," Stover said. "I'll be right back in New England in the same kettle of fish. Maybe I should fight now and get it over with. Do you believe fighting a viable alternative to living in New England?"

"I work for *The New Boston Times*," Francine said. "We're not supposed to have an opinion."

They came to the crossroads now at Breed's Meadows. One road led to Canada, the other to Breed's and Bunker Hill—life on earth as we know it.

"I don't know," Stover of Yale said, standing stock-still at the crossroads, "which way to turn."

"Well, don't lean on me, Stover," Francine said in the deadly quiet before the battle. "If it were me, I would toss a coin and settle it."

"I don't have a coin."

187
THE
LONG
NAKED
DESCENT
INTO
BOSTON

188

THE
LONG
NAKED
DESCENT
INTO
BOSTON

"Neither do I," Francine said.

"In that case we'd better join the bunch," Stover of Yale said, turning toward the battle. "They tell me it's cold as hell in Canada anyway."

So for the want of a coin the Revolution was won, Francine thought.

At Breed's Hill, the Patriots had built a gorgeous series of forts, considering that they had never done it before.

There was a Frenchman, the Emperor of China told the King of Spain, by the name of Redan who specialized in building forts. His trick was to build a perfect style of fort that was impossible to take and then develop a way to take it. Then from what he had learned from that, he would build a better fort. That is how the art of fort-making evolved into what it is today. All the credit is due to André Redan and very little to us.

Francine quit this profane discussion on the art of war to make her way to the rear. She did not quit the battle in pique or petulance in protest over women being excluded from Harvard and everywhere else. She quit the battle because Poxe had warned her not to risk life and fair limb until the paper had discovered which way the ball was bouncing.

So Francine drifted to the rear on this memorable day, June 17, 1775, and would have nothing to tell her grandchildren of particular interest excepting the whore in New Haven experience. Which was not true.

But even now, reinforcements were arriving in the form of Braxton and Lee. Dilsie had remained behind to hold the fort, and Gretchen, Nathan, and Poxe were still up in the air, without lunch but getting a bird's-eye view of the whole shebang.

"Didn't you think to bring lunch, Gretchen?" Poxe said.

"No, I brought no lunch," Gretchen said. "Are women supposed to remember everything of importance while men's minds wander?"

"Yes."

"Well, I've got something in a doggie bag left over from Franklin's dinner. You know how Benjamin's mind wanders when he's thinking about electricity and he is supposed to be thinking about eating."

"Let us see what Franklin did not eat," Poxe said.

Franklin had not eaten a ham on rye, one-half slice of dill pickle, and something that looked like potato chips he was personally inventing and never ate whether he was thinking about electricity or not. A half-bowl of soup and a quarter-tankard of ale were also left for the doggie bag.

"But how did you get the soup and ale into the doggie bag?" Nathan said, resting on his spyglass and thinking.

"I didn't," Gretchen said. "I just wanted to tell you, although unable to show you, how bad Benjamin's appetite is since he got back from Paris. He used to be able to eat like a horse."

"I know," Poxe said. "He never used to leave anything for the doggie bag. All of the dogs, women, and slaves in his house are as thin as a rail. But be that as it may, let us eat what he left this time and thank God for small favors in spite of Gretchen's forgetfulness. Then we can get back to the Revolution. If that is agreeable to everyone? We don't seem to have any choice, do we? We can't get this damn balloon down, can we? But I have an idea," Poxe said. "An idea that will not only put the *Globe* and Jackson out of business, but as an added attraction, win the Revolution. I hate to do this to the British. Some of my best friends are British."

"Go ahead and do it anyway," Nathan Hale said.

189

THE
LONG
NAKED
DESCENT
INTO
BOSTON

twenty-four

As we have already learned, Francine seems to have disappointed us by moving to the rear. Dilsie was still back holding the fort, and Lee and Braxton were going to the war as fast as the Tory boatman could get them there. But no one of our direct concern was at the first battle foray, so let us turn it over to someone who was actually there for a change. Not some historian or some fiction writer penning bullshit about just before the battle, mother, but a certain Robert Trent who was on that hill when the British came up like the thunder 'cross the bay:

"Some of us became frightened and ran. We do not know whether those who stuck to their guns did so because they were more frightened of being frightened than actual fright. We will never know. The eternal mystery. But God bless everyone who stuck and may their souls tarry in peace. Each of them."

Or Peter Brown's account: "About nine o'clock at night we marched down to Charlestown Hill . . . and about half after five in the morn, we not having about half the fort done, they began to fire (I suppose as soon as they had orders) pretty briskly a few minutes, and then stopped, and then again to the number of about twenty or more. They killed one of us, and then they ceased till about eleven o'clock, and then they began pretty brisk again; and that caused some of our young country people to desert, apprehending the danger in a clearer manner than the rest, who were more diligent in digging and fortifying ourselves against the cannon. We began to be almost beat out, being tired by our labor and having no sleep the night before, but little victuals, no drink but rum. . . .

"They fired very warm from Boston and from on board, till about two o'clock, when they began to fire from the ships in the ferryway and from the ship that lay in the river against the Neck to stop our reinforcements, which they did in some measure. One cannon cut three men in two on the neck of land. Our officers sent time after time after our cannon from Cambridge in the morning and could get but four, the captain of which fired but a few times and then swang his hat round three times to the enemy, then ceased to fire.

"It being about three o'clock, there was a little cessation of the cannons' roaring. Come to look, there was a matter of forty barges full of regulars coming over to us. It is supposed there were about three thousand of them and about seven hundred of us left, not deserted, besides five hundred reinforcement that could not get so nigh to us as to do any good hardly, till they saw that we must all be cut off, or some of us, and then they advanced.

"When our officers saw that the British regulars would land, they ordered the artillery to go out of the fort and prevent their landing if possible, from which the artillery captain took his pieces and went right off home to Cambridge as fast as he could, for which he is now confined and we expect will be shot for it.

"But the enemy landed and fronted before us and formed themselves in an oblong square, so as to surround us, which they did in part, and after they were well formed, they advanced towards us in order to swallow us up. But they found a chokey mouthful of us, though we could do nothing with our small arms

THE
LONG
NAKED
DESCENT
INTO
BOSTON

192

THE
LONG
NAKED
DESCENT
INTO
BOSTON

as yet for distance and had *but two cannon and nary gunner.* And they from Boston and from the ships a-firing and throwing bombs keeping us down till they got almost round us."

Now from a British officer's point of view, a Captain Rawlings: "Our troops advanced with great confidence, expecting an easy victory. As we were marching up to attack, our artillery stopped firing. The general on inquiring the reason was told they had got twelve-pound balls to six-pounders, but that they had grapeshot. On this, he ordered them forward and to fire grape.

"As we approached, an incessant stream of fire poured from the rebel lines. It seemed a continued sheet of fire for near thirty minutes. Our Light Infantry were served up in companies against the rock fence without being able to penetrate. Indeed, how could we penetrate? Most of our Grenadiers and Light Infantry the moment of presenting themselves lost three-fourths, and many nine-tenths, of their men. Some had eight and nine men a company left, some only three, four, and five.

"On the left, Pigot was staggered and actually retreated. Observe, our men were not driven back; they actually retreated by orders."

Now Gentleman Johnny Burgoyne's point of view from his vantage point on Copp's Hill: "As our first arm advanced up the hill, they met with a thousand impediments from strong fences and we were much exposed. We were also exceedingly hurt by musketry from Charlestown, though Clinton and I did not perceive it till Howe sent us word by a boat and desired us to set fire to the town, which was immediately done . . . our battery kept an incessant fire on the height. It was seconded by a number of frigates, floating batteries, and one ship of the line.

"And now ensued one of the greatest scenes of war that can be conceived. If we look to the height, Howe's corps ascending the hill in the face of the entrenchments and in a very disadvantageous ground was much engaged. To the left, the enemy pouring in fresh troops by thousands over the land, and in the arm of the sea our ships and floating batteries cannonading them. Straight before us, a large and noble town in one great blaze. The church steeples being of timber were great pyramids of fire above the rest. Behind us, the church steeples and heights of our own camp, covered with spectators of the rest of our army which was not engaged. The hills round the country covered with civilian spectators . . . The roar of cannon, mortars, and musketry, the crash of churches . . . and whole streets falling together in ruins to fill the ear; the storm of the redoubts . . . and the reflection that perhaps a defeat was a final loss to the British Empire in America to fill the mind, made the whole picture a complication of horror and importance beyond anything that ever came to my lot to be witness."

Braxton and Lee, when they got to the hill, wanted to know why some Patriots ran and others did not. It was easy to get a convincing story from the deserters. Certainly those who had been hit by cannonball were not feeling up to snuff and those who had been stuck through with a bayonet were no longer eager about war. People like this had an excellent reason to advance to the rear. But what about those who threw their muskets away at the first crack of the first shot? Like Thomas Hardly from Maine: "My damn gun would not work. I got a flash in the pan three times straight. I do not know who sold these guns to the army but they should be shot. But it is probably myself who will be shot for desertion. My only hope is that the firing squad that shoots me will use the same guns from the same manufacturers who should be shot. I hope that my firing squad gets these guns that flash in the pan also."

Albert Flax said he quit the redoubt because of a family problem.

Lyle Wilkins said he ran because he just realized what war was like.

Dick Helms because he wanted to think things over.

David Willard because "I am a born coward and it's too late to change now."

James Reed said, "It's a damn silly question to ask."

Braxton and Lee finished the interviews and ensconced themselves on Bunker Hill across from Breed's Hill under old farmer Bunker's wild cherry tree. They were eating cherries to quiet their nerves when Braxton had the sudden idea to bottle the cherry juice and sell it as a cure for fornication after the war. Wild cherry juice spiked with three-fourths alcohol. Women drink a lot more than people realize. With this concoction a

193
THE
LONG
NAKED
DESCENT
INTO
BOSTON

194

THE
LONG
NAKED
DESCENT
INTO
BOSTON

woman can say, "I feel a touch of fornication coming on. I think I'll take a shot of Braxton's Wild Cherry Piss without anyone being the wiser." A cannonball whizzed by. After the war you could set up a Cherry Piss factory in New York and another in Boston to cut down on the shipping costs. "I'd better stop calling it Braxton's Cherry Piss or people will not take the product seriously. What do you think, Lee?"

A hailstorm of British bullets passed overhead.

"I think you are frightened," Lee said. "That you are scared and you are trying to brave it out—here, have some more cherries."

"Do you think old Bunker will object to our stealing his cherries?"

"When I was a lad in Virginia," Lee said, "as I told you before, the Washingtons lived over the mountain from us in Vernon. Everyone said that young George was a fine lad but he was addicted to chopping down cherry trees. After chopping the tree down, George would march up to the person who owned the cherry tree and tell them, even before he was asked, that he could not tell a lie, that it was his very nibs that had done it. There were no reform schools at the time, so George went scot-free. I don't see how old farmer Bunker can object to our eating his cherries when no one in the Colonies objected to, or at least couldn't make a case against, George chopping whole damn cherry trees down. George used to throw coins, too, across the Potomac as though money were going out of style. Some neighbors who lived on Vernon Mountain said George was just another spoiled rich kid who would never amount to a hill of beans. My family always said that George would grow out of it and that every kid deserved a second chance. Our parson named Weems said there was enough good material in George for a book."

"Who's scared now?"

"I admit I'm scared," Lee said, looking up from his drawing and watching the bloodied Patriots pass. Lee made notes on his drawing to denote the color scheme that he would fill in later. First it would go as a black and white block print for the paper—HORROR AT BREED'S HILL. Then he might get a silkscreen print out of it, or when there was time, a painting in oil or watercolor. After the war there would be a market for this kind of memorabilia by an artist who was here.

"I should have stuck to my guns and gone to Paris to study," Lee said. "Instead of that, my parents insisted I go to Harvard and I gave in. If I didn't go to Harvard, they said, I'd end up like the Washington kids and never amount to a hill of beans. I should never have gotten into newspaper work. It's nothing but a way to make a quick shilling, but with only a Harvard education, there aren't many opportunities available. Haven't you noticed, Braxton, that after you have been in the newspaper game for a few months, you wake up one morning believing the stuff you wrote?"

"Yes, I guess that's why everyone else thinks we're crazy. To get a better understanding, everyone should be forced to work for a newspaper for a few days, then they would be in a position to forgive and forget. Notice, Lee, that the Patriot retreat is in full swing. I think I have enough copy on why the deserters took off. Dilsie can headline it WHY THE FLEERS FLED. I'd like to get something now on WHY THE STAYERS STOOD for the next day's follow-up. We have got to be careful what we write, because the readers will get what Poxey calls a truth feedback from their friends and relatives who were here. That can be very threatening to a paper's credibility. In the French and Indian Wars the truth feedback almost put the *Globe* out of business. Poxey never forgot that. Poxey always says no matter what happens to put you off the track, a good seasoned newspaperman will stick as close to the lie as possible, so that the people who were here will finally be convinced that they were not here. You're aware, I know, Lee, that no one has won a battle in this war yet and maybe never will. Try to tell the dead on both sides on Breed's Hill they won and see what they say. But the paper insists on a victor even if it means the battle goes into overtime. I'm going to get an on-the-spot interview with some of those who stood. Try to get a quick face sketch of them for me, Lee, as they talk."

A bloodied Patriot with red hair to match staggered up and placed his gun against the tree carefully as though he owed his life to it. "Shit," he said.

195
THE
LONG
NAKED
DESCENT
INTO
BOSTON

196

THE
LONG
NAKED
DESCENT
INTO
BOSTON

"Where are you from?"

"Waterbury."

"Why did you stand? Not retreat ass over teakettle?"

"It's interesting that you should ask that question."

"Well?"

"Every man will have to go through the experience himself to find out. The normal tendency in battle is to run away ass over teakettle, but I suppose there are those of us who are not normal, who have a tendency to tarry. It could be some childhood experience we are blocking out, some innate tendency to tarry, but we should not rule out damn foolishness simply because the word has been overdone. I don't see why I should tarry here and deprecate myself for *The New Boston Times* after risking getting my ass shot off for the Revolution, do you?"

"No."

"I'd better run along. The British are right behind me, or they were a moment ago," he said, picking up his musket.

"Don't rush off," Lee said. "Have some cherries."

"I hope we haven't said anything to offend you," Braxton said. "Do have some cherries."

"No," the red-haired Patriot said. "I enjoyed our little talk. But I'd better run along or my wife will wonder what happened to me. I told her I was going to drink some beer with the boys or go down to the Mystic and fly a kite. You know how women worry when they hear there's been a Revolution."

"Can I get your name?"

"No, remember," the Patriot said, wiping his musket stock red with a bloodied handkerchief and moving off, "remember I am supposed to be flying a kite."

"Of such enigmas and quick images are wars made. You couldn't print that; no one would believe it. It's true, as Poxey always says, you have got to stick to the lie, otherwise the reader will think the paper is crazy. As Poxey says, what does the public want? My God, what does the public want?"

On the other side of Bunker Hill waited Francine for the boys from the *Times*. Now that all the redoubts on Breed's Hill had been taken by the British, the British were chasing the American defenders round and round Bunker Hill, trying to capture whoever was left or stick some Patriots for good measure. The Patriots were going so fast round and round Bunker Hill that many were thrown off the hill by centrifugal force, landing in the Back Bay or Charlestown none the worse for wear. A British sergeant who had just lost a Patriot to centrifugal force came up to Francine, who was composing rhymes to kill time in a strawberry patch. The British sergeant placed his long spontoon against Francine's breast. A spontoon is a long lance with a blade and spear on the tip used by officers on both sides because a sword is worthless in battle, merely something carried to dazzle the peasants and impress the ladies on your time off. A spontoon is thought by some to be a symbolic extension of the penis, but as our Colonel Conant warned, it can also be used to chop off your head or make a hole clear through you, depending on the mood of the spontoonist.

"Get that damn spontoon off me," Francine said.

The spontoonist, a certain Sergeant Reed from Liverpool who had taken the King's shilling after a drunken night in Bristol, was not to be put off by Francine's words. He had had a very frustrating day, trying to get up Breed's Hill and chasing the Patriots round and round Bunker with nothing to show for it.

"Remove your furbelow," the sergeant said.

"I durst not," Francine said, pulling her furbelow even tighter.

There had been many contradicting editorials recently in both the *Globe* and the *Gazette* on how to foil a rapist. The *Times* itself had been quiet about rape, which was becoming endemic in the Boston area excepting Hahvid Yahd where nothing happened one way or the other. Jackson of the *Globe*, after the *Times* had been quiet too long, accused the *Times* staff of being at least partly responsible for the rape boom.

The *Gazette* had advised Francine and all Colonial dames to pull on the attacker's yonker and scream. The *Globe* said in an article by Doctor Glanders that if you pull on an attacker's yonker and scream, you are done for. You might as well cash in your chips. And anyone who advised that kind of nonsense should be put in the stocks and remain there till the cows come home. And then they could be released for a short time to do the milking and then clapped right back again. You pull his yonker at your own peril. The American Medical Association, which had just this

197

THE
LONG
NAKED
DESCENT
INTO
BOSTON

198

THE
LONG
NAKED
DESCENT
INTO
BOSTON

very week established its first chapter in Boston, advised paying your fee in advance and then asking advice. So Francine, along with all Colonial dames, was caught in a quandary, what with the *Gazette*, the *Globe*, and the American Medical Association pulling and tugging at each other and the *Times* remaining suspiciously silent. It left a young girl at sixes and sevens about how to cope, particularly in a neat strawberry patch with a soldier's spontoon pressing her.

"All right, knock it off," Lee said. "You've had your fun."

Sergeant Reed of Liverpool turned, as though he had been struck smartly, to face a likely looking lad of about five and twenty with soulful blue eyes that seemed to be searching for something in an odd way. He was well built and wore a purple buskin and yellow pantaloons such as you might see among the youth group any Saturday night at the Rose and Crown. But there was something in his eyes, something that a philosopher or even Doctor Glanders would find difficult to explain—something soulful—that caused the British sergeant to relax his grip on his spontoon.

"You've had your fun," Lee said. "Let's just call it a day and let bygones be bygones."

"If you think it was fun to go up Breed's," the sergeant said, "with everyone in the Colonies shooting at you, you have another think coming."

"He has a point," Francine said.

"Do you always have to take the side of the British?"

"Fair is fair," she said. "After all, Lee, it was me who was being stuck with the spontoon. It was my virtue that was at stake. He has had a very hard day and was confused. It's not every day everyone in the Colonies takes a shot at you. Call it temporary insanity. Then he's probably read books telling how soldiers rape everyone in sight after a battle. Blame the books, blame Little Brown, Lee. Blame yourself, Lee. You are part of *The New Boston Times* that remained silent on the subject."

"I'm sorry," Lee said to the sergeant. "You have had a very hard day. I didn't catch your name?"

"John Reed," the sergeant said, extending his hand. "Do you know this young lady I was spontooning and about to rape?"

"Yes," Lee said, "she is an old colleague of mine."

"Cut the old, Lee," Francine said.

"I'm sorry. I didn't know," Reed said.

"I be Amos Lee," Lee said, "of *The New Boston Times*, and this be another colleague, Isaac R. Braxton. Braxton, this is Reed. Reed is with the British Army. Reed, this is Braxton. Braxton is with the *Times*."

"Then ye be all with the *Times*," Reed said. "What brings you here?"

"The Revolution."

"Can I take a look at your spontoon?" Braxton said. "I have never seen a spontoon close before. Just pictures."

"We're not supposed to loan our spontoon to anyone," Sergeant Reed said. "Lord Percy's orders."

"Lord Percy is not around now."

"All right, I guess it don't do any harm," Sergeant Reed said, passing his spontoon to Braxton.

"This is quite a gadget," Braxton said. "Who invented it? Did Franklin have a hand in it?"

"No, it's an old weapon," Reed said. "It was supposed to be obsolete a long time ago. I believe it was used by the Athenians in the Peloponnesian War."

"Well, the Peloponnesians knew a thing or two," Braxton said. "This would have punched quite a hole in you, Francine, if Lee and I had not come up in the nick of time. Was the spontoon widely used in the Seven Years' War?"

"Yes," Sergeant Reed said. "You know, come to think of it, Lord Percy told us to mop up on the Patriots before they all escaped to Roxbury. Can I have my spontoon back?"

Braxton held on to it, examining it.

"Give him his spontoon back, Braxton," Francine said.

Braxton passed back the spontoon.

"Pleased to have met you," Reed said. "Wait, here's my card if you're ever in Boston. I'm with the Seventeenth Lightfoot."

"If you're ever in the vicinity of the Rose and Crown, give us a buzz," Lee said.

When Reed disappeared around Bunker Hill, Braxton said, "That's about the nicest rapist I ever met."

199
THE
LONG
NAKED
DESCENT
INTO
BOSTON

twenty-five

Pomfret and Pomeroy, being very decent chaps who had the luck to be brought up in a decent household and taught all the virtues in Newark, New Jersey, were not corrupted by Boston or the latest saying by either side. They were of course tilting toward the British, because with all the talk of freedom and liberty by the Patriots, there had been no talk of abandoning slavery. Not a whisper.

Today, while General Gage was occupied by the unpleasantness at Breed's Hill, Pomfret and Pomeroy decided to take Gage's launch to Noodles Island and do what they could to succor and comfort Mrs. Gage in her quarantine there.

The distance between Griffin's Wharf and Noodles Island on a foggy day is about seven miles. On a clear day it is slightly more, don't ask me why. Gage's launch was manned by eight Spaniards captured in the Seven Years' War. That must mean, Pomfret thought, there was one good year when the British captured two. Today, the 17th of June, 1775, was a foggy day and the Spanish slaves had been fed an extra ration of rum so the distance to Noodles Island was covered in jig time.

Mrs. Gage caught the rope on the landing dock and told them the quarantine master was in bed with a case of mumps. She said she had contracted mumps herself since she had been held in quarantine and she had seen the firing on Breed's Hill and the burning of Charlestown and wondered "what all the fuss was about."

"The man is fighting a war," Pomfret said.

"What about?"

"First we want to make you all comfy in bed with a nice cup of tea," Pomfret said. "The idea of your coming down to the dock in your condition is beyond all bounds of reason. A great deal has happened since you have been at sea and we will fill you in, but now you must avoid a death of cold. Do you have any mustard plasters?"

"No."

"Any living relatives who should be notified in case you kick the bucket?"

"General Gage."

"We've already thought of him," Pomfret said.

"You two think of everything," Mrs. Gage said, leading the way to her two-bedroom white Colonial cottage on a hill overlooking a cabbage patch.

"Do you grow cabbage now, Mrs. Gage?"

"Only when I feel like it," she said, "but I am dying to know what all the fuss is about on the mainland."

"After we get you to bed with a nice cup of tea," Pomfret said, "we will tell you such tales that will make you stop up your ears, weep for your King, and make every woman rue the day she ever gave the lineaments of life to a male child. Black or white, red or yellow."

"The times are out of joint," Pomeroy said. "O cursed spite that ever we were born to set them right."

"Wait," Mrs. Gage said, stopping on a knoll in the midst of a

201

THE
LONG
NAKED
DESCENT
INTO
BOSTON

202

THE
LONG
NAKED
DESCENT
INTO
BOSTON

budding hawthorn bush. "You both, Pomeroy and Pomfret, have led much too sheltered a life. As household slaves you have been protected from reality. You probably read Latin and Greek and know the Bible backwards, but I was brought up in the army and the ways of the world do not shock me. Males are on this earth to stay, at least for the time being, and we must make the best of it."

"You should have seen what the man did on Breed's and Bunker Hill this afternoon," Pomeroy said.

"I know only too well the manner in which men are capable of behaving," Mrs. Gage said, "but women must learn to take the good with the bad."

"Yes, I suspect both Pomeroy and myself," Pomfret said, "have been overprotected from the vicissitudes of life and have concluded wrongly, it seems, that people the world over should be as kind, considerate, and thoughtful of others as they be in Newark, New Jersey."

Mrs. Gage explained Noodles Island to Pomfret and Pomeroy as they made their way up the narrow path strewn with honey-suckle and wild rose to the white cottage. The path commanded a perfect view of the King's fleet and Dorchester Peninsula. You could still see the tea slick from the latest tea spill in Boston Bay that was ruining the beaches. With so many tea ships running the British blockade, there were bound to be collisions in the dead of night. Not since the all-male Boston Tea Party, where the men got their jollies polluting the bay, had conditions been this bad.

But Mrs. Gage, too, pointed out the amenities of being on Noodles Island. There was peace and quiet here and a chance to think. True, the supply of books was limited and there was no gossip excepting an occasional note in a bottle from a ship-wrecked sailor on Manhattan Island. But there were compensa-tions in a life of quiet ease and contemplation away from the hustle and bustle of modern eighteenth-century life.

"I suspect I was not made for these modern times," Mrs. Gage said.

They arrived at the cottage just in time to avoid a rain shower, and Pomeroy and Pomfret set about making Mrs. Gage comfy. There was wood to be brought in, a fire to be made. The cat to be let out. The goldfish to be watered. The grandfather clock to be wound. Letters to be read and answered. Prayers prayed. Hymns sung. Turning stones that had been left unturned. Righting wrongs. Catching up on the fan mail and doing all those things that are neglected when a person has the mumps.

But at last Mrs. Gage was all comfy in bed with a nice cup of tea and said, "Now tell me what all the fuss is about on the mainland."

Pomfret put aside *Paradise Lost*, which he had been reading aloud, removed his glasses, and said, "You would not believe it, madam."

"Try me," she said.

"Do you remember a John Hancock and a Samuel Adams?"

"Yes."

"A Henry Knox who had the bookstore before Brown? A Benjamin Franklin who owns part of the *Times* and flies a kite frequently—something to do with electricity?"

"Yes."

"Do you remember a young man from Virginia, a Thomas Jefferson who writes well and who Scoop Jackson claims travels with an attractive mulatto named Sally Hemings?"

"Yes."

"A man who always shows up in uniform, his name has slipped me."

"Washington," Mrs. Gage said.

"A financier named Haym Salomon?"

"Yes."

"Two radicals, a white named Tom Paine and a black named Crispus Attucks?"

"Don't keep me in suspense," Mrs. Gage said. "What manner of trouble have these people gotten into this time?"

"They have started a Revolution," Pomfret said.

Mrs. Gage twitched a tear from her eye and Pomfret brought her a glass of gin to quiet her nerves.

"I suppose it had to happen sometime," Mrs. Gage said. "The children leaving their mother country. But Americans could not have picked a worse time for this divorce. Everyone in the Ministry has a touch of gout and King George himself is crazy and in deep trouble with his mistress."

"I am sorry," Pomfret said. "We didn't know. Have another sip of gin. I'm certain if the Colonists knew about this at the time

203
THE
LONG
NAKED
DESCENT
INTO
BOSTON

204

THE
LONG
NAKED
DESCENT
INTO
BOSTON

they would not have started the Revolution. These things can always be put off."

"Prince Charles of Wales tried to assure me personally that the King is not crazy, that the King is simply being discreet," Mrs. Gage said. "I had Lord Randell arrange an audience for me with the King on his mistress's day off. The King struck me as being crazy as a bat."

"Not as a bedbug?"

"No, as a bat," Mrs. Gage said.

"That is a pity," Pomfret said. "Can I get ye another tot of gin?"

"Yes, I could stand another slug," Mrs. Gage said. "It's not every day you are hit with a Revolution."

"A touch of vermouth?"

"I'll take it straight."

"One or two olives?"

"Hold the garbage," Mrs. Gage said. "Tell me, Pomfret," she said from her mumps bed, "how is Mrs. Loring doing?"

Pomfret pretended interest in the gin.

"I said, what in the hell is Mrs. Loring up to?"

"Tut tut," Pomeroy said. "Don't get excited in your condition."

"I'll get as goddamned excited as I please," Mrs. Gage said, rising from her bed of pain where Pomfret and Pomeroy had placed her and striding to the window in her gold wrapper and looking out over her cabbage patch, over the Boston Bay browning with the latest tea spill, looking over Boston itself and all the way to the mischief on the mainland.

"Hell, I don't care what Mrs. Loring is up to," Mrs. Gage said. "I couldn't care less. Gage is a lousy lay. I apologize for the language."

"Tut tut," Pomfret said. "I'm sure you exaggerate."

"All generals are lousy in bed," Mrs. Gage said, tapping her now empty gin glass on the windowsill.

"I'm sure that is an unfair generalization," Pomeroy said.

"The hell it is," Mrs. Gage said. "Clinton is lousy, Howe is lousy, Braddock was lousy, God rest his soul in peace. Burgoyne is—well, Gentleman Johnny is not bad if he puts his mind to it."

"You see," Pomfret said, "although everything is not peaches and cream, everything is not topsy turvy either. Pomeroy and myself like to think positively. I am sure that we can't lump all generals into one bed. I am certain generals vary in their sexual performance as much as people."

"Not so."

"You came up with General Burgoyne."

"I did? It must be the gin. Johnny is no prize catch either. Goddamn that Mrs. Loring, who in the hell does she think she is? Excuse the army language, gentlemen."

Pomfret and Pomeroy got Mrs. Gage back to her bed of pain and propped her up with pillows so that she might see the latest tea spill and any mischief that might occur on the continent. "How is Madame de Tocqueville doing?" Mrs. Gage said. "Has she got Lord Percy's ass in a sling yet with her military advice? You must excuse my language, gentlemen."

"Madame de Tocqueville," Pomfret said, opening up John Milton's *Paradise Lost* again, "is in fine fettle. Now why don't you see if you can get a little rest?"

"I don't want any goddamn rest," Mrs. Gage said. "What else happened when I was at sea?"

"Well, the American Colonists are trying to write a Declaration of Independence from England in Philadelphia."

"What balls the Colonists have," Mrs. Gage said.

"No, Mrs. Gage, dancing is not permitted in Philadelphia."

"What balls they have," Mrs. Gage repeated.

205
THE
LONG
NAKED
DESCENT
INTO
BOSTON

twenty-six

Poxe had just told Nathan, Gretchen, and God that there would be hell to pay if they did not get down in time for the Declaration of Independence. Where were you, Daddy or Mommy, when the Declaration of Independence was signed? We were naked over Boston.

At this very moment, Hancock and Adams, Jefferson, Franklin, Paine, and the whole gang were busy as bees scurrying in and out of the State House in Philadelphia, trying to make head or tail out of all of the suggestions that were piling in. Spies from the British Central Intelligence Agency were there in false beards, planning to invade from Sheep's Bay if the Declaration came off.

The Un-British Activities Committee was there with bells on, taking down names and bribing porters to go through Tom Jefferson's wastebasket and Franklin's pockets, and noting what women left whose room at the William Penn at what time and why. The BCIA were confused by their own false beards, wigs, and noses and bribed each other and pummeled each other in dark alleys and stole secrets from each other and had each other arrested and thrown in jail. They arranged prostitutes for each other with excursions on Delaware Bay. They kidnapped each other and laundered money in the Delaware River with which they bribed each other, and the danger, Jefferson said, was that once this thing gets started in the States it's going to be tough to stop. The Colonial Bureau of Investigation, the CBI, was ever on the alert to catch a Revolutionist, and followed each other around in sundry and interesting cloaks and disguises at great cost to the King, but of much entertainment to the theatrically-minded Philadelphians. But the Colonial Bureau of Investigation was not all thundersheet and clowns. It was headed by a fathead named J. Edgar Coolidge, from Delaware and Lackawanna who kept a file a yard thick on each of the members of the Continental Congress, telling who slept with who and all the whys and wherefores.

"And it still exists today—those files, that is," Franklin said, putting down his pen with which he was improving Thomas Jefferson's first draft of the Declaration of Independence. "The Colonial Bureau of Investigation, the Un-British Activities Committee, and the British Central Intelligence Agency are hot after us Revolutionaries. Are you sure you want to go through with this, Tom? You don't want to take off for Canada while the going is good? The King, being a forgiving monarch and wanting to bind up old wounds, I am sure will give amnesty all around as soon as things blow over. The King really only wants to nail Hancock and Adams. What do you say? Last chance." Franklin picked up Jefferson's rough draft of the Declaration of Independence. "All right, if you want to push ahead with this scheme, Tom. You say here in your first statement, 'A Declaration by the Representatives of the UNITED STATES OF AMERICA in General Congress assembled.' Is that really what you want to open with? It doesn't quite turn me on. Now you go on to say, 'When in the course of

207
THE
LONG
NAKED
DESCENT
INTO
BOSTON

208

THE
LONG
NAKED
DESCENT
INTO
BOSTON

human events it becomes necessary.' What becomes necessary, Tom? All right, here we go: 'for one people to dissolve the political bonds which have connected them with another'—not bad, but kind of a dull opening, don't you think? What about, 'Resistance to tyranny is closeness to God'? What about, 'Liberty is born in the blood of Patriots'? Too strong? You think that might cut down on volunteers? No mention of blood at this point? All right, now you go on to say, 'which have connected them with another.' Another what, Tom? You don't finish the sentence. I would put a period there. And I wouldn't be afraid to start the next sentence with 'And.' 'And to assume among the powers of the earth the separate and equal station to which the laws of nature and of nature's god entitle them, a decent respect to the opinions of mankind requires that they should declare the causes which impel them to the separation.' That's kind of long-winded, Jefferson, and badly punctuated, don't you think? Why can't we just say what we want to say and get on with it? I wish Tom Paine was here. Not that I don't appreciate the time and effort you put into this, Tom, but if you expect the delegates from Massachusetts to understand anything but one-syllable words, you've got another think coming. Now why don't we just skip that and get right into: 'We hold these truths to be self-evident that all men are created equal,' whatever that means. Don't mention that to Hancock, Tom. Are you sure you don't want to include women here too? Still mad at them? 'And are endowed by their creator with certain inalienable rights; that among these are life, liberty, and the pursuit of [property?] happiness.' I like that change. The pursuit of happiness sounds sexy. And now you go on to say, 'That to secure these rights, governments are instituted among men, deriving their just powers from the consent of the governed.' Now doesn't that mean, Tom, that every Tom, Dick, and Harry will have as much say as we do? Not that I think we're any great shakes, but don't you think we should put some kind of qualification in there—a poll tax or something? They're doing that in the South already, according to Washington. George wouldn't like much the idea of having to ask every male redneck's consent whether or not to declare war on the Indians. All right, we'll just let it go as a good phrase. I'm sure the President will declare war on anybody he wants to anyway, without asking around. Are you getting tired, Tom? All right, we'll put this aside for now and get back to it in the morning. I hope none of this leaks to the Press."

"Well," Dilsie said at the bar of the Rose and Crown, "we have got to get out a paper somehow, some way, which means we have got to cut down on the booze and get going into a long descent into Boston that will sell papers. The cash flow is nil. What do you think, Brown?"

Little Brown put down his bar rag and leaned across the rum to Dilsie. "I always told Poxey to have a newspaper made up and ready to go in case something like this happened."

"In case Poxe was unavoidably detained," Braxton said.

Francine came in and said she had last seen Poxe's balloon trailing in the direction of Noodles Island, but it had dropped some notes at Copp's Hill and she had them here and would read them if everyone would shut up.

Mr. Loring stopped whistling Mozart.

"I am over you now," Francine said, reading Poxe's note, "both literally and figuratively. My friends and colleagues Gretchen and Nathan are standing by like faithful dogs in my hour, days, of trial. This must be a historic moment for all of us (we must be setting some kind of balloon record). I would appreciate it very much, to use an expression of Francine's, if you would get off your Puritan asses, stop lolling at the Rose and Crown, and get a paper out. Headline should read: EDITOR POXE REPORTS BRITISH STOPPED AT BUNKER HILL BUT PATRIOTS SEEM OUT OF STEAM AFTER RETREAT FROM TOP OF HILL TO BOTTOM OF OTHER SIDE. PANIC. PANDEMONIUM. BLAME LACK OF PRACTICE IN EVOLUTIONS OF DRILL. PATRIOTS WERE OVERCONFIDENT. INITIAL REPULSE OF BRITISH BLAMED IN DISASTER. GENERAL ARTEMAS WARD WOULD LIKE REMATCH. TROOPS WERE OUT OF CONDITION. TOO MUCH WHORING, DRINKING BLAMED. DISRESPECT FOR OFFICERS. CONTEMPT FOR GENERALS. WOULD LIKE TO GO HOME. WAR NOT FUN AFTER ALL, PRIVATE INDICATES. MANY COULD JUMP TO BRITISH IF BETTER OFFER MADE. THE REVOLUTION SEEMS TO HAVE HAD IT FOR NOW. MUST BE BETTER WAY TO EARN LIVING, WOUNDED SOLDIER HINTS. MAYBE KING NOT TOO BAD, DYING PATRIOT INDICATES. REVOLUTION MAY BE CANCELED

209

THE
LONG
NAKED
DESCENT
INTO
BOSTON

210

THE
LONG
NAKED
DESCENT
INTO
BOSTON

"Here's another note Poxe dropped at Atley's Wharf:

"SPOTTED GEORGE WASHINGTON COMING TO THE RESCUE. PASSING THROUGH NEW HAVEN. FINE FIGURE. SHOULD INSPIRE CONFIDENCE DESPITE 0 AND 5 RECORD IN FRENCH AND INDIAN WARS. WASHINGTON HAS EARNED SOBRIQUET HONEST GEORGE THROUGH CONFESSIONS OF CHERRY TREE ACTIVITY. GEORGE ACCOMPANIED BY SMASHING LOVELY WAGON DRIVER NAMED KAY WINTERS, BUT GENERAL INSISTS MARTHA WILL FOLLOW WITH CLEANING PARAPHERNALIA AFTER THE WINTER THAW. MARTHA RELUCTANT TO FACE NEW ENGLAND FUEL SHORTAGE. WASHINGTON INDICATES TO THIS REPORTER THAT INDIANS' WOOD CARTEL INTOLERABLE AND COLONIES WILL NOT SUBMIT WILLY NILLY TO ECONOMIC STRANGULATION AND FREEZING TO DEATH. INDIANS OFFER TO BUILD SAWMILL BY BARNSTABLE'S ARTSY-CRAFTSY RESIDENTS. THE SMOKE IT WOULD CAUSE AND INDIANS' WAR WHOOPING AND LIVING IN TENTS WOULD THREATEN PROPERTY VALUES. ALMOST AS BAD AS LIVING NEAR THE IRISH, OUR OWN DISTINGUISHED NEW ENGLAND LITERARY FIGURE LOWELL CABOT LORING WAS HEARD TO COMMENT

"Dilsie," Poxe's note went on, "see if you can tear down the makeup for tomorrow's paper and print this. I believe that our readers are more afraid of the Indians that they know not than the British that they know too well. Plus the fact the Colonists are more afraid of freezing their asses from the Indian-caused wood shortage than having their asses shot off by the British. Think about this. But print it. Things go well enough up here, considering the altitude. Nathan is learning to spy, and Gretchen and I have fallen in love. I assure you it is not puppy love. After all, I am forty-one going on forty-two and Gretchen is eighteen going on nineteen, and that all adds up to a lot of years. It is not something brought on by the high altitude. We have both given it a great deal of mature consideration, and God willing, we plan to marry soon after we descend. If she can get an annulment from the rustic in Maine. I don't believe their marriage was consummated. Gretchen doesn't think it was. Something happened one night, but she suspects it was Indians prowling around the place that dropped something. Dilsie, don't print the part of this note about Gretchen and me. Use your own judgment about Washington's affair and Martha. We don't want to get sued. All the *Times* needs now is a lawsuit. Can't you say someone close to general indicated, or it was learned from a usually reliable source? Dilsie, we all miss you and the gang. Nathan regrets he can't be with you. And if we should die up here or in trying to land in Boston, apologize for me to those two, Braxton and Lee, for calling them dumbos. I am sure they will both be heard from when our country settles down. Maybe Lee should stick to painting naked women and Braxton should write historical novels. Anyway, I don't believe newspaper work is their cup of tea. It certainly has been hard on me. Anyway, encourage them for now until the newspaper can meet a decent payroll and we can steal some men like Jackson from the *Globe*. Dilsie, I am counting on you to get out tomorrow's paper. Are you covering the independence thing? Until we make our descent into Boston, I remain your loving Poxey, Editor in Chief, Somewhere over Boston."

"Well," Dilsie said, tapping her plumed pen on the bar and staring at Braxton and Lee. "Poxey has mixed several stories as well as several metaphors in his dispatch. It will take a lot of editing. He started with Washington's triumphal entry into New Haven, then he had to throw in some bits about George's love life to pep it up. And then out of the blue he brings in the fuel shortage and gets in his opinion about the Indians and his prejudice against the Irish, then he bitches about our not covering the independence thing. Who does he think is willing to traipse off to Philadelphia this time of year with no expense account to listen to a lot of radicals cook up a document no one can understand. I don't think there is reader interest there, do you, Braxton?"

"I believe the paper has a responsibility to print what the reader should know."

"Balderdash," Dilsie said. "What do you think, Lee?"

"I go along with Braxton."

"You two sticks together, don't you? What do you think, Francine?"

"Well, I suppose the paper should have some relevancy, Dilsie."

"I never heard of a paper making any money with that attitude," Dilsie said. "I see now why Poxey picked me to take over. I can understand why the *Globe* does so well and that New York paper that prints all the news that's fit to throw out. *They*

211
THE
LONG
NAKED
DESCENT
INTO
BOSTON

212

THE
LONG
NAKED
DESCENT
INTO
BOSTON

gets ahead in this world. Still, I don't want to run over you," Dilsie said, going over and warming her hands at the fire. "We will mention independence on the back page and promise a Monday morning follow-up. By that time the readers will be so excited about Washington's grand entry into Boston they will have forgotten what the war is all about. Agreed? Does that make you all happy? Lee, I would like a picture of the New Englanders freezing to death from the fuel shortage and the Indians living it up in the forest with all that wood to burn. Braxton, do a piece on the Indians' offer to build a sawmill on Naragansett Bay and mention all the garbage that would be dumped into the ocean and spoil the beaches just when the New York crowd are beginning to think of Massachusetts as a cheap place to live. Say something good about the Indians, but bring in how they are being misled by the British into thinking they own this country and can charge anything they want for their wood. Mention Indian economic strangulation of the Colonies again, but not from left field. Francine, do a tearjerking piece on how all this is going to affect women. Lay off the propaganda stuff about women's rights. The men will shut this paper down the first peep out of us. Despite the fact that the British Intelligence Agency will help our cause if they think women will spread chaos in America, we had better lay low on our consciousness-raising activity until all the men are committed to killing each other. Then we can stop sucking and start biting, but for now just stick to the things women are supposed to be interested in, like having a lot of babies that will starve to death if the high prices continue, worrying about their loved ones at the front who aren't paying a pence in alimony, and wondering whether to sleep with an American or a British soldier with all the feedback you get from the natives no matter which way a girl jumps. Put in all that bilgewater you usually find on a woman's page. I figure if we can't beat the *Globe*, we will join them. I think that's the way Poxey would want it. Now can we have a moment's silence to implore Providence or whoever is running things that our prayers will all be answered and Poxey et al. will make a successful descent into Boston?"

"I don't know," Braxton said, "whether I want Poxey to stick his oar in right now. You're doing a good job, Dilsie. What do you think, Lee?"

"Poxe can stay up there a while as far as I'm concerned," Lee said.

"Francine?"

"I'm willing to give a moment's silence for the old son-of-a-bitch," Francine said. "If that's all ye want."

"The ayes have it."

"Don't I vote?" Brown said.

"Go ahead."

"Aye."

"You, Lowell?"

"Aye."

"Braxton and Lee?"

"Aye."

"The dog?"

The dog barked aye.

"The ayes have it. And if there are no objections from the floor, it be so ordered. We of *The New Boston Times* do observe one minute of silence to implore Providence and/or those responsible to bring back our loved ones in one piece so that we can get on with the war in peace. Amen."

All of the people in the Rose and Crown got up and shook hands with each other and made small talk and then moved over to the fire and congratulated Dilsie on her new job. Dilsie warned Francine to keep obscenities out of her copy until after the war. Charles Vasherton—or was it Washington?—she had learned was a straight arrow who might close the paper down if he had a good excuse, particularly if he was getting a bad Press. "I have nothing against the new general," Dilsie told Lee, "but we will have to watch our 'p's' and 'q's' until we see which way the wind blows. I would like to do an in-depth human interest story on the new general before Martha shows. You know how wives put words in their husbands' mouths. Anyway, I think Charles—or is it George?—will be more open with us without Martha."

213
THE
LONG
NAKED
DESCENT
INTO
BOSTON

twenty-seven

Benedict Arnold came in the Rose and Crown with a British Central Intelligence agent. The BCIA man was disguised as a young girl prostitute just in from Morristown, New Jersey, and trying to learn the ropes. It was an excellent cover. Lowell Cabot Loring began whistling Mozart. Dilsie went through the book-store to the *Times* room and sat at Poxe's editorial desk. Benedict Arnold followed her, and the BCIA man in the guise of an amateur prostitute sat opposite Lowell Loring and listened to Mozart.

"Sit down, Arnold," Dilsie said, first clearing his chair of busted pica type. "What's on your mind? First tell me why you're running around with the BCIA."

"It's a girl I picked up on the Boston Common. She is new in the city. You think she's with the BCIA?"

"*He* is with the BCIA. A Charles Colton. We are thinking of doing a feature on him and blowing his cover. But Poxe thinketh he's more important to us alive than dead, so we're sitting on it. What can I do for you, Benedict? Are you still looking for a job?"

"Yes."

"Money is awfully tight, Arnold." Dilsie reached down to the lower drawer of the desk and took out the application file and looked for an "A" for Arnold, "B" for Benedict. "Here we are," she said. "Assistant Ethics Professor at Yale. How does that pay?"

"Poorly."

"Still, there's hopes for tenure."

"Yes."

Dilsie tapped her forefinger on Arnold's file. "I feel I should warn you, Arnold, that the newspaper business can be rough, not exactly the place for ethics. Bad language. A rough business."

"I am sensitive to that. What does it pay?"

"Moderately."

"How moderately?"

"In round figures?"

"Yes."

"Well, Poxe gave me a pound note before he went up."

"Well, that's pretty good," Benedict Arnold said.

"I want to warn you," Dilsie said, "that Poxe does not throw pound notes around like straw." Dilsie shuffled Benedict Arnold's file. "To put it mildly," she said.

"Ye think I should think about another business?"

"To put it mildly," Dilsie said. She went through the file until she found "H" for Hale, "N" for Nathan. "We had another Yale chap in here the other day, a likely Jewish lad, a Nathan Hale. Mr. Poxe had no opening but suggested spying. Something like that wouldn't interest you?"

"No."

Dilsie flipped through Arnold's file. "I see you have a good

215
THE
LONG
NAKED
DESCENT
INTO
BOSTON

216
THE
LONG
NAKED
DESCENT
INTO
BOSTON
recommendation from Francine's father. Although I see he adds as a footnote, 'Not to be trusted.' What do you suppose he meant by that?"

"I haven't the slightest idea," Arnold said. "Probably a pet peeve."

"What does Francine's father teach?"

"He is a Professor Emeritus in Creative History."

"Any good?"

"I took his course for credit."

"Duller than shit? Excuse the newspaper language, Arnold. If you hang around Francine, that's the way you gets to talk."

"Francine's father tends to ramble," Arnold said, "but he did convince me that all history is creative. It's just that some is duller than others."

"An interesting point," Dilsie said. "You know, Arnold, I'm intrigued with your curriculum vita. Assistant Professor of Ethics. A perfect cover."

"For what?"

"Traitor," Dilsie said.

"I am insulted, madam."

"What are you doing out with the BCIA?"

"A girl I picked up in the Common, that's all."

"If you got a job on the *Times*, it would give you access to a lot of important misinformation."

"I am insulted, madam."

"I believe in getting to the point, not kicking shit around—pardon the language. I have self-confidence. I learned self-confidence from a parson's son in Punkhatasset that I blew apart. You see that blunderbuss?"

"Yes."

"Well, until I used it on the parson's son he had self-confidence. He attacked every girl in Punkhatasset. He always got right to the point."

"May I go now?"

"No," Dilsie said, "you stay right here, Arnold. I'll be back in a minute."

Dilsie left the office, crossed through the bookstore without a nod to Brown, and went into the Rose and Crown, noticed the BCIA man was missing, and got Braxton away from Lee and told him to go down to the BCIA office and run a check on Chuck Colton. "Something fishy is going on," Dilsie said. "I think there's a story."

"When I finish my drink."

"Now," Dilsie said.

When Dilsie passed back through the book shoppe, Little Brown wanted to know what was up. "Later," Dilsie said.

When Dilsie entered the *Times* office, there was Benedict Arnold standing next to the press with her blunderbuss pointing at her.

"Are you sure you're doing the right thing?" Dilsie said.

"I believe so," Arnold said.

"Well, there is no charge in that blunderbuss," Dilsie said. "That blunderbuss was standing in the corner with the muzzle down, which means in any blunderbuss that the shot will run out. That's one of the reasons the blunderbuss is obsolete."

"I didn't know," Arnold said, putting the blunderbuss aside. "But you had no right to insult me."

"Insulting people is part of the newspaper game, Arnold. You will have to get used to it, particularly if you plan to get into public life. Now you will have to run along. I am a busy man—I mean woman. As Francine says, my consciousness still needs raising. If you're looking for work, Arnold, the new general—Vasherton I think his name is—will be in town tomorrow. Look him up. He is hiring big. Congress has loaded him down with money."

"Money?"

"Yes. How are things with Peggy? Still expensive?"

"How did you know?" Arnold said from the door.

"The *Times* knows everything, Arnold, but we won't print it if you behave yourself."

Arnold slammed the door, knocking down some of Brown's best sellers.

And Brown is pissed, Dilsie thought.

Braxton hurried along Prince Street to get to the BCIA office before they closed. Prince was crowded with Redcoats still coming back off Breed's or Bunker Hill. Their traffic clashed with the usual office-closing Boston traffic at five o'clock. They should

217
THE
LONG
NAKED
DESCENT
INTO
BOSTON

218

THE
LONG
NAKED
DESCENT
INTO
BOSTON

stagger off-hours, Braxton thought. He noticed, too, how many carts were going by with only one driver, which clogged the traffic. There should be a public transit system, Braxton thought. Here it is already the eighteenth century and we still haven't got around to solving our urban transit problem. And look at the smog.

When Braxton got to Chuck Colton's BCIA office, Colton was still there, but his secretary had already left and Colton was reaching for his coat. On the wall along with the coat, Braxton noticed, was all the working paraphernalia of the profession. Fake beards in three distinguished colors, including, for some strange reason, green. I suppose in case camouflage is needed in a haymow, Braxton thought. There were also pinned to the wall, each in its proper place, false teeth, false eyes, false noses, false breasts, and false penises in sundry sizes. A horse's head that could be slipped over your own. Goat horns and a horse's ass that attached to the rear. But the *pièce de résistance* that took up the centerfold of the wall and distinguished a national organization from a mere private detective outfit were several sets of false pubic hair in astounding measurements but subtle shades, all marked PROPERTY OF THE BCIA.

"Have a seat, Braxton," Colton said.

"I want to hit you with this right away, Colton," Braxton said. "What were you doing out with Arnold?"

"Arnold is a dumbo," Colton said, combing down his real hair. "If Arnold told you I picked him up on the Common, he is telling you the truth for now. But Arnold is a dumbo."

"But if you abuse a man like that, it can lead him to take desperate measures."

"I am not responsible for that," Colton said. "Why should you care, anyway? It will make you a good story whatever happens to Arnold. A newspaper should be neutral. Or are you taking sides?"

"Maybe I am taking sides," Braxton said.

"That's bad business," Colton said, sliding his comb in his back pocket. "We British are going to win this one and then you'll be up shit creek. Another thing, Braxton. Stay out of that balloon Poxe is spying on the British with. We plan to shoot it down. The BCIA already has twenty-eight million pounds to salvage the balloon from the bottom of Boston Bay and discover the secret of what holds a balloon up."

"Twenty-eight million pounds?"

"Yes. Parliament was against the idea, but the BCIA stole the twenty-eight million out of petty cash. Just because Parliament was elected by the people, Parliament has somehow got the strange idea it should run the country. Another point, Braxton. No matter who wins this one, it's not important."

"No?"

"No, we men are simply killing off each other. It's all in the family. It's a form of male genocide. We don't know what causes it. The important war is being lost."

"You mean the women are quietly taking over?"

"Not very quietly," Colton said. "Look around your office. Notice anything happening? Who ordered you to come and see me? All right, after the war when the men have stopped killing each other, the men will come to their senses and fire some of the women, but not all. By that time some of the women will know too much and will spill the beans. Other women will be the only ones who know how to run the country. Those that are fired, you notice, keep very quiet so as not to draw attention to themselves until the next war. Women believe in two steps forward and one step backward. That's the motto of their Revolution. They're patient bitches; in a couple of hundred years and ten more wars, women will be in the driver's seat."

"I haven't noticed anything unusual," Braxton said.

"Look around, Braxton, you're fighting the wrong war. Do you care for some snuff?"

"No, I don't use it," Braxton said.

"Getting back to your Benedict Arnold," Colton said. "We British can use him, but only if he gets a good job with the Patriots. His price is very high, you know. Peggy is into him for a fortune. Don't believe all his Professor of Ethics at Yale bullshit. We checked him out. And while I'm at it, Braxton, try to discourage young Nathan Hale from going into spying on the British. We wouldn't want to hang a nice Jewish boy like that."

"He's not Jewish."

"We don't want to hang anybody," Colton said. "We would

219

THE
LONG
NAKED
DESCENT
INTO
BOSTON

220

THE
LONG
NAKED
DESCENT
INTO
BOSTON

like to stop this war right now. Can't you speak to Washington? Get a ceasefire?"

"I'm afraid it's too late," Braxton said. "George has already made up his mind."

"Could you get at him through Martha?"

"Martha is mad at the Tories. They've been cutting her at parties. Why didn't the British give Washington a commission? I think at one time that would have kept him happy."

"Because the British Ministry is made up of damn fools," Colton said. "Are you getting a story out of this? Does what I'm saying make any sense?"

"I'm getting something, I guess," Braxton said. "I don't know what Dilsie will think of it."

"What a woman will think of the idea of a ceasefire? There's your Revolution, Braxton. I've got to be running along. Don't go up in the balloon."

twenty-eight

The good people who had been writing the Declaration of Independence had not been remiss. They were still going at it hammer and tong. They also serve who only sit and write. Whilst the boys on both sides were traipsing up and down Breed's Hill, Franklin was not only inventing things but editing Tom's independence copy as well.

Whilst Washington marched to the rescue at Boston and Mrs. Loring pondered military problems with Gage, Dilsie was deep into tomorrow's editorial and a signed column of her own as well.

In England, King George the Third was considering

222
THE
LONG
NAKED
DESCENT
INTO
BOSTON
options—a tax rebate to the Colonists or a wood tax or fuel rationing, giving women the vote or putting all women in jail, arresting George Washington or making George Washington King of the Colonies, making a Colonial infant phenomenon Ambassador to Ghana or enforcing the Townsend Act excepting the tax on tea to show the King was fair but still had balls, eliminating the tax on tea or doubling the tax on fuel. In other words, the good King was carefully examining all of the options in an English mountain retreat among the snowballs, and he then told Lord North he planned to take his program to the American people and ram it down their throats. "Let the American people themselves decide who's crazy now," King George the Third said.

"That's a good title for a song," Lord North said. "But all kidding aside, Your Majesty, shall we withdraw our troops from the Colonies? Send over some German troops? Cancel all Colonial taxes? Tax the hell out of the Colonies? Send the infant phenomenon to Ghana? Keep a low profile and hope that everything blows over?"

"I vote for keeping a low profile and hoping everything blows over," King George the Third said, placing a snowball on his nose and sipping a nice cup of tea. "I'm sick of all these options. I think Washington is trying to make a name for himself, don't you? Why didn't we give him a commission and pick up his expenses? No one told me he was a free agent and could have been picked up on waivers. Why doesn't Franklin go back to inventing things? Jefferson to his mistress? John Hancock to his insurance business? Washington to lecturing his three or four hundred slaves on freedom and liberty? The infant phenomenon to acting? Sam Adams back to jail? The American newspapers to printing a word of truth for a change of pace? I will tell you why, my dear minister—because the Americans are bored and I have absolutely no one to blame for that but myself. Instead of attending to the Empire, I have been living it up with Minnie MacGregor, the Scottish Firecracker, and I must confess I have enjoyed every minute of it and hardly missed the Empire at all. Have you noticed how nice and quiet it's been around the palace without an empire? I may resign. Let the Colonies stew in their own juice. What will America do when they haven't got King George the Third to kick around any more? On second thought, send more troops. See if you can get Parliament to appropriate three hundred and seventy-five million more pounds. Our credibility is at stake. It's the domino theory. If America goes, then the whole Empire will go down the drain."

King George the Third tossed his snowball to Lord North and all the royal retinue retired to the King's mountain retreat to have another nice cup of tea.

Meanwhile, Pomfret and Pomeroy had left Noodles Island, but not without promising the ailing Mrs. Gage to fetch Tom Paine for company. Young Wild Tom would read to her from his new book, *Common Sense,* and try to get her mind off the trouble on the mainland and help her forget her mumps and Mrs. Loring and get a good night's rest.

Right now, Dilsie was probably the only one in the British Empire with her mind on the ball. But she was trying to get out a newspaper, meet tomorrow morning's deadline, meet a payroll, while seemingly everyone else in the Empire was shooting at everyone else for ducks. Half the staff of *The New Boston Times* was sailing around in a balloon. The other half was supposed to be getting an in-depth interview with George Washington, but they were probably at the Rose and Crown with Little Brown, guzzling Colonial Big Sweet Mama Shake-ups. But Dilsie was being unfair and wrong, which is excusable because she was under the stress of getting out the *Times* by herself.

Unfair and wrong because even now as Dilsie accused Francine, Lee, and Braxton with curses not loud but deep, our heroes were approaching their rendezvous with he who would become—unbeknownst to them at the time or they would have been more prompt—the Father of Our Country. True, they were discombobulated. Poxe had cautioned them some time ago that Washington, being from Virginia, had a deep Southern accent. That there would be a problem in communication. That Washington would say "woe," meaning war, and "y'all," which translated into English means everyone. But our heroes had a fall-back in Lee, who had been brought up near Vernon and had spoken Southern fluently before Harvard had ruined him. With a little practice it would all come back.

Outside of Hartford, Washington sent ahead a line of skir-

223
THE
LONG
NAKED
DESCENT
INTO
BOSTON

224

THE
LONG
NAKED
DESCENT
INTO
BOSTON
mishers and some snipers to clear out the Press. After three shots, Scoop Jackson took off. Then Washington's press information officer rode up to our heroes on a swift sorrel mare and told them that the shooting at the Press was all a mistake— inoperative; that the general did have a word for them.

"What's that?"

"No comment."

"We broke our ass to get out here to Hartford," Francine said. "We don't want to talk to a wise-ass information officer. If the general has his eye on being the Father of Our Country, the least he could do is tell us where he stands on the issues."

"The general is new at this job," Washington's press officer said. "Why don't you give him an opportunity to get it all together without making a damn fool of himself? As for the general having his eye on being the Father of Our Country, remember he didn't ask for the job. You can quote the general as follows: 'I could not pass the cup when destiny and a lot of people I know made this plea to my honor, my courage, and my debt to this time and place for which I will forever be grateful, keeping in mind I didn't ask for the cup in the first place, and in the second place—' "

"Did he say that?"

"That's what he indicated," the officer said. "Now why don't you newspaper people clear out and let us get on to Boston and get a good night's sleep?"

"The British Army is in Boston."

"They told us in Philadelphia the British had been beaten at Bunker Hill."

"At Breed's Hill, and try to remember Breed's Hill and Bunker Hill are not in Boston. They are out on the Charlestown Peninsula," Lee said.

"Why didn't someone tell us this?" the press officer said.

"And the Patriots," Francine said, "got their ass whipped on Breed's Hill and Bunker Hill. They ran all the way to Roxbury."

"Why didn't someone tell us this?" the officer said. "All they told us were lies about the body count. Apparently the Patriots killed more British on Bunker Hill than there are people in England. In Philadelphia, everybody is celebrating the end of the war. Revere told us when the British tried to go up Bunker, the Patriots mowed them down like hay."

"That's true," Francine said, "but the British kept a-comin'."

"Well, this puts a new light on everything," the officer said. "I don't know whether or not we want to go ahead with this thing. Do you mind waiting while I go back and tell the general what's happened? I'll only be a trice."

"Quick ass," Francine said.

The press officer turned and said, "You ladies and gentlemen represent the—"

"*Times*," Braxton said.

"The general will appreciate this information in terms of the lies he heard about Bunker Hill in Philadelphia, and I trust he will have something to say to you in terms of appreciation."

"We would feel honored," Braxton said.

In a long trice the officer was back with General Washington. And Washington was everything the book said he was, and more. He rode his horse like a centaur. He would supply the Patriot ragamuffin rustics hiding in front of Boston not only the élan of leadership but the panache of glory that was needed. His searing green eyes could at first glance—your glance, not his—gradually take on the warmth and humanity beneath his stern demeanor. Although not in his stocking feet while riding his horse, six-foot-three was not an exaggeration of what he stood unhorsed, probably much more. Washington was very impressive. He impressed everyone. He impressed even these newspaper people. That is very difficult to do. Newspaper people are a cynical bunch. They can spot a phony. The *Times* people knew immediately they were in the presence of an awesome man. They had touched history. After all the lies and dissembling about the war, they were at last in the presence of a straight arrow.

"Can I be of some possible service to you, ladies and gentlemen?" Washington said. "First, let me say I place great value on the intelligence about Bunker Hill you have supplied. Although I am disappointed, I intend to press on. Can you inform me of the condition of the road into Cambridge?"

"The British have mined the Medford road," Lee said, "so take the Roxbury cutoff. When you get to Harvard College, turn left at the first green and white house. That street will dead-end into General Ward's house."

"Don't I know you?" Washington said. "Aren't you—let me

225

THE
LONG
NAKED
DESCENT
INTO
BOSTON

226

THE
LONG
NAKED
DESCENT
INTO
BOSTON

think—aren't you Amos Lee of the North Vernon Lees?"

"Yes."

"I'll be damned," Washington said. "It's good to see you. Are there any other lads from Virginia here?"

"A few."

"I guess things are pretty much of a mess up ahead."

"Yes."

"Well, we'll try to get things straightened out," Washington said. "Why don't you people lead the way—I don't believe we've met."

"This is Francine Wilkes, a reporter and a very good one, and this is Isaac Braxton, our writer."

"Delighted," Washington said. "All with the *Times*?"

"Yes."

"A fine paper, I suspect," Washington said. "Now you people run ahead and we'll follow. I'll put some flankers and skirmishers out in front of you in case there's trouble." Washington trotted his horse away, then turned and said, "See you in Cambridge," and then, "By the bye, I apologize for the press officer."

"It looks like a long war, sire."

"You can say that again," George Washington said.

Francine, Braxton, and Lee trudged down the road, proud as peacocks. Francine turned her horse on the others and said, "Wait till Dilsie finds out we've got an 'in' with Mister Cool. She'll blow her stack. This is the best thing that happened since Poxey took off. I can't believe it—that Washington dude is a little doll. The war is won, I hope. Why not? This General George Washington is a living doll."

twenty-nine

At Cambridge, Washington was immediately surrounded by assistant professors of history and young teens seeking autographs. Some merely wanted to touch the hem of his garments and others inquired into Martha's health. Neighbors brought in fresh flowers and small gifts of frankincense and myrrh, packets of snuff wrapped in gold foil, and advance copies of the Declaration of Independence to be autographed.

Francine, Braxton, and Lee had arrived early—Washington had been held up by the Massachusetts Colonial troopers for

228

THE
LONG
NAKED
DESCENT
INTO
BOSTON

speeding and by autograph seekers at Watertown, and the front end of his horse had come out of alignment at the Roxbury cutoff—and the three intrepid reporters were forced to inform General Artemas Ward that he had been terminated.

"You mean fired?" Ward said.

"There are other jobs."

"Where can a general find a job in today's market?" Ward said. "I hear Washington took my job at a salary cut."

"Washington will take no financial remuneration. Just expenses."

"If a person is willing to work for nothing, anybody will hire him," Ward said. "Wait till the other generals hear this. Patriotism is one thing," Ward said, "but with today's inflation how is a man going to make it? Steal the harpsichord," he told his mistress, "and tell the Mayflower draymen to move out the spinning wheel, the butter churn in the library, the dog in the yard, and everything in the spare bedroom. I don't want to leave anything for that son-of-a-bitch."

"That's right," his mistress said.

"Wait," Francine said. "General Washington deserves your respect. Give him a chance. I don't like your goddamn language."

"That's just too fucking bad," Ward's mistress said, slamming a pinafore into a steamer trunk. "Does the Mayflower supply blankets to protect our goods? They charge enough. When generals will work for nothing, there's no point in being a mistress any more. A general can always parade around on his goddamn horse on his day off, but what can his mistress do without pence?"

"Washington gets expenses."

"Well, that's not too bad," Ward's mistress said, changing her tone from saucy scorn to a hint of respect and curiosity. She had peroxide hair and a bright ribbon and a pennyfeather in her purple Easter bonnet Ward had coughed up. "Why didn't you think of expenses, honey?" she said to Ward. Her name was Peggy and she was, had been, thinking of jumping back to Benedict Arnold anyway. "With just expenses alone, honey, a girl could do all right. What's that balloon doing up there?"

The Mayflower people had already slammed almost everything in the house into the falling-apart wagon they had brought over on the *Mayflower*. Now the Mayflower driver wanted to be paid in advance for smashing everything.

"No dice," Ward said.

"That's right, don't take any of his shit," Peggy said. "Don't pay until the goods are delivered in perfect order. He's already loaded the harpsichord ass-backwards on top of the dog. Don't pay the son-of-a-bitch in advance."

"Company's orders," the driver said.

"Fuck the company," Peggy said.

"Company's orders."

"I give the orders here," Ward said.

"That's right, honey."

"You've been terminated, sir."

"No, I've been fired," Ward said. "But until that man shows up, I'm in charge of everything."

"That's right, honey. Driver," Peggy said, "you deliver all that shit in perfect shape to Twenty-three Prince in Boston and we'll write you out a bum check on the Colonies. They still owe you money, don't they, baby?"

"Yes," General Ward said, "but they won't pay for moving."

"Poor baby."

"What do you want me to do?" the driver said.

"You can throw all that shit in Boston Bay as far as I'm concerned," Peggy said. "What's that damn balloon doing up there?"

"Let's not be hasty," Ward said. "Will you take a postdated check?" he asked the driver.

"No. We must be paid in gold before we deliver. Company's orders."

"When the fuck is anybody going to see any gold?" Peggy said. "I'd like to see some gold myself. I haven't seen anything but Continental paper since the goddamn Revolution started. Gold!"

"Watch your language. Washington will be here any minute."

"I can't drive into Boston anyway," the Mayflower driver said. "The British have got a checkpoint and I have a heavy overload. Anyway, no Americans will be permitted to enter Boston as long as the Revolution is on."

"I believe I can take care of that," General Ward said. "I am

229

THE
LONG
NAKED
DESCENT
INTO
BOSTON

230

THE
LONG
NAKED
DESCENT
INTO
BOSTON

certain the British are in the market for a used general. I've got a uniform that belongs to me, two swords, and all that stuff on the Mayflower wagon. What more could they ask? It will save the British the expense of shipping a general over from London. I hear they're hiring a lot of Germans that can't even speak the language. What do you say, my good man?" he said to the Mayflower man. "Will you trust me?"

"I'll trust you," Peggy said.

"I'm asking the driver," General Ward said.

"Company's orders," the driver said. "I must be paid in gold. In advance. Or it comes out of my pay packet. On top of which I may be thrown in durance vile. Pay now, patch your things together later. That's the company motto. Remember, everything is insured with Hancock."

General Ward removed his gold general's surcoat, rolled up his general's Belgian lace and linen sleeves, curled his general's lip, and was about to thrash the lower-class insolent minion to kingdom come when a loud hush was heard in the antechamber. George Washington had arrived. The *Times* people took out their plumes to get it all down. The crowd in the pink drawing room divided in the middle, forming an open lane with a shaft of light that suddenly appeared in the skylight, illuminating the way. Angels darted about, and soft music could be heard in the distance.

But George Washington, born to the frontier of hardy stock, ignored all this foofaraw, which was probably imagination anyway. George Washington turned out to be just folks. But beneath the plain homespun House on the Prairie surface all could sense, all could feel almost palpably, the hidden fire in the man. You had to know, I mean really know, Washington to know what I mean. This assemblage felt then what I'm telling you now; it was a kind of mystical experience. People who have studied Indian mysticism will know what I mean. It's kind of like going up in a balloon on your day off without guide ropes and feeling free, free, free and knowing that out there someplace beyond the beyond something very big is happening that you understand but nobody else does. The crowd did not bow, sensing Washington's democratic high regard for the little people. Somehow they knew he felt just like one of them. What more could a man ask from the powerful and the rich? Washington, they felt, had a very high regard for women too and understood all their problems. The fire that burned deep within him even seemed to heat up the room a bit, and when the little people stepped back, they did it out of respect for the man as well as for the uniform he stood as a symbol for, but in some respects because of the heat. No one will ever know. Things like that make historians' work difficult, and give the devil his due, they are the first to admit it. Washington surveyed the scene. I think everyone who was really there will agree on that part. The *Times* people touched their fountain plumes to the pad; the balloon passed over again. And Washington said, "What's all the fuss about?"

There was an absolute silence with only the faint hum of the balloon overhead.

"Come, come," Washington said.

Now the Mayflower driver flung himself down at the feet of our George Washington, but with a kind of humility instead of humiliation. All the little people sensed the difference and did not feel inadequate but felt that the driver, in view of the circumstances, was doing the right thing.

"Forgive me, sire," the Mayflower driver said. "I was trying to gouge these people."

Washington raised his arm in the manner we have all seen our Savior do when stuck for a line.

"What people?" Washington said.

"The general who is moving."

"But I've only just arrived," Washington said.

"The guy Congress just fired," the driver said, "is moving."

"They told me in Philadelphia there was nobody in charge here," Washington said.

"Yes," Lee said, handing his plume to Francine and stepping forward. "You are relieving General Artemas Ward in front of Boston. The British can break out at any moment and arrest us all for breaking ye law and order. Hang us, maybe. It would be legal."

"They told me in Philadelphia, Lee, that the British had been defeated once and for all on Bunker Hill and this was just a

231
THE
LONG
NAKED
DESCENT
INTO
BOSTON

232

THE
LONG
NAKED
DESCENT
INTO
BOSTON

clean-up operation. They don't give me anything straight. We Southerners have got to stick together. Have you noticed a prejudice against Southerners, Lee?"

"Somewhat."

"I have already," Washington said. "Young man, get on your feet."

The driver stood on his feet, cap in hand.

"Now take this poor general's belongings to Boston and put it on my expense account."

"Yes, sire."

Washington turned and placed his hands on General Ward's shoulders. "I didn't ask for this job, Ward. I'm sure you'll find something to do. I have found in life that what we consider setbacks at the time can be turned into opportunity. All of us have hidden resources that we hadn't spotted before. Maybe you weren't cut out to be a general after all. Maybe Providence has something bigger in store for you." Washington sensed that he was losing his audience, so he cut it short with, "We all hope so, Ward."

"Thank you, sire."

"How did the British move up Bunker? Did they try to create a diversion to conceal their main thrust?"

"It was Breed's Hill, and no, sire, there were no diversionary tactics. The British just kep a-comin'."

"There's nothing anyone can do about that, Ward, except quit. You did the right thing."

"Thank you, sire."

Washington touched Lee on the arm to follow him into the back drawing room where he could breathe. They sat across from each other on a pair of Louis XIII love settees that Peggy didn't like and had left.

"These settees are better than orange crates, sire," Lee said.

Washington ignored him. He was thinking of something else. Washington tried to pull off his boots and failed. Now he placed his head between his hands and leaned forward, all played out. "Lee, you're going to have to tell me the whole true situation. I've been lied to all along the line. I still plan to take charge of the rebellion, Providence and Congress willing, but we Southerners are going to have to stick together. At this time, Lee, I do not expect much help from anyone else." Washington got off one of his boots and examined it, then said, "Lee, I got a copy of your *New Boston Times* in Hoboken. If what your paper says is true, we have already lost the Revolution. Now can you tell me what your editor is doing up in a balloon?"

"No, sire."

"I understand, Lee."

"Thank you, sire."

"I understand, Lee, the need for a Free Press, but both you and I, Lee, are country. Just folks. Your editor is a Boston man?"

"Yes, sire."

"Then why don't we shoot him down?"

"The war, sire, is against the British."

"You're certain it does not involve a prejudice against the South?"

"Not at this time, sire."

"You know, Lee, I never was one for Revolutions. Can't you think of a different name for this war? Anything but a Revolutionary War. You know, Lee, when I think of Revolution, I think of young people from Columbia University with beards throwing bombs. I don't think Martha will like the idea very much of my being involved in a Revolution. I told her it was just a regular war like we're always having."

"I'll speak to Paine," Lee said.

See if you can get Young Wild Tom or your editor to call the Revolution something else," Washington said. "The French and Indian Wars was a good name. Everybody hates the French and the Indians. The War of the Roses was a good name—you can almost smell that name."

"I'll speak to Poxe," Lee said.

"Then you will shoot him down?"

"No, sire, the British are taking care of that."

"Good. I'm happy that someone up here is doing something. Your paper says the Patriots have no uniforms."

"True, but the *Times* is working to get them uniforms. I don't suppose you would consider being in charge, sire, if your troops have no uniforms."

"You can say that again," George Washington said.

Lee, Braxton, and Francine got through the British lines using

233

THE
LONG
NAKED
DESCENT
INTO
BOSTON

234
THE
LONG
NAKED
DESCENT
INTO
BOSTON

Press passes. They walked right through the Rose and Crown, past Scoop Jackson and past Mr. Loring whistling Mozart, through the book shoppe, not listening to Brown's complaints about sales, and into the *Times* office and found Dilsie hard at work.

"Did you get a story?" Dilsie said.

thirty

Pomfret and Pomeroy got back to Boston from Mrs. Gage on Noodles Island and stopped in at the Tory apothecary Doctor Glanders to fetch some medicaments for Mrs. Gage's mumps.

"The best and the cheapest prescription I know of will not cost you a farthing. It's a formulation," Doctor Glanders said, "that goes back to the Ming Dynasty—a good swift kick in the ass. I don't know why a kick in the ass makes the mumps disappear, but it always does. We don't know why acupuncture

236
THE
LONG
NAKED
DESCENT
INTO
BOSTON
works either. Modern medicine, you would think, would have made some progress in the last three thousand years, but it hasn't. The only thing we drug companies have come up with is higher prices."

"Well, that's something," Pomfret said.

"The drug companies need a tax write-off as an incentive to search for drugs. It takes a lot of money to search for drugs. People don't realize how much it costs," Doctor Glanders said, pouring a dark flask of yellow piss into a test tube of human sperm, "to develop an antiacid and an antigas in mint and orange flavor. My firm, Upcharles, is working on an aphrodisiac now that should double the population of America by 1975. In only two hundred years, Upcharles Aphrodisiac will put the population of America at two million."

"Where are they going to put 'em all?" Pomfret said.

"Mr. Poxe suggested in last week's Sunday *Times* that we transport the surplus population to other planets via the balloon."

"Science fiction."

"No," Doctor Glanders said, "Poxe is under attack in the scientific community for what is called in the technical jargon of the medical journals 'bullshit.' But we have discovered in the past that yesterday's bullshit is frequently today's science." Doctor Glanders shook the flask of sperm till it turned green, which is evidently what he was looking for because his face turned into a huge grin the way the Israeli scientist Isaac Newton must have reacted when he stumbled on gravity while looking for a shortcut to Leeds.

"Only yesterday, while petting the cat, I had the good luck to come upon a gimmick to protect sensitive hemorrhoidal tissues. The trick, of course, is to go back to a more normal form of sexual intercourse. But people won't pay for that information. People want something in a bottle that sells for four shillings and has been advertised widely in the *Times*. I've found a medicinal use for something the people in Pennsylvania can't make heads or tails of that keeps coming up in their backyards near Titusville. They call it pet-roleum oil because their pets get stuck in it. I've discovered that it will protect hemorrhoidal tissues; now people can do whatever they want to in bed. It will come in mint or orange flavor and can be used as an antigas or an antiacid, or patients can do whatever the hell ye want to with it."

"Will it cure the mumps?"

"No," Doctor Glanders said, holding the flask of green sperm up to the light. "Have ye ever seen green sperm before?"

"No," Pomfret said. "I can't say as I have. What good is it?"

"At this point in time we don't know," Doctor Glanders said. "But that is how pure science works, in contradistinction to applied science. A pure scientist, which I like to call myself, invents green sperm. An applied scientist like our friend Benjamin Franklin invents a practical application for green sperm and gets all the credit. Newspapers like the *Times* see to that."

"We were just looking for something to cure the mumps," Pomfret said.

"Well, you won't find it here," Doctor Glanders said. "As long as the *Times* carries on a vendetta against the drug industry, you won't get anything out of me come hell or high water. Does Poxe realize how much costly research goes into simply developing an effective antigas and antiacid in orange or mint that will at one and the same time protect the sensitive hemorrhoidal tissues?"

"I don't believe he does," Pomeroy said.

"It is not a semantic happenstance," Doctor Glanders said, changing the window display and the subject at the same time. "It is not a semantic happenstance that people from Maine are called Mainiacs. It is also true—and I believe it follows—that people who go up in balloons can't keep their feet on the ground."

"I never thought of that," Pomfret said.

"That's about it," Doctor Glanders said. "How do you like the new window display?"

"How will people know it's green sperm unless you put a sign on it?" Pomfret said.

"People aren't as dumb as you think," Doctor Glanders said. "Now, you wanted a specific for the mumps?"

"Yes."

"Is the patient a good Tory or in rebellion against our gracious King, our noble King?"

"I'll try 'in rebellion against our noble King, our gracious King,' " Pomeroy said.

237
THE
LONG
NAKED
DESCENT
INTO
BOSTON

238

THE
LONG
NAKED
DESCENT
INTO
BOSTON

"No," Pomfret said. "Mrs. Gage wanted us to dig up Tom Paine so she could hear the other side of the argument, which must mean in her heart of hearts she's a Tory now."

"Why didn't you say that before?" Doctor Glanders said. "We will have Mrs. Gage on her feet again in a trice, as good as new." Doctor Glanders reached down from the shelf a bottle of Pennzoil. "I want her to take a heaping teaspoonful of this pet-roleum oil before bed and before breakfast and following intercourse. Keep the pet-roleum oil away from pets. I will write these instructions clearly on the label in Latin so that there is no confusion or misunderstanding. If she follows instructions carefully, she should be able to leave her bed of pain and be on her feet again in a few months as good as new."

From the balloon, the *Times* people saw Pomfret and Pomeroy leave Doctor Glanders and cross to the Rose and Crown, and all the *Times* people in the balloon wondered what was up.

thirty-one

George Washington wasted nary a moment upon his arrival to command the Patriot threadbare but dedicated troops in front of Boston. "Are the Patriots highly motivated?" Washington wanted to know. Washington had leaped right in without catching up on his sleep or partaking of a mouthful of victuals. He was in conference stern with Henry Knox, who you will remember formerly owned the Boston bookstore before he palmed it off on Brown. Henry Knox was into artillery now in a big way, and

240
THE
LONG
NAKED
DESCENT
INTO
BOSTON
Washington hung on every word, keen to know from whatever source he could. Washington never heard of artillery before. Cavalry either. There was no imaginable use for these things on the frontier. The French and Indians, Washington's opponents in the French and Indian Wars, until now had probably never heard of those things either. But Washington, eager to learn, showed great interest in both subjects. Lafayette was coming over to take care of cavalry. A footloose German, Baron von Steuben, was threatening to come over to fill in temporarily until the Colonists got the hang of all of the evolutions of the drill. And here was good old fat jovial, God bless him, Henry Knox giving up the book business just when it was about to pick up to take on the thankless job of artillery for George.

"How can we lose?" Washington said.

"Without sufficient motivation we can lose," Knox said.

"Try to get hold of a Thomas Paine," Washington said. "Have you read his new book?"

"Yes, I don't believe a word of it," Knox said.

"Yes, he does get carried away," Washington said. "But I think *Common Sense* is exactly what the doctor ordered for the troops in terms of motivation. Can you get hold of him?"

Knox made a note on his pad: Seek out Tom P.

"He used to hang out with the newspaper gang at the Rose and Crown in Boston, but since the war I don't know what's happened to him."

"But Boston is behind the enemy lines," Washington said.

"That never occurred to me," Knox said.

"It didn't occur to me either until just now," Washington said. "By the bye, Knox," Washington said, "do you have any artillery for your artillery?"

"No, that never occurred to me until you brought it up."

"Then why don't you hop up to Saratoga and get some?"

"All right."

"But before you go, Knox, look into the Tom Paine matter, will you?"

"All right."

Of course, as any qualified historian knows—but it bears repeating here—Knox did not go to the Rose and Crown. Pomfret and Pomeroy did. Knox took off for Saratoga without a fare-thee-well.

Pomeroy and Pomfret entered the Rose and Crown. It was filled with British tommies just back from the Revolution, discussing the pros and cons of what had happened on the hill. They had all received a cash bonus for their victory, which would be deducted from their veterans' pensions, but now they were all slopping up Rum Flips as though they were about to go out of style.

"That's an unfair supposition," Paine said.

Pomfret and Pomeroy had at last found our hero, Tom Paine, the young man who by his grit and wit, and in spite of all the evidence to the contrary, would lead our young country to a place in the hierarchy of nations. Not with a quick sword but with a steady pen. They also serve who only sit and write. In spite of the cynicism that overtakes some of us. In spite of the truth. Where a true heart beats, the sun will always shine through, and its fertile warming rays allow us to surmount many obstacles, both the real and the unreal.

"That's an unfair supposition," Paine said.

"What is?" a Tory corporal with a bandaged head said.

"You need a new bandage," Paine said.

"What is an unfair supposition?"

"What you said."

"What did I say?"

"That I am a demagogue," Paine said.

"Defend this," the bandaged British corporal said. "On page seventeen: 'The King a beastly tyrant;' and here on page thirty-one: 'The King an insane monarch.' On page forty-seven again: 'The King issued four drunken proclamations.' Now where in God's name, Paine, do you show one bit of evidence for this?"

"You're taking what I said out of context," Paine said.

"Can we have a word with you, Tom?" Pomfret said.

"Hi, Pomfret!" Paine said. "I'm sorry," Paine said to the bandaged British corporal, "I didn't catch your name."

"Leadbetter."

"You should get that bandage changed, Leadbetter," Paine said.

241
THE
LONG
NAKED
DESCENT
INTO
BOSTON

242

THE
LONG
NAKED
DESCENT
INTO
BOSTON

"We have with us—" Pomeroy said.

"Hi, Pomeroy!" Paine said. "This is Leadbetter."

"We have with us some medicaments for the mumps," Pomeroy said. "Maybe we could find something among them that could patch up Leadbetter's head." Pomeroy unwound the tattered bandage from the British corporal's head, exposing his busted noggin.

"My, my, you have taken a bad fall," Pomfret said.

"I was going up Breed's Hill," the British corporal said, "innocent as you please, when someone hit me from behind with an axe."

"We will have you as good as new again in a nonce," Pomfret said. "Did your mother know what you have been up to? That Breed's Hill has always had a bad reputation outside of Old Southie," Pomfret said. "There's no worse place for trouble." Pomfret kept up this irrelevant small talk to distract the brave corporal from the pain of detaching his bandage and applying the Pennzoil.

"That feels much better," the corporal said.

"You're going to be all right," Pomfret said.

Mrs. Gage had had a hard night on Noodles Island with only Bill Shakespeare's *Macbeth* to read, which is not the most cheerful book in the world when you're down with the mumps. She had walked over to the lighthouse to comfort the Tory quarantine master and lighthouse keeper, who had a worse case of mumps than she did, with a nice cup of tea. The Patriots had accused the Tory quarantine master and lighthouse keeper of being a homosexual and a lesbian for taking this cushy job from the British.

"Now, it stands to reason," the Tory quarantine master said, "if I was a homosexual or a lesbian, I would have brought a nice boy or a nice girl to the lighthouse to help with the light housekeeping. Instead of that I am quite alone—you can search the place if you want."

"I don't care," Mrs. Gage said, "whether you are a homosexual or a lesbian or need help with your light housekeeping. That is your affair. What does concern me is that if the Patriots win the war, they are going to crack down on everyone with a different cut to their jib; everyone who is not male, white, or twenty-one. I have heard if the Americans gain their independence, they are going to ignore the King and elect some poor boob to run this country."

"Why in God's name would they want to do that?" the lighthouse keeper said.

"And institute Prohibition."

"Against what?"

"Everything, I believe," Mrs. Gage said, "beginning with liquor, women's rights, and all the more interesting forms of sex."

"Why in God's name would they want to do that?"

"We don't want to be prejudiced against the Patriots," Mrs. Gage said. "To be fair, if you have a Revolution and you happen to win it, the people expect you to do something, even if it's only taking away their rights. The liberty and freedom to put people who disagree with you in jail. But I'm being unfair. I'm sure Young Tom Paine can make out a good case for the males killing each other. We Tories tend only to see one side of things. How are your mumps?"

"Better," the lighthouse keeper said.

"Tom Paine may nip out and see us today."

"I don't want to see him," the Tory said. "I have already made up my mind I am for law and order."

"Pomfret and Pomeroy—bless their black souls—are going to try to dig up a specific for our mumps from Doctor Glanders," Mrs. Gage said.

"Doctor Glanders is a quack. I hear he is trying to sell green sperm and a specific for hemorrhoidal tissue in orange and mint."

"The green sperm is pure science," Mrs. Gage said. "It is not for sale, it's just a window display. As Doctor Glanders keeps saying, that's the way pure science works. You have to kick things around and sleep on it, then someone like Franklin finally figures out a way to make money out of it. That's American progress. Another reason for independence. They know the British are holding them back from stealing the Indian land. The Americans call it Manifest Destiny. Still, as I say, we are prejudiced. I wish Paine would get here with the Patriots' point of view and the stuff from Doctor Glanders."

"Glanders is a quack."

243
THE
LONG
NAKED
DESCENT
INTO
BOSTON

244

THE
LONG
NAKED
DESCENT
INTO
BOSTON

"It's a pity," Mrs. Gage said to the Tory quarantine master and lighthouse keeper, "but you and I don't seem to have anything in common excepting the mumps. When Tories fall out, then the Patriots will elect some poor boob to take over the country."

"And I couldn't care less," the Tory said, touching the mump on his neck. "If all Tories are like Doctor Glanders, I don't care if the nuts take over the country. My old friend Old Melville and I are even beginning to lose interest in our organic garden. Everything is beginning to taste like wild hickory nuts. I have half a mind to join the Revolution myself."

"I'm sure you wouldn't do anything like that," Mrs. Gage said, fetching a fresh ice pack. "Try this," she said. "Doesn't that feel better? Now why in the world would you do a thing like that? Join the Rebels?"

"It's difficult to explain things to a woman," the Tory said, "but a man just reaches a point where he doesn't care any more. He figures if a good Revolution comes along, he will join it even if only to get out of the house. Then he figures it doesn't necessarily have to be a good Revolution. It's common sense and only stands to reason that you can't agree with every point in a Revolution. So a man will settle for the first Revolution that comes along. Beggars can't be choosers."

"As I said, all we seem to have in common is the mumps," Mrs. Gage said. "I will trot down to the wharf and see if I can spot Young Wild Tom Paine and Pomfret and Pomeroy with the medicaments."

"Glanders is a quack," the Tory said, "and so is Paine."

Mrs. Gage, quite out of patience, slammed the lighthouse door in her fellow sufferer's face, causing the whole lighthouse tower to shake and the big whale-oil light to flicker and make the people up in the balloon wonder what was up. Whale oil was cheap in the Colonies, with plenty of whales to slaughter, so it didn't pay to turn out the light in the daytime. The whale oil was delivered by Old Melville, a sacrilegious Tory who wanted his son to become a writer and get out of the whale oil business, "what with the whale conservationists on our ass." Old Melville was one of the few visitors Mrs. Gage had seen, and Old Melville just dumped the whale oil in the whale oil tank and fled the mumps. He said he didn't want his son to catch it. That is why Mrs. Gage was so much looking forward to Young Tom Paine's visit to break the monotony.

As Mrs. Gage walked along the lily-strewn path from the lighthouse to the wharf, she remarked the typical New England day—you couldn't see ten feet. When there was a break in the weather, you could see all the black piss in Boston Bay. The latest tea spills from Hancock's ships. Hancock had promised to the clean air and the clean water nuts that he would put double bottoms in his tea ships so that after his tea ships collided, everything would be as good as new. But because of the expense, he had canceled that order (inoperative), explaining to the clean water and clean air nuts that with the war on poverty and the war on the British, the people should not be asked at this point in time to bear the extra expense of tuppence on tea, which the company would have to pass along to the consumer in order to show an unfair profit. "If free enterprise is not what the Revolution is about, then I don't know what the Revolution is about. The people have got to make up their minds whether they want a Revolution or cheap tea. They can't have both." So you can understand why Mrs. Gage's mind was all in a dither, what with all this kind of talk in the Colonies on top of the mumps. She did so much want to be fair to the Patriots and try to understand their point of view. But outside of their slogans, they didn't seem to have one. "I suppose that is the way men are. The British don't seem to have a point of view either. They're just both going at it hammer and tong and the devil take the hindmost. What do men want? My God, what do men want?"

Mrs. Gage stood on a flower-bedecked knoll that overlooked Noodles Inlet and waved to the launch that flew the Cross of St. George and was rowed by the Spanish slaves captured by Lord Nelson's grandfather in the Bay of Biscay at the start of the Seven Years' War. I hope this one doesn't last that long, Mrs. Gage thought. She waved furiously to the men standing up in the British launch, hoping they would spot her through the tea spill. The three men without mumps must not be allowed to escape in the New England fog and tea spill. Although we will never

245

THE
LONG
NAKED
DESCENT
INTO
BOSTON

246

THE
LONG
NAKED
DESCENT
INTO
BOSTON

understand men, it is always handy to have several around the house in case of an emergency such as sex or to fetch a poor girl a nice cup of tea.

The two blacks, Pomfret and Pomeroy, were standing on the forecastle, chanting out the beat to the rowing "Spanish slave white bastards" now that the shoe was on the other foot. They, Pomfret and Pomeroy, stood like admirals of the ocean sea. A young white lad who must be Paine was bouncing up and down on the poop and repeating himself as though he were stricken with St. Vitus Dance. At last Mrs. Gage could make out what Young Wild Tom was saying:

"Don't tread on me!"

So that is what all the fuss is about, Mrs. Gage thought. I've often wondered. To hear that young lad shout, you'd think he had some fresh slogan nobody had ever thought of before. My grandmother in Ipswich used to shout the same slogan to my grandfather, and that was over a hundred years ago. No, there is nothing new happening under the sun this day in Boston. Still, they are having quite a bash. You can hear the guns popping away now. But I will go down to the dock, tie up the boat, lift the men ashore so that they don't get their tootsies wet and catch their death, and do all the things women do to show we female slaves are happy and the thought of our own freedom never crossed our minds.

"Grab this," Pomfret said, and tossed the rope.

"The blood of the slain and the weeping voice of nature cries 'tis time to part!" Tom Paine said, waiting to be lifted ashore.

Oh Christ, Mrs. Gage thought, and me down with the mumps, too. He forgot "Everything that is right or reasonable pleads for common sense." The Revolutionists can drown, for all the hell I care, in Hancock's tea spill. I won't lift them ashore this day. But she carried them ashore and kept their tootsies dry and cursed them under her breath for the day she was born.

And the Spanish slaves muttered to each other in Castilian, shocked to hear a woman talk this way—and in *los Estados Unidos tambien!*

thirty-two

"Do you see what I see, Nathan?" Poxe said from high over Boston.

"You mean Jackson returning to the *Globe* with a scoop?"

"No."

"You mean the Tory lighthouse keeper on Noodles Island playing with Old Melville's son Herman?"

"No."

248

THE
LONG
NAKED
DESCENT
INTO
BOSTON

"You mean Gretchen in deshabille?"

"No, I mean over there, Nathan. It looks as though the British are going to make a foray against Dorchester Point. If the British sally out, they can get behind Washington at Roxbury. Then all of Knox's bastions, barbettes, chevaux-de-frise, counterscarps, fascines, and demilunes will be facing the wrong way, and then Paine's packet of clichés will be just so much bullshit. Paine's book will die and Little Brown's publishing house will die, and we of *The New Boston Times* will have to think of another circulation gimmick if the British get behind those French words."

"What do all those French words mean?"

"Forts, Nathan. If the British get behind them by way of Dorchester Point and Phipp's Farm over there, then the Patriots' French forts are useless and can be taken from their unprotected rear."

"I believe Phipp's Farm is still posted," Nathan said.

"I can't make out any NO TRESPASSING signs with the naked eye, Nathan. Take a look at Phipp's place through the glass."

"No, I don't see any postings now," Nathan said. "See what you see, Gretchen," Nathan said, passing the glass.

Gretchen squinted through the scope, standing and looking like an ad for White Rock Colonial Soda Water, with her breasts like rocks not swaying in the breeze, because as everyone who has been up in a balloon knows, you move, you travel, and are part of the wind so that there is never any sensation of even a breeze, you being part of the whole affair.

"No," Gretchen said. "Phipp's Farm is no longer posted. The signs must have blown down in the last storm. The British are free to come and go as they please."

"The Americans, I regret, never paid any attention to those NO TRESPASSING signs," Nathan said. Nathan was never one who believed all is fair in love and war. A sign is a sign. The ends do not justify the means. Fair is fair. What's good for the goose is good for the gander. If the British respect NO TRESPASSING signs and the Americans do not, isn't someone trying to tell us something about this Revolution? Is it all futile? Are we perchance on the wrong side?

"I suppose," Poxe said, "we have got to keep telling ourselves there can be no representation without taxation or vice versa, whichever the case may be."

"Nevertheless," Nathan said, "a sign is a sign. You either respect them or you do not. If you start a country without respect for signs, where will it all end up? It seems to me that, on the surface at least, the British have a sense of fair play and we do not. Now, Mr. Poxe, how are we going to rationalize ourselves out of that?"

Poxe realized he was dealing with someone who was true-blue. A straight arrow. A type he had never encountered in the publishing game. A type who would lay down his but one life to make a point and never regret it at all. Somehow I will have to find a way to cope with this civilian—Poxe always called anyone not in the publishing game a civilian—some way to make Nathan realize that if the British have the right to cross Phipp's Farm free and clear, they will get behind Washington's counterscarps and fascines and the jig will be up. We might as well all go home and count our chickens, make up and kiss the King's ass, pay that extra tuppence for tea, apologize to His Worship for the unpleasantness at Lexington and Concord and Bunker Hill, and forget the whole Revolution happened.

"Is that what you want, Nathan? Do you want to go back to playing kiss the King's ass?"

"No, but fair is fair," Nathan said. "Despite your newspaper vulgarities."

"Am I being vulgar, Gretchen?"

"Yes," Gretchen said. "A king is a king, and as long as we have a king, perhaps we should show him proper respect and not talk about him in newspaper language."

So, Poxe thought, watching down on cloud-covered Boston, watching Prince Street, watching Scoop Jackson come and go in the pea soup—the whole camp, the whole balloon seems to have turned against me. Where is your Revolution now? Soon General Gage will be behind the Patriots and the Rebels will have to throw in the sponge. General Gage knows Washington is new at this game and Gage is taking advantage of Washington's greenness with an enveloping operation by Dorchester Point, which Ward forgot to fortify, then across Phipp's Farm in a trice, and then it

249
THE
LONG
NAKED
DESCENT
INTO
BOSTON

250

THE
LONG
NAKED
DESCENT
INTO
BOSTON
will be trick or treat for poor George. Washington showed such promise, too. If he could only get in four or five years of practice without the British lowering the boom on him right at the beginning, I'm sure he could pull this Revolution out. Washington is resolute. An excellent father figure—certainly Gage or Lord Percy can't hold a candle to him. I wonder what happened to Percy after the beating he took at Concord, and I wonder how you punctuate this sentence without help from Dilsie or some other copy editor who can cut the mustard. Washington is not only resolute and an excellent father figure, but will learn this war business, too, if the British will only give him half a chance. I must do an editorial on that one day.

"Gretchen, can you take a note?"

"No," Gretchen said.

"Temper, temper," Poxe said.

"How can you marry me when we land," Gretchen said, "when you're still married to Mrs. Poxe—Theodosia, I believe you said her name was?"

"Would you believe," Poxe said, fumbling at his chest, "that my wife completely slipped my mind?"

"No."

"Would you believe," Poxe said, still searching in his hairy chest for his wife's locket of hair, "that I simply haven't thought of her in a coon's age?"

"No"

"Would you believe," Poxe said, coming up with something he fished out of his hairy chest—but it turned out on close inspection to be an ivory cross (I must be getting religion, Poxe thought)—and he said to the sex we all fear, "Would you believe, Gretchen, that Theodosia traipsed off to Asbury Park without so much as a by-your-leave and left me holding the bag? That I have a clear case against her of child, I mean husband, abandonment that will stand up in any court except a British court, and that is why we all have to fish or cut bait and win this Revolution so a man can get some justice around here, to say nothing about the high taxes and all that. Paine can word this better than me—or I, which is correct? I or me? If Dilsie would edit Paine, we could get a book that would boom Brown into a best seller for starters and would be a complete eye-opener to all the readers who are wondering what the Revolution is about. Do you see my point, Gretchen?"

"No."

Just like a woman, Poxe thought, fingering his ivory cross. No logic. "You, Nathan?"

"No."

Just like a civilian, Poxe thought. They never understand the problems of getting out a newspaper. They think you can win a war with martyrdom alone. They don't understand the necessity of the lies that any good newspaper supplies to any good cause. What I will do is divide and conquer Nathan and Gretchen. I love and cherish them both, but Nathan is dead wrong and I am right as rain when I say all is fair in love and war and resistance to tyranny can be mighty helpful to the newspaper business.

"What do you say to this, the both of you," Poxe said, squinting through the spyglass at Phipp's Farm, "that we tell old Phipp that the British will trample his new winter wheat crop to death unless he posts it. That way we are simply stating a fact and not taking sides. It should appeal to the conservationists, and if Phipp's winter wheat fails, the women and children on both sides will go naked and starve unless we have a mild spring. What do you say to that, Gretchen?"

"Well, it makes sense to me," Gretchen said, "particularly the part about the women and children going naked and starving unless we have a mild spring."

Women are not as dumb as I thought, Poxe thought, hugging his ivory cross for luck. "Nathan?"

"Fair is still fair," Nathan said.

Why, the young son-of-a-bitch is back to that, Poxe thought. No wonder there is so much anti-Semitism in Boston.

"Fair is fair," Nathan said. "Your plan is not founded on equity. Your motivation is not to help Phipp save his winter wheat or to keep the women and children on both sides from going naked and starving unless there is a mild spring. You simply want to stop the British from lowering the boom on Washington. You couldn't care less about Phipp losing his winter wheat to the trampling soldiers or the women and children begging naked in the streets of Boston for bread unless there is a mild spring. You couldn't care less, Poxey. Fair is fair. Give the British their due.

251
THE
LONG
NAKED
DESCENT
INTO
BOSTON

252

THE
LONG
NAKED
DESCENT
INTO
BOSTON

Fair is fair. The British may never have the opportunity again to lower the boom on Washington, and I regret to say I believe they should have equity in this matter. The British thought of it first and they have already demonstrated their fairness in respecting signs at Lexington and Concord. They might have won that one hands down if they ran around helter-skelter as the Americans did, shooting at everybody that moved. They showed their fairness then by not shooting at any target that was not clearly identified by Lord Percy in writing. This may sound strange coming from Nathan Hale, but I regret to say the British should be given a fair shake."

"Now that we have all come to a mutual disagreement," Poxe said, "we will tell old Phipp to post his farm. All in favor say 'aye.' The ayes have it. With any luck at all we should begin our long—wind and Jackson permitting—naked descent into Boston any minute now. Take this message, Gretchen. We will drop it on Phipp's noggin."

Poxe dictated: "Dear Phipp. Your farm is naked of posters and everyone is watching. No, seriously, Phipp, the British really are coming this time—no bullshit. This is not another Paul Revere false alarm. The British will trample your winter wheat from hell to breakfast and there will be no crop disaster loans this time. King George is fed up with our Revolution shenanigans. They tell me down at the office that if you farmers can make a good crop, you can clean up this fall by price-gouging both sides. Wheat is already bringing two pounds ten shillings a bushel in New Haven—Colonial Farm and Boston Meal Bread ten shillings the loaf, with the sky's the limit unless the British stick their oar in and interfere with free enterprise. Sign it, 'Death before dishonor,' " Poxe said.

thirty-three

Yes, it is true it did look as though Jackson would scoop *The New Boston Times*. Yes, it is true the British were up to some mischief at Dorchester Point. Yes, it is true the British had worked out a plan that was awfully clever. Yes, it was true that Mrs. Loring had done the British spade work. But it was equally true that Generals Gage, Howe, Clinton, and even Gentleman

254

THE
LONG
NAKED
DESCENT
INTO
BOSTON

Johnny had thrown in their two cents. How could the British lose with such a fine array of generals with seven years' practice in the Seven Years' War? And with nothing to lose excepting America, which they didn't care much about anyway. The British generals had all gathered in the Rose and Crown after having carefully swept out all the lower classes and arranging flowers and everything nice with going-away presents for General Gage, who was going to head the attack and come in behind all those French names when no one was looking. General Gage was in fine fettle when he rapped with his gavel on a puncheon of wine for law and order.

"Come, come, gentlemen," Gage said. "If we all want to get on the next boat to England, there is still this matter of the Revolution to be taken care of. I know it's embarrassing to many of you who have friends and mistresses on the other side, but let's get on with it."

Everyone was seated at the flower-bedecked tables to celebrate the battle tomorrow that would end the Revolution once and for all—seated according to name, rank, and serial number, but Mrs. Loring had been careful to place no one below the salt, which left most of the tables empty at one end. Lord Percy was there, dressed to the nines in his new bonnet and second-hand marshal's baton. Madame de Tocqueville was loyally by his side despite the fact that Percy hadn't taken a bath in three months. Lee was sketching the scene from the bar, and Francine and Braxton were trying to make sense of the goings-on for tomorrow morning's edition. Dilsie was safe in the office, correcting proofs, straightening out syntax with the help of Doctor Johnson's Unabridged, which she had stolen from Brown. Brown was pissed off and rearranging his books according to subject matter and sexual proclivities of the author. Brown did not realize history was being manufactured in the next room, and Dilsie, like most blacks, was so busy with the work of the world she didn't give a damn. Or as Dilsie was misquoted later in one of Brown's cheap penny-press novels that sold well, "Frankly, Scarlett, I don't give a damn."

In this main banquet room of the Rose and Crown that had been reserved for the Rotarians but preempted by the British, Gage was still banging away for law and order. Benedict Arnold, along with Peggy and Chuck Colton of the BCIA, had taken a quiet table in the corner with one candle.

"The King's Ministry has decided to investigate the BCIA," Colton said, "but fortunately they have selected me to head the committee. They're worried about the money we stole to dredge up the balloon."

"The BCIA investigating yourselves. Let's have a drink to that," Arnold said, "and don't look so worried, Peggy dear. I'll get that appointment to West Point, you just wait and see."

"My God, I hope so," Colton said. "The BCIA hasn't overthrown a government in a long time now. The people in England will wonder what we have been up to. Where all their good money has gone. My God, Arnold, it will be your ass if you don't get that job at West Point."

At the center table, groaning under the weight of flowers and war trophies from the Seven Years' fandango and beneath the plaque saying "The Boston Rotarians meet here every third Thursday of the month," sat Clinton, Howe, Burgoyne, dressed in full regalia and trying to steal the show from Gage.

"The way I see it, if it was me," Clinton said, "we should move this whole shooting match to New York and divide the Colonies in half."

"What would that accomplish? New Jersey doesn't care about Pennsylvania anyway."

"I mean separating Maryland from Massachusetts."

"They don't care about that either," Howe said.

"But I care about it," Clinton said. "Do you notice this champagne has a funny taste?"

"They say New York is a very expensive town to live in now," Howe said.

"It's all tax deductible," Burgoyne said.

"What do you think of Gage's idea to take Washington from the rear?"

"It's not only a vulgar idea," Burgoyne said, "it's also illegal. Phipp's Farm is posted."

"I hear all the NO TRESPASSING signs blew down in the last storm."

"Well, that puts a new light on the matter," General Howe said. "I don't think this champagne tastes funny. I just think it's

255
THE
LONG
NAKED
DESCENT
INTO
BOSTON

256
THE
LONG
NAKED
DESCENT
INTO
BOSTON

the mood we're in. After Gage gets his ass whipped tomorrow, everything will taste good again."

"Certainly you're jesting, Howe," Clinton said. "You certainly don't have designs on Gage's job."

"Of course not," Howe said. "Who is that asshole sitting over there all by himself whistling Mozart?"

"That's Lowell Cabot Loring, the Dean of New England Poets."

"Well, he looks like an asshole to me," Howe said. "I think it would be a good idea to move this whole clown act—so fondly referred to by our King as the British Army, even though half of it is made up of Krauts who can't speak anything we can make out—move the British Army to Halifax before we invade those Tories in New York. Give New York a chance to lower the price of their theater tickets anyway. How is your play going, Johnny?"

"Did you ever try opening in Boston?" Burgoyne said.

"Who is that asshole over there all by himself reading the paper?" Howe said.

"That's Scoop Jackson of the *Globe*."

"Well, he looks like an asshole to me," Howe said. "Who is that we see in the mirror?"

"That's you, Howe."

"Well, I look like a fine figure of a man to me," Howe said.

Gage was still pounding the wine barrel for law and order, threatening to bring the Boston Rotarians' sign down on all their heads, but no one was paying him any heed. At a hundred dollars a plate, they thought they were entitled to make some noise of their own.

"All right, you guys," Francine said, jumping on top of the bar and lifting her dress to attract attention. "You guys have fucked around long enough. Give Gage a chance. The Boston Rotarians are waiting to get in. After all, this is their night for the hall. This is the third Thursday of every month. The British Army is here because the Rotarians were generous to let you in in the first place."

There was a shout from the British Army of "Hear, hear, that's a good girl! Fair is fair. Give the generous Rotarian chaps a go at the Rose and Crown. This champagne tastes funny anyway, don't you think, Clinton?"

General Gage at last got his law and order and the drunks were willing to listen.

"Listen," Gage said. "I've got good news for you."

"Tell us the bad news first," General Howe said.

"No, it's all good."

"Then let's hear it," Howe said. "What have you got for openers?"

"The operation to come in behind Washington's rear is off."

"I never cared for that anyway," Howe said. "What is on?"

"I'm coming to that."

"Give Gage a chance," Francine said. "Are you taking this down, Braxton?"

"Tell them to speak slowly," Braxton said.

"What's on?" Howe said.

"He's coming to that," Francine said.

"What about all the time and energy we wasted bribing that Patriot, old Phipp?" Howe said. "Does all that go down the drain?"

"Last night," Gage said, "Washington fortified Dorchester Point."

"The bastard," Howe said.

"All of our movements have been observed aloft and reported to Washington," Gage said.

"What does aloft mean?"

"*The New Boston Times* balloon."

"Why didn't the British Army think of something like that?" Howe said. "Must the British Army always be a couple of generations behind the times?"

"Fortunately," Gage said, "the American Army is careful also to keep several generations behind the times."

"That's fair of them," Howe said. "I didn't think the Colonials had it in them."

There was faint applause for the American Army and a few toots of "Hear, hear."

"The observation balloon was entirely the idea of *The New Boston Times*," Gage said.

257
THE
LONG
NAKED
DESCENT
INTO
BOSTON

258

THE
LONG
NAKED
DESCENT
INTO
BOSTON

There was a slightly bigger applause for *The New Boston Times*.

"But the British Army, under my direction," Gage said, "has not been asleep at the switch."

"That's something new," Howe said. "A pleasant surprise."

"We had already planned to get a balloon of our own. When who should show up in Boston Harbor yesterday on the latest boat from Pedomonde, Germany, but guess who?"

"Who?"

"Our own Professor Hortzkoller. Can I introduce him now?"

"I don't see how we can get out of it," Howe said.

"Professor Hortzkoller has invented the collapsible dirigible and he thought to bring it along with him on the off-chance we might be interested in surplus war equipment. Apparently Germany has it coming out of their ears."

"I don't see any dirigible," Howe said, looking around the banquet room. "Not that I'd recognize one if I saw one, but I certainly don't see anything that big."

"The professor left it on the boat."

"A likely story," Howe said. "After the Phipp deal fell through and Washington fortified Dorchester Point, I'm not going to buy another pig in a poke."

"I saw the dirigible with my own eyes," Gage said.

"Are you sober for a change, Gage, or is this the peach brandy speaking?"

"Sober as a judge," Gage said. "I tell you all the news is good. If you speak to this dirigible in German, it will expand as big as Boston."

"Then we will foil the Patriots and hang them on their own petard?"

"Yes, I tell you all the news is good," Gage said. "Does anyone here speak German? Professor Hortzkoller never seems to have picked up much English. I wish they'd screen these people before they send them over."

"Braxton, you speak some German, don't you?" Francine said. "Why don't you help out?"

"My German is rusty," Braxton said, looking up from his plume. "Anyway, I don't want to help the British."

"Braxton speaks some German," Francine announced, "but he finds himself tilting toward the Patriots."

"We all do at times, old man," Howe said. "It's nothing to be ashamed of. It's only human. The Patriots have some excellent slogans. I have tilted toward the Patriots myself at times, and I'm sure every Patriot has tilted toward the British on an off day— although I can't think why. Anyway, that's beside the point. The point is, you're only being asked to give this German chap a chance to explain his fool gadget. That certainly shouldn't embarrass you with your Patriot friends or compromise your alleged newspaper."

"All right," Braxton said.

"That's a good boy," Gage said.

General Gage asked Professor Hortzkoller to step up to the bandstand—the drum of the Colonial All-Gas Band was still there with their sign on it—and Gage prevailed upon the good German professor because of the ladies present to remove his silk hat and button his fly.

"Now that isn't asking too much, is it?" Gage said.

Professor Hortzkoller was introduced to Generals Howe, Clinton, and Burgoyne and the common folk. Cigars and brandy were passed out by Francine, and everyone settled down to a good evening with the German collapsible dirigible, which might, just might, despite Gage's blundering, pull this war out yet.

The good professor, with the aid of blackboard and chalk supplied by Francine, gave the lift equation of the dirigible, figuring the ambient air computated at 78 degrees F. Buoyancy is derived through Archimedes' principle as follows:

$$B = WA - Wg$$
$$= V (CA - Cg)$$
$$= V (CA - C_A T_A/T_g)$$
$$= VCA (1 - T_A/T_g)$$

Where:

B = Aerostatic buoyancy of the gas in a balloon.

WA = Weight of air displaced by balloon.

Wg = . . .

"Hey, Hortzkoller," Gage said, "you can knock off the technical crap for now."

259

THE
LONG
NAKED
DESCENT
INTO
BOSTON

260

THE
LONG
NAKED
DESCENT
INTO
BOSTON
Professor Hortzkoller, through Braxton, went on to explain that the collapsible dirigible mounted two cannon, three rockets, five slingshots, two grappling irons, four boarding hooks, a boarding board for when the enemy balloon was seized in the air, then a spare plank so that when the pirates and/or Rebels were seized, they could be forced to walk the plank and make the long naked descent into Boston much quicker than they ever dreamt in their wildest dreams.

They would create quite a splash in Boston.

"I don't know," Gage said. "This seems to me cruel and unnecessary punishment. After all, they are not pirates. If you were to meet the enemy chaps on the street, I am sure they would seem like rum fellows. Because of poor judgment and exposure to Paine, they happen to be on the wrong side, but that doesn't allow us to kill them in cold blood—fair is fair."

"Being on the wrong side in a war," Howe said, "is a very important matter. There are two sides to everything, and in a war you have to take one side. That's a law. A law that stands to reason. Common sense. But the idea of killing people I find most distasteful. The thought makes my hair curl. My teeth stand on end. Outside of a penny-dreadful play, the idea of making people walk the plank is contrary to all my upbringing. Something you read about in children's storybooks or see in one of Johnny's plays."

"Only in my Boston play," Burgoyne said.

"Be that as it may," Howe said, "I find the thought as cheap as a periwig and thundersheet, not only distasteful to me personally but to my honor in toto."

There was some applause at this remark.

"I think you want my job, Howe," General Gage said.

"I wouldn't touch it with a ten-foot pole," Howe said.

"Why don't we leave it to the judgment of the aeronauts who capture the enemy ship?" General Clinton said. "Let them decide on the spur of the moment what is to happen to the Rebels. Then if our chaps do something simply awful to the Rebels, the General Staff, of which at this point in time I am proud to be a member, is released of all responsibility. On the other hand, if some credit is due, I am not above taking it."

No applause greeted General Clinton's comments. Not so much perhaps because of what he said, but maybe the way he said it. That is why, Braxton thought, it is important to be an eyewitness to the Revolution—because it is important to see as well as hear, to feel as well as just be here. It is why history is distorted when being handed down from one historian to another, all with tenure and using callow students to do the research. As Francine would say, history gets fucked up. George Washington becomes a monument. Jefferson a fornicator. Paine a nut. Benjamin Franklin an inventor in search of the Declaration of Independence. If you knew these people, I mean really knew them, none of this stereotyping is true. I admit Paine seemed kind of a nut to me until I got to know him, I mean really know him, then suddenly everything fitted together and he made a lot of sense. Common sense. If our own historians screw up the truth about our own heroes, imagine what a version they'll come up with about these British. Who are not really bad chaps at all when you got to know them. I mean really know them.

"I believe now," Gage said, "that it is you, General Clinton, who want my job. I mean really want my job."

"I wouldn't touch your job, Gage, with a ten-foot spontoon," Clinton said.

They broke up the meeting, leaving Professor Hortzkoller with his foot standing in the air.

Braxton got Francine into Brown's bookstore's dark back room, not only to get away from those military nuts on both sides but to try and make head or tail of what went on. "In the first place," Braxton said, "I did not translate everything to the British."

"Why not?" Francine said.

"Listen," Braxton said, "it's not a collapsible dirigible at all. It's not even a dirigible."

"Why not?" Francine said.

"Because, as the professor told me, the dirigible has not been invented yet, to say nothing of the collapsible dirigible."

"Why not?" Francine said.

"A lot of people are working on it, but no luck," Braxton said.

261
THE
LONG
NAKED
DESCENT
INTO
BOSTON

262

THE
LONG
NAKED
DESCENT
INTO
BOSTON

"You see, the dirigible is a rigid structure in the shape of a cigar, encapsulated in an envelope of silk. Inside the structure are many small free balloons to give the—let's call it creature—buoyancy, commonly called lift—"

"Spare me the details. I'm only a woman," Francine said. "And get your hands off me."

"So the creature is not a dirigible after all, but what the professor referred to as *Der Blimp*. Which is really only a common Montgolfier hot-air balloon of a different shape."

"A horse of a different color."

"Yes, people frequently are confused and mistake a blimp for a dirigible. But they are as different as night and day. The professor believes that if the Patriots believe *Der Blimp* to be a dirigible, then they will not know how to shoot it down, because as most men know—certainly a man as clever as George Washington—a dirigible has many of these free balloons inside the structure and it would take a month of Sundays to shoot it down. Whereas *Der Blimp*, being only actually a hot-air balloon in disguise, could be plinked down with a spontoon if Poxey can get close."

"But I don't think Poxey has a spontoon," Francine said.

"If only we could get him one."

"How are we going to get him one?" Francine said.

"I guess there's no chance. But I hate to see the Revolution lost over the lack of a spontoon."

"Let Poxey take his licks," Francine said. "He stuck us with the newspaper to get out. Knox stuck Brown with the bookstore. The Patriots are stuck with Washington for better or worse. This is Seventeen seventy-six. It's tough all over. Let Poxey take his licks. Poxey never did tell Gretchen about his wife, Theodosia. He's leading the poor girl on."

"I'm sure he told Gretchen about her—either that or it entirely slipped his mind," Braxton said.

"Shit," Francine said.

"Do you mind if I put my hands on you again?" Braxton said.

"Go ahead," Francine said, and then she said, "Wait a minute. Look over there. Do I see a spontoon?"

It was the spontoon of the British soldier who had tried to rape Francine in the strawberry patch on Bunker Hill. He had come to the Rose and Crown with his spontoon when the heat of battle was over, realizing what an un-British, what an ungentlemanly thing he had tried to do to Francine in the strawberry patch, loaded with guilt and feeling the least he could do was give Francine his spontoon as a token of his great remorse. He had left his spontoon against a pile of best sellers in Brown's shoppe— unable to face her, but knowing that every morning Brown looked at the lastest best-seller stack to see how much the pile had shrunk. The British soldier had left a note in the spontoon: "From James Reed of the 17th Lightfoot for Francine in fond memory."

"If we can get that spontoon to Noodles Island," Francine said, "I'm sure Pomfret and Pomeroy will find a way to get it to Poxe. Blacks are born with a sense of rhythm and they are natural dancers and on a clear day should be able to toss the spontoon—if Poxe catches a down draft—into his balloon basket. Go fetch the spontoon, Braxton."

"Do you mind if I put my hands on you again first?"

"Go ahead," Francine said.

"Is this your spontoon?" Brown said.

"Thank you," Francine said. "Continue doing whatever you were doing, Braxton. Then we will get this spontoon to Poxe. If you must have a Revolution, the least we can do is win it."

263
THE
LONG
NAKED
DESCENT
INTO
BOSTON

thirty-four

The only thing that happened between the Battle of Bunker Hill and the British evacuation of Boston—I mean really happened—was the failure of three of Gentleman Johnny Burgoyne's plays, which is reason enough to leave Boston. But there was also this: an unrecorded event—unrecorded for obvious reasons we will soon learn—that not only decided the outcome of the Revolution—who won and why, etc.—but fixed the fate of generations yet unborn.

"Do you see what I see, Nathan?" Poxe said.

"What's that?"

"That object over Boston back there. It looks like a dirigible."

"The dirigible hasn't been invented yet."

"That's what I thought, too," Poxe said, "but it sure looks like one. How do you make it out, Gretchen?"

"I make it out a dirigible," Gretchen said, "or I'm a monkey's uncle."

"You see, Nathan, we haven't been seeing things. Someone must have invented the dirigible."

"Well, I'll be a monkey's uncle," Nathan said.

"We must not get excited," Poxe said. "I believe that as long as there is a will, there is a way."

"I regret to say I forgot to bring along a spontoon."

"Everyone knows, Nathan, that a spontoon is useless against a dirigible. A simple hot-air balloon such as we have, yes. But a dirigible, as everyone knows, is made up of many free balloons for buoyancy, sometimes called lift, concealed inside the envelope, and it would take a month of Sundays to spontoon each separate balloon. Right, Gretchen?"

"If you say so," Gretchen said.

"Although I recall reading in the sporting page of last year's London Sunday *Times*," Poxe said, fingering his ivory cross in thought, "that a certain Kraut by the name of Doctor Hortzkoller, I believe it was, was working on what he was fond of calling *Der Blimp*, which is actually a Montgolfier hot-air balloon in disguise. Do you suppose that is what we are seeing now?"

"If you say so," Gretchen said.

"What's got into you, Gretchen?"

"When I was working my fingers to the bone, burning your shirt to keep this Montgolfier up, I ran across this note in your handwriting to Theodosia. Shall I read it?"

"God, no," Poxe said.

"It says, 'Theodosia Honey, if you run off to Asbury Park with the girls without feeding the dog, it's all over between us.

265

THE
LONG
NAKED
DESCENT
INTO
BOSTON

266

THE
LONG
NAKED
DESCENT
INTO
BOSTON

Unbeknownst to you, I have run into a very sweet dear, dear package at my office called Gretchen—because that is her name—Gretchen Greenwinter. We plan to run off someplace where neither of us is known and raise a family or whatever is customary under the circumstances. If it doesn't rain. You can see I am confused because my heart is all aflutter.' Signed, 'Formerly your sweet Poxey.' "

Gretchen burst into tears. "I am not crying, Poxey, because I am mad at you," Gretchen said, "but because I am mad at myself for having misjudged you so. I am crying also because of joy to have found an honorable man."

They fell into each other's arms in happy sobbing.

"Jesus Christ," Nathan Hale said, "break it up, won't you? The British are coming."

And indeed they were. Poxe unwound himself from Gretchen and grabbed Nathan Hale's spy telescope and had a good look. "Indeed they are," he said, "and she has two cannon mounted on her port gondola. This means trouble."

"If you say so," Gretchen said. And she threw herself at Poxe again. But Poxe stood her off while watching the British coming on. "What we do here today," Poxe said, "will be little noticed or long remembered, but I believe the Revolution hangs on it. And I know I can count on every man jack to do his duty."

General Gage and General Howe and General Burgoyne and General Lord Percy and all the members of their staff were standing on the aft deck of the good ship *Der Blimp*. Mrs. Loring, Madame de Tocqueville, and their entire retinue of serving maids, footmen, coachmen, and general roustabouts were having a quilting bee in the main cabin of *Der Blimp*. They had a cozy fire going in the fireplace and were quite oblivious to the Revolution outside. But perhaps it was that they were trying to block it out.

General Burgoyne entered the main lounge now in his new uniform. His hair was tousled from the Boston breeze, which gave him a Byronic look. He seemed to be swaying drunkenly, but it was only to keep his balance in the normal swaying of the gondola swinging beneath *Der Blimp*.

"What have we here?" General Burgoyne said. "This is no time to shut yourself up inside. It's a beautiful day out. If we lose the cloud cover, we will be able to see New York."

"We have seen New York," Madame de Tocqueville said.

General Burgoyne sat down, took out a silver and pearl-studded snuff box, snorted a sniff, and joined the circle of gossip.

"This is woman talk, Johnny," Mrs. Loring said. "I don't think it would interest you."

"Everything interests me," Burgoyne said. "Excepting the Revolution. I should never have opened my play in Boston at this time."

"Any time."

"That's unfair, madam. I believe my play will prosper in New York."

"I would take it on the road first and iron out the kinks."

"Kinks?" Burgoyne said, staring out the window at Roxbury.

"Those Tory critics in New York will murder you if you go in with that turkey."

"Turkey?" Burgoyne said, standing up and noting the cloud cover was lifting.

"Sit down, Johnny," Madame de Tocqueville said. "You're rocking the gondola. What else is new?"

"Gage is being fired," Burgoyne said. "Don't let this get around, but Howe is going to take over the whole circus. He plans to open in New York in July, but first he's going to Halifax to get the bugs out of the British Army. New York will be tough, he knows that."

"New York is not tough if you prepare for it," Mrs. Loring said. "I must get to know Lord Howe better. I might be able to lend a hand."

"Why didn't they give my Lord Percy a shot at command?" Madame de Tocqueville said. "The British are going to lose the war anyway."

General Burgoyne continued to stand. The British might lose the war down there, but he was determined if possible to try and salvage something out of this skirmish. He pretended to be looking down at the country louts practicing the evolutions of the drill for the girls of Cambridge, but he said to the swaying sewing bee, "I believe you young ladies have a fear of Revolution, and as Doctor Glanders has observed, you are masking it as a fear of flying. That you are behaving like chatterboxes to hide that fact. I wonder what will happen to Doctor Glanders and all his Tory ilk

267
THE
LONG
NAKED
DESCENT
INTO
BOSTON

268
THE
LONG
NAKED
DESCENT
INTO
BOSTON

when we British clear out and the Rebels catch hold of him? Have you ladies noticed that all the doctors are Tories? And the lawyers, too. And the pickpockets. A fine lot."

"Sit down, Johnny, and tell us about your lousy play."

General Burgoyne quit the main lounge, slamming the door, shaking *Der Blimp*, and rattling the glass in der cocktail lounge of der good ship *Der Blimp*. It was getting harder and harder to think in the King's English.

"What's up, Johnny?" Lord Percy said on deck.

"What's up out here?"

"The usual," Lord Percy said. "We are closing on the enemy balloon now. See it over there?"

"Yes."

"Professor Hortzkoller has got the cannon loaded, all ready to go."

"Grape?"

"No, he thought he would try a six-pounder if it wouldn't disturb the ladies too much."

"Nothing would disturb that bunch," General Burgoyne said.

"You seem perturbed, Johnny. Did something happen in there that you would rather not discuss at this point in time'?"

"No, nothing."

"It was something about the play, I hope. You have got to face it, Johnny. You can't open in New York or even Halifax with that turkey. The critics will murder you."

"Let's get back to the Revolution."

"No, I tell you as a friend, Johnny, you need a second act. The Revolution can wait."

"I would rather not discuss it now," General Burgoyne said.

"As you wish, Johnny," Lord Percy said, striding away and joining the professor at the cannon.

"What's gotten into Burgoyne?" the professor said.

"Something happened in the gondola he would rather not discuss."

"It will blow over."

"These things usually do," Lord Percy said. "I thought you didn't speak English."

"Not in front of all those people at the victory banquet last night," the professor said. "But up here I feel free to make mistakes."

"In grammar, I hope you mean, not in handling this thing."

"It's not a thing," the professor said.

"What is it?" Lord Percy said. "Let's clear this up once and for all. Is it a dirigible or a balloon?"

"It's neither. It's a blimp," the professor said.

"Is that good or bad?"

"Bad."

"You mean they can knock us down with a spontoon?"

"Yes." The professor stroked his beard. "If they have a spontoon."

In *The New Boston Times* balloon, everyone was scurrying about, not trying to find a spontoon, which they already knew they forgot to bring, but trying to get more lift to escape the six-pounder they could see approaching from Medford on the port side.

"We can't find a spontoon," Poxe said, "so we've got to find more lift. You wouldn't consider jumping out, would you, Nathan, so Gretchen and I could be alone for a while?"

"No."

"That's all—just no?"

"Yes."

"No regrets?"

"No."

"*The New Boston Times* means nothing to you, Nathan?"

"No."

"Listen, my love," Gretchen said to Poxe, "Nathan is obviously going to hang tough. Why don't you think of some other way of getting lift? I know you have a seminal mind."

"I was only thinking of *The New Boston Times*."

"Think about us," Gretchen said. "Think about our future."

"Do you suppose Dilsie's getting the paper out?" Poxe said. "Something like INTREPID FLYERS SAVE CAUSE IN RECONNAISSANCE OVER ENEMY CAMP. THEY ARE MY EYES, WASHINGTON HEARD TO SAY. POXE OF NEW BOSTON TIMES QUOTED, 'WE WILL STAY UP AS LONG AS NEEDED.' FEAR FELT FOR PATRIOT AERO-

269
THE
LONG
NAKED
DESCENT
INTO
BOSTON

270
THE
LONG
NAKED
DESCENT
INTO
BOSTON
NAUT LIVES BY BOSTON POPULACE. CONGRESS SHOULD ACT INSTEAD OF SITTING ON ASSES, A SOURCE CLOSE TO THE TIMES OPINED. FEAR FELT FOR LOSS OF AMERICAN CREDIBILITY AT THIS EARLY STAGE OF GAME. FEAR FELT FOR LOSS OF SEMINAL MINDS IF BALLOON BUSTS. FEAR FELT FOR NOT ONLY LOSS OF SEMINAL MINDS BUT WHOLE DAMN REVOLUTION. A SOURCE CLOSE TO THE TIMES LEARNED THERE ARE THREE IN THE BALLOON, ALL FRIENDS OF THIS REPORTER—GRETCHEN GREENWINTER OF BANGOR, MAINE, NATHAN HALE OF NEW HAVEN, HIERONYMUS POXE OF BOSTON. 'WE HATE TO SEE THEM GO,' A SOURCE CLOSE TO THE TIMES STATED.

"Do you think I have a seminal mind, Gretchen?" Poxe said.

"I certainly do, my dear Poxey."

"Then," Poxe said quietly, "that gives me the strength to go on."

"What's up?" Howe said, approaching the professor from the rear as he was aiming the cannon that said on its breach "Krupp's Works."

"Does Krupp's Works mean that someone by the name of Krupp is working somewhere, or does it have something to do with the place where the cannon was manufactured?"

"It's where the cannon was born," the professor said. "The Krupp's Works."

"I still find it confusing. Is there any chance of getting a shot at *The New Boston Times* balloon today? The women want to get down as soon as possible. They have things to do. The way this thing is bobbling about, I don't imagine you can get a straight shot."

"A Krupp has an automatic cannon stabilizer," the professor said. "When we go *boom*, they go *blop*."

"The women will be pleased to hear that," General Howe said. "Let me run off and tell them. Can you manage by yourself?"

"Yes, go ahead," the professor said.

In the main lounge, the women were not particularly pleased to learn that the Revolution would soon be over. They had taken that for granted. They did want to hear more about the weather out there and whether or not it was safe to hang something out to dry.

"I think so," Howe said. "Do you know what occurred to me on the way to *Der Blimp* this morning?"

"No, what?"

"That maybe I shouldn't take this command job. If we shoot this balloon down, there will certainly be other balloons."

"I have been assured," Madame de Tocqueville said, "that the Patriots are using the only balloon they have got. And don't imagine problems, Lord Howe. Everything will turn out all right in the wash. My mother always said, 'One balloon at a time.' And if everything goes haywire, you will think of something new, Lord Howe. You have a seminal mind."

"Do you think so?"

"Yes."

"Well, that gives me the strength to go on," General Howe said. "Have you observed that the professor is closing in on the enemy balloon fast?"

The ladies put aside their drinks and knitting and stood up to have a good look.

271

THE
LONG
NAKED
DESCENT
INTO
BOSTON

thirty-five

"Will you all come in here?" Dilsie said. "We have an editorial question to decide. How far do we want the paper to tilt in the direction of the Patriots in view of the turn of events?" Dilsie said when she got the *Times* gang out of the bar and into the office.

"I'm still willing to go all the way," Braxton said.

"Well," Lee said, "in for a penny, in for a pound."

"That's what makes our ass go round," Francine said.

Dilsie said, "Please don't talk, anyone, while I'm interrupting. If you can locate Revere, have him deliver the spontoon to Noodles Island. Even if Pomfret and Pomeroy can't throw it up there, or through reasons of conscience refuse to throw it up there, there should be a Boston Irishman out there who can. Those tall Celtics are always throwing things through peach baskets. Right now I want two of you to hop over and do an in-depth human interest story on the new Patriot general. We will need it for the obits. He is a Southerner and sensitive to the fact, so don't harp on it. I believe he is a South Carolina boy."

"Virginia," Lee said.

"His name is Vasherton something?"

"No, it's Washington."

"Doesn't he have a first name? Charles?"

"George."

"You sure?"

"Yes."

"It wouldn't do to get his name wrong," Dilsie said.

"That's right," Francine said. "If the paper called our savior Vasherton Something, the historians going over old newspaper files would think *The New Boston Times* had shit for brains."

"Correct," Dilsie said. "I want Francine and Lee to hop over the lines to Cambridge and do an in-depth on Vasherton. If he doesn't last long in charge, we will always have it for the files if he makes a comeback. Check up on his whole army—you know, who's who in the zoo—that kind of filler for the Sunday paper. Lee, sketch some pictures of Vasherton."

Before Lee and Francine crossed the British checkpoint on Boston Neck, they went upstairs to the bed to collect some artist's junk Lee needed for the pictures and got into a sex thing. It all started when Lee told Francine he would like to do a bare-assed sketch of her for the Sunday centerfold in case the Revolution was called off.

"The Revolution won't be called off, Lee," Francine said. "The Media are much too involved and the Rebels are closing in

273
THE
LONG
NAKED
DESCENT
INTO
BOSTON

on Boston. Why don't you be honest with yourself, Lee? You
need some sex, don't you? All you have to do is say so. What's

"That's the way we were brought up," Lee said.

"Is Vasherton like this, too?"

"George Washington," Lee said, balancing himself in awe on
all in sex at this point in time. He is only interested in saving our
country. I believe the history books will bear me out."

"That's nice," Francine said.

"Not that George Washington is not a regular fellow," Lee
said. "He enjoys a joke as well as the next man. Why do you
think he volunteered to take over what is laughingly called the
American Army?"

"That's not funny, Lee."

"We were buddies at Vernon," Lee said.

"I can't imagine Vasherton being anyone's buddy, can you,
Lee?"

"Not now," Lee said, "but I can't imagine a person changing
that much. George was older than I, but we used to toss silver
sovereigns across the Potomac together."

"Good wholesome fun?"

"Washington was a straight arrow."

"Then he hasn't changed."

"Not really that much," Lee said.

"A big bore."

"Not when you get to know him, really know him," Lee said.
"If you want a word, I would say 'resolute.' "

"I was afraid of that," Francine said. "Then Jackson of the
Globe got Vasherton down pat in yesterday's *Globe*?"

"Yes," Lee said.

"That leaves the *Times* up shit creek?"

"Yes."

"Lee, you have lost interest in having sex this morning,
haven't you? Is that what thinking about your Vasherton has
done to you?"

"I guess so," Lee said.

"It's amazing the influence that man has," Francine said.

"My God, Francine," Lee said, struggling to put on his pants at the window. "Look up there."

It was Poxe. Despite the fact that he was being pursued by the British with their two Krupp cannons blazing away, he had the sheer courage to hurtle his balloon over Cambridge, apparently to drop a message of importance to the general on what Poxe had observed lately with no thought for the safety of his own life and limb.

"It's amazing the courage that man has," Francine said.

"Look down there, Francine, at Griffin's Wharf," Lee said, pointing. "The British are evacuating Boston. That's what Poxe observed and is warning Washington about with no thought for his own safety. Although Howe is aloft in *Der Blimp,* he has secretly ordered his troops to prepare for a pullout. The British are abandoning Boston, Francine! We've won! We've won! The deed is done! Poxe is warning Washington to play doggie. To lie low. Not to waste any more lives. But to get his brass band together for the grand entrance into Boston. We must set this type: REVOLUTION SMASH IN MASSACHUSETTS. SELL-OUT IN CAMBRIDGE. BOSTON STANDING ROOM ONLY. WASHINGTON INDICATES TO THIS REPORTER BETWEEN AUTOGRAPHS AND HAPPY TEARS THAT BACKERS NO LONGER NEEDED. NEW YORK NEXT TRIUMPH. ROAD COMPANIES PLANNED FOR WHITE PLAINS, BRANDYWINE, VALLEY FORGE. SHOW TO FINISH IN YORKTOWN. REVOLUTION WORLD SOCKO. FRANCE MIGHT TRY ONE. RUSSIANS INTERESTED. AMERICAN ORPHANS ROUNDED UP TO LEAVE WITH BRITISH—MANY CHILDREN OF BRITISH SOLDIERS. TORIES PLEAD FOR SPACE ON DEPARTING SHIPS. 'WE FEAR BLOODBATH,' DOCTOR GLANDERS INDICATES. RIGHT NOW BOSTON TIMES SPY BALLOON PLANNING TRIUMPHAL LONG NAKED DESCENT INTO BOSTON.

"We've somehow got to get to Dilsie through the crowded streets," Lee said, clutching his trousers. "This is a stop-the-press."

"Our bed is in the same building as the *Times,*" Francine said.

"I forgot that," Lee said.

In the pressroom, Dilsie on hearing the news from Lee finally got the press stopped and kissed them both. "You have both scooped Scoop Jackson of the *Globe.* Now get thee both hence to

275
THE
LONG
NAKED
DESCENT
INTO
BOSTON

276

THE
LONG
NAKED
DESCENT
INTO
BOSTON

Vasherton and indicate his first reaction. Sketch his expression, Lee. This will bomb his mind. I can't tell you how happy I am. The British running away means that Burgoyne's play will fold, to say nothing of the effect the British pullout will have on all of history. And the *Times* caused it and got it first!" Dilsie said, jumping up and down on a type case. "First, first, first!"

"Don't ruin the type, Dilsie."

"But don't you see?" Dilsie said, hugging Lee much to Francine's chagrin. "This means Scoop Jackson is finished. The *Globe* is up shit creek. Thanks to Poxey, the *Times* is in the driver's seat and we will all live happily ever after—after Poxey makes his long naked descent into Boston."

But Poxe was not yet about to make his descent into Boston, naked or no. He had his hands full trying to escape *Der Blimp.* Poxe, exercising much tact and diplomacy, had got Nathan and Gretchen to accept the fact that it would not be all peaches and cream from here on out, despite the fact that the rustics below were dancing in the streets of Cambridge. Poxe also had got Nathan and Gretchen to consent to the overflight above Washington to drop a note to warn him of the British pullout. And Washington had not reacted as you might think. When our General Washington at last found Poxe's note in the snow and got his glasses out and read it, he did not take any credit in the victory for himself, but got down on his knees and thanked Providence. Washington skipped thanking Poxe. Not that he dismissed Poxe's efforts out of hand; he was simply in a hurry, we suppose. That could account for why history until now skipped Poxe, too. Thus the need for this book. Anyway, Washington busied himself getting his brass band organized to enter Boston and hiding from the busybodies from *The New Boston Times.* "I must get Hancock to take care of Poxe's relatives if the British shoot him down," George Washington said to himself when he was finished kneeling in the snow.

"Did you see Washington kneeling in the snow?" Poxe said.

"I didn't even realize it was snowing," Gretchen said.

"It's not snowing up here," Nathan said, looking through his spyglass, "but it's apparently snowing down there. Otherwise how could George Washington be kneeling in the snow?"

"Listen to Nathan, Gretchen," Poxe said. "Nathan makes a lot of sense. Nathan, can you think of some way we can get *Der Blimp* off our ass? They're about to blow us out of the sky."

Francine and Lee did not get themselves hence to interview Washington immediately, as Dilsie had directed them, but stopped off to have a snort at the Rose and Crown to wet their whistles for the road. There they ran into Paul Revere, who refused to take the spontoon the British soldier had given to Francine to Noodles Island. He said he was tired of being a messenger boy, sick of being used, and was no longer going to neglect his huge family and silver pot business, and anyway he would not lift a finger to help *The New Boston Times,* which had still not given him credit for the Lexington–Concord ride. The fact that the *Times* had nominated Paul not only as the best rookie of the year but also the best supporting actor in a serious comedy did not help. "Tell Poxe he can shove the spontoon up his—"

"Cut it," said Young Melville, who was writing a book in the corner of the Rose and Crown. Lowell Cabot Loring began whistling Mozart, fearful there would be a confrontation. Young Melville put aside the book he was writing and marched up to Francine. "I will take the spontoon to Noodles Island," Young Melville said, "with the next whale oil delivery to the lighthouse."

"I don't want to interfere with your writing," Francine said.

"Brown won't give me an advance on the book anyway," Young Melville said. "I was trying to finish it before the whale becomes extinct, but if Brown doesn't care, I don't care."

"What are you going to call your book, Melville?" Braxton said.

"Something Dick," Melville said.

"What about Big Dick?" Francine said.

"Too vulgar, but I'll speak to Brown about that in the morning," Young Melville said, marching off with the spontoon to catch his father's next whale-oil boat to Noodles Island.

Brown leaned over the bar to Francine and Braxton. "Herman wants to call his whale book *Moby-Dick.* I never heard such a lousy title, did you? But he'll deliver your spontoon. He's got a character in his novel called Queequeg who carries one of those things all the time. Herman's not much of a writer, but he

277
THE
LONG
NAKED
DESCENT
INTO
BOSTON

278

THE
LONG
NAKED
DESCENT
INTO
BOSTON

certainly has a way with whales. It's very difficult to get Herman to think Revolution, but a spontoon is right up his alley. Now, what can I do for you people?"

Little Brown served them two Colonial Big Sweet Mama Shake-ups and a Rum Flip and got them on the road again. Then Francine and Lee had to stop off at Glanders' apothecary to check out whether Pomfret and Pomeroy were really on Noodles Island and why. Glanders told them Pomfret and Pomeroy were on a mission of mercy with Tom Paine to comfort Mrs. Gage on Noodles Island. Poor Mrs. Gage was down with the mumps, which at least justified her long quarantine; this was all news to Francine and Lee but would be too late to make tomorrow's edition. Glanders was also depressed about his being a Tory and wondered whether it was too late to switch. He had already learned that Howe was fleeing and leaving the Boston Tories to the vengeful Patriots—to the bloodbath. And maybe if he, Glanders, switched sides now, no one would be the wiser. "When does Poxe plan to make his long naked descent into Boston, do you know?"

"Maybe never," Lee said.

"But I thought the whole shooting match was over."

"Not by a long shot," Lee said. "Poxe is still very much in trouble. The British Der Blimp is still after Poxe, and it is rumored that when they catch him, they are not only going to make him walk the plank over Boston Bay, but Gretchen and Nathan Hale as well."

"But that's barbarism and against the Paris Accords," Doctor Glanders said, examining his green stuff.

"The British plan to call the balloon spies pirates," Lee said. "It all came out at last night's British one-hundred-dollar-a-plate banquet."

"What are dollars?" Doctor Glanders said, placing the green stuff back in the window display.

"Dollars are the new American money."

"Are dollars worth anything?"

"Not much," Lee said.

"Then it's all so much poppycock, just a lot of talk if the American dollar isn't worth anything. But you said a lot of people paid one hundred of them for a plate?"

"There was chicken and peas on the plate," Lee said.

"Still, it's a lot of them for chicken and peas. What did you say they are calling them?"

"Dollars," Lee said.

"I still can't make up my mind whether to switch sides or nay. What do ye think, Lee?"

"I don't know. What do ye think, Francine?"

"I don't know," Francine said, exiting to feed her nag.

"Which way is the wind blowing?" Doctor Glanders said. "Do the Patriots have a Chinaman's chance?"

"Not at this point in time," Lee said. "I don't see how Poxe is going to get out of walking the plank."

"Well, you have cheered me up a great deal," Doctor Glanders said. "Now, Lee, is there anything I can do for you, man to man, before Francine gets back? Condoms? French ticklers? Things that women wouldn't understand."

"Women understand," Lee said. "What do you think a French tickler is for?"

"You may be right. You know," Doctor Glanders said, picking up the bottle of sperm, "I haven't found any use for this green stuff."

"I must go."

"Before you rush off," Doctor Glanders said, "if you're going by George Washington's place, why don't you dump off some medicaments as a gift from me. That way, no matter who wins the Revolution, I will have a sheet to the wind. Just say they're gifts from Doctor Glanders, and do take Washington a few bottles of this green stuff and see if he can make head or tail of it."

"It will be a pleasure," Lee said.

As Lee went from Doctor Glanders' to the British checkpoint, all of Boston rocked from the battle overhead. Shrapnel fell all over Boston from the grapeshot, and six-pounders bounced thirty feet in the air after they hit the cobblestones. At night the sky flashed with fire and no man slept, no cock crew, no ghost walked—there was only man-made thunder and lightning overhead, deciding whether this nation or any nation so conceived and so dedicated could long endure. Poxe was dropping notes all over Massachusetts "to be delivered to George Washington," keeping the general in touch with exactly what was happening in the battle

279
THE
LONG
NAKED
DESCENT
INTO
BOSTON

280

THE
LONG
NAKED
DESCENT
INTO
BOSTON

above and to the British beneath. Washington asked the army to set aside a day of prayer as well as the usual prayer breakfast to see if that would possibly help Poxe. You never know about these things until you try. Sometimes God and Washington got along fine and sometimes they did not—it depended on what kind of a day Washington was having. As Washington told his troops many times, don't ask God for everything. Try and see if you can do a little something for yourselves for a change. But this day, Washington, without wings or a balloon of his own to help out above, was plainly worried and sat in his tent and brooded and read Poxe's messages and brooded some more and wished he had wings so he could be in the thick of it instead of sitting here like a bump on a log. At ten o'clock that morning, Washington had put red hats on the Green Mountain Boys and had them spell out in Harvard Yard various messages of encouragement to Poxe, but outside of that, General Washington felt absolutely helpless and out of it all. It's funny, Washington thought, how history is decided by circumstances over which we have absolutely no control. One lucky shot by that six-pounder yesterday and our Revolution would have gone down the drain. People don't realize that.

When Francine and Lee reached the British checkpoint, all hell had broken loose and there was so much consternation with the British looking at the heavens above that Francine and Lee were able to trot through the British lines without so much as a by-your-leave.

thirty-six

On Noodles Island, Tom Paine was in the midst of saying to Mrs. Gage, "Everything that is right or reasonable pleads for separation from England—the blood of the slain and the weeping

282

THE
LONG
NAKED
DESCENT
INTO
BOSTON

voice of nature cries 'tis time to part! Even the great distance which the Almighty hath placed between England and America is a strong and natural proof that the authority of one over the other was never the design of Heaven."

"Let me think about that, Young Wild Tom," Mrs. Gage said.

They had all rushed down to Noodles Beach when the cannon-ading started to get a better view. The lighthouse keeper and Herman Melville's father were already there to see what was up. Mrs. Gage introduced Paine, Pomfret, and Pomeroy to the keeper and Old Melville—"I don't think you've met, have you?"

"We've met your boy but we've never met you," Pomfret and Pomeroy said to Melville's father.

"I haven't met anybody," Tom Paine said. "Has anyone read my book?"

"I don't read much unless it's about whales," Old Man Melville said. "Has anybody seen Herman? He brought me the nicest harpoon today. What's all that noise up there?"

The battle above was now passing over Noodles Island, and even the Spanish slaves who rowed the British launch took more than a passing interest. All eyes watched heavenward. And with the *boom boom boom* of the cannon above, you could not hear a farthing drop below.

"Look," Tom Paine said. "The *Times* hot-air balloon is being torn to shreds by the cannon on *Der Blimp*."

"Yes."

"I believe," Tom Paine said, "the day of the Montgolfier hot-air balloon is over."

"Yes."

And then something startling happened that brought tears to the eyes and great shouts that could be heard from the Boston shores. Although the hot-air balloon had been torn to tatters and was fluttering like a torn rag in the sky under the pounding of the cannon, somehow under Poxe's urging and her own sheer guts, Gretchen was crawling up the netting that surrounded all of the balloon and from which the basket hung and was writing in huge lettering a slogan that stopped everyone's heart, including the Spanish slaves who understood no English but realized some-thing big was happening. George Washington from just outside his tent saw it and realized that, with everything else going haywire, this Gretchen was exactly the shot in the arm the Revolution needed. With everyone else lying down on the job and switching sides, here was a young girl who had the moxie to bring a touch of guilt to all of us. Washington dismissed Betsy Ross, who was trying to sell him a flag, and watched Francine and Lee approach bearing gifts from Doctor Glanders.

"How are you doing, old buddy?" Washington said to Lee. "You know someday we should start a university called Washington and Lee. How does that sound to you?"

"Very good, sire."

"Oh, Lee," Washington said, jumping up, "don't be a stiff shirt. As long as there is no one else around, I would rather you treated me as an equal. I very much feel the need at times to relax with an old buddy."

"Very well, sire." Try as he might, Lee could not feel equal to a monument. You would have had to be in the presence of George Washington yourself to know the awe that Lee felt despite their boyhood friendship.

"Look up there, the both of you," Washington said in a commanding voice. "Up there is a young girl with the courage to put us all to shame."

What Gretchen had writ on the balloon was: RESISTANCE TO TYRANNY IS OBEDIENCE TO GOD. Even *Der Blimp* had stopped firing temporarily out of respect for her courage. Or her nakedness.

Washington removed his blue and white tricorn hat and placed it over his heart. The others did the same. Washington looked straight ahead for one minute of silence. The others did the same. Finally, General Washington broke the ice. "Did you see Betsy Ross's new flag, Lee?"

"No."

"I find her flag a trifle busy, but I like it," Washington said, and then noticing the medicaments, "What is that Tory Glanders trying to cover his tracks with now?"

"A bottle of green stuff."

"Throw it overboard," Washington said. "Glanders is a quack. Lee, if you know that girl up in the balloon who had the guts to do what she just did, tell her for me that it is the noblest gesture that I ever had the honor to witness."

283

THE
LONG
NAKED
DESCENT
INTO
BOSTON

284

THE
LONG
NAKED
DESCENT
INTO
BOSTON

"Very well, Your Worship."

"Oh, Lee, what ever happened to our friendship?" Washington said.

At the beach at Noodles Island there was equal consternation at Gretchen's act. Everyone simply stared at everyone else in amaze. Dumbfounded. The shores of Boston, too, were silent out of respect for Gretchen.

On board *Der Blimp,* General Howe, even in the heat of battle, said, "It wouldn't look too good if we shot the Patriots down now. Let's just board them with our grappling hooks and boarding board and then we can use the boarding board to make them walk the plank into Boston Town."

"After that young girl's display of courage," the professor said, "how can you, Howe?"

"How can I, Howe? You bet your life Howe can," Howe said. "How do you think I became a major general? The British Army shows great acts of individual courage such as we have just witnessed all the time. But the other side has never shown the proper respect for our courage. There are times in a man's life when he needs to be hard."

"Yes," Madame de Tocqueville said, "I wish the general would explain that need to my Lord Percy."

"And another thing," General Howe said. "If we let the Patriots off scot-free, King George would never speak to us again and I wouldn't blame him."

"Neither would I," General Clinton said.

"Burgoyne, shall the Rebels walk the plank?"

"Agreed."

"Percy?"

"Agreed."

"Gage? Gage?"

"General Gage has been fired."

"Then we are all agreed."

"No one asked me," Professor Hortzkoller said.

"Professors don't count," Howe said. "Get out the grappling hooks."

Over the professor's protest, the grappling hooks and walking plank were gotten out and the poor tattered balloon was seized and our heroes were forced to board *Der Blimp* at the point of spontoon in a high wind across a narrow plank placed carefully between the air ships for just that purpose.

"Have you anything to say before the Englishers dump you in der drink?" the professor said.

"Let me handle this," General Howe said. "I am in charge here. Yes, what do you people have to say for yourselves before you walk the plank? I hate to do this, you know."

"My only regret," Nathan Hale said, "is that I have but one life to give for my country."

"A likely story," Howe said. "We have heard all that before. Listen—I didn't catch the name?"

"Nathan Hale."

"Can I call you Nathan?"

"Yes."

"Listen, Nathan, do you realize the shenanigans your country has been up to, starting with your big tea spill in Boston Harbor? Do you want to start a country that pollutes the whole world? Think about it. And if you don't give a damn about ecology, think about the problem of your Patriots winning. Then, like the British, America will get into this empire thing and spend its total income on the army. Have you ever heard of distant strange places where promises must be kept and obligations met or your empire will lose its credibility?"

"I never heard of those distant strange places."

"Neither have I," Howe said, "but after you polish off the Indians you will have to find someplace to go for an encore. Think about it, Nathan. There's still a chance for you to get out of this."

"I don't know what you're talking about," Nathan said. "I am only sensitive to the fact of this girl Gretchen's great act of courage in the face of certain death. I can only repeat what I said. My only regret is that I have but one life to give for my country. Correction: I only regret I have but one life to *lose* for my country."

"Well said," Burgoyne said. "Even if you didn't say it that way the first time, you should have. It's more euphonious. I think Hale should be allowed the honor of being the first to walk the plank. Agreed?"

Everyone agreed.

285

THE
LONG
NAKED
DESCENT
INTO
BOSTON

286

THE
LONG
NAKED
DESCENT
INTO
BOSTON

"Can I say something before I die?" Gretchen said.

"No," Howe said. "Women always want to keep talking. I don't think you could top what Nathan Hale said anyway. Any statement you might make would only confuse the record. It would be anticlimactic. But go ahead—ruin everything."

"I don't want to steal the play away from Nathan," Gretchen said. "I only want to thank dear Poxey for the kindness and consideration he has shown to me and all members of my sex. I hope the sisters in the future will remember Hieronymus Poxe and set aside a day for him in commemoration—July fourth—instead of Washington or somebody. After all, Poxey was the first American to hire women on any large scale, and despite the fact that the pay was low, you can't expect a pioneer to have his consciousness raised in one jump. My only regret—I'm sorry, Nathan—is that I didn't get in the haymow with Poxey to show my appreciation more. I'm sure it would have been a revealing experience for not only Poxey but for the both of us—"

"You've run out of time," Howe said.

"Just one more thing," Gretchen said.

"No, all get in line to walk the plank."

"I only wanted to say," Gretchen said, "that I forgot to sweep the office. I don't know why, but it didn't cross my mind till now. I don't know what got into me."

"Forgiven, dearest," Poxe said, kissing her.

"Break it up and everyone stand in line to walk the plank. I hate to do this," General Howe said.

"My God," Mrs. Gage said. "Look what's happening up there. Howe is dropping our heroes into the drink and I didn't bring my bathing suit to help rescue them."

"You can use mine," Old Melville said.

Everyone rushed around, trying to find a bathing suit in order to rescue our heroes, and the Spanish slaves braced themselves to row the rescuers out for the pickup.

"There will be no pickup if I can't locate my bathing suit," Mrs. Gage said.

"I said you could use mine," Old Melville said.

"Here's a spontoon, if it will help," Young Melville said.

But Mrs. Gage had already stripped to the buff and jumped into Boston Bay, such was her haste to be of succor. Everyone else boarded the Spanish slave ship and was rowed out peacefully, with Mrs. Gage swimming alongside.

"You shouldn't have put yourself to all this trouble, my dear," Poxe said when Mrs. Gage collared him and pulled him to the slave ship.

Mrs. Gage went to and fro, to and fro, until she had picked up all the survivors, and thank God all had survived.

"What happened to our hot-air balloon?" Poxe said to one of the slaves.

The Spanish slave said he didn't speak English, but Pomfret said that the balloon had caught on the Noodles Island lighthouse—what there was left of the balloon.

"We'll have the ladies patch it up and we'll have another go. This time with a spontoon," Poxe said.

Out of modesty, Mrs. Gage was still swimming alongside the slave ship as it made its way back to Noodles Inlet.

"Don't mind us, Mrs. Gage," Poxe said. "We've been in the buff ourselves for days."

At Noodles Island the women patched up the Montgolfier until it was as good as new, and within hours our heroes took off again, this time armed with the spontoon Young Melville had brought.

"She's coming up again," Lord Howe said. "What do you make of that, Professor?"

"It means," the professor said, "that while they were on board with us they observed this was not a dirigible but a *Der Blimp*. Just another gas bag."

"You mean they're out to get us?"

"Yes," the professor said, "and this time they'll probably have a spontoon."

"In that case," Howe said, "the better part of valor would probably be for us to get down and clear out of Boston before this whole thing blows up in our face."

"Wise choice," the professor said.

"After Boston, I think I'll like New York. What do you say, Johnny?"

287
THE
LONG
NAKED
DESCENT
INTO
BOSTON

288

THE
LONG
NAKED
DESCENT
INTO
BOSTON

"I'd like to try the road for a few weeks."

"No time. Take her down, Professor," General Howe said. "Ladies, we are going to try our luck in New York. Are you game?"

All were game for New York, particularly Mrs. Loring, who had taken a shine to Howe. Howe had taken a shine to Mrs. Loring, too. Mr. Loring was probably down there someplace whistling Mozart, wishing them well.

George Washington was above all things a person of rectitude, and part of his appreciation at the idea of the British clearing out of Boston was that Boston would be free of sin; at least it would return to a level of sin that could be coped with. Still, if the British went to New York, that might bring more sin there, and there was already enough sin in New York to sink a ship. Nevertheless, Washington thanked God for small favors and was delighted at the turn of events brought about by *The New Boston Times* and all the *Times* stood for, and he ordered a tremendous celebration to greet the long naked descent into Boston.

It has long been said by people of low birth and historians who have debased their profession that the Father of Our Country was a tightwad who padded his expense account with fine wines and victuals from foreign countries and paid for naught out of his own pocket. "Charge it to the Colonies, Gimbel." But such was not the case this April 1, 1776, in Boston, Massachusetts. Washington dug into his own meager fortune for the bash to celebrate the return to earth of our heroes. History is silent, but we do know that Washington sold two of his slaves at this time for a cash flow. Whether Martha put the money into the kitty to pay off the Vernon mortage or all of it went into *The New Boston Times*'s homecoming we simply don't know.

People came from all over the Colonies to witness the descent, some from as distant as Jamaica and Niagara Falls. Jamaica, Long Island, of course, but that's still pretty far. Indians came in from the forests bearing wood to relieve the fuel shortage. Until that day, New England had been entirely dependent on foreign fuel. Great bonfires were lit. The brass bands from every local Middlesex village and farm showed up. The

Masonic Lodgers, by whom Washington had been given the Third Degree, were there in full Arab regalia, including the latest lampshade hats. The religion of your choice was represented by the Jews, including the Orthodox, the Reformed, the Unreformed, and the Utterly Hopeless. The Christians were represented by the Christ Child in short pants. Free shoppes were set up all over the Boston Common. The carriage companies gave five-hundred-dollar rebates. Little Brown set up an autograph stand for Tom Paine. POXE FOR KING buttons and tee shirts were distributed free by milkmaids from Providence, Rhode Island. Billy Cracker held an evangelical crusade in the Boston ice rink after the ice had been taken out and free popsicles distributed. Billy said he would talk till hell froze over or Poxe descended in the glory of the light. Crap games were set up, houses of prostitution were built and then torn down at the request of George Washington. Pickpockets and muggers came from as far as Brooklyn, and the Danbury Hat people gave away free frisbees and hula-hoops with the purchase of each picture of a naked lady. Candidates for the Continental Congress were bribed openly by the fuel companies until the money came out of their ears. But the bands and the brand-new uniforms of the New England Patriots were the splendor that stole the show. Coaches and managers from all over the world had been hired and fired to drill the Patriots—Steuben from Germany, Pulaski from Poland, Lafayette from France, Franco Harris from Pittsburgh. The Patriot uniforms were designed by Coco Chanel, Rembrandt, El Greco, Hart Shaffner & Marx, and Levi-Strauss. Francine added her touch, too—a simple black dress with long sleeves, cut short at the ass in order to carry more ammunition.

But the main attraction was the speakers' stand, fashioned of Mohawk Indian wood and bearing the speakers—you guessed it—Pomfret and Pomeroy, Dilsie, Gretchen, and Francine, Braxton and Lee, Lowell Cabot Loring, whose poetry reading had almost singlehandedly commenced the Revolution, George and Martha, Thomas Jefferson in the latest, Benjamin Franklin to the nines, Dolly Madison, Rutherford B. Hayes, Sr., his son Sammy Davis, Jr., Sam Adams, John Adams, John Jay, Aaron Burr with pistol, Alexander Hamilton with sword, farmer Jimmy with teeth,

289
THE
LONG
NAKED
DESCENT
INTO
BOSTON

290

THE
LONG
NAKED
DESCENT
INTO
BOSTON

James Madison, Sir Hubert Humphrey, Doctor Glanders, the Knights of Columbus, Benedict Arnold, Peggy, Patrick Henry, Haym Salomon, the King of Spain and the Emperor of China. Have I missed anybody? Everyone who signed or took the Fifth and refused to sign—on the respectful grounds that it must incriminate them—the Declaration of Independence was there. You name it—anybody who was somebody and everyone who was no one—they were all there to witness this final long naked descent into Boston.

There was a big silence over all of Boston.

"Here they come," George Washington said.

And indeed they were coming, but what shook the mind of every Bostonian on this memorable day of days was the sign that Gretchen had writ with the moral support of Nathan Hale and the financial backing of Poxe. A sign on the side of the balloon bigger than Boston Bay, bigger than all of us, encompassing not only the balloon but all of our hopes and dreams, a sign, Dear Reader, we will forget at the cost of our American soul, a sign that this day was emblazoned in the heart of each of our countrymen as though emplanted there by a sharp spontoon. Everyone in the world rose to his feet as the balloon came into full view over Boston and the writ slogan emblazoned on the side could be read: PROCLAIM LIBERTY THROUGHOUT THE LAND AND TO ALL THE INHABITANTS THEREOF.—Dilsie Firstchild

"Here they are," George Washington said.

When the full impact of the slogan hit them, the Bostonians tore Boston apart.

That is why Boston is in the shape it is today.

When the full impact of the happening in Boston hit them in New York, the New Yorkers tore New York apart. That is why New York is in the shape it is today.

When the full impact of the happening in Boston hit all of America, the Americans tore the British Empire apart and started one of their own.

That is why America is in the shape it is today.

"No more editorials," Poxe said. "The important thing is that you read *The Long Naked Descent into Boston* first in *The New Boston Times.*"

Written and Directed by:

Times Reporter: Isaac Braxton   *Isaac Braxton*

Additional Dialogue: Francine Braxton   *Francine Wilkes*

Rewrite: Dilsie Lee   *X*

Art Work: Amos Lee   **AMOS LEE**

Editorial Secretary: Gretchen Poxe   *Gretchen Greenwinter*

Approved by the Editor in Chief of The New Boston Times:

Hieronymus Poxe,
on this day
July 4, 1776

P.S. Memo to all Editors, Publishers, and Dear Readers:

OUR LIBERTIES WE PRIZE

OUR RIGHTS WE SHALL MAINTAIN

Hieronymus Poxe

291
THE
LONG
NAKED
DESCENT
INTO
BOSTON

END

ALBERTSON COLLEGE OF IDAHO
PS3555.A7.L6
The long, naked descent into Boston /

3 5556 00035185 8